To Judie,
To the mother of
the bride — nice
wedding — Clean Y...
Cheers! Sue

CLEANING
CLOSETS

By
Susan DeBow

"Dialogue"
PUBLISHING, INC.

ISBN 13: 978-0-9764904-4-9
ISBN 10: 0-9764904-4-7
LCCN: 2007905286
Copyright © Susan DeBow, 2007

First Edition, 2007

Dialogue Publishing
16990 Cherry Crossing Dr.
Colorado Springs, CO 80921
http://www.dialoguepublishing.com
info@dialoguepublishing.com

Editing by Dorrie O'Brien, Grand Prairie, Texas
Cover design and book layout by Gail Cross, Desert Isle Design, Mesa, Arizona

Printed in the United States of America

1 2 3 4 5 6 7 8 9 10

For Nick

Acknowledgments

When I think of writing, not only this book, but also my writing career, the word "generosity" comes to the forefront. It has been through the generosity of many people's expertise, support, time, and friendship that I have been able to grow as a writer.

For a long time I didn't think I could write a novel. The committee in my head argued, "Yes you can. No you can't." It wasn't until I went to Anam Cara, a writer's retreat in Ireland, and silenced this committee enough to hear my own voice, that I knew I could write a novel.

To get a feel for this process, picture a small two-wheeled rickety donkey cart, with me sitting in the back of it, being pulled, not by donkeys, but by fabulous people. There have been times when I stopped the cart and tried to get off, but have been encouragingly nudged back on by my writer friends, editors who have become friends, long-time friends, new friends, and family. Thankfully, the cart and the novel made it to the finishing line and to a wonderful publisher.

It's time now to put names to the people who have so graciously helped push and pull me through this world of writing.

My friend Sue Booth Forbes, the person who started and runs Anam Cara, the writer and artist retreat in Ireland where my life changed one night while performing West Side Story in her living room. She has given me and countless other writers hope and a haven, words of wisdom and boy, have we had some laughs. Everyone needs a Sue Booth Forbes in their life.

To Tracy Clark, my mentor, who plucked my work from a pile and has worked with me for almost ten years. She is kind and generous and is the person who lets me know if my writing "sings" (or not!). In all of this time, we have only met and spoken once. The rest has been by Internet.

Wendy Beckman, I appreciate your feedback, humor, and friendship. And my writing group, Wendy, Jan, and Sandy, sisters in the pursuit of writing, laughing, and a good buffet.

Barbara Stahura, a writer extraordinaire, who I walk hand in hand with through the writing jungle. She encourages me when I have my days where I think I might quit writing and become a plumber. Keep the faith.

Thank you Pat Mirabelli, my friend, for reading an early draft and meeting me for our Diet Cokes in the afternoon.

To my editors who have supported me, and have become my friends, thank you. Ellen, Judy, Denise, Bob, and Leslie, you have each made me a better writer.

Sue Lutz Hamilton, and Dialogue Publishing, thank you for your support and the opportunity. You are a pleasure to work with.

I have to mention Betsy Wurster, my best friend since kindergarten. She doesn't read my work but I love her anyway!

To my kids, Ben, Chris, Andrea, and Rachel, now grown, who fill my world with hope and love and seem proud to tell people their mom is a writer. I have to thank my grandchildren Lanna, Ella, Connor, and Danny, because the mere mention of their names makes me smile. And thank you to Erin and Danielle, my daughters-in-law, who are wonderful wives and mothers and I am glad to have you in my life.

And for over thirty-five years I have had the support of a man who has been a true believer. Nick, words cannot express my gratitude and love. And your back scratches sustain. Now we can do that road trip.

On with the show!

Chapter 1

Getting Ready

Lydia stared out the window at the pile of firewood, next to the slab where the garage once stood, frosted with an ample layer of winter meringue. A tire swing hung from a branch of a half-dead oak tree.

She'd thought the grandkids would use the swing, but they never had. Instead, they'd sat on their bottoms playing Gameboy or Nintendo, eating Gummi Bears, asking her why she didn't buy Mountain Dew. Sometimes, in her attempt to look "hip," she popped a Puckerball into her mouth, turned toward her grandchildren, and stuck out her Leprechaun-green tongue. They thought she was a riot. Their parents didn't.

She reached for a bottle of aspirin, extra-strength, tapped two into her palm and swallowed them with a chaser of diet cola, hoping to prevent the headache she knew would come when the real estate agent appeared. Aspirin, diet cola, and prayer were Lydia's trinity of salvation for dealing with the world. After taking the first two parts of her elixir, Lydia pulled out a kitchen table chair, sat down, leaned her elbows on the table, clasped her hands together, bowed her head, closed her eyes, and prayed aloud.

"Dear Lord, do you want to know what I did today? I unclogged the kitchen drain. Oh, I know you already know, but I'm lonely and

I just need someone to talk to and since you're the one who took Walter from me, I think listening to me is the least you can do.

"If I sound edgy, it's because I am. It's been eight hundred and three days since Walter died and there's still not a day that goes by I don't think about him. There are days when I swear I hear him fumbling with his keys to unlock the front door, or when I'm upstairs, I call, "Walter? Is that you?" as I'm sure I hear him opening the cupboard door in the kitchen and emptying his change into the jar. But then nobody answers and I wonder if I'm going insane. At least insane with loneliness.

"It's not that I don't ever talk to anyone else. I do. But it's not the same as talking to someone who cares that you wake up every morning and gives you a kiss goodnight. Besides, I don't think the checkout clerk at the Dollar Store is really interested in hearing me explain my kitchen drain victory.

"I tried to tell Grace about my plumbing triumph but before I'd finished, she said, 'Why didn't you just call a plumber?' bursting my bubble. She had no idea what an accomplishment it was for me to be self-sufficient. And if I'd've told Tim what I did with the drain, he would've chastised me for not calling him.

"Also today, God, I was thinking about faith. I'm not sure why. I was running laundry through—actually, I spent a good hour trying to get a grape juice stain out of the tablecloth, and I almost got it all out, when the word "faith" popped into my head. See, that's the kind of thing I would also tell Walter about. Anyway, where was I? Oh, I mentioned how I was thinking about faith and I realized faith is really quite a ponderous subject. It weighed me down more than the laundry basket full of wet towels I carried from the second floor. It seems faith is such an easy word to say, but a hard thing to have. As I folded the towels I asked myself, what is faith? I suppose faith is believing without proof. Then I thought about how so many important things in life are things we can't see: love, sadness, hope, fear. They aren't tangible like a couch or a refrigerator

"Sometimes I wonder if faith isn't just a man-made ideal designed to keep all of us from packing it in when our lives seem full of despair. I mean, if I didn't have faith, would I still get up every day? Do you realize how difficult it is for a mother to lose her son and a wife to lose her husband? And yet I get up every morning believing this life you gave me is worth living.

"Oh, I'm rambling. And I'm tired and I have so much to do, so I'm going to move on with my prayer so you can move on to the next person.

"Thank you for my children: Grace, Tim, Sherry, and Sugar, all of whom I love dearly but don't know how to deal with. Grace is as bossy as ever. She thinks you put her in charge of telling us all what to do. She's even arranged for a real estate agent to come to my house tomorrow to try to talk me into selling our family home. Would it be a sin if I played 'not home'?

"Tim lets his wife walk on him like he's a freshly cut backyard. I'm convinced that's a big factor in why his hairline is receding. Sherry, the sweet dear, is getting quieter and quieter. I'm concerned for her. And Sugar, well, I pray for a visit from her, magenta hair and all.

"Be with my son Buddy. I wish you'd give Buddy back to me. I miss him. I miss him so much. I think about who he was and who he would have become. And I feel cheated.

"Be with my treasured cat Binky. And my dear friend Madeline, who undergoes a hysterectomy at four this afternoon even though I told her it is best to have surgery in the morning before the surgeon's feet, eyes, and hands get too tired. Be with Carol, my hairdresser for the last twelve years, who's going through her third divorce. Also, I ask you to watch over my friend Bonnie, who's turning the big Five-O and thinks her life is as good as over. I especially ask for help in keeping my sharp tongue from doing the devil's dirty work, calling slow drivers and rude cashier's names like moron ....
. . and worse.

"And as always, be with Walter. I miss something different about him each day. Today, I missed his whistling, even though I hated it when he was alive. He loved to whistle the theme from the movie *The Bridge over the River Kwai*. Whenever he whistled, I told him his whistling hurt my ears. And he'd always respond, saying, 'You'll miss it when I'm gone.' And I do. I really do.

"Until later, amen."

Lydia looked at the clock on the stove. "Nine-thirty. We've got two and a half hours to clean this old house, Bink. Think we can do it?" Between talking to herself and Binky, her cat, she was amazed at how much conversation she actually had.

"You know what they need to invent, Bink? A caffeine patch. I could sure use one right now. A bolt of high-octane caffeine." She bent down to pet her kitty. "Kiss, kiss," she said. She groaned as she straightened herself back up.

She cranked on the radio to the local oldies' station. Lesley Gore's "It's My Party" played. "Ooh, yes, Leslie, baby," Lydia said. She turned on the disposal and pushed down the hazelnut coffee grounds she had dumped into the sink. The disposal drowned out the radio. She turned up the volume.

She lifted the saucepan that had been soaking and squirted it with detergent and swirled the edges and bottom with a scouring pad. Her hips swayed to the music. She did a little shoulder action as she rinsed out the remnants of last night's tomato soup and lay the dripping pan in a dish rack. She sponged off the avocado-colored counter, then wiped out the inside of the sink. The smell of the lemon detergent and stale coffee grounds argued for prominence in the air.

Grabbing the broom from the pantry, she put it up to her mouth, holding it like it was a microphone. She sang, "Nobody knows where my Johnny has gone, but Judy left the same time." She lowered and tightened her grip and spot-swept the floor, aiming for a pile of toast crumbs under the table. As she sang, "It's my party and I'll cry if I want to, cry if I want to," she let go with a powerful thrust of the broom. The breeze made a collection of dust and cat fur dance across the floor like windswept tumbleweed skipping down the main street of a ghost town.

Her mind switched tracks. *When did Grace develop such a strong, overbearing personality? Who does she think she is taking other people's lives into her own hands, working them like they were putty? She wasn't like this when she was little.*

Or was she?

The more she thought about Grace's penchant for pushing people around, the more she realized this change didn't happen overnight. No. It developed gradually. The truth was, she'd ignored it. In her role as mother she didn't want to hurt Grace or any of her other four children's self-esteem. Self-esteem, those two magic buzz words of parenting. They were to Lydia and Walter like the words "college education," had been to their parents. She and Walter had been raised during the time when a college degree was perceived as a virtual guarantee for a successful, balanced, happy life. But Lydia had seen and known many people who had college degrees and still made muck out of their lives. She could make a list.

Same with self-esteem. Give your kids self-esteem and they will be successful, balanced, and have a good life. So Lydia never called her kids idiots (even if they were), she gave them choices instead of orders (would you like to brush your teeth now or in a few minutes?), and sang their praises for behavior that in past generations would be expected (Sugar, thanks so much for cleaning up your room. You should be so proud of yourself.). She told her kids how wonderful they were. She looked for each one's special talent and praised it to high hilt. She fed her kids breakfasts of self-esteem, lunches of praise, and dinners of compliments. The kids ate it like sugar. But eventually Lydia sensed this steady diet of candy-coated reality had produced cavities of arrogance and entitlement and parents who groveled at their children's feet.

She put the broom back in the pantry, shut the door, and leaned against it. She closed her eyes. *Grace is just trying to help*, she thought. Maybe it was time to move. Maybe this house was too big for her after all. And maybe, just maybe, Grace wasn't too far off the mark when she blurted out, while driving home with her mother from Port Huron Mall, that when Walter died, not only did she lose her father, but she lost a good part of her mother, too. "And that's totally unfair," she'd said.

Lydia looked at the clock, again. Almost ten. Time to engage in suburban-style chemical warfare. She bent down to get her bucket and cleaning supplies from under the sink. Unintentionally, she knocked over a stack of baked-black cookie sheets. "Damn," she said. She accidentally grabbed a can of ant and roach spray instead of furniture polish because she didn't have her glasses on because they were broken.

Her hand made its way around an ever-expanding collection of hard sponges. She grabbed her red rubber gloves and snapped them on with a surgeon's skill, reached for the furniture polish, two old diapers, a squeegee, glass cleaner, tile cleaner, bleach, air freshener, and toilet bowl cleaner, and placed them in her official cleaning bucket.

There was a knock at the door. "Oh great," she said, looking at Binky. "Who in the world could that be?"

Chapter 2

The Realtor

Lydia marched down the hall. Her goal was to get rid of whoever was at the door so she could get back to cleaning. This place was a mess. Her modus operandi since Walter died was to throw everything into the nearest closet. She'd decided long ago not to look at cobwebs as clusters of dirt. Instead, they were fairy doilies, God's curtains.

"You're delusional," Grace told her. And maybe she was. But whose business was it, anyway? If she wanted to be delusional, so be it. If she wanted to be a hermit, so be it. And if how she lived her life didn't suit her kids or anyone else, so be that, too.

The knock at the door became insistent, like a woodpecker.

"I'm coming already," Lydia said.

Lydia and Walter Calypso and family had moved into the house at 147 Chippewa Street twenty-seven years ago, after Walter had been named principal of Port Huron High School. They were drawn to the neighborhood for several reasons. It was convenient to shopping, the library, the beach, and both of the schools where they worked.

On Sundays, they used to drive through the neighborhood and look longingly at the older homes, many being renovated by young families such as theirs. They drove slowly in order to avoid hitting kids who rode Big Wheels, hopped on pogo sticks, chased balls, and sometimes played on the street. Lydia loved to go through the area just past dusk when people had turned the inside lights on but hadn't yet shut the shades.

Lydia tugged at the door. It wasn't easy to open. Over the years it had weathered and wasn't plumb anymore.

"Hello, Liddy. My name is Bitsy Esterhaus," the woman said. "It's nice to meet you. I've heard so much about you from Grace. You know she and I met when she was an attorney for Great Lakes Title Company."

Bitsy stepped inside. She wore a red tweed suit and a tennis bracelet Lydia was certain she had seen for sale on QVC. When she entered the foyer, Bitsy extended her hand. Waving her red-glove-encased hands in front of her, Lydia said, "Sorry, I was cleaning." She smelled Bitsy's gardenia-scented perfume.

"Lovely window treatments," Bitsy said, reaching for one of the gold swags hanging above the picture window. She rubbed the fabric between her fingers. "Chintz?"

"No, actually a polyester and rayon blend."

"Oh. Faux chintz."

"Yes," Lydia said, "faux chintz." She had never heard of such a thing. "I am sorry," she said, finally removing her gloves. "I wasn't expecting you until noon. That's when Grace said you'd be here. Noon."

"Noon? Oh no, there must have been a miscommunication. I said around ten-thirty. I have a Rotary meeting at noon."

"But my house, me, we're not ready." She felt like she was a little kid in school making excuses about a poorly written assignment.

"Don't worry about it. What difference does a couple of hours make?"

"A lot."

Ignoring the obvious clue that it might be better if she came back at another time, Bitsy placed her personal computer on the marble-topped washstand Walter's grandmother had brought from England when she'd come to the United States in the late 1800s. Walter had insisted the piece was over 200-years-old. He'd loved to tell the age of everything, how much it cost, and where it'd come from. For a long time, Lydia considered this trait a harmless foible, until Walter bragged to their card club about the great bargain he got on the mink coat he'd bought her for her fiftieth birthday. "It only cost fifty bucks. Got it at the Crème de la Crème consignment shop." Lydia knew it made Walter feel big to tell such stories, but it had made her feel small.

On the table were three books. One was about the doors of Boston. Lydia thought doors were a strange subject for a book, but she'd received it as a retirement gift from the English department. There was a book containing a photo compilation of John Deere tractors. This book had been a favorite of Walter's. The third book was about sisters, given to her by her psychic sister in Houston, the one who hadn't spoken to Lydia since she'd rejected her offer to act as a medium.

She watched as Bitsy moved the books so she could open her laptop case.

Binky peeked her head around the door. Lydia had planned to put the cat in her travel case before the real estate agent arrived but she hadn't had time since Bitsy had come so early.

"Meow," Binky cried as she strode into the room. Ignoring Lydia and Bitsy, Binky stood at the base of the floral-patterned sofa, arched her back, rounded her shoulders, stuck her tail high in the air, jumped on the seat, then hopped up to the back of the sofa, lay her heavy yellow body down, agile as a gymnast on a balance beam, dropped her tail, and swung it like a metronome. She turned her head toward Bitsy, and looked at her as if to say, "I hope you weren't planning on sitting here."

Bitsy turned and to Lydia's surprise, picked up Binky. "Hey, pretty puddy cat."

Lydia was surprised the Realtor seemed to like cats. "I can put her in the other room," she said, reaching for Binky.

"Nah, she's fine," Bitsy said, nuzzling the cat.

Lydia was beginning to like this gal, even though she didn't want to.

After putting Binky down on the floor, Bitsy got back to business.

"The market is really hot right now. Things are moving lickety-split. And it isn't even spring yet," she said, clicking her fingernails on the laptop keys.

The click, click, click, made Lydia think of the song, "Fly Me to the Moon." Lydia told Walter she'd never go into outer space even if NASA paid her a million dollars. But at the moment, flying to the moon sounded pretty good. She was tired of dealing with mornings that were too quiet, when her only company was an anchor person sitting in a little box talking about things that had no relevance in her life. She hated having coffee alone. And she missed Walter, his irritations, his snoring.

Reality returned when she heard Bitsy say, "I'll be logged on in just a sec."

"Would you like a cup of coffee?" Lydia asked, praying Bitsy's would say yes so she could go into the other room. The gardenia perfume was giving her a headache.

"Sure. Cream and sugar, please. Or half and half will do."

"I have faux cream," Lydia said, trying to show she had a sense of humor.

"Pardon me?"

"Faux cream, like faux chintz curtains. You know… two-percent," Lydia said, chuckling, pleased with her own quick wit.

"Oh, well, that's fine. That's what I should be using anyway."

Lydia went to the kitchen. She sensed that giving this agent a tour of the house was going to be like getting weighed in public. Humiliating. During her last visit to the beauty shop she'd heard Val, the manicurist, tell a couple of people that the Department of Motor Vehicles was going to start weighing people when they got their driver's licenses renewed. Lydia swore that if that happened, she'd take the bus.

Lydia walked into the living room carrying the coffee and a couple of slices of Entenmann's cherry strudel on a small silver tray her daughter, Sherry, had dug out of the closet to serve guests who stopped by the house after Walter's funeral. As she set the tray down on an end table, Bitsy mentioned a house she'd just sold two streets over, on Cherokee. "I sold it for four hundred thirty-five thousand. But of course it has a pool and guesthouse; a very unique property. It was totally updated with the newest amenities like granite countertops and a steam room."

Lydia didn't listen. Instead, she wondered why, throughout her married years, she'd rarely used the pretty things she and Walter had collected. Why was she so afraid things would get chipped or scratched or marred or broken? They had china from her mother, a beautiful cut-glass Waterford pitcher they'd gotten as a twenty-fifth anniversary gift, and even a set of four-hundred thread count Egyptian cotton sheets she wouldn't use because she was afraid she'd ruin them.

Thud.

"Oh my, are you all right?" she asked as she noticed Bitsy losing her balance while reaching behind the sofa.

"Is there a plug back here? My computer battery appears to have died. Technology. I have a real love-hate relationship with it. Do you use a computer?"

"Egad, no. My kids keep telling me I need to move into the twenty-first century, get a computer and go—what is it they say? Wireless?—but I'm a yellow-legal-pad sort of gal. There's a socket closer to the other end of the couch. Let me plug it in for you."

"Oh, thanks. The battery says it will last four hours, but of course it runs out of juice if I just look at it."

Lydia took the computer plug, leaned over the couch and nearly fell into Bitsy's lap. "Whoa," she said as she momentarily lost her balance.

By the look on Bitsy's face she could tell the poor woman didn't know whether to catch her or push her away. Bitsy perched her tortoise-shell-colored half-glasses toward the edge of her nose, tilted her head forward and smiled. She had something between her teeth. A poppy seed. Seeing the seed made Lydia work the front of her own teeth with her tongue. She noticed Bitsy's eyebrows arched in a slightly odd place. But on her, the eyebrows sort of worked.

The phone rang.

"Hello, Mom? It's me."

"Uh-huh," Lydia answered.

"Is Bitsy there yet?"

"Uh-huh."

"Well, what do you think of her? She's great, isn't she?"

"Uh-huh."

"Have you talked about selling the house?"

"Uh-huh."

"I'm going to drop Kelly off at dance and then drive on over. Say, is Bitsy near you?"

"Uh-huh."

"Let me speak to her. Okay?"

"Uh-huh."

Lydia handed Bitsy the phone, then got up and walked to the piano, which was covered with family photos. Some faced left, some faced right. Grace had told Lydia the arrangement looked helter-skelter. Lydia countered with, "There is a method to my madness. I want it to look like the people in the photos are talking to one another." Grace and Guy and their three kids faced Sherry and Joe and their kids Danny and Markey. Tim, his wife Helen, and their two children, Heather and Brady, were posed as though they were talking to Lydia and Walter, whose photo was taken when they celebrated their thirty-fifth anniversary at an all-male production of *Guys and Dolls* at the Hidden Valley Dinner Theatre. "Next time read the fine print in the ad," Walter had told Lydia.

Lydia's favorite photo of Buddy, taken when he was sixteen, a year before he'd died, stood alone in the center. He was on a dock, shirtless, smiling. He held a string of Walleye. Golden rays from the sun silhouetted his sunburned face and shoulders. Sugar's photo sat left of center, facing an autographed photo of Katie Couric. Lydia had received the picture of Katie at Christmas. It was a gift from Sugar. Until she was fired, Sugar had been in charge of the teleprompter for one of the news programs. One day she'd had to take something to Katie's office. While she was there, she'd told Katie how much her mother admired her. Katie gave her an autographed picture. It was Lydia's favorite present that year.

She started to wipe dust off the piano with her sleeve. But she stopped. *This is stupid*, she thought.

She watched as Bitsy kept talking to Grace.

Yes, she was ticked that Grace had sent this Bitsy to her house and yes, she was not thrilled Bitsy showed up so early, but she could see why Grace liked this woman.

"Oh yes. It's lovely. Uh-huh. Yes. She is a delight," Lydia heard Bitsy say. "Sort of quiet though," Bitsy whispered into the receiver. "I haven't looked around yet. Just doing a little preliminary chit-chat... you know. Then tour. Then a market analysis. How about if I give you a call later? Uh-huh. I will... Don't worry. I'll take good care of her."

Bitsy handed Lydia the portable phone. "Not sure how to turn this thing off," she said, adding, "That Grace is such a jewel. Such a good daughter. Sounds like she really takes good care of you." Bitsy leaned forward, peered down over her glasses, and looked at Lydia. "She certainly loves her mother."

Lydia was a bit embarrassed, so she just nodded.

As Bitsy continued fiddling with her computer, Lydia thought about how since Walter died, Grace, and the other three kids, confused love with control, a helping hand with suffocation, and her needs with theirs. In the reshuffling, the rights and privileges she had earned as a mother and adult had disappeared.

Grace had made it perfectly clear she was finished mourning her father's death. It was also obvious she thought it was high time for her mother to move on, too. "You need to sell the house and move closer to us," Grace said. Lydia suspected Grace's motives had something to do with free babysitting. Grace had hinted that she would love to resume her career as an attorney. The reason she hadn't done so was because her husband, Guy, said he didn't want the kids "left like orphans" at daycare.

Lydia's second oldest, Tim, was certain his mother would do better in a condominium, or a planned development where the grass was cut, snow removal was taken care of and outside maintenance would be done, all for a monthly fee. Heaven knows that would take the burden of his mother's problems off him. Lydia understood this, but had she really called upon Tim for help all that often? She didn't think so.

Sherry told her mom she thought she should go back into teaching. "You loved teaching," Sherry said. And Lydia had loved teaching. That is, up until the last few years before her retirement when all of the changes in the profession caught up with her. Many of the students didn't give a flying Fig Newton whether they passed or failed. Regardless of their grade, they knew they would go onto the next level anyway. She got tired of the administration breathing down her back about higher test scores without consideration as to whether the students learned to think. And the parents. Good Lord. Half the students came from broken homes. From her vantage point, it was obvious many parents didn't have a clue how to raise a child. They didn't even know how to raise themselves.

Sherry didn't know any of this because she was away at college during that time.

Then there was Sugar, Lydia's youngest, who had picked up a drug habit instead of a degree at Antioch College, and who had spent the last two years living in a ramshackle, fifth-floor walkup in New York. She seldom heard from Sugar. And she wasn't sure why.

The only child who didn't seem to be telling her what to do was her son Buddy, who had broken the unwritten law that a child should not die before his parents.

"Shall we start with a tour?" Bitsy asked, standing and pulling the bottom of her brown suede jacket down over her wide hips. Lydia knew the feeling. She was always trying to pull sweaters, shirts, and tops down over her hips, which were, as her mother told her, "born for birthing."

"Well, this is the living room."

Bitsy scribbled notes on a yellow legal pad. "Tell me about this room."

What's to tell? A room is a room is a room. "What do you mean?"

"Oh, just some of the special features. You know, like new carpet or special lighting or features like the fireplace. Is it wood or gas burning? Does it have a gas line? Things like that."

"Oh. No, it doesn't have a gas line; it is wood-burning. I haven't used it in a long time, though."

"Any particular reason why not?"

"No. Well, yes, actually. Walter always made the fires. He was a Boy Scout, a semi-professional pyromaniac."

Bitsy laughed. "I had one of those, too. My son. Except his thing was firecrackers. Set a bunch off in the basement. About five thousand dollars later, you couldn't even tell what part of the basement burned."

"Aren't kids grand?" Lydia commented. Dang. This Realtor was a real person, not the stereotype she suspected Grace would send. "Shall we go into the dining room?"

"Sure. Just let me finish my notes."

Bitsy stood in the living room finishing writing while Lydia went to the dining room and opened the closed drapes, shut to keep the cold air out. Walter had insisted on closed drapes during the 1980s when energy prices skyrocketed. She hated keeping the drapes drawn because it made the house so dark and it made it difficult for her to see the world, but every time she opened them on a cold day, she heard Walter's voice saying, "It's costing a fortune."

Lydia turned on the chandelier and dimmed the light so it wouldn't be too bright. She didn't want Bitsy to see the thick layer of dust on the buffet. She straightened the papers on the dining table, bills mostly, coupons that she'd clipped but had forgotten to use, and birthday cards she bought for her family and friends whose birthdays were coming soon. She mailed birthday cards at the beginning of each month so she wouldn't forget to send them. No matter what day of the month your birthday was, you'd receive your card by the fifth.

"This isn't a bad-sized dining room," Bitsy said, turning the dimmer switch to make the light brighter. "Room for a hutch, buffet, table for how many? Eight?"

"We've had sixteen seated at the table. The table has three extensions."

"Wow. That must have been a bit snug. Or they didn't have hips as wide as mine."

"Oh, I guess it was a tad tight, but it is a great room for holiday dinners."

Lydia was proud of her dining room. The two-bedroom house they had lived in before hadn't had a dining room. It was one of the aspects of this house she loved.

"Nice view out the window. Ooh, but only single-paned glass. Not so good." Bitsy traced her hand along the edges of the windows, checking for broken seals. "I'm afraid to ask what your utility bill is." Without waiting for a reply, she added, "Will you be leaving the chandelier or taking it with you?"

Take the chandelier? Had Grace told this woman she was going to sell for sure? Nothing like getting your home sold out from under you, she thought. "Sure I'll take it. If I ever move." The chandelier was one of the few things she'd gotten after her parents died. It was an expensive chandelier. The price she paid was a three-year estrangement with one of her sisters. "What did Grace tell you, anyway?"

"That you wanted to sell your house."

"I never said that. I told her I didn't know what I was going to do. She told me you were just coming over to give me some idea of what houses around here are selling for."

"Well, maybe she just assumed you'd be selling. I know she thinks you *should* sell."

"Yes, I know that. But as far as I know, it is *my* name on the deed, not hers."

"Oh, I am so sorry. It is obvious I've struck a nerve. I hope you realize I'm here to help you, not hurt you," Bitsy said, her voice taking on a low, soft tone. "It seems that you and Grace might not be on the same page."

"That's for sure. Forget the same page, Grace and I haven't even been on the same chapter for quite a while now. Maybe she means

well, but it's as though she thinks she's the only one with a brain."
Lydia put a hand over her mouth. "Oh, I'm sorry. I shouldn't have
said that. You don't need to hear our family laundry. I don't know
what has gotten into me."

"No need to apologize. I have a family. I have sons and daughters
and I know the drama that comes with a family. My kids only stopped
telling me how to live my life after I told them if they didn't knock
it off I'd take them out of my will. Of course, I was just kidding,
but they didn't know that. Worked like a charm. But, nevertheless,
if you do decide to sell, and we do put your house on the market,
if you're going to take the chandelier, we can put a sticky note on it
or you can replace it before the house goes up for sale. Also—I hate
to be the bearer of bad news—but this wallpaper is really dated; it's
quite a busy pattern. And unfortunately, many prospective buyers
can't imagine their own furnishings in a home if it's decorated too
much like the current owners."

Lydia wanted to wilt.

When she and Walter had looked at this Victorian, wood-frame
house, it had been covered with chipping crème de menthe-colored
paint. Every room had different styles of wallpaper. The dining
room had bird-of-paradise swooping over a green-striped, tropical
background. The living room was decorated with red velvet-flocked
hibiscus. Their bedroom was papered with the most vibrant and
obnoxious lavender she and Walter had ever seen. They both thought
it was hysterical that the ceiling in the master bedroom had a huge
mirror on it. "Now that's an interesting touch in a Victorian house,"
Lydia had said at the time. And the bathroom with the pink-and-
black tile that someone painted sea shells on? Even that didn't make
them not buy the house.

"You mean having wallpaper someone doesn't like makes people
not buy a house?" Lydia asked. "Don't buyers look at a house's
character, a place for them to fulfill their dreams?"

"For better or worse, we're past the days when generations of
families lived in the same house forever. We live in a transient society.
People move in and six month later they're transferred to Omaha.

And with over fifty-percent of marriages ending in divorce, well, it's a changed world from when you bought this place."

"In other words, you're basically saying if I sell, I'll need to strip the wallpaper off all the walls and replace it?"

"Yes, m'…"

"And what would I replace it with?"

"Something neutral. Buyers these days want a clean slate. They want to be their own artists and start with a plain palate. Houses, well, homes, are statements these days. They say, 'This is me. This is who I am and what I have achieved.'"

Boy, was Lydia getting an education. When she and Walter bought this house, they were simply looking for a good place to raise their family. "I just don't know about this," Lydia said as she walked into the kitchen, each step becoming heavier along the way.

"That's just the way the world of real estate works these days. People want what they want and they want it when and how they want it. They want better than what their parents had and they want it sooner than their parents had it. Bigger and better. It's the American way."

"I guess you're right."

She leaned against the wall. She thought about how she had seen it with her kids. Not so much Sugar, who definitely set her own standards, but certainly Grace, and Tim, and maybe Sherry, although not so much Sherry, either, because she was barely hanging on by a thread, financially. But Grace? Definitely Grace. She had moved five times already and she was only thirty-three. Each place was bigger and better. Grace had told her mother that since Guy was a lawyer with Taft, Lincoln and Adams, a prestigious firm in Sandusky, they needed to live to a certain standard. "We work hard for it and we're going to have it, by God."

Lydia hated it when Grace said "by God." But she kept her lip zipped. Lydia worried about Grace and Guy's lifestyle, how they sometimes robbed Peter to pay Paul and used credit cards even to buy food. Walter would never have approved of that. She worried Grace spent money to fill a void.

Well, to be fair, Lydia worried about everything. Since she had retired it had become her full-time profession.

And Tim, perhaps it wasn't so much Tim, but his wife Helen who was never satisfied with what they had. She loved throwing every new SUV in the neighborhood in Tim's face. She wanted new carpet because Brady, their son, spilled grape juice on it. Helen had called Tim at work and went on and on how the carpet was ruined by that stain and they would have to get the whole first-floor carpet replaced. After Tim mentioned what happened to his mother, Lydia called Helen and suggested she use spot remover and a good steam clean.

Two weeks later, Lydia noticed they had gotten new carpeting.

"How about the carpet? How old is it?" Bitsy asked.

The question jolted Lydia out of her trancelike state. "Gosh. It isn't new, although it seems like we just got it yesterday. I think we bought it about six years ago, not long after Buddy died. Weird, isn't it? Your son dies so you buy new carpet. Actually, I think that's when we replaced several things. The summer after Buddy died. Walter thought buying things might help me get over his death. But of course it didn't." Lydia wanted to kick herself for giving out so much information.

Bitsy took Lydia's hand. "I understand."

Lydia pulled her hand away. *No, you don't,* she wanted to say. But she didn't. Instead, she stood stone-faced and thought about the many well-intentioned people who came to Buddy's memorial service, looked through her eyes, held her hand like a slab of bacon, and said, "I understand." But they didn't understand. And this woman didn't understand, either. None of these people could understand. Not unless they too had a child who had killed himself.

Bitsy walked into the kitchen. Lydia followed.

"I haven't seen a stove like this in a long time," Bitsy said. "Does it work?"

"Works like new. Looks like new, too, don't you think?"

"Well, yes, it does. Did this come with the house?"

"Oh, no. We, Walter and I, bought it at an auction in Waynesville. We fell in love with it."

The 1934 Detroit Jewel Bitsy was ogling over had slender legs and a smooth, shiny backsplash that leaned forward to cover the burners if they weren't being used.

Bitsy touched one of the knobs. "Ivory?"

"No, Bakelite, an early form of plastic." She loved telling people that. Lydia lifted the porcelain lids off the burners and the griddle in the middle. She turned one of the Bakelite knobs and flames shot out.

"It looks old but new. Did you use it much?"

"All the time. Cooking's one of my hobbies; well, it was, when I had people around to feed. Walter and I cooked together."

"I must say this is a beaut. Quite a collectible," Bitsy said as she moved toward the sink.

Lydia's shoulders relaxed when she talked about the old stove. Something about this well-worn kitchen, peeling paint and all, made her feel safe.

Then Bitsy asked with a wink, "You won't be taking that with you, will you?"

"I wish I knew," Lydia said.

Bitsy went about her business. "Dishwasher. Disposal. Exhaust fan. A nice-sized pantry, or it would be, if it wasn't so overflowing. You have enough foodstuffs in there to feed China." Bitsy tried to shut the pantry door, but it pushed itself open. "The kitchen is a bit small."

"I never thought of it as being small. Our whole family sat around this table."

"Today, the kitchen is *the-a-ter*. It's the hub of the house, the room where most people entertain," Bitsy said, making a grand gesture with her arm.

Lydia laughed at Bitsy's theatrical display. "What about the living room? Isn't that the room where you're supposed to entertain?"

"Not anymore." Bitsy said, "That was then. This is now. Life is much less formal these days. No one wants to be stuck back in the kitchen working when everyone else is in the other room. That takes away the mojo."

"The what?"

"Mojo. Sex appeal."

Lydia knew she'd been out of the flow of things since Walter died, but now she felt as though she were living in a world she didn't understand at all. Sex appeal at a dinner party? No wonder so many marriages ended in divorce. People were worried about mojo instead of a good Beef Bourguignon. Good Lord, what was the world coming to?

Lydia's shoulders drooped as she walked out of the kitchen and into the hallway. She wasn't sure how she would muster enough energy to show Bitsy the entire house. With barely a movement, she opened the door to the den. She didn't want Bitsy to see the hole in the wall that had been there since Tim knocked his elbow through it when he and Buddy were rough-housing.

Bitsy peeked her head in the den without entering. She stood in the doorway and took notes.

"This would make a nice office," Bitsy said. "Is there hardwood under the carpet?"

"Actually, there is linoleum over the wood and under the carpet. The owners before us had put down linoleum. Orange linoleum. Walter tried to remove it but it was a mess, so we just put carpet over it. He was going to fix it when he had more time.

Lydia led the tour room after room—Bitsy following, adding notes to her stenographer's notebook. Another room on the first floor, one that was supposed to be a guestroom, was covered floor-to-ceiling in fabrics and patterns. A dress-making mannequin stood in front of the window. A tape measure was draped over her shoulder and a wide-brimmed Victorian floral hat sat cockeyed on the round head that someone had put on top of the neck. The wood head with a painted face had on a blonde wig on under the hat. Bitsy laughed when she saw the expression on the mannequin's face that looked like someone had pulled her cinch too tight.

"This looks like a hub of activity," Bitsy said.

Lydia felt her face turn red. "Oh my word, this is a mess." Bending over, she picked up some red plaid taffeta she had begun to make a

Christmas tree skirt from… two years ago. There was also a basket of yarn in various colors and textures. Stacks of fabric and notions lined the walls.

"You'll have to excuse this mess," Lydia said, sinking under the realization of the many projects she had started but hadn't finished.

Bitsy picked up a pattern that was by the sewing machine. "This would look good on you," she said. "In a nice, bright yellow."

Lydia smiled.

"But," she added, "When you sell, you really will have to do something with all this stuff. Perspective buyers would be overwhelmed."

Lydia and Bitsy walked upstairs, Lydia holding onto the handrail for support. At the top of the stairs, to the left, was Grace and Sherry's old bedroom. It was the only room that had some semblance of order. Bitsy didn't even comment on the striped wallpaper. Sugar's room, the smallest bedroom, still had posters of punk rockers on the walls. The bed was made but you could barely tell because so many clothes and boxes were stacked atop it. Lydia kicked a couple of pairs of old grunge boots out of the way so Bitsy could enter. By this time Lydia wasn't even listening to Bitsy's comments. She had zoned out.

Bitsy took hold of the doorknob to open the boy's room. Lydia quickly placed her hand over Bitsy's, at first preventing her from turning the doorknob.

"No," Lydia said. "We can't go in there. We just can't."

Bitsy looked confused. Her eyebrows arched even more than normal.

"Is there something wrong with this room?" Bitsy asked.

Lydia shook her head. "No," she said. "I just don't want to go in there. I just can't." Her eyes had welled and her voice had become thin.

In a quiet voice, Bitsy told Lydia that in order to give her an accurate analysis, she really did need to see the whole house. She said this as she placed her hand on Lydia's shoulder.

"It's just that this room has a lot of memories," Lydia said.

"I understand," Bitsy said. "We can make it quick."

Lydia opened the door and followed Bitsy into the room. And

true to her word, Bitsy stayed only a couple of minutes.

Bitsy poked her head into the hall bathroom that all of the kids had shared. The stool, with the worn Humpty Dumpty, all five of the kids had used when they were little to stand on to brush their teeth was next to the sink. Lydia stood in the doorway.

Looking at it, Lydia could still see each of her kids standing on it, carefully squeezing out toothpaste onto their small toothbrushes.

The last room was Lydia and Walter's room which had a half-heartedly made bed and a multitude of clutter. Lydia picked up her flannel nightgown she had dropped on the floor and laid it on the bed. Bitsy walked around the room, looked to see what type of view there was out the window, and made more notes. *She must be writing a novel,* Lydia thought.

Bitsy said she thought she had seen enough for this visit. Lydia felt a miniscule of relief when they walked back downstairs. After they were on the first floor, Bitsy walked back to the dining room and looked out the large picture window.

"What's the matter?" Lydia asked, joining Bitsy in her search for she didn't-know-what.

"I don't see a garage. Don't you have a garage?"

Lydia felt the room temperature drop to zero. Her face drained of color. "It was over there," she said, pointing to the back left corner of the yard. "We used to have a garage over there."

"Well, what happened to it?"

"It was, a, just, a, old and um, falling apart so we tore it down," Lydia sputtered.

"Eeh. You know, that might have a negative effect on the resale value of your property," Bitsy said. "Garages are big these days."

When Bitsy finished looking out the window, Lydia pulled the dining room drapes closed. This time not to keep the cold air out, but to keep memories at bay.

Before she left, Bitsy told Lydia what she thought the Victorian house would sell for if it were "in top condition," and if she invested in a new garage. Lydia was taken back by the number. Bitsy said she'd put information together and make a list of things Lydia should do to get the house "ready to go." Lydia wanted to say "go where?" She pictured her house pulling up stakes and trotting down the street, taking a shortcut between the Gleason's Tudor and the Marabelle's Mediterranean until it ran out of breath and plopped down only one street over. She kept this thought to herself.

"Well, thank you for your time," Bitsy said, as she packed up her laptop. "I can tell this wasn't easy for you."

Lydia helped Bitsy with her coat.

"It was a pleasure meeting you," Bitsy said, extending her hand.

This time, Lydia held her hand out, too.

After she shut and dead-bolted the front door, Lydia walked into the kitchen. She put the salt shaker and pepper mill back in the middle of the Lazy Susan that was in the middle of the table. She noticed the peppermill needed filling. She took a wedge of cantaloupe from the fridge, ground some pepper on it and took a bite. She sat down in one of her garage-sale chairs and counted fourteen pink paper pouches of Sweet 'n Low she had saved from going through fast food drive-thrus. She adjusted them so they all faced the same way in the milk glass bowl. She pinched off some crumbs from the strudel Bitsy had left untouched and dumped the rest into the stainless garbage can Walter had gotten for free when he'd purchased a one hundred-forty-nine piece set of knives off the Home Shopping Network.

Restless, Lydia got up and walked to the living room. Binky followed, climbing on to his mistress as she sat on the piano bench, then jumped off Lydia and onto the piano keys, making a sound like a chord in a horror movie. Lydia would have loved to have gone upstairs, taken off her shoes and pants to lie down, but Grace had said she was coming and Lydia knew that just as soon as she dozed off, her daughter would arrive. So she did the next best thing. She unbuttoned her pants in an attempt to relieve the feeling of suffocation she had felt all morning.

"Ah, there are some benefits of living alone," she said as she unzipped her zipper a couple of inches. "Freedom."

She turned toward the piano, pulled the cover over the keys, causing Binky to jump to the floor, folded her arms and placed them on the piano and lowered her head to rest on her arms.

If only she could shake the embarrassment she had felt when Bitsy opened the hall closet and a baseball mitt had fallen on her head. She winced. Thankfully, Bitsy had laughed. But when she'd opened her bedroom closet, you'd have thought she was afraid a rat would jump out and bite her ankles. The expression on Bitsy's face was priceless when she opened the linen closet and the vacuum hose broke loose and flailed about as if it were inhabited by a ghost.

"Poor Bitsy. I hope she doesn't tell Grace."

Most all of the closets in the house were as overstuffed as the stockings Lydia used to fill for her kids at Christmas. She hadn't been able to bring herself to clean them for years, not since Buddy died. To her they weren't just "things" that were in these closets, miscellaneous merchandise that had no meaning, no life or weight. They were the trail that told she and her family existed.

It wasn't just a baseball mitt, a singular item, with only one remembrance. She had taken both Tim and Buddy to buy their baseball mitts. She'd taken them to baseball signups and she had made brownies for the team picnics and sold raffle tickets to her friends to try to help raise money for a new backstop and she helped Tim oil his glove even though she thought that would make the glove slippery and she remembered the crisis when Buddy thought his glove was stolen and they offered a reward for its return.

And the errant vacuum? That was her mother's vacuum. It was better than all of the new upright vacuums she and Walter had bought and boy, did it do a job on the stairs.

"You certainly have a lot of 'stuff,'" Bitsy had said as she chewed around the house like a termite.

"It might appear to you to be clutter," Lydia said, "but what you're calling clutter is my life."

There was Buddy's purple shirt with Harmon's Insurance arched above the number thirteen, (his favorite number); he'd worn it to Little League games the year the team won the championship. Lydia

tried hard between ball games to remove the grass stains and the
smell of a young boy's sweat, and she was upset that even after using
the strongest cleaners, the sweat smell remained. But after Buddy
died she was grateful the smell hadn't left. At least once a year, on
the anniversary of his death, Lydia went to Buddy's closet, took the
folded shirt off the shelf, brought it to her face and buried her soul
in her son's scent.

The pink tutu Grace had worn and pirouetted in as a doll in Miss
Casteel's annual dance recital was in one of the closets. And there
was the retainer Sherry had hated to wear it because it made her lisp.
When Bitsy had opened the door to Walter's closet, Lydia'd recoiled.
She could feel the words Bitsy hadn't said, "Why haven't you cleaned
that closet? Gotten rid of his stuff?"

Lydia'd wanted to run. She'd wanted to crawl out of her skin, skin
that didn't feel like her own anymore, skin that had been massaged
so deep with grief it had grown old. She wished she'd had the guts to
say, "Get out of my house, my home, my life. I don't need someone,
anyone, coming into my home, judging me. Not you. Not my kids.
No one. Only God."

Chapter 3

A Matter of Grace

Grace shepherded Austin and Kelly into her silver Town and Country minivan. Kelly, whose caramel-colored hair had never been cut and was braided and wound like a climbing rose around the top of her head, hopped into the van and helped her little brother Austin up and across the backseat, boosting him into his car seat behind the driver. Kelly was five, Austin was three. Kelly was slender like Grace. Austin's body was plump and round like a soaked bean.

"Mommy, Austin's sitting on the seatbelt thing and I can't get it out," Kelly said.

"Just relax, Kel, I'll be there in a minute. I'm strapping Gigi in. I can't be two places at one time," Grace said as she plopped the carrier containing Gigi onto the leather car seat.

Gigi was short for Giselle, who'd been conceived fifteen months earlier, in Paris, after a stroll along the Seine and a bottle of Champagne Bollinger Grande Annee Brut 1995. In a dark, mood-laden café swirling with smoke and throaty conversation, over a dinner of escargot, rack of lamb, and crème brulée, they discussed how they thought that two children, a boy and a girl, were plenty, the perfect family and that after they returned from Paris, Guy would get a vasectomy. That was after one glass of wine. But by the time the bottle was empty, passion trumped planning and off to their room they went where the smell of lavender wafted in the air, flames from the fireplace did the tango and they slid in and out of each other all night long on creamy silk sheets in a four-poster mahogany bed.

When they found out Grace was pregnant with their third child, Guy decided to put off the vasectomy until after the baby was born. "That's a mistake," Grace had told him. You should just go ahead and get it done now."

But Guy pleaded he was too busy. He'd get it done later.

Grace gave a heavy sigh. Kelly scrunched her nose and squeezed through the front seats and sat in the passenger seat. "Shotgun," she said.

"Where'd you hear that?" Grace asked.

"From Markey and Danny. They call it whenever they get in the car."

Her cousins. Grace's sister Sherry's boys.

"Danny says if you have to ride in the backseat alone you're the nigger."

"Kelly! Kelly Mumford! Don't you ever say that again."

"What? Shotgun?"

"No. The word…the word…" She could barely bring herself to say it. "N-i-g-g-e-r. That's not a nice word. It hurts people's feelings."

"But it doesn't hurt my feelings, Mommy. Whose feeling does it hurt?"

Grace didn't have time to go into the meaning of the word or why it shouldn't be used. They were late. How could she explain racism and prejudice while she had three kids in the car and a zillion things on her mind in order to get ready for Bunko, which was at her house tonight? And how could she tell Kelly about how much it hurt her, when, as a child, she was the victim of racial slurs because of her dark skin and hair?

"It's just not nice, that's all. I'll tell you why later." She could ring her nephew Danny's neck. That's part of the reason why she hated to get together for family functions like birthday and holidays. She was afraid of what her kids would pick up from her sister Sherry's kids or Sherry's husband, Joe, the family bigot.

Her sister's kids ran rampant. Talked back to their parents. At Thanksgiving, Danny had burped during grace. And what did his father Joe do? Laughed. Sherry said nothing. Grace had wanted to pop the little bugger. She and Guy never liked or approved of Sherry's husband. "A total redneck" Guy called him. Grace agreed. He reminded her of a scab picker. Someone who finds something that is trying to heal and then picks away at the wound until it bleeds. Over and over until it turns to cancer.

Joe was also the only family member who ever mentioned Grace's adoption or the fact that she was Hispanic.

Kelly bent over and picked up her Barbie backpack, opened it, got out her Princess Barbie, closed the pink bag, put it on the floor, and snapped her seatbelt. Sometimes being the older sister was not fun.

Austin turned around in his car seat and stood up.

"Sit down, Austin. Right now," Grace said, giving Kelly an evil eye as if to say, "He wouldn't be doing this if you had strapped him in."

Kelly held her Barbie to her nose and said, "Bad girl, Barbie." She spanked her doll.

Grace wound the seatbelt through Gigi's car seat and clicked it in place. She put a pacifier into Gigi's mouth and shut the door.

"Me want a mimi, too," Austin said.

"No. Big boys don't use mimis."

Grace swooped around to the door behind the driver, (thank God they finally put two back doors on vans) opened it and grabbed the elastic waist of Austin's Osh Kosh B'Gosh jeans, swirled him around, pulled his short, upside-down bowling-pin shaped legs out from under him, and slid him down the back of the car seat. "There, you little wriggle worm. Let's get you strapped in. We're going to be late to Kelly's dance class." Austin twisted in protest. "Sit still, Austin, I mean it."

He stuck his lower lip out like a window ledge, and squinted his chestnut-speckled eyes, just like his father's, not at the brightness of the sun glaring on the snow, but at his mother's command. Grace had no time for this display of displeasure. She had no time for displays of pleasure, either. She was too busy being tired, irritated,

distracted, and sick to her stomach. Being pregnant made her feel
that way. But only part of her nausea was due to morning sickness.
The other part of her distress was the result of a conversation she'd
had with Guy the night before.

Guy had arrived home at a halfway reasonable hour, nine-thirty,
which was a lot better than the last two nights when he hadn't come
home at all. He'd told Grace he was working on a "huge" case and
they'd be working "well into the night," therefore he would spare her
the disturbance of his rolling in late. He'd stay in the hotel suite his
firm leased. It was down the block from his office.

Grace would rather he came home, even if it was in the wee hours
of the morning, but what she wanted obviously didn't matter.

Guy poured himself a glass of red wine and sat down in a leather
recliner.

"Where's the remote?" he asked, looking at Grace. "You didn't want
a glass of wine, did you?" he said, obviously as an afterthought.

"The remote's probably on the end table under the magazine,"
she said, "and I would love a glass of wine…but I can't have one."

"Why not?"

"Because I'm pregnant," she said.

"You're what?"

"I'm pregnant."

"You're shitting me," he said.

"No, I'm not. The doctor told you to use a condom for two weeks,
but no, you couldn't. I remember your words exactly, you said, 'Don't
worry, nothing's going to happen. I'm fixed.' And now look what's
happened. Not to mention, I told you when I was pregnant with
Gigi that you should go ahead and get the procedure done."

Guy gulped his wine. "Don't go blaming me. You know as well as
I do that you could have done something, too, used your diaphragm
or whatever that thing is."

"You certainly have selective memory. I told you the diaphragm
didn't fit anymore. Not since Gigi was born and you said, 'Don't
worry, I'll just use condoms until I get fixed.' And when I told you
that you had better wear a condom because of what Dr. Eubanks

said, you said, 'Forget it, I'll take my chances.' So you took your chance and blew it! For both of us!" Her voice shook. She stood and held onto the back of the couch.

"This is bullshit. I'll sue that incompetent bastard."

"He wasn't incompetent. You were. You simply couldn't do what you were told."

He was quiet for a moment. "Well, there's an easy solution."

"No."

"No what? You don't even know what I'm going to say."

"Yes, I do. But I'm not going to even say the word."

"What? Abortion? You don't have to say it. You just have to do it."

And with that he thrust his glass down on the end table, got up out of the chair, walked by Grace and said, "This is bullshit. Pure bullshit."

She hadn't even turned the car on, yet her mind was already a million miles away. She plopped a Barney video into the DVD player, pushed play, gave Austin a picture book, made sure his hands held the book, and then squeezed the door shut. "You're fine," she said as she opened the driver's door, stepped in, sat down. She lifted her bottom off the seat to adjust her navy-blue peacoat. She sighed, opened her purse, and waded through the mess of gas receipts, Kleenex, (used and unused), gum wrappers, nail file, fuzz-covered mimi, until she felt her leather gloves on the bottom. She pulled them out, shook off the lint from an old Kleenex and put the left one on first, then the right one. But they felt odd. She jerked the right one off, turned it inside out and pulled off a hairy cherry Lifesaver. She adjusted her rearview mirror so she could see Gigi sucking her mimi, eyes at half staff. Then she moved the mirror so she could see Austin picking his nose.

"Stop picking your nose, Austin," she said.

"Booger."

"Just leave it alone 'til I can help you."

"Booger." He took his left finger out of his nostril and replaced it with his right index finger.

"Austin, that's disgusting," Grace said.

"Disgusting," Kelly repeated.

"You buckled up?" Grace asked Kelly.

"Uh-huh."

"You mean 'yes.'"

"Yes."

"Finally. We're off."

Grace backed her minivan into the turnaround, stopping a foot short of the basketball hoop. She threw the car into forward and hit the gas pedal. The tires spun on some ice.

"You *do* have your dance bag, don't you?" Grace asked.

"Yes."

"Do you have your tap shoes and ballet slippers?"

"Uh-huh."

Grace didn't correct her uh-huh. "I hope we're not late. You know Mrs. Casteel doesn't like it when anyone is late." She made sure no traffic was coming from the right side as she turned onto Fairview. Grace had taken lessons from Mrs. Casteel when she was Kelly's age. She'd learned correct posture, how to hold her head and hands and make an entrance. Perceiving herself as the Twyla Tharp of the Midwest, Mrs. Casteel didn't walk into a room, she swooped.

"Don't be late, Barbie," Kelly said, pinching her doll's arms.

Grace didn't like it when her daughter talked to her doll like that, but right now she didn't have enough time or brain cells to stop her. The doctor said not to worry, Kelly would outgrow it, but still she didn't like it. And shouldn't she be able to modify her own children's behavior?

Gigi sounded like a suction cup slurping and popping her mimi. Austin continued excavating his nose while Kelly brushed Barbie's hair. Grace tried to stay focused. And on time.

"Kel, I'm running over to Grammy's. I'll be back when your lessons are over."

The dance lessons lasted two hours and included tap, ballet, and jazz.

"'Bye, Mommy. Tell Grammy I says hi," Kelly said as she unbuckled her own seatbelt, opened the big car door, shut it, and walked around the front of the van into the dance studio.

"Will do." She had two hours to drive to her mother's, which was twenty-five minutes each way. Hopefully her mom would tell her to leave the kids so she could go to the store. She didn't really want to go to her mother's right now, but she sensed by her mother's tone on the phone that she was peeved with her about the real estate agent.

Grace waited until she saw Kelly walk over to Mrs. Casteel. Looking at her daughter through the window she noticed how young and small she looked. At home, perhaps because the other two children were so small and young, Grace treated Kelly as though she were older and more mature than she really was. It wasn't until she saw her daughter stand next to Mrs. Casteel that she realized Kelly was barely more than a baby herself. She expected a lot of Kelly, she expected too much of everyone, really. She talked to people, her kids included, in lawyerly tones. She gave directives. Wanted to discuss facts, not feelings.

Thank goodness Gigi and Austin were quiet on the way to her mother's. It gave Grace time to think. Time to try to figure out when her marriage had gone so off track. What was it that had made Guy, who had once seemed to treat her so well, now treat her with such disdain?

Sitting at a traffic light, Grace remembered how she and Guy used to jokingly refer to their life BC…before children. It was easy for her to drift off to memories of when she and Guy would talk for hours, share emotional intimacies, and feed each other the first bite of strawberries or mangos or grapes or plums. Sometimes they'd just lick one another's finger and savor it like it was filet mignon. Eventually they would collapse onto the bed or forest floor or car seat and their bodies would become loose with lust and juice and interweave as if neither had bones.

It was a period when time didn't matter. There were no babies crying and no mortgage payments to worry about. A big decision was whether to have caf or decaf, coffee latte, or mocha cappuccino.

It was during that part of their relationship when both Grace and Guy believed in each other more than themselves.

But then the kids came. Grace quit her job and Guy began living for his. "After Austin was born," Grace said out loud. "That's when things began to change."

At a traffic light, Austin said, "Mommy, we there?"

But Grace didn't hear him. Her mind had switched back in time to something that, when it happened, she'd thought was just an innocent incident. But now, in retrospect, it was more like evidence. Evidence that something was amiss in her marriage.

It was January twenty-third. Grace remembered the date well because it was the day after Austin's first birthday. Guy had called at about six-thirty to tell her he wouldn't be home that night.

"I'm just going to stay at the firm's suite down the block," he said. "It's snowing like the dickens and I have to be back here at seven, so, it just makes sense to me not to drive home."

"But it's not snowing that much," Grace said. "The snow's not even sticking on the streets and besides, you promised you'd be home so I could go to Bunko."

"What's more important, my career or your social life?"

"That's not a fair question. Of course your career's important, but I haven't been out on my own for weeks and—"

"I hope you're not blaming that on me."

"I'm not blaming it on anyone. It's just that—"

"Grace, I can't discuss this now. We'll have to talk about it tomorrow when I get home from work. The last thing I need right now is a whiny wife. The woman I married was not a whiner. Now buck it up and I'll see you tomorrow."

Grace hung up the phone, trying to hide her tears and anger from Kelly and Austin, who were sitting at the table waiting for their dinner.

"What's the matter, Mommy?" Kelly asked. "Why are you sad?"

Grace regained her composure. "Oh, Kel, Mommy's fine. It's just that Daddy won't be able to make it home tonight so Mommy can't go out to Bunko and see her friends. That's all."

"I'll be your friends," Kelly said.

Grace had leaned over, hugged her daughter, and kissed her forehead.

At about eleven-thirty that night, when she couldn't get to sleep, Grace had decided to call Guy at the hotel. Even though she was hurt and angry with him, she still wanted to hear his voice.

"Hello," the voice on the other end of the line said.

"Guy, it's me," Grace said, softly, her head nestled in the pillow.

"Yeah, Grace, what's wrong?" Guy said.

"Nothing. Well, I can't sleep and I just wanted to hear your voice. That's all. The kids are in bed with me. Austin's squirming and Kelly's snoring. You should hear her."

"Uh-hum," Guy said, as if he were distracted.

Grace heard mumbling on the other end of the phone.

"Guy, are you alone? You sound distracted."

There was a pause. "It's just the TV. The weather girl."

"Oh."

"Oh, what?" Guy asked, defensively.

"Oh, nothing, I guess. I just thought you'd maybe want to talk to me."

"Now's just not a good time, Grace. I'm dead tired and I want to go to bed. I'll see you tomorrow."

Click.

And that was that. No goodnight, I love you, or anything. Just click. And although for the longest time she had believed the voice in the background was the weather girl, something about that night didn't ring true, but it was only now that she was realizing it.

Looking back on it, Grace also realized it was around that time when Guy's behavior toward her changed. Compliments were replaced with criticisms. "Don't tell me you're wearing that," Guy would say just as they were going out the door to a dinner party or business function. "Why?" Grace would ask. "Because it makes you look fat," would be Guy's response. And of course he'd do this when there was no time left for her to change clothes, so Grace would go to the event and feel self-conscious the whole night while Guy did his best John Kennedy charisma routine on all the people in attendance.

Grace thought about how through the years the way Guy touched her had changed. Before Guy would hold her hand, put his hand on the small of her back and if he saw a runaway eyelash on her cheek, he'd tenderly brush it away. Now, he rarely touched her at all, except to have sex. But even then, it was as if his hands were on automatic pilot. And when sex was finished, he'd roll over to his side of the bed satisfied, and she'd roll to her side wet with tears of loneliness.

Guy's work hours became even longer, and the "business travel" began. And then, instead of drinking a cup of coffee with her in the morning and kissing her goodbye and saying "I love you," when he left, Guy began telling Grace, "I'll get coffee at the office," and instead of giving her a kiss before he went out the door, he'd say things like, "See you later," or "I'll be working late tonight."

But as soon as she was convinced Guy didn't love her, he'd do some grand gesture that reeled her back in. There was the sparkling diamond tennis bracelet delivered by a chauffer with a box of Godiva chocolates; the dining room set she had told him she wanted but he told her they couldn't afford, delivered while he took her to lunch at Pigall's, the finest French restaurant in Sandusky; and then the trip to Paris, that led her to believe she had the best husband and marriage in the world.

But between those moments of standing at the summit, feeling as though she truly was the one her husband loved, Grace lived with the reality of everyday life, as she watched a darker side of her husband emerge.

Expecting too much of others had always been Grace's way. She and her friends at Bunko discussed it. They discussed everything. Families, parents, siblings, in-laws, and sex were some of the favorite topics discussed in the group of neighborhood ladies called the "Bunkettes." The group met on the third Thursday of the month at a different club member's home each month. The hostess made appetizers and dessert. They drank wine and gossiped and rolled dice to see who could get sets of different numbers. Mindless, Grace knew, but Grace remembered how her mother used to come home from her bridge games in such a good mood. She thought maybe playing such a mindless game might be good for her; make her relax.

She couldn't imagine her mother's Bridge Club ever having the kind of discussions the Bunkettes had. She was certain the Bridge Club kept their discussions to recipes and spousal achievements, whereas the Bunkettes spent the evening gossiping, discussing whose husbands had been asked to leave, what diet program they were each on this month, and sex. They always talked about sex. That always got the biggest laughs of the night.

Last month, when Bunko was at Clare Porter's house, her cousin, Carly Harding, who lived across town and sometimes subbed for a regular Bunko player, dished about her sex life. Carly, after four raspberry wine coolers, spilled the beans on how she and her husband, Kevin, engaged in a few *ménage a trois*. The first tryst was an accident, she said, or at least that's what she thought at the time. "It was my birthday," Carly said. The other three women at the table continued nibbling on crackers spread with crab dip or pimiento spread. For a second, Estelle, seated at Carly's table, drew dirty looks as her noisy jaws and cracker-crunching nearly drowned out Carly's confession. "Must be lockjaw," Estelle said as she took a sip of wine. "Sorry." She set her cracker down. Carly took the time to take another drink of her wine cooler.

"As I was saying," she said, scrunching her shoulders and giggling, "it was my birthday. Kevin said he'd arrange my whole celebration. I was turning the Big Three-O you know, and I'd been crying for days. So I thought he was going to arrange a surprise party for me. You know, family, friends, big cake and stuff. Whose roll is it, anyway?" Carly said looking around the table. "We better keep the game going or we'll get in big trouble."

"It's my turn," Estelle said. "I'll keep rolling if you keep talking." Estelle picked up the dice and rolled. "What number are we on?" she asked Vicki, the woman seated next to her.

"Three's."

"So I'm getting all excited about what I'm sure will be a huge surprise party. When Kevin booked us a room at the hotel I thought, wow, this is going to be big."

"Next. Your turn, Carly, roll the dice," Estelle whispered.

"Oh, sure." She rolled the dice but kept talking. "The afternoon of my birthday, a Saturday, can you believe how lucky I was that my thirtieth turned out to be on a Saturday? That afternoon—I have two three's," she said interrupting herself. "Did you mark that down?"

Ginger, the one keeping score, nodded her head and said, "Got it."

"Well, Saturday afternoon about four, Kevin said, 'I've got something for you to open,' and so I walked into the bedroom. He hands me this box. It was professionally wrapped with perfect edges and a lovely bow. So I opened the box. It was a teddy, not the kind you hug, but the kind you wear. It was little and black and had a push-up bustier and garters and everything. There were also fishnet stockings in the box. So I said thanks and gave him a kiss and he said, "Put 'em on." I said that I would do that when we got to the hotel but then he said, 'No, put the stuff on now. I want you to wear that *to* the hotel.'"

By now, Lindsay, who had been at another table in the family room had come into the kitchen to refill her snack plate. She stopped at the table and listened. Before long there was a throng of cackling, but fully engrossed women listening to Carly. Grace came in, too. She leaned against the breakfast bar.

"So did you put it on and wear it?" Lindsay asked.

"I asked Kevin, 'What will I wear over it?' And he pulled out another box. It was huge and it was wrapped better than the other one."

"What was in it?" Estelle asked, before biting down on a carrot stick.

"I'm getting there," Carly said. "Don't rush me."

Some of the ladies laughed. Others seemed frustrated at the slow speed at which Carly's story was being delivered.

"I opened it very carefully. Didn't rip the paper at all. I figured I could use the shiny yellow paper again."

"Tell us what was in the blasted box," her cousin Clare demanded.

"It was a mink coat. Full-length. That's what was in the box."

Oohs and aahs came from the group. Except for Ginger, a card-carrying member of PETA, whose face turned sour.

"Kevin said, 'I guess that solves the problem of what you should wear over the teddy,'" Carly said, and then added, "So that's what I did. At that point I figured we'd probably go to the hotel room first, before we went downstairs to my party in the hotel."

"How'd he know what size?" Lindsay asked. "My Jake wouldn't have a clue as to what size teddy I wore. Not to mention, he bought me a vacuum for my last birthday. I guess he figures those are one-size-fits-all."

Grace remembered how Guy had bought her a teddy when they went to Paris.

"Okay. We need the rest of the story," another one of the women said. "All this buildup and it's going nowhere yet."

"I need another wine cooler," Carly said, starting to get up out of her seat.

"You need a cup of coffee," her cousin said, just loud enough for the couple of women standing around her to hear.

"Get Carly another wine cooler," Estelle said.

When she saw that someone was going to bring her a drink, Carly sat back down and went on with her story.

"The teddy was a tad snug, but Kevin said it looked fine; great, as a matter of fact. But have any of you worn one of those things? My boobs were pushed up under my chin. Could have set a tray of drinks on 'em. And the thong felt like I was wearing one of those wire cheese-slicers. Thought it would cut me in two. What was embarrassing was I didn't have a clue how to use the garters. I mean, I'm a pantyhose girl. But I did the best I could. The only thing I was missing was a bunny tail and ears."

"You wore that to the hotel?" Mimi, who hadn't said a word, asked.

"With a mink coat over it, I sure did. With high heels, too. I forgot to tell you, he'd bought stiletto heels. They were so high I thought I'd get a nose bleed when I wore them. And you know, Kevin's my height, so I towered over him and my boobs were right under his nose."

"This is lovely and all," Lindsay said, "but when are you getting to the sex part?"

"Soon, hon, soon. So Kevin and I are driving to the hotel and I thought I'd play along. I reached over and touched him, you know, there. And before I knew it his dick was so stiff he could have steered the car with it. I opened my mink and flashed him a couple of times. And by the time we got to the hotel I didn't know if we'd make it to the room. He said, 'Don't worry about your stuff. I'll get it later.' Can you pass me a pretzel, Estelle? I think I need something in my stomach."

Estelle pushed a bowl of pretzels in front of Carly.

"Thanks. Where was I?" she asked.

"You had just gotten to the hotel."

"That's right. Walking through the lobby, I said to Kevin, 'Don't you need to go check in and get a key?' He said that wouldn't be necessary, that he had everything arranged. So I figured that he'd had rose petals strewn all over the room and a big bottle of champagne was probably on ice. In the elevator, I kissed him and then he started fondling me. Fondling is a funny word, isn't it? Then he put his hand under my teddy."

"Was anyone else in the elevator?" Mimi asked.

Carly was so into weaving her story that she didn't acknowledge Mimi's question.

"So we're mauling each other going down the hall and he said, 'Stop. This is the room.' I asked 'Don't you need the little plastic thing to open the door?' He said 'No. Just relax.' He turned and knocked on the door. That was odd, I thought, but maybe he had a bellboy setting things up so I didn't say anything. Anyway, by then he'd nearly pulled my boobs out of my outfit. But I was into it so I didn't care. And then the door opened."

"And?" Lindsay, Mimi, and Estelle asked in harmony like they were the Lennon sisters.

"And. The guy who answered was definitely not a bellboy. He was tall and built like a god and…"

"And what?" Mimi said.

"And he was *naked*."

"Totally naked?" Estelle said.

"Stark."

"My God, what'd you do?" Lindsay asked, chewing her pretzel faster and faster.

"My mouth dropped to the floor below. Especially when Kevin said, 'How do you like your birthday present?'"

"Oh, my God. I would have died," Lindsay said.

"I damn nearly did."

"So did you go in?"

"Of course. What was I supposed to do, stand in the hallway in a state of undress? I didn't think twice about it, especially after I heard people getting off the elevator."

The whole group listened intently, as though Carly were delivering a tornado warning.

"Before I knew it Kevin had his clothes off and instead of a bed strewn with rose petals I noticed a video camera set up on one side of the room. Kevin started undoing the zipper on the back of my teddy and the other guy unfastened my garters. I ended up like the peanut butter in a sandwich."

"What about the surprise party?" Mimi asked.

"That was the only surprise I got," Carly said, then added, "God, why am I even telling anybody any of this?" She excused herself. "I think I'm going to vomit."

Vicki, one of the Bunkettes, a Sunday school teacher at the First Church of God, said she didn't know if they should have egged Carly on; that it wasn't a Christian thing to do. Clare said she'd never seen her cousin in such a state. She suggested that since it was late, perhaps the group should forget finishing the game and retreat to the dining room for coffee and tiramisu.

"Good idea," Grace said. She was tired and she knew Guy would be waiting up for her, not to talk, but to have sex.

The table was beautifully set with Noritake cups, saucers, and dessert plates. Someone asked Clare what pattern this was. Another commented on how lovely the floral centerpiece of yellow carnations, orange lilies, and purple iris brightened the bleak winter weather.

Tiramisu was passed out; hazelnut coffee and French roast decaf were offered and poured. Grace and Estelle asked for tea.

Five minutes passed. Carly had not returned from the bathroom.

The Bunkettes took a survey to see how many had ever partici-
pated in a *ménage a trois*. Of course the pledge of honor was said. "I
do solemnly swear that information divulged tonight will be locked
up in the vault and not shared with anyone outside this room or
I shall face the wrath of the Bunkettes and be forced to resign in
shame. Amen."

Out of twelve ladies, two hands went up. Glenna, a massage
therapist with four kids said she and her husband Bob, a policeman,
were members of a swinger's club that met once a month in
Sandusky. The other one who raised her hand was Tatiana, a Mary
Kay representative, whose husband Harry used to be on Port Huron
City Council. He was forced to resign when he was caught paying a
prostitute with a check.

Grace said nothing. Just because her husband wanted that kind
of action didn't mean she had to confess to the Bunko group. Still,
she turned red. Between bites of tiramisu she thought about Guy's
insatiable sexual needs. She was worn out trying to meet them.

The ladies sipped their coffee and oohed and aahed over the
tiramisu. Estelle told Clare she wanted the recipe and Clare responded
by saying, "Costco."

Seven minutes passed and still no Carly. Then ten. After fifteen
minutes, Clare said, "I'm going to go check on Carly."

"Good idea," several exclaimed. They had all finished eating dessert.

Clare set down her coffee cup, placed her white damask napkin
on the table and excused herself. She walked down the hall to the
bathroom, expecting to see the door closed. But it wasn't.

"Carly? Carly?" she called. She walked into the bathroom as though
she expected Carly to jump out from behind the towels and say "Boo."
She turned off the bathroom light and moved toward the living room.
Carly was passed out on her floral chintz couch, snoring, lying flat on
her back, one of her legs on the couch, the other hung off the side.
Clare lifted Carly's leg and arm onto the couch, took the throw her
mother crocheted for her from the loveseat and covered Carly.

Clare walked back to the dining room and told the women about
Carly's condition. The women quietly walked their coffee cups to

the kitchen, retrieved their coats from Clare's bed in her first floor master, and left.

Two weeks after the Bunko meeting Grace got a call from Carly.

"I'm sorry to bother you," Carly said, "but I need an attorney. I'm filing for divorce. Do you think you can help me?"

"Divorce? I'm so sorry," Grace said. "I am an attorney, but not a practicing one. I'm just a mom these days." The words caught in her throat. She hated not being able to say, "Certainly, come to my office and I'll take care of it."

"I didn't know. I thought you did both," Carly said. She cleared her throat and said, "There's something else I need to talk to you about."

"What's that?" Grace said.

"It's not something I want to talk about over the phone. Maybe we could get together?"

"You know, Carly, I'd love to, but I'm so swamped this week. How about some time next week? Would that be soon enough?"

"I guess so. Call me when your schedule eases up. Okay?"

"Will do."

But Grace didn't call the next week or the week after.

Grace tried to open the front door to her mom's house, but the door was locked. Holding Gigi in one arm and Austin's hand with the other hand, she turned and used her elbow to ring the doorbell. She had forgotten that it didn't work. "Damn," she said. She let go of Austin's hand, opened the storm door and knocked.

"Come in," she heard her mother yell.

"I can't. The door's locked."

A few seconds passed. She heard her mother's footsteps.

Grace didn't like it when she had to knock to get in the house where she grew up. It made her feel like a stranger, not family. Although she knew it was for safety's sake, that didn't take the feeling away.

"Austin, sweetheart," Lydia said as she leaned over and scooped the snow bunny into her arms. No matter what went on in her life, her grandchildren made her smile.

"Hi," he said, pointing to his nose. "Booger."

Lydia wanted to laugh at Austin's declaration but she knew her daughter would get angry. "Let's get you a tissue," she said. Lydia didn't look at her daughter as she got a tissue for Austin. She was glad for the distraction of the booger. "Here, pumpkin, let's get rid of that nasty thing," she said as she wiped Austin's nose.

"Yucky," he said.

"Yes, yucky."

Before she took off her coat, Grace said, in her interrogating tone, "What did Bitsy say?" She slowly peeled the coat off her cashmere sweater that had become statically charged from the lining in her coat. She removed her leather gloves and rubbed her hands together and scuffed her shoes on the carpet so she wouldn't shock the baby when she bent over to unwrap her. Gigi sat in her car seat like a noodle cooked past al dente.

"Austin, what does the cow say?" Lydia asked, either ignoring Grace or stalling. "Not much," Grace said. If curtness was a sweater, his mother's answer would be wearing it.

Not knowing when to retreat, Grace continued, "Well, I'm sure she had something to say. Did she talk to you about selling your house?"

"No, we talked about my career as a film star. Frankly, I think my house offended your real estate agent friend's sensibilities."

"Come on, Mom, you're imagining things. What are you talking about?"

"Bitsy, your friend Bitsy, seemed to have the distinct impression that I was for certain going to sell my house." She raised her eyebrows, tilted her head down, and peered over her glasses, right at Grace.

"Well, Mom, you need to sell this house. It's too big. Look at all of the repairs that need tending to and aren't getting done. And Mom, to be honest, doesn't it seem to you that instead of healing and getting on with your life since Daddy's death, you're going the other way? Withdrawing. Frankly, you're dragging down yourself and your kids and grandkids."

"So that's it. I'm dragging everyone down, am I? Does my mere existence bother you kids that much? Am I not allowed to mourn the loss of my husband? I hadn't even gotten over your brother's death and then your father died." It sounded like someone had put a rubber band around her throat. "Besides, I have gone on with my life. It's just a *different* life."

"Of course you're allowed to mourn, but, Mom, at some point you've got to move on. And it's been over two years since Daddy died. Did you read any of those books I bought you about grief and mourning? They said after a year or so you'd probably start healing. And I mourned Daddy's death, too, and Buddy's, but you've got to put a time limit on this stuff. It's like you've chosen a life of mourning. And all any of us kids want is for you to be happy."

"So you think I've chosen a life of mourning? Do you think I enjoy it? Mourning isn't something that you choose, Grace, it's something that happens to you. Death makes it happen. Outliving your child makes grief happen. Not living out your dreams with your husband makes grief happen. It's not a choice like what color suit should I wear to the office."

Grace knew she had waded into treacherous emotional territory and it wasn't going well. She saw it on her mother's face. Her complexion, which usually looked as if honey beige foundation had just been applied, now looked sallow. And how long had it been since she'd seen her mother's hazel eyes beautifully made up with taupe shadow and mascara?

Austin moaned. He was hungry. Gigi fussed. Grace looked at the anniversary clock on the piano. As usual, it read seven thirty-seven. She then checked her watch to see what time it really was. Time to feed Gigi. Austin's moans turned to a pathetic, fake-sounding cry, Gigi wailed, and Grace heard her mother sniffling. Great. Just great.

"For Pete's sake, Mom, you took what I said the wrong way," Grace said, wishing she had kept her big mouth shut and waited for her brother and sisters. Grace had an idea to gather her siblings and hold a "mourning intervention," similar to the kinds they had for alcoholics and drug addicts.

"Oh, I think I took it just how it was given."

"I just meant…" Grace said while sitting down, and opening Gigi's diaper bag to retrieve a bottle, "I just meant to say, it's not just me, but Tim and Sherry and Sugar, and we're all worried about you. You live in this big house alone. You hardly go out. I'm not sure what you do. You've changed. And haven't you noticed the neighborhood has changed? What would Daddy say? You and Daddy wouldn't have allowed this behavior from us. If you saw us floundering and wasting our lives and getting knocked down by disappointment you'd tell us to get up and move forward. Your famous words were, 'This too shall pass.' But Mom, you're not letting this pass. Mourning death has become your life. It makes me sad and frankly, it pisses me off!"

Austin sat next to his sister on the piano bench, hitting the piano keys with his stubby fingers. "Row, row, row," he sang between bites of animal crackers.

Lydia walked to the window. "Did you say you have some errands to run? If you need to go, just go. Leave the kids here with me." She walked over and took Austin's hand and helped him scoot off the bench. "I'm going to give him some pasta pickups in the kitchen."

If the kids hadn't been there, Grace would have followed her mother into the kitchen and pursued the conversation. Forced it, even. But she was tired and her day wasn't half over. She waited a couple of moments, then sat down at the piano bench, the same piano where she had learned to play Chopin's "Mazurka in B Minor" and more importantly, "Heart and Soul" with Sidney Meteor. Gingerly, she took her left hand and placed her fingers in position for a C major chord. But she didn't push the keys down. Instead, with her left hand, she tapped the keys lightly enough not to produce a sound. Then she got up and fed and burped Gigi, kissed her, set her in the car seat, carried the car seat into the kitchen and placed it on the table. She blew a kiss to Austin, who sat in a highchair on the other side of the table. She looked at her watch and said, "I'll be back in an hour."

Chapter 4

Truth's Gremlins

An afternoon and an evening passed since Bitsy Esterhaus, the real estate agent, had come. Grace came and picked up the kids, Kelly in tow. Lydia was thrilled to see Kelly. She loved her granddaughter's hugs and kisses. They were real kisses, not the windswept ones on the cheek she got from her grown kids.

Grace said little. She thanked her mom for watching the kids, bundled everyone up, and left.

The Stouffer's chicken teriyaki still sat on the floor, uneaten by Lydia and rejected by Binky. Until today she hadn't thought about selling her house. She'd read articles in magazines and books on grief that said you should never make a big decision such as selling your house for at least a year after a spouse's death. *So what if it's been nearly two and a half years? Not every widow sells the house they live in, do they? It's home, for crying out loud.* But if the idea was such a bad one, why couldn't she put it out of her mind; go on as if Bitsy Esterhaus had never come to her home? House. Home. "What is a home?" she asked as she walked from room to room, flipping on light switches, peeking her head into the rooms to make sure no boogiemen were hiding, waiting to strike until she was asleep. She checked all the outside doors and made sure the deadbolts were in place. She turned on the outside lights, then went to the kitchen and wiped the counters. "Ant traps," she said. "Don't forget to set out the ant traps." She set the thermostat to sixty-seven.

She'd always thought she knew what a home was. Now she was confused. Was her home this big old house she loved or was it the people who had passed through its doors?

The house was quiet. She enjoyed the quiet. When the kids were all home she had pleaded with God for just a moment's peace and quiet. Every day stereos blasted, doors opened and closed (sometimes by slamming). The refrigerator door constantly opened and closed, which drove thrifty Walter nuts.

She could still hear Walter yell, "Tim, stop it with the trumpet."

"But I've got to practice," Tim yelled back.

"Not at midnight, you don't," Walter screamed. Lydia remembered thinking that if Tim's trumpet playing didn't wake the neighbors, Walter's tuba-sounding voice would.

"Did you see my history book?" "Who ate my M&M's?" "Sugar, did you steal my blue sweater?" "Last one in the car's a rotten egg." "Mommy, I had a bad dream. Can I sleep with you and daddy?" "What time will the Easter bunny come?" "Mommy, come see the tent Gracie and I made."

And the parties. Buddy's thirteenth birthday party. He'd invited his entire class. She'd decorated the first floor in balloons, crepe paper streamers, and posters. She laughed, thinking about how she had walked into the den and found Eric Brewster, Buddy's best friend, one of the boys killed in the accident, on the floor making out with Schuyler Thomas, the little girl next door.

"Uh-hum," Lydia said.

Eric hopped off Schuyler. Lydia never saw Eric move that fast, before or after.

Grace's sweet-sixteen party was quite the occasion, too. Lydia let Grace take care of the invitations. Walter was none too pleased when fourteen boys and only four girls showed up. Lydia told him, "Grace is no fool."

The house had seen its share of sadness, too. Wakes after Buddy and Walter's deaths. Over two hundred people stopped by on the afternoon of Buddy's funeral. They brought condolences and food. Tim said he never wanted to see Jell-O as long as he lived. There were so many Jell-O salads that, after everyone left, Sugar and Sherry and Tim took the salads outside and had a food fight. Walter was on his way outside to stop them when Lydia stopped him. Tears flowing, she said, "Let them go, Buddy would love it."

She turned off the kitchen light and walked to the stairs, but instead of going right up the stairs, she turned and looked around. Memories were everywhere. She held on to the newel post. She saw Walter stripping and varnishing it. She looked in toward the living room. If someone asked her to, she could have told them when and where she and Walter had purchased each piece of furniture and knick-knack.

Walter didn't believe in credit cards, so improvements on the house were made as cash became available. Both he and Lydia spent almost every weekend for two years scraping and removing paint from the oak woodwork in the five-bedroom home. It took seven months to refinish the banister and newel posts going up the stairs. The previous owners had painted all the woodwork black. "Looks like the Adams Family lived here," Walter had said.

She and Walter loved the old house. Except when they hated it. Repairs were never complete. They'd fix the water heater and then the gutter would come loose. Just when it seemed like things were caught up, a pipe would break in the upstairs bathroom and cause water clouds to form on the ceiling in the dining room.

There were times when Walter wanted to sell the house, buy a new one with modern plumbing and amenities. But Lydia said no. This was home and always would be.

The closest Lydia came to selling the house was after Walter sat her down on the sofa and told her they wouldn't be able to afford to go on their dream trip to Ireland. The money they had saved for the trip was going to have to be spent on having the main wooden beam replaced with a steel one. "Termites," he'd said.

"Don't tell me this," Lydia had said. "You can't take this trip away from me. From us. We need it."

When she was young, she'd seen pictures of Ireland in a coffee table book her parents had kept in the living room. She loved the idea of leprechauns and shamrocks. And after she read *Angela's Ashes*, she was certain she and Walter had to go to Ireland. She found the melancholy of Ireland so romantic. She had high hopes a trip to Ireland would be just the ticket for her and Walter to leave the sadness of Buddy's death on the shores of America while they rekindled their passion on the Emerald Isle.

Walter said he understood, but he also couldn't weave gold from straw.

Lydia was angry with him. And furious at the house. "Maybe we should just go ahead and sell this big old thing," Lydia had said. It was all she could do not to break every window, knock holes in the walls, and torch the place. "This house controls our lives more than the kids do."

Walter had responded by saying, "Houses are like kids. Sometimes they need us the most when they deserve us the least."

She hated to admit it, but Walter was right.

They repaired, refashioned, and remodeled. They bandaged house wounds the way they bandaged their kids' skinned knees and elbows. They replaced broken window panes the same as they healed their children's growing pains. They listened to the house creak and groan. They knew how the poor old thing felt. Tired. Just as they made vows when they married, they made a vow to stay in the house through tight budgets and windstorms, broken window cords and seals, holidays that pushed the walls out with cheer, and times when even the walls knew to be quiet because its residents were in mourning.

Lydia said to Binky, "Maybe this big old lug of a house *is* too much for me." She turned to head up to bed. "How many times have I climbed these stairs?" she said. "How many times? I bet a million."

She got into bed and pulled her Downy-smelling chenille bed-spread over her shoulders and up around her ears. Although she thought she looked better with longer hair, over the last couple of years she'd become a prophet of functionality. Short hair, sensible shoes, high-rise cotton underpants, leisure bras that didn't lift and separate, but simply kept her breasts from sliding under armpits, clear nail polish instead of colored, and microwaveable, one-serving dinners with unknown sauces the consistency of Plaster of Paris. She used to wear her hair longer in the winter and shorter in the summer. But when Walter died, so did her seasonal change of hairdos.

Longer hair helped protect her ears from the sheer winds that took a shortcut from Canada to the States by cutting across Lake Erie. The winds traveled through the streets of Port Huron, leaving lakeside trees looking like they had a bad case of rheumatoid arthritis.

She rolled onto her right side toward what had been Walter's side of the bed. Binky sprawled out in Walter's spot. She stroked the cat's fur. It was the color of autumn wheat, gold and smooth. It reminded her of the drives she and Walter took in the country. They'd searched antique shows and yard sales for their next treasure. Finding a wooden chair covered with layers of putrid-color paint, was like finding a ruby under a pile of earth. Most of these were billed as "antiques," but weren't. They were simply old chairs. They'd offer five bucks, seven, max, keeping their excitement about the item between the two of them, make the deal and throw their purchase in the back of their Astro mini-van and away they'd go. Before they were out of the driveway, they saw the chair stripped and sanded. They debated what color to paint their latest *objet d'art*. Walter stripped and sanded and Lydia painted. She loved using different colors: red, green, black, peacock-blue. Sometimes she painted a dahlia or rose on the piece. She learned how to paint roosters and flowers in a Tole painting class.

One thing she did not like to do was paint any two pieces alike. Therefore, none of their kitchen chairs matched. She believed that each chair had its own distinct personality, just like her kids.

It took her a long time before she developed the confidence to use a set of mismatched anything. Her mother would have rather died than use items that didn't match. She said the Eleventh Commandment was, "Thou Shalt Have Matching Sets of Everything."

Lydia slowly found her own eclectic style. She gained confidence when she saw Martha Stewart on television stand with her shoulders back, chest out, exuding the beauty and personality of serving guests on mismatched sets of plates. Lydia was buoyed by Martha's approval, but still, she found herself defending her style to her kids, (mostly Grace) who complained about having to sit on mismatched chairs. "Looks like we can't afford a matching set," Grace said with that little tsk, tsk in her voice.

"These chairs have history," Walter replied in defense of their acquisition. "One day these will be collector's items."

"Yeah, right," Grace said. She rolled her eyes and cast a glance of adolescent contempt to the ceiling.

"Contrary, that's what Grace is. Contrary. Don't you think so, Binky?" Lydia was certain Binky nodded. She hadn't used the word contrary in ages, but it was such a fitting description of Grace. And bossy? Good Lord.

She thought about Walter, as she'd done every night since he died. The comment Jan, her sister, had made this morning during a phone call came to mind. "You know, Lydia, I don't want to be cruel, but it seems you love Walter more now that he's dead, than you did when he was alive. Seems you've forgotten the years where, well, you know what I'm talking about."

"Nonsense," she'd said, "Walter was a wonderful husband. And unintentional or not, that was a cruel thing to say."

As she lay there in the dark quiet of the night when truth's gremlins come like floaters across the closed eye, she knew that what her sister said contained some truth. But when she'd buried Walter, along with his body, she'd buried his sins, too. In doing so, she'd placed his memory on the throne of death's delusions. She chose to remember the good because that is what she thought forgiveness was and that is what she had promised God she would do.

How she would love to call Rita, her dearest friend who left her life as quickly as she had come into it. Rita always knew how to straighten out her knotted mind.

Suddenly she couldn't get Rita out of her mind.

From the outside Lydia and Rita didn't have much in common. Lydia was married. Rita wasn't. Lydia believed in monogamy. Rita said, "Pff. Unnatural." Lydia loved small towns. Rita walked around singing "New York, New York." If asked her age, Lydia would reply without shame, "Fifty-two." But when someone asked thirty-seven-year-old Rita her age, she'd snap, "None of your damn business."

They were opposite in appearance, too. Lydia stood five-seven; at least, that's what was on her driver's license. Rita, after morning stretches, barely reached five foot one. Rita flaunted her nearly perfect figure. If Lydia so much as uttered the word "cheesecake," her midsection expanded two inches. She was none to pleased with her thighs, either, calling them descendents of the great Sequoias. The one thing the women had in common was hazel eyes, but you'd never know—Rita wore blue contacts.

During summer vacation Lydia wore Capris, sleeveless shirts, and flip-flops. She raced from baseball game to soccer practice to track-and-field meets. An adventure was loading the station wagon with five kids, one husband, seven suitcases, two large coolers, pillows, blankets, car games, Cheetos, and a large supply of Dramamine before driving twelve hours to Atlantic City where all she wanted to do was bury her head in the sand until it was time to go home.

Summer breaks for Rita meant traveling the world wearing bangle bracelets, backless sundresses, and high-heeled sandals adorned with rhinestones. She traveled alone, preferring out-of-the-way haunts instead of familiar tourist spots. Naps were *de rigueur*. If she saw something she wanted, she bought it. If she saw a man she desired, she went after him.

"I've got to stop thinking of Rita," Lydia said. Easier said than done. Lydia still didn't understand why Rita disappeared from her life without a goodbye. It was if she'd been watching *The Twilight Zone* where people thought they knew people but suddenly they would disappear.

"Enough," she said.

Lydia scrunched her eyebrows down, forming a teepee in the middle of her forehead. Usually it was the child who wanted to break away from the parents. Live the life they wanted, find out who they were without living in someone else's shadow. But this was the opposite. She told her friend Madeline, the one scheduled for the hysterectomy, "My life has become a Robert Altman movie. It has no beginning, no middle, and no end. And the person who's editing it is horrible. In short, it's a visionless series of events linked together by my mere existence."

Madeline said, "That's quite profound. Too bad I don't have a clue what you mean."

They both laughed. Lydia was sorry she had said what she said because it was apparent Madeline didn't understand her abstract, yet very real thoughts. She also knew that if she made the same remark to Rita, Rita would have known exactly what she was talking about.

She had a headache. "Maybe praying will help," she said.

She called her morning and nightly prayers "bookends." She began and ended each day with maxi prayers, long, drawn-out affairs that were intended to cover most everything that needed praying for. She prayed for the world at large, starving children in Africa, for an end to violence in northern Ireland, the AIDS epidemic, genetically modified meats, the president, even if she couldn't stand him, the old, sick people she read the newspaper to in the nursing home, the folks she delivered Meals on Wheels to, and for Cleveland Indian victories. She didn't mention all of these things in one prayer. She rotated prayer subjects like they rotated dairy products at Albers.

She prayed for planes flying overhead, that the captains didn't have a fight with a spouse before takeoff. Recently, she'd added cruise ships to her litany, praying people wouldn't pay all that money and end up puking their guts out. She'd prayed for years that God would be with Little League coaches and teach them patience and kindness—especially dealing with *her* kids.

Sometimes she thought God probably put earplugs in when he heard her coming.

She prayed about personal things. She asked God if she should call a plumber about the backed-up drain. She hinted that it would be a really nice gesture on His part if He took care of the problem Himself. Once after such a prayer, she woke up to an unclogged sink.

She asked for forgiveness because she didn't give Sondra Gribsby all the ingredients in her recipe for her highly praised coconut cake. There was something about Sondra that Lydia didn't like, so she told her the recipe called for double the amount of pineapple juice needed, thereby causing the cake to have the consistency of a chest cold.

She prayed that the suspicious-looking mole on her grandson Danny's back was merely an unruly freckle. She'd told Sherry she should have the doctor look at the mole. Sherry insisted the mole was nothing. But Lydia couldn't stop thinking about what happened to poor Kathy Bakewell, a fellow teacher, whose seven-year-old son got melanoma and ended up having his left leg removed.

After Buddy's death, she prayed for the strength to live and after Walter died, she prayed that God would let her die.

The bookends began with the Lord's Prayer. She felt the Lord's Prayer, although divine in spirit and beautiful when sung (especially the rendition sung by Charlotte Church), was very general and failed to allow for specifics. She was also afraid that if all she said was the Lord's Prayer, God might get her confused with someone else.

She was raised Methodist. When her children were young, the family attended the First United Methodist Church. After Buddy's death, church appearances by any member of the Calypso family were scarce. Because of the circumstances of Buddy's death, Lydia felt that whenever she walked into church, instead of experiencing love and acceptance, she felt inquisitive stares and judgment. She decided at that time that she didn't need a church. But she did need God.

She became a do-it-yourself Born-Again Christian after Walter died. On a day when a sweater and jacket were necessary due to the late fall chill, Lydia marched herself down to the shores of Lake Erie. She looked around to make sure no one was in sight, and then she removed her loafers, shimmied out of her corduroy jumper and turtleneck, quickly pulled off her navy leotards and walked into the lake. She strode out into the water until it was up to her chest. *That* was farther out than she thought it would be. She had to make a decision. She wanted to go for a full submersion, but if she walked out much farther, she might get caught in a current and be swept out into the lake and drown. The point was to be saved, not drowned, so instead of venturing out any farther, she dunked her head in the cold water, then swam like a dervish back to shore.

Walking out of the lake, dripping, and smelling slightly fishy, Lydia's somber mood broke when she thought of what Walter would say about what she'd just done.

Walter was not a church-goer. When he was little, his mother made him go to a neighborhood Pentecostal church. He hated it. He told Lydia that "All the old ladies had their skinny hair pulled back in these bun-things. They wore no makeup and looked like they'd just stepped out of the *Night of the Living Dead*." He was entranced one time when his mother dragged him to a tent revival and "Lo and behold," he had told Lydia, "they had a snake-handler. This preacher guy went nose-to-nose with a rattler while a couple of younger women lifted their arms to the Lord, screaming 'Hallelujah,' right before they passed out dead on the floor."

"You mean the women died?" Lydia asked, her face reacting in horror.

"No. They just passed out, but to a nine-year-old kid, they sure as hell looked dead."

He had told Lydia he wished faith and belief came as easily to him as it seemed to come to her. But after Vietnam, whatever faith he had held onto as a child was gone. "I wanted to vomit whenever I'd see photos of LBJ walking out of church," he said. "All of those presidents, Nixon, Kennedy, whoever the hell they are, they all put their suits on and parade into and out of church so the press can see them and then they send young men to lose their arms and legs and lives in wars that should never have been. Those presidents pray at the altar of power, not God."

It broke Lydia's heart to hear Walter talk like that. She had no idea how anyone could live in this world without faith, if not in people, then in God. If she hadn't had her faith after Buddy died, she was sure she would have died, too.

Lydia had observed throughout their marriage that Walter didn't let the outside world, or even his kids, know how he felt about faith. She suspected that he sensed that within his role as an educator, his views might not be welcome, especially in the heart of the Midwest. And with his kids, Lydia thought that he didn't want his cynicism about faith to become theirs.

Every Sunday, when she was getting dressed to go to church, Lydia would say to Walter, "Sure you don't want to come with us?" And he'd say, "No, thanks. You're my God ambassador. Pray for me." He always said it with a smirk in his voice, but Lydia believed this smirk hid his fear and he truly wanted her to pray for him. So she did.

As she lay in bed unable to sleep, Lydia remembered how she and Walter had never talked about death, other than his silly asides, so when he died, Lydia was conflicted as to how to handle his funeral. Should she have a church service or would Walter feel more comfortable with a few words said by friends at the funeral home?

It was during that awful time, when decisions had to be made quickly, that Lydia realized how much she didn't know about what her husband believed. Not that she hadn't tried. She'd started early in their relationship trying to engage him in conversations about life and God and the world, but Walter resisted. "How do you think God got here?" Lydia asked him one night shortly after they were engaged, after they had made love in a cove hidden by rocks on the shores of Lake Erie.

"I have no clue," he said.

"Well, aren't you curious?"

"Not in the least."

"Don't you ever wonder how we got here? How the stars and the moon and the planets were formed?"

"Nope."

"Well, what about God? Do you think he's in everyone? And destiny. Walter, do you believe in destiny?"

"My gosh, Lydia. What are you doing? Writing a book? I have no clue. I'm not even sure God exists."

"How can you say that? Look around us. Look at those stars shining over the lake. How can you not believe in God when you look at that moon that shines light down so we can sit here and gaze into each other's eyes?" Lydia slid her hand under Walter's untucked shirt and rubbed the soft skin on his side between his back and stomach.

He flinched.

"What's the matter?" Lydia asked.

"That tickles. How about if you just rub my back?"

"I will if you answer the questions."

"I *am* answering the questions."

"No, you're not."

"Sure I am," Walter said. You just don't like the answers."

"It's not that I dislike your answers. It's just that I don't understand them."

"There's not much to understand. They're pretty simple."

"That's not what I mean," she said as she rubbed in circles on his back.

"What *do* you mean?"

"Oh, I don't know. It's just that I think of this kind of stuff a lot," Lydia said.

"I can tell," Walter chided.

Lydia pinched him.

"Ouch."

"Sorry."

"I don't understand anyone who doesn't, at least sometimes, think of this kind of stuff."

"I don't think about that stuff because there are no answers," Walter said, matter-of-factly.

"But sometimes, Walter, it's not a brain thing, not something you can see. It's something you feel, like faith. It's believing in something bigger and better than us."

"I understand what you're saying. For you it's more of a heart thing. But for me, it has to do with the brain. Either it exists or it doesn't. And for me, if there's no scientific proof, well, let's just say

I'm skeptical. And if you saw what I saw in 'Nam, I doubt you'd be much of a believer, either."

"But that seems like such a lonely, sad way to live." She removed her hand from inside his shirt. For a moment she closed her eyes and bowed her head, as if she were praying. Then she opened her glossy eyes, lifted her head and looked out at the lake. It was as calm and still. "But if you don't believe in God, what do you believe in?"

"You," he said, as he took her chin in his hand, turned her head toward his and kissed her. "And us," he added.

So many nights since Walter died had been spent like this, reliving scenes from her marriage. Sometimes the scenes comforted her and made her drift off to sleep with a smile on her face, but other times, her thoughts led her to bad dreams that seemed to have partial truths that caused her to question the memory of her marriage. She was certain that it was Freud and the devil that volleyed her dreams back and forth, playing tricks on her, trying to put a wedge between her and Walter and God.

For the first year after Walter's death, Lydia kept trying to rehear the last conversation she'd had with her husband. Had she told him she loved him when she left before him that day? Did she give him a kiss goodbye or did she purposely leave the house, believing she could give him a kiss later? Why did it matter so? she often asked herself. Walter knew she loved him. She had told him so, often, at least during the last couple of years, after the years of angst and confusion and worry of raising five children had subsided and since Walter had quit drinking and since she had once again become the most important person in his life. It was almost as if Walter, too, had been born again, not in a religious sense, but within their marriage. Lydia had been stunned but thankful about whatever had made Walter mellow, because now they could have the future that they had waited so long for.

Lydia was glad that each month now there were more nights where she would fall into bed, say a prayer, and then drift to sleep relatively quickly. But tonight was not one of them. She looked at the ceiling, which often became the movie screen of her mind. She saw each room in her house. She thought about how each room had a different scent. The living room, especially on damp days, smelled of old fires and of rose potpourri by the piano. Whenever she walked through the living room she grabbed a handful of the crisp dried flowers and squeezed them, hoping to bring their fragrance to life again. The dining room smelled like vanilla-scented candles. She always kept candles on the table. When she opened the drawers of the buffet, the smell of old linens and mothballs overwhelmed the vanilla smell.

The kitchen had many smells. Saturday meant the smell of fresh baked bread. Sunday was pot roast. Wednesday night was stringy barbecue that cooked all day while everyone was at school. And Friday was pizza night. It wasn't just that the smell of food was delightful. It was what those smells signified. Family. Friends. Never ending laughter and lives. Then she recalled the smell in the kitchen today. Bleach. Ant traps. Bitsy's perfume.

"You smell like puppy-dog tails," she'd told Buddy, trying to get him to understand the importance of hygiene. Without trying, she smelled the air left in his path when he walked by her after a shower, spiffed up for a date, a cosmopolitan of shampoo, deodorant, clean socks, and cologne.

Closing her eyes, she smelled the tangy scent of Walter's Old Spice, the way his hair smelled after he washed it with a bar of Grandpa's Pine Tar Soap. She smelled his breath and the peppermint mouthwash. Before Buddy died, Walter used the mouthwash before they made love. After Buddy's death, Lydia noticed Walter used the mouthwash to mask the smell of alcohol.

Walter upped his drinking after Buddy died. At first she envied his release. If she could have drunk, she would have. That way they could both swim to alcoholic oblivion together. But she couldn't drink. It made her sick. Plus, there were the other kids. Someone had to keep the family a family.

Walter told Lydia that until he went to Vietnam, he'd never had a drink. "I don't want to be like my mom and dad," he'd said.

In a letter she received from Walter, he mentioned how many

soldiers drank and did drugs. "I'm not going to do that stuff," he'd said. But after five months of seeing people die or getting so badly wounded they prayed to die, Walter wrote to Lydia, "I've learned to drink with the best... and the worst of them."

People who knew Walter when he was an army medic said it was truly remarkable that after 'Nam, he could return to the States and live as normal a life as he had. Before he went overseas, he'd wanted to become a doctor. But when he returned, he'd told Lydia, "I've seen enough blood and guts for a lifetime. I want to work with the living, not the dying. Besides, to be a doctor, you need faith. And I have none." So he went back to college to become a teacher. He got his master's and then doctorate.

Lydia supported him all the way. She was so proud when he told her, "Maybe I can teach these kids how not to hate."

Lydia began, "Our Father... Our Father, who art in..." *In, in? In what?* She lost her place. She tried again. "Our Father which art..." She changed who to which, hoping that would get the flow going. Again, the words drifted off into space. She tried another time. No luck. Shifting in bed, she squirmed from her side, onto her back and then placed her folded hands under her breasts. Just as she began the prayer again, her nose itched. She scratched it. Then, like bubbles popping up to the top of boiling water, itches popped up across her forehead, her ear, her cheek, all over her face and neck. She took both hands and rubbed her face. She wanted to scratch off the top layer of skin so she could stop the itches at their source. But these weren't surface itches like when someone is tickled with a feather. No, these itches were deep like nerve endings having panic attacks. The itches went to her feet. She tried to distract herself by praying, when what she knew she needed was a good rub of Calamine lotion. "Our Father who art in Heaven. Hallowed be thy name," she said, stepping up the pace. She tried to keep her words from breaking loose and becoming lost like a child in a store. Blast. Another itch. Her concentration broke again. Nerves? Binky opened his eyes and looked at her as if to say *"Please settle down; you're affecting my sleep.*" Tick, tock, tick, tock. Big Ben clucked on. "Shut up," Lydia said to both Binky and Big Ben. She wanted the itches to go away. She wanted this day to go away and tomorrow to come. And why couldn't she remember the Lord's Prayer?

She reached over and touched the brass lamp on the nightstand. It went on with her touch. No chain, no reaching up into the lampshade in the dark, trying to find the switch, no clapping. Thank goodness no clapping.

When he was alive, Walter's gadget collection included "Clapper" lights. Clap on, clap off. He went clapping from one room to the other. Drove her to distraction. But at least the "Clappers" served a purpose, unlike the Chia plants he lined the family room window with from Christmas until February when the neglected foliage curled like pubic hair. His Chia collection included the one goofy grinning head, a sheep, a dog, and a unicorn. Every Christmas he turned their kitchen table into a little Chia nursery, spreading out newspaper, setting up his terra cotta pots and smearing each one with goop that would turn into "pet fur." Lydia complained, but Walter told her it was no worse than her peanut brittle mess that stayed all over the table for two weeks straight.

The week after Walter's funeral, Lydia instructed Tim to remove all the Clapper light gizmos. She and Grace carted the Chia plants to the garbage. She sent Sherry to the Lighthouse to buy new lamps for the nightstands on the sides of the bed. In spite of her grief over Walter's death, she was glad she no longer had to go around the house clapping to turn a light on or off.

The art deco dresser she bought at a garage sale stood against the wall, facing the foot of the bed. The top was covered with moisturizers for every body part. Most of the beauty products were a year and a half past their expiration date. There was a jar of beeswax to soothe elbows, cotton balls with mint oil to soothe tired eyes, Oil of Olay to soothe her skin, something to soothe everything except what really needed soothing.

An earring tree sat in the corner. Gold hoops of every size, covered with dust, hung like nylons from a shower rod.

Lydia scooted herself up on the bed, pulling Walter's pillow behind her so she sat upright. Binky meowed. He didn't like having the pillow removed from under his tail. Except for the light that shone on the left side of Lydia's face, the room was dark. She shifted her head from one side to the other, looking at the hollow reflection in the mirror over the bureau. She couldn't believe it was hers. She had grown into the habit of looking past herself in mirrors or at least focusing on just the one area she was dealing with: her hair, an eyebrow, the blush on a cheek, or lipstick on her mouth. She had not looked at the sum of her parts for a long time. Of course there were moments when she felt human, a viable part of the world, but more often than not she felt like a used jigsaw puzzle bought at a garage sale, the kind with pieces missing.

The corners of her mouth drew in a downward crescent. She was never one to wear a big smile. What she used to call "laugh lines" now appeared as deep crevices, the kind mountain climbers fear they will fall into.

She lifted her head and stretched. She worked her hands around her neck. She felt once-taut skin hang loose, forming little pleats. Her skin felt thinner. She tilted her head back to see if the sacks of skin beneath her jaw line went away.

"My God, I have jowls."

The shock of seeing jowls had one redeeming value: It stopped her itching.

"This must be how it feels to be a giant leaking balloon in the Macy's parade. Deflated."

It was obvious she wasn't going to get to sleep now. She thought about counting her blessings but decided that took too much energy. Sometimes when she couldn't sleep she counted the cracks in the ceiling. Made believe they were constellations. She swore there was a Big Dipper above her bed.

She touched the lamp two more times to get it to its brightest level, then dropped her feet to the floor and into the pair of size-nine tan moccasins she kept at the side of her bed. With her elbows on her knees, she glanced at the clock. It was nearly midnight. She thought about going downstairs and turning the television on but she knew the only shows on that late were reruns of *Baywatch Tokyo* or infomercials about buying real estate with no money down. No, she didn't want to go downstairs.

"Maybe I'll read," she said to Binky.

She picked up a *Ladies Home Journal* from a stack of magazines she kept on her nightstand and flipped to the article "Can This Marriage Be Saved?"

Lydia scanned the article and laughed. She recalled the time she and Rita drank a bottle of Blue Nun and decided to make up a letter and send it to "Can This Marriage Be Saved?"

This month's article was about a wife who was tired of her husband's jealousy. It reminded her of when she and Walter first dated. He was so jealous of her friend, Phil. Phil Boynton. She'd dated Phil in high school but they'd both opted for friendship over romance. Even after they were married, Walter was jealous of Phil. In one of the letters he sent from Vietnam, he said he was certain Phil would try to replace him when he was gone. Lydia laughed when she'd read that. Then she felt guilty for laughing because the last thing she wanted Walter to do when he was overseas was worry.

The letter. *Where was that letter I wrote Walter that explained how he meant the world to me and that Phil was just a friend and if this marriage was going to last, he was going to have to understand that I intend to have both female and male friends? And where's Walter's letter he sent back to me? The letter where he told her me he was sorry and that he loved me and that although he hoped he would be enough for me, he now understood that part of the reason he loved me and was attracted to me was that when he saw me around other people, I brought smiles to everyone's faces and it would be very selfish and stupid of him just because of his insecurity to want me to be anyone less than who I was.*

Walter said he saved every letter Lydia wrote him. He locked the letters away in a gray metal file cabinet in his closet. For posterity, he'd said.

Lydia realized she wasn't reading the article but staring at a full page advertisement that warned, VAGINAL CREAMS CAN CAUSE CONDOM

FAILURE! She read further. *Vaginal creams containing vegetable or mineral oil can cause condoms to burst upon contact with air. These substances cause decreased condom integrity.* Lydia wondered when condoms had ever had integrity. In her world, "rubbers" were the contraception of last resort. Of course that was before HIV and AIDS. Walter hated condoms, said that when he used them it felt the same as trying to cover his size-twelve foot with a size-ten shoe.

She stuck the magazine back in the bed stand.

Walter said he was glad when the time came when they could throw birth control out... and he and Lydia could make love with freedom and fancy and live with the chance that one day the love they shared would develop into a baby.

Six months, a year, eighteen months, two years passed but no baby. Lydia took her basal temperature and prenatal vitamins to get her body ready. She tried not to worry. Once, Walter handed Lydia's faith back to her when he told her God would give them a child when He thought they were ready. But by the third year of trying and testing and probing and prodding, Lydia said she didn't care about God's plan, she wanted a baby, now. And maybe they should adopt.

For months, Walter said no, which caused many arguments. And what was even more frustrating for Lydia was that she had known Walter's position about adoption since before they were married because they had discussed it. So she couldn't even argue, "But before you said you would."

Once, when they were talking about what size family they each wanted, Lydia had asked Walter, "Suppose, just suppose, we can't have children. We would adopt, wouldn't we?"

"Not necessarily," Walter said. "Besides, I'm sure we'll have no problem having kids."

"But what if we can't? We would adopt, wouldn't we?"

"Right now, I'd have to say no," Walter said.

"You mean you wouldn't even consider it?"

"I'm not saying I wouldn't consider it, but it's not something I want to do. I really don't want to raise someone else's mistake."

Walter's response flabbergasted Lydia.

"Mistake? A baby's not a mistake. They're innocent little beings who deserve to be brought up by people who love them. Every child has that right."

"Well, maybe so, but…"

"But what?"

"What if I couldn't love the baby?"

"You would, Walter. You would," Lydia said.

"I don't know. I just don't know. I just don't think I'd want to do that."

Lydia had resigned herself to keep trying to get pregnant even though she was worn out from the emotional toll it took on her, Walter, and their relationship. She was almost glad when July came and it was time for Walter's annual trip down to Las Cruces with his veteran buddies. Lydia told her sister Jan, who knew of her inability to get pregnant, that she was glad Walter was leaving so she didn't have to have sex.

"It's been about as exciting as sorting laundry," Lydia told her. "Walter seems to have lost his enthusiasm. It's like when I tell him we need to make love, he acts as if I've just asked him to cut the grass."

"Liddy, girl, just relax. It sounds like you both need a break. Besides, once you do get pregnant, and I'm sure you will, you'll never have a good night's sleep again," Jan said.

"That's easy for you to say because you're part rabbit. If a guy looks at you the wrong way, you get pregnant."

"Well, there are problems with that, too," Jan said, laughing.

Lydia had prayed that Walter would have a change of heart about adoption.

"Dear Lord,

"I know you have a plan for each of us, and I'm trying not to be impatient or argue with you about that plan, but God, you must know how much I want a baby. And not just a baby, although you know how wonderful it must be to touch your cheek against a baby's skin, but I want to raise a child, watch that baby turn into a toddler, an adolescent, and even a teenager. The thought of going through this life childless almost paralyzes me. All I ever wanted in my life was to have my own family. I don't care about fancy houses or cars or clothes. I realize a child is a precious gift. You know that if you bestow that blessing on us, I, we, Walter and I, will cherish the little soul you give us.

"As I said, I'm not sure what your plan is, but if it isn't in your plan for me to bring our own child into this world, please soften Walter's heart to let him understand that no matter how a baby comes into this world, it deserves to have loving parents. Let him realize as soon as a baby looks in your eyes, it attaches itself to your soul.

"Until tomorrow, amen."

Lydia had thought it a miracle when a couple of months after returning from his trip to Las Cruces, Walter said he thought adoption was the way to go.

Chapter 5

Statements of Concern

L uckily, Maria Sanchez, Grace's housekeeper/babysitter was available to stay late and feed the children and put them to bed the night of Grace's Bunko party. At the last minute, Guy had called and said, "Sorry, but I can't make it home on time." It had something to do with a last-minute meeting, he said.

Grace had taken the easy way out on refreshments. She'd bought them. But some of them had to be reheated and others she had to add spoonfuls of sour cream and garnish at the last minute. Even though she had bought hers at the Dilly Deli, an expensive gourmet shop that smelled of imported Italian salamis and moneyed yuppy patrons, she knew they wouldn't taste as good as the ones Clare Porter had served last month at her house. Grace remembered seeing Clare's menu and stack of pages of recipes cut from magazines, tacked to the bulletin board. When someone had mentioned, "Ooh, these cheese straws are divine," Clare had yelled out *"Southern Living!"* When someone else mentioned how good the little puff pastries with spinach and artichoke in them were, Clare yelled *"Gourmet!"* Grace knew she'd be answering "Dilly Deli!" all night.

By the time she'd placed the chocolate-covered raisins, Crunch 'N Munch, and butter mints in bowls around the living and dining rooms and made sure the cold hors d'oeuvres were cold, and the hot ones, hot, all Grace wanted to do was go to bed. Sitting with a bunch of cackling women, rolling dice, and watching them drink too much wine was not what she wanted to do right now.

It was midnight by the time Grace cleared the last coffee cup and saucer off her dining room table and put it in the dishwasher.

Guy still wasn't home.

The Bunkettes had left about eleven-fifteen, that is, all except Nadia, the wife of a colleague of Guy's.

"I thought I'd stay and give you a hand," Nadia said, stifling a yawn.

"Don't worry. I'll just clear off these last few plates, then call it a night."

"Are you sure? You seem really tired and preoccupied tonight."

"I am tired. I was hoping I wouldn't fall asleep playing." She laughed. "That would have looked great. Hostess falls asleep and crashes into Bunko table."

Instead of leaving, Nadia picked up a plate with the remnants of the Boston Cream Pie Grace had served. She poked her finger into a crumb and licked her finger.

"Really Nadia, I can get this. It's getting late and I'm sure you want to get home."

Nadia put the plate on the counter and took a noisy breath. "All right, I'll cut to the chase. Is everything all right between you and Guy?"

Grace turned sharply. "*Why* do you ask that?" she said, snapping the china cup onto the granite counter.

Nadia shrugged a nervous shrug. "I don't know. Well, yes, I do know. Peter mentioned that Guy was sometimes spending the night at the firm's hotel suite at the Porter House. He thought it was odd and mentioned it to me so I thought I should mention it to you."

"Guy's been very busy. The Dolby case has been very time-consuming. And some of the depositions have run so late he and I both agreed it would be better for him to stay closer to the firm," Grace said, knowing she wasn't telling the entire truth.

"But the Dolby case wrapped up two months—"

"There were a lot of after-the-fact issues that went on following the trial."

"Oh, I'm sure," Nadia said, her backtracking obvious. "Peter's always got his nose in other people's business, you know. He just loves gossip. He's worse than a little old lady. I just thought, oh never mind. You're right; I should be on my way."

Grace let Nadia rattle on, but she wasn't listening. Guy mentioned to her just this morning that he was still working round the clock on the Dolby case. A case she just now learned had ended two months ago.

"I hope you don't think I was out of line mentioning this to you," Nadia said as she put on her black leather car-length coat and wrapped a red silk scarf around her neck. "I was just concerned."

Grace responded to Nadia's statement of concern with an arch of her eyebrows. Without talking, she escorted Nadia to the front door. She supposed she said "'Bye," but she wasn't sure.

After she closed the door and clicked the deadbolt, she turned off the porch lights and the walkway lantern, removing any welcoming sign. She walked across the custom-made Italian tiles of the foyer and into the living room where the lamps were still on. The house was so quiet she could hear the click of the switch as she turned off a lamp. Passing the lovely baby grand piano, she stopped to look at the group of family photos. She picked up the latest photo taken soon after Gigi was born nine months ago. She studied each person's face. Where are the smiles? she wondered. Why doesn't anyone look happy? Then she put the photo back and picked up one of her mom and dad. It was the last photo taken of them before her dad died. Lydia was sitting on Walter's lap, kissing his cheek.

She carried a bowl of butter mints into the dining room and placed it on the table. The table sat twelve comfortably before adding any leaves in it. Even though she was tired from taking care of the children and Guy had spent two or three weekends that month in New York working with clients, she had insisted on having the family Christmas at her house. She thought having it at home would give her mother a break, but later she learned from Sherry that Lydia was sad and a bit miffed about breaking the tradition of having the holiday at her house.

Mrs. Sanchez worked overtime helping get the house ready. She and Grace wound greens around the upstairs banister. Grace called in a professional tree decorator and had the twelve-foot tree trimmed in white and gold. And Mrs. Sanchez roasted a fifteen-pound rib roast.

In spite of laborious and expensive preparations, Christmas dinner didn't live up to Grace's expectations.

She had assumed everyone would be glad to come to her beautiful new house. But hers wasn't a home where you could flick your leg over the armrest of a chair like her mother's was. Guy was in a foul mood because he found the bill for the Christmas tree decorator fifteen minutes before guests arrived. Kelly had a fever and vomited on her cousin Danny. Markey put a glass of juice (he would rather have had pop but Grace didn't keep pop in her house because she didn't want her kids to drink it) down on the coffee table without putting a coaster beneath it, causing Grace to have a near conniption fit. And all Sherry's husband did was comment on what he perceived was the cost of things.

"I'll bet that piano cost a whole month's salary," he said to Guy, who instead of showing any modesty, said, "Depends whose salary you're talking about."

Her mother kept asking if there was anything she could do in the kitchen; slice something, stir anything, assemble whatever. But Grace said, "No, no, no. You are here to relax."

"I feel so useless," Lydia told Sherry.

Sherry was thrilled to be doing nothing. It wasn't often that she got to sit in a chair and drink a glass of wine. "I'd love to feel useless," she said, laughing.

Grace was surprised she had kept her head in the Bunko game tonight as well as she did, especially with all she had going on in her mind. She had ticked off her mother; she had forgotten she was supposed to take Allison Spencer home from ballet so Allison's mother, Carolyn, was pissed off at her, too. And then there was Guy, who was irate with her because she had become pregnant again.

"Mommy, I'm thirsty," Grace heard Kelly say.

"I'm coming, Kel," Grace said, calling up from the bottom of the stairs. "I have to turn off the kitchen light."

She walked back into the kitchen, filled a glass full of tap water and switched off the light. As she walked up the stairs she looked up. Kelly stood at the top of the stairs, holding her small turquoise blanket and the raggedy teddy bear that had once been her mother's.

"I can't sleep, Mommy."

Those were words Grace did not want to hear. She knew exactly what would come from her daughter's mouth next.

"Can I sleep with you?"

Grace said, "I don't know honey." All she wanted to do was lie in her bed alone and go right to sleep. She had not felt well the last week. She had not kept any food, except soda crackers, down all day. And she was exhausted from getting ready for the Bunko club. "Kel, hon, Mommy's very tired."

"Please, Mommy. I dreamed about the bad monkeys again."

"Oh my. Not them again."

"They were chasing me. Can I sleep with you?"

"Of course you can. Come on."

Kelly took a sip of water and then climbed on her mommy's bed.

Grace had been asleep an hour at most when she heard the garage door open. She tried to roll over but had no room to maneuver as Kelly had nuzzled up as close to her as she could. Grace thought about getting up and confronting Guy about where he had been until all hours of the morning, but instead she decided to lie in bed and act as though she were asleep. She had no energy for a confrontation. She would accuse. He would deny. He would tell her she was paranoid. She would call him a liar.

But instead, Guy came into the room and walked to the bathroom and brushed his teeth. As he approached the bed he saw Kelly, picked her up, and carried her back into her bedroom. Grace listened as he shut Kelly's door. He came back and got into his side of the bed.

Grace made sure her body was facing away from his. She didn't say a word. And she didn't plan to. She heard Guy making coughing noises. Intentional. Trying to get her attention. But she didn't move or acknowledge her husband's presence. She knew every move and sound he'd make before he made them. Her body tensed as she felt the bed shift with his weight inching toward her. Her stomach tightened. She squeezed her eyes shut tight. She didn't want him to touch her. But a fight in the middle of the night, or sex, were the only two choices she had. And frankly, sex took less energy.

He put his hand on the small of her back, then, moving his hand in circles, he inched it toward her bottom like this was some sort of romantic seduction.

Grace didn't move. She was frozen stiff, as if an intruder had just entered her room. She tried to make her mind dissociate from her body. She'd done that a lot recently, detached herself from the unpleasantness of her life.

Guy pulled his body closer and closer and wedged it into her backside. She smelled his cologne. She wanted to elbow him in the groin. Bastard, she thought. He breathed into the nape of her neck, kissing it like a butterfly, lifting her hair and blowing across her hairline. His breath smelled like peppermint toothpaste.

She played dead.

It didn't dissuade him. He moved his hand up and around her body, reaching for her breasts. They were sensitive to his touch, but not in a pleasant way. They were tender because she was pregnant. She knew he was trying to get her attention but she resisted. With his breathing quickening, he drove his hand down her still body and tried to reach between her thighs. Grace closed them as tightly as she could. With his left hand he grabbed her shoulder and rolled his wife over and with his right hand he pried between her legs.

He placed his lips on hers to kiss her but she jerked her head away and said, "No."

But that didn't stop him. He worked her legs apart, flattening her on her back and as he got on top of her he moaned, "I need you. I need you."

"You son of bitch," she said.

Chapter 6

Cuckoo

Lydia woke the next morning on Walter's side of the bed. When she got up to go to the bathroom she nearly killed herself tripping over the pile of clothes she had dredged from her closet and thrown onto the floor. She didn't remember doing it, but apparently she had thrown out a Scrabble game, several purses, two floral arrangements that at one time she had taken apart, and a tambourine. With her eyes half closed she walked over the pile of stuff and caught a strap from a sundress on her foot. She tried kicking it off but ended up bending over and pulling out the spaghetti straps that had gotten stuck in her toes. Still with eyes half closed, she trudged into the bathroom.

She put her robe on and walked down the stairs, following the smell of freshly brewed coffee to the kitchen. She was glad she had set up the coffee pot the night before. She switched on the small television she'd had Tim hang under the counter in the kitchen after Walter died. If she couldn't have Walter join her in a cup of coffee, she could have Katie. Walter wouldn't allow a television in any room designed for eating; he said viewing the trash on the idiot box would cause indigestion. And heartburn. But Lydia opted for the chance of heartburn over the dreaded silence of loneliness.

"There has been another bombing at the Turkish Embassy," the newscaster said. She turned the volume down. "I don't want to hear this kind of thing first thing in the morning. I'll keep the sound down 'til Katie comes back on."

Now all she needed was her raisin toast covered with a very fine film of butter and a generous topping of strawberry jam. She took two slices of raisin bread out of the bag she kept in the refrigerator, dropped them into the toaster, adjusted the setting to just past midway and pushed the squeaky lever down. She took out the butter and put it in the microwave for ten seconds to soften it, poured a cup of coffee into an English china cup decorated with hand-painted red roses, placed it on its matching saucer and carried it to the table. She always poured her coffee before she went out to get her newspaper as this allowed the coffee time to cool off to the perfect sipping temperature. She'd wait to put the cream in the cup until she got back from getting the paper because if she put it in before she went, the coffee would become too cool. She had this down to a science.

She walked through the living room and opened the curtains. It looked like it was going to snow. Again. That is all it had done since Christmas. Clouds hung low, pregnant, and overdue. She tightened the belt on her robe and stepped onto the front porch to retrieve the newspaper that was on the sidewalk. The wind tried blowing her robe open as she gingerly bypassed patches of snow that had blown onto the porch.

The street was quiet. She had hoped she could scamper out and back in quickly before the neighbors saw her. She was a sight: She hadn't brushed her teeth, combed her hair, washed her face, or shaved her legs. The newspaper, in its plastic bag, was covered with windswept snow. She picked it up and shook it off, causing crystal-like snowflakes to tingle on her hands. Turning around to go back into the house, she heard the sound of a car crumpling the snow and turning into her driveway.

"Grace. What are you doing here so early?"

"I figured you'd be up, so I decided to come over. Well, actually,

I told Bitsy to meet me here. I thought it would be good if all three of us got together to discuss your selling the house."

"Grace. I didn't say I was— Oh, for Pete's sake… I'm freezing. I'm going inside."

"That's fine. Bitsy is here now," Grace said, acting as though what her mother had said didn't matter.

Bitsy's Lexus turned into the driveway. By the time she parked, Lydia was in the house ready to ring Grace's neck. And Bitsy's.

Lydia was in the kitchen when Grace and a sheepish-looking Bitsy walked in.

"Hello, Bitsy," Lydia said, a noticeable chill in her voice.

"Hello. I'm sorry to be here so early again," Bitsy said, looking apologetic. "But Grace insisted. And she said she had cleared it with you."

"Oh, it's fine, Bitsy. Don't worry. My mother's up early. And I have other things to do today so, let's just get to it. Did you bring the information about what needs to be done to get the house on the market? And the contract?"

"Grace!" Lydia said. Her voice was as brittle as the china cup she held in her hand. "May I see you in the other room? Now?"

"Ooh, I smell coffee," Grace said, taking her coat off. "Let me get a cup."

"Grace. I said *now*."

"Jesus, Mom. Settle."

It was obvious Bitsy felt uncomfortable. She still hadn't taken off her coat and she kept clearing her throat.

"Bitsy. I don't mean to be rude, but this really isn't a good time."

"Mom, Bitsy came all the way over here on this crummy day. The least you can do is listen to the plan she's put together to sell your house."

"Grace. If you don't come into the other room right now, I am going to—"

Lydia walked past a shell-shocked Bitsy and into the other room. Grace followed her mother.

"Don't worry," Grace whispered to Bitsy. "I'll calm her down."

"What are you doing?" Lydia asked in a hard whisper "It is eight-thirty in the morning. I'm not even dressed, and anyway, where are the kids?"

"Relax, Mom. Guy's mother called last night and asked if I wanted her to watch the kids for a couple of hours this morning. You know they've been in Florida for the last month so they haven't gotten to see the kids. So, when Bitsy called and told me about her visit yesterday and said she'd put the information about selling the house together, I decided we needed to just get going with this."

"Grace. Bitsy seems to be a lovely woman. But the point is, I am not selling my house right now."

Grace raised her eyebrows. "You don't have to sound so harsh about it. I'm just trying to help."

"But I didn't ask for your help, Grace. At this time I don't need help, at least the kind you are forcing on me."

"I'm not *forcing* anything on you. I've been *offering* you help. There's a big difference between the two, and honestly, I don't know why you choose to look at my concern and interest as being anything other than helpful. The bottom line is, Mother, you need to sell this house and change your life."

"Grace, I appreciate your concern. But I feel like you're trying to push me out of my house. My home."

"I am not."

"Well, it seems to me that you are."

"I'm only trying to help you see some options. See some things that frankly, I think you're unable to see."

"And you think selling my home out from under me is showing me an option?"

"Mother, I'm not selling your house out from under you."

"That's what it appears."

"Well, then. If you think I'd do something like that, that gives me a good idea of what you think of me."

Lydia stared into Grace's brown eyes and Grace stared right back into her mother's hazel ones. Voices that had started out as whispers had grown to full throttle, louder than the den had been exposed to in years.

There was silence.

Then Grace added, "Sometimes, Mom, I think you choose to see me as the bad guy for reasons I just don't know. If Tim would have done what I've done, you'd've accepted his help with open arms."

"That's not true and you know it. I would have responded the same way."

Lydia knew Bitsy was getting an earful but she didn't care.

Neither Lydia nor Grace heard the cuckoo clock in the hall cuckoo nine times. Bitsy apparently did.

"Grace. Lydia. I don't mean to be rude, but I really think I should leave. It sounds like you two have some things you need to work out."

Lydia knew more than enough had been said and that nothing was going to be settled, not in both of their emotional states.

Bitsy, still with her coat on, said, "I have the information written down in this envelope. I'll leave the information here for you to go over at your convenience."

"That sounds good," Lydia said. "I would appreciate that."

For the first time that morning something was going her way.

Bitsy looked at Lydia. Then at Grace. And without waiting for anyone to say anything else, she turned to walk out. "Please don't let a house tear you two apart." Bitsy buttoned her coat and walked down the hall and out the front door.

Grace shook her head and looked as though tears would fall if she spoke. She grabbed her coat off the chair and put it on. She tied her red plaid scarf around her neck.

Lydia took a deep breath. "Should I put on a fresh pot of coffee?"

She couldn't see Grace's face but saw her shake her head. "No. I'm leaving."

Lydia looked at Grace's back. She looked at her petite form, strong posture, and beautiful coal-colored hair that hung to her shoulders. Her looks belied her personality. Lydia had always gotten a sense of pride when she watched how her daughter could, within minutes, have people wrapped around her finger. Cool confidence behind a warm smile. Lydia had always enjoyed how different Grace was from Tim or Sherry or Sugar and how Buddy used to be.

Lydia walked the few steps across the kitchen toward her daughter. She wanted to give her a hug. Holding out her arms for an embrace, she said, "Grace, are you all right?"

Grace didn't go into her mother's arms. Instead, she whisked past saying, "I'm fine. Just fine."

Lydia thought Grace was far from fine but she knew unless her daughter wanted to tell her what was really wrong, she wouldn't. The only thing Lydia did know to say was how she felt. "I love you, Grace."

There was silence.

Lydia repeated herself. "I love you, Gracie."

"Do you, Mom? Do you love me?" Grace asked as she tugged her shoulders, breaking away from her mother's hands. She spun around and rushed past her mother. "Does anybody really love me?"

Before Lydia had time to react, she heard the front door close, bringing with it a gust of cold air. As cold as the air was, the sound of her daughter's voice was more chilling. She had never heard Grace sound that way.

Chapter 7

Calling Tim

Lydia picked up the phone to call Tim to see if he might know what was wrong with his sister. Grace and Tim seemed to be the closest of all of her children. Maybe he could lend some insight as to what was causing his sister to act this way. But she put the phone back on the cradle. Maybe she should think before she started bringing other family members into this. Besides, how could she talk with this Pennsylvania-sized lump in her throat?

Tim's secretary, Janice, buzzed Tim and told him he had a call on line two. He was wrapping up a meeting with Kenny Johnson, a supervisor in the processing department. "I'm sorry I had to be the one to tell you the news, but I've got a directive from high up the food chain that says that until profits and expenses get more in line, we're all going to be getting cramps from this belt-tightening. Hopefully, this will be temporary."

"I hope so, too," Kenny said. "I hate to see anybody get laid off and I hate to be the one to do it."

"If you need anything, let me know. And keep me posted on how it goes. We don't need a disgruntled employee coming back at us with a Uzi in his hands."

"You got that one right," Kenny said as he walked out the door.

"Mr. Calypso, you have a phone call on line two," Janice said again.

"Thanks, Janice," Tim said. "Tell whoever it is that I will be with them in a minute."

"Certainly."

Tim scooted his executive-style leather chair back, put his hands on the edge of the desk and stood. He removed his charcoal worsted wool suit coat and hung it on an antique coat tree that was in the corner of his corner office. His parents had given him the coat tree when he was named vice-president in charge of production at the Sudbury Tomato Company. Tim prized the coat tree; it had been his great-great-grandparents'. Walter said it had come from Derbyshire, England. According to his dad, it had been in the family for over a hundred and fifty years.

He removed his glasses, which had been a permanent fixture on his face since he was nine when his younger brother Buddy had accidentally hit him in the left eye with a model airplane. Though Tim lost ninety-percent of his sight, he'd forgiven Buddy with relative ease. But Buddy never forgave himself. He told several people, including his oldest sister, Grace, that maybe the world would be a better place if he wasn't in it.

Her response at the time was "Well, you should feel bad. Look what you did. You *blinded* your brother."

Tim cleared his throat and picked up the phone, hoping the caller wasn't George Tinsley, another vice president telling him he was going to need to get rid of more "dead weight."

"Tim Calypso."

"Morning, Tim."

"Oh, hi, Mom," he said with relief. "What's up?" Gone was his octave lower voice tinged with gravitas that he used around the plant to sound managerial. He sat back down.

"Nothing much," Lydia said.

"That's good. Is this just a good-humor call? I could sure use one," he said, letting his body relax from its state of high alert. He scooted his chair back across the hard plastic runner and threw his legs up onto the desk.

"Why? Do you have a lot going on at work? Are you getting your rest?" Lydia asked, sounding a bit hovering.

"Just the usual. Problems, problems, problems," Tim said, adding, "I guess that's what I'm paid to handle, though."

"And you're very good at it, too." Lydia didn't have a clue as to what problems he was talking about, but that didn't matter. He was her son and he was good at whatever he did. That was the way it was. At least in her mind. "How are Helen and the kids?"

"Fine. Except Heather has a cold, Brady has a goofy rash on his left arm, Helen has cabin fever, and some sort of fungus between her toes that she insisted on showing me at breakfast. Other than that, we're in great shape."

"That's good," Lydia said. There was no tone in her voice

"Okay, Mom, what's up?"

"What do you mean what's up?"

"I mean what's up? I just told you Heather is sick, Brady has an unknown rash, and Helen has cabin fever and an unidentifiable fungus and you said that's good."

"Oh, I'm sorry. Did Helen take the kids to the doctor?"

"Okay, Mom. 'Fess up. I can tell something's wrong."

"Why do you think something's wrong?"

"Crying is usually a give away."

Lydia didn't acknowledge if she was crying or not. "Listen, Tim. I hate to bother you, especially at work." It was true, she hated to bother her son while he was working as she knew he was very busy, but it was almost impossible to have a coherent conversation with him when he was at home, what with the kids, the two dogs, and his wife vying for attention in the background.

"That's okay, Mom. I'm glad to focus on any problems that don't deal with tomatoes or employees."

"I don't know, Tim. Grace is acting strangely. I guess I was hoping maybe you could shed some light on what's going on with her. And before I forget, there is something else I need to talk to you about, too."

"What?" Tim said.

"One question at a time," Lydia said. "Have you talked to Grace recently?"

"Let me think. Was it Friday? No. I talked to her Saturday. Saturday about noon. She called and asked if I could get together with her over the weekend. She said she had something she wanted to talk to me about."

"So did you? Did you get together and talk?"

"No. I asked if it was something that could wait because that's when Heather started coming down with a cold and Brady had basketball practice and I had to help coach because the real coach, his coach, was going to be out of town on business. I told her maybe this weekend."

"What'd she say to that?"

"She said okay. She sounded a bit disappointed, but you know Grace, she's always disappointed if things don't go her way. Why do you think something's going on with her?" Tim pulled his feet off the desk, then leaned over and put his elbows on his knees. The phone was lodged between his shoulder and ear.

Lydia told him about how strange Grace had acted at her house yesterday after her Realtor friend had come by. "And then this morning, when she stopped by with that Realtor again, when I told her I loved her, she said something to the effect that she thought nobody loved her. It was quite strange."

Tim didn't say anything.

"Is this about something I did or said or something? Or is her life in disarray and I don't know about it?"

Tim laughed. "Mom, on any given day, all of our lives are in disarray."

"You know what I mean."

Lydia tried not to sound miffed at Tim's apparent nonchalant answer. He was acting just like his father. "Until you know for sure there's something wrong," Walter used to say, "don't worry."

"I'm serious, Tim. Do you know what's going on? She keeps trying to get me to sell the house and, well, here is the second question. Had you and Grace and Sherry planned on having some sort of grief intervention with me because you all think I've gone off the deep end since Daddy died? Grace said *all* of you want me to sell the house. She also said I'm bringing the family down with the way I act." Her throat tightened as she spoke. The whole notion of an intervention made her angry.

"Mom. Listen. I have no plans to get together with anyone to have any 'intervention.' Anyway, aren't those for alcoholics and drug addicts? I mean, for Pete's sake, you know if I have a problem with anything you do I just come over and talk. I don't need a committee to get your attention. You know that. Don't you?"

"I thought I did, at least until Grace brought up that silly intervention thing. And she mentioned it at least twice."

Tim's phone buzzed. It was Janice, the secretary.

"Mom, I really hate to do this, but I've gotta go. Tinsley's on the other line and he said it's urgent. I'll call you back as soon as I can. You gonna be all right?"

"I'll be fine. Get back to your work. I shouldn't have called."

"Sure you should've. You're my mom."

Chapter 8

Circumstances

Lydia pushed the button on the phone down without hanging up the receiver. If she set the phone back in the cradle it would seem as though the conversation was finished, which it wasn't.

It was eleven o'clock and she still hadn't gotten dressed. Although she knew she had clothes on, a nightgown, robe, and slippers, she felt naked. It was as though she had gotten a second-degree burn on her heart. It was open and raw, with nerve endings exposed. She didn't know what to do.

Should she call Sherry and talk to her, ask her what was up with her sister? No. What good would that do? Grace and Sherry weren't close. It was not as if they talked every day, or at least that was the impression Lydia got. Grace complained often to her mother about Sherry. "Sherry's kids are out of control," Grace would say, or "Doesn't it bother you that Sherry's house is so dirty? Not messy. Dirty."

The fact was, Grace was a snob. Lydia hated to think that, but that is certainly how it appeared. She had tried on numerous occasions to un-barb Grace's wires by explaining to her that not everyone was as lucky as she was. Not everyone's husband had a great job. And that Sherry did the best she could.

"People need to be responsible for their decisions," Grace had said during the discussion. "Personally, I think some people just enjoy being victims. I think Sherry does."

"I don't think that's true at all." Lydia had said. "Sometimes there are circumstances that we don't know about."

"People make their own circumstances. And they suffer the consequences."

Lydia felt uncomfortable talking about one of her children behind her back. But Grace loved to talk about them. To Lydia, it was as if the only way Grace knew to make herself look good was to put someone else down. Lydia appreciated the fact that Sherry never talked ill of her older sister, or any of her siblings, for that matter. She had even heard Sherry tell people how much she admired Grace. Sherry seemed proud to tell all of her friends that her sister was a lawyer, and that if her sister wanted to, she could probably be a movie star, with her Hispanic style, toast-colored skin, and flair for the dramatic.

It caused Lydia unease that none of her daughters were close. All three had catapulted into orbits of their own. It was like the three of them had never shared the same world. Grace lived on planet, "Do it My Way." Sherry lived on planet, "Could I Please Have One More Hour of Sleep" and Sugar, well, Lydia wasn't sure, but thought she lived somewhere in Lala-Land.

Lydia had this vision of what a family should be. But reality seemed to have played a bad joke on her as far as family and friends were concerned. She tried to figure out where along the line the breech was made, but she didn't have a clue. She made herself sick sometimes wondering where she had gone wrong. With her and her sisters, she knew exactly what caused their divisions. But with her own kids, everything was speculation, except with Tim, who laid his cards on the table.

She walked across the kitchen to go upstairs and finally get dressed. Why, she didn't know. She wanted to hibernate until spring. After hanging up from Tim, she decided there really was nothing she could do to remedy the Grace situation, at least not right now. So for the next hour, she decided to put it out of her mind.

Or at least she would try.

As she walked past the table she saw the large manila envelope Bitsy had left.

"Liddy" was written in flourishing hand on the front middle of the envelope.

She picked up the envelope and unwound the string that kept the clasp closed. Clearing away the crumbs from her toast, and after wiping her hands on a piece of paper towel, she opened the envelope. She was hoping Bitsy had just written her a thank you note that said it was nice meeting you. She wasn't ready for anything other than that.

She opened the envelope and pulled out a letter, a brochure, and a checklist of "Things to do to get your house ready for sale." She picked up her tortoise-shell reading glasses she'd bought at the Dollar Store, put them on and started to read.

Dear Liddy,

It was such a pleasure finally meeting you and seeing your house. Your home is lovely. It shows a lot of love. But I have to be honest, before we can put it on the market and get top dollar for it, there are some items that must be addressed. For your convenience I've enclosed a short list of things that need to be taken care of before we put that "For Sale" sign in your front yard.

Grace also mentioned to me that she wants me to show you a few small, one-story houses that are for sale near her. She said she would love to have you live closer to her so she can be near you. I will call you to set up a time.

As I see it, the items on the list shouldn't be a big deal, except maybe the new carpet (I detected quite a bit of cat odor; definitely a buyer turnoff), but I could arrange with Bob's Carpet Barn to take care of this for you. I have a special arrangement with Bob. So let me know.

Sincerely, Bitsy Esterhaus
Executive Sales Vice-president
Prestige Plus Real Estate Company

Lydia lifted her glasses and wiped her eyes with the back of her hands. She scanned the list of things Bitsy said needed to be done.

"What am I going to do, Binky?"

Binky meowed.

She needed something stronger than water. She went to the fridge, got out a bottle of Ruby Red grapefruit juice and poured herself four ounces. Four ounces were how much she was supposed to have if she wanted to stay on her diet. Of course her diet varied. Some days she was on Weight Watchers. Other days she tried to adhere to Atkins, and every once in a while she pulled out her old Richard Simmon's Dial-A-Meal. Sometimes she wished she were a pioneer on the prairie where food choices were minimal. But then she'd remember she hated rattlesnakes and those were rampant on the prairie, so she really was better off in the here and now.

She took a bite of toast. It didn't hit the spot. "Forget this," she said as she went to the pantry and grabbed a bag of Oreos, her heavy-duty therapy.

With one Oreo in her hand and one in her mouth, she resumed reading Bitsy's "To Do" list. Her eyes scanned down the list. She was so emotionally exhausted she didn't bother taking the Oreo apart and first eating the icing. Instead, she popped the whole cookie in her mouth.

She read the first five items on the list.

1) Remove dated drapes and replace with up-to-date window treatments.

"Ha," she said, "Walter's probably rolling over in his grave now."

2) Remove and replace rusty heat registers.

3) To make the rooms look larger, move half of the furniture to a storage unit. Note: A friend of mine owns "U Lock, We Store," which is only a mile from your house. Tell him I sent you and he will give you a deal.

4) I noticed the toilet in the upstairs hall bathroom ran. Call a plumber and get that fixed. Also have him give the other plumbing a once-over.

5) Mildew is a problem. You need to use a good, strong bleach mixture and scrub down your bathroom and kitchen walls.

She couldn't take any more so she searched the pages for the bottom line. The bottom line was this: In red, boldface print, Bitsy had handwritten, "The first thing I would recommend for you to do is clean your closets."

Chapter 9

Marblehead

Grace didn't want to go home after she left her mother's house. She didn't want to go to the mall even though she had a babysitter and she needed a new dress for one of Guy's work functions. She didn't want to go to her friend Sheila's, like she was supposed to, to talk about the plans for the charity auction for the Great Lakes Children's Hospital. The fact was, she didn't want to go anywhere. She wanted to evaporate like the snowflakes did when they fell into Lake Erie, never leaving a mark or a memory. She felt as if all she were doing was creating messes in people's lives because her own was so out of control.

The tears that fell when she left her mother's were dry now, leaving her face feeling pasty. Her make-up was a mess. And she didn't care. Guy insisted she put makeup on every morning when she got up, whether she was going out or not. "I don't want you looking like a housewife," he had told her, which she found interesting since he insisted that she be a housewife and keeper of the kids even though she had told him she would prefer to work at least part-time. So even on the weekends, she made sure she got up before the babies, sat at her chintz-draped dressing table and put on Olive Dew moisturizer, matching powder, taupe eye shadow, cocoa eyeliner, *Arizona Sunset* blush that was made especially for Hispanics, and clear lip gloss while Guy lay in bed snoring. When she finished putting her makeup on, she tried to slip unnoticed out of the bedroom so as not to awaken Guy because if he stirred, which he did most of the time, he would want sex, when all she wanted was a cup of coffee.

Guy couldn't get enough sex. Rough and tumble. Whether she wanted it or not. Like last night. Grace told her therapist she could probably count on her fingers the number of times Guy had actually made love to her after they got married. Most of the time he just wanted sex. Not slow, stare in your eyes, gentle foreplay, "Was it good for you?" sex. Just raw, rough sex. The kind that left her sore, hurt, and angry. But when she mentioned anything about it to him, he'd glare at her and say, "You know you want it, I can see it in your Hispanic eyes," which made her furious. One time after he made such a comment, she flung her arm up to slap him. He was too fast, and she missed. That's why the recent trip to Paris stood out to her so. Guy had actually been loving and tender, yet passionate, when they made love, which made Grace hopeful things would be different. But when they returned home, he went back to his old pattern.

During the last year, Guy tried pressuring her into having group sex. He couldn't understand why she was so adamantly against it. He told her that other couples in the law firm he worked for had group sex, not together as that might interfere with business relationships, but he knew they were swingers. Even Peter, one of the partners.

She didn't tell anyone about Guy's comments or actions, half out of fear and half from embarrassment. But she did find it interesting when Carly mentioned her *ménage a trois* at Bunko. Maybe it was her just not being adventurous. Maybe Guy was right, perhaps she had become boring and predictable and maybe she deserved this difficult marriage because she wasn't worth anything better.

Grace had decided to see a therapist after she'd scared herself one day while she and the kids were driving down the road and she'd had this overwhelming urge to push the gas pedal to the floor and steer the car into a tree. The feelings frightened her so that she'd had to pull the car into a McDonald's parking lot and sit there. Her grip on the steering wheel loosened as her palms began to sweat. She didn't even know if she should drive home, but who could she call? Guy would be incensed at the inconvenience; her brother Tim was out of town on business; and her mother would freak out. And she couldn't call her sister Sherry because how many times had she told her sister, who despaired over her own life, to 'Just get your act together'?"

"What's wrong, Mommy?" Kelly had asked when she saw her mommy breathing big gulps of air, sniffling.

All Grace could say was "Mommy has a headache and I think I need to get a Coke."

"Can I have one, too?" Kelly had asked.

"May I," Grace corrected. Even in this state of possible tragedy, Grace was going to make sure her kids used good grammar. "I will get you juice, not Coke."

"He's never hit me," Grace had told her therapist, in an attempt to defend why she stayed with her husband. "It's just the things he says make me feel like I'm being cut with a knife. I don't know, maybe I've brought it on myself by not living up to his expectations."

Grace couldn't say her husband wasn't a good provider. He was. He bought her expensive clothes and perfume. He was decent to the children, although she wished he would spend more time with them. But, as she told the therapist, "Maybe me telling him he should spend more time with the children is putting undo pressure on him as he really is trying to build his career so we can all could have a better life."

When the therapist asked her what she meant by a "better life," Grace stuttered a bit before saying, "He always told me he wanted to live in a house, a large Tudor house on the lake. And he wants to go to Europe at least once a year and he wants the kids to go to private school because he said public schools are awful and he says 'My kids are going to get the best.'"

The therapist challenged her by asking, "Well, what do you think a 'better life' is?"

Grace couldn't answer the question. Sitting in that chair, she felt as though she wasn't a part of the earth or in her own body and she had no idea what a "better life" was. "I suppose I haven't thought too much about it," she said.

"I think it's about time you do," the therapist said. "It appears to me that you have lost your identity. You've buried your true self behind achievements, your husband, and your children, anything that allows you to not see or feel who you really are."

Grace asked the therapist, "How can I be so good at understanding facts and the complex issues of the law and how can I be good at helping other people sort out their problems, but when it comes to my own life or the lives of people I love, I fail? Miserably. And how is it that even after growing up in a home where my parents told me I could be whatever I want to be, I could feel like so much of a nothing?"

The therapist said, "Welcome to the club, Grace. You're not alone in your feelings. Unfortunately, self-esteem and self-worth aren't something that can be given as a gift by parents, teachers, or well-intentioned people. In the end, self-worth is something you have to give yourself. It's something most of us have to work on constantly. Even me."

Grace's eyes widened. "You don't mean to tell me you don't have self-esteem?" Grace asked, looking at the therapist with a cocked head and squinted eye.

"Sometimes. That's part of the reason I see a therapist, too."

"You're kidding."

"No, I'm not. Grace, a lot of this doesn't have a thing to do with how smart you are or what you achieve. It's how you see the world. How you react to things that are in your control and things that you have no control over whatsoever. Sure, it can have to do with chemical imbalances in the brain, but so much of it depends on how we think. And our thinking is something we can control. Frankly, it's about the only thing we can control. We often don't have the distance and objectivity we need to analyze situations without becoming emotionally embroiled. We are told we can 'be' anything, but 'being' doesn't necessarily address the issue of who we are. And that *is* what's important: Finding out who we are and accepting ourselves after we find out who that is."

Finally, Grace had opened the window for the therapist. "Abuse isn't always physical. There's sexual abuse and emotional abuse, both of which can wreak just as much or more havoc as physical abuse," the therapist said. "Victims of emotional abuse, just as those who are victims of physical abuse, have the misconceived notion that they are responsible for the abuse that is being placed on them. And sexual abuse has nothing to do with love. It's all about power. And each of the abuses produces a victim."

Grace recoiled. Victim? Did she say victim? The thought was repugnant to her. She was a lawyer, for heaven's sake. Victims are weak.

In the sessions to come, each time the therapist said the word "victim" Grace distanced herself from the word. It got to the point that when she was sitting in a chair at the therapist's office it seemed she was representing another person, a Grace she didn't see or understand at all.

She defended this other Grace as though she were appearing before a judge. Instead of the conflicts in her head resolving themselves, Grace became more confused. Who was the real Grace? What did she want? And how could she get whatever it was she wanted? Did she have a right to find out? And how could she find out for sure when she didn't know from whom or where she really came?

The therapist said she might get worse before she got better.

Grace drove around nearly forty-five minutes before she realized she had no idea where she had been or where she was going. It was as if the car was on automatic pilot and she was just a passenger. She couldn't remember if she had stopped at red lights, turned left or right, or gone in circles. She sensed it wasn't a blackout, but a zone-out. Part of her was conscious, but reality wasn't in the picture.

She noticed she was driving out of town, on St. Rte. 23, heading along the lake up to Marblehead Lighthouse. Her car drove like it had a mind of its own. She drove by Pickett's Farm Market that was boarded up and hidden by unplowed snow, closed for the season. Oh, how good a fresh tomato would be right now, she thought. She couldn't stand the winter tomatoes she bought at the grocery store. They tasted like what she imagined the fake fruit on her mother's dining room table would taste like.

In the summer, she'd drive to Pickett's with her kids, just like her parents had done with her and her brothers and sisters. She had bought tomatoes and green beans and corn on the cob. Kelly loved to eat corn on the cob. Grace had taught Kelly to chew the corn all the way along one side, making a ding sound like the return on a typewriter, and then chew it back the other way.

She laughed when she remembered how Buddy had, on a dare from Sugar, taken a big bite out of one of their mother's plastic pears and then carefully rearranged it back in the bowl beneath a red and green apple and a bunch of grapes so that Lydia wouldn't see the hole he had made in it. Now she wanted to kick herself for tattling on Buddy to their dad.

For some reason, she and Buddy were always at odds. Maybe she picked up her sense of disdain for him from their father. She watched how he treated Buddy. Nothing Buddy did was right, and she, maybe to show her allegiance to her dad, also sided against her brother. She'd talked to her therapist about this too, trying to understand why she had always aligned herself with her father, even when she thought he was wrong. "That's pretty natural," the therapist said, "most daughters are daddy's girls." Grace could understand that dynamic if she and her dad had had a real biological connection, but they didn't because she was adopted.

She passed Froto's Mini-Race Track. Her stomach sank. That was where Buddy had worked the summer before he died. It was abandoned now. Boarded up. It never reopened after the accident and the lawsuit that followed.

Although the heat in the car was on full blast, Grace shivered as she passed Froto's. She and her friends sometimes went to Froto's to see Buddy and the "hot" guys who hung out there trying to speed their way through life. Buddy said the guys loved to hang out there because of the smell of the gasoline and the roar of the engines. "A guy thing," he called it. "That's as close to Grand Prix as these dudes will get." He'd laugh.

Grace's mind flashed back to when the whole family had celebrated when Buddy was named assistant manager at Froto's. Lydia made a devil's food cake and Buddy's favorite meal, spaghetti and meatballs. Buddy got to sit at the head of the table.

Almost every achievement and milestone was celebrated in the Calypso house. When she was little, the milestones ranged from pooping in the potty to losing a tooth. As the kids got older, cakes, and special dinners marked anything from Buddy winning a kickball kick championship to Sherry selling the most Girl Scout cookies. If Sugar avoided getting a "D" on her report card, that was feted, too. *Boy, they really stretched some of those things.*

She wanted to carry on that tradition after she got married and had children. It hadn't happened, though, because Guy said he thought the idea was stupid. Grace had tried to start the tradition after Kelly lost her first tooth. She bought a "Barbie" cake and made a small crown for Kelly out of construction paper decorated with glitter. Guy flipped out. Not in front of the kids. He had more control than that. But that night, after dinner, he'd said to Grace, "I told you we weren't going to do that shit." And then he wanted to have sex.

She pulled into the parking lot by the lighthouse. The gravel and ice crunched beneath her tires. No other cars were there, so she parked in the spot closest to the pathway to the lighthouse.

Why Marblehead, why the lighthouse? Marblehead is a place you go in the summer when the lake is blue and boats with red and blue and yellow and green sails pass along the horizon and children play along the shore, watching the waves crash and break over the boulders that have been moved into place to keep the shore from eroding. Who in their right mind would want to come to Marblehead in the dead of winter when the sky is a gruesome gray and snow is blowing sideways and the winds blow through you like you're a tennis net? Grace's mind couldn't stop.

She sat in the car a few minutes and tried to figure out what she was doing here. She questioned if she were in her right mind. Then, as any good attorney would, she thought, what is a right mind, anyway? Why had she come to Marblehead, a frigid windswept mass of white concrete when she could have gone anywhere else, someplace toasty like the coffee shop in town where, throughout the winter, they have a blazing fire going in the stone fireplace? It was as if something were drawing her to the cold dark waters of Lake Erie. And she didn't know what it was.

She tried to look out the window, but since she had turned off her windshield wipers, the window was covered with snow. It was really coming down. She was mesmerized by it. Her thoughts went vacant. She didn't wonder if Kelly and Austin were being nice to Guy's mother. She didn't look at her watch to see if it was time for Gigi to have a bottle.

She didn't think about Guy or the question he asked as to whether she thought her *real* mother was fat. And then he added, "Aren't those slacks getting a little tight?"

He had said this to her just this morning while she was getting dressed to go to her mother's house to meet Bitsy. When he'd said that, Grace felt as though she were going to vomit. Of all of the cruel things he had said, this had to be the cruelest. But all she could bring herself to say was, "Lydia's my *real* mom. And you know how I feel about that."

But when she walked out the door, she heard Guy say, "No, she's not."

Grace unhooked her seatbelt, opened the car door and listened to the symphony of air whistling outside her car, across the lake, and through the branches of the barren trees. It sounded like a kettle drum, beginning slowly, then growing louder, more resonant. She watched the choppy waters of the lake jitterbug toward the shore, whitecaps changing partners with each new gust of wind. Such a vast expanse of nothingness, she thought, looking out across the lake. Just like life.

Normally every waking moment of her day since she was born, or so it seemed, had been taken up with thinking. Her brain shifted thoughts faster than an Indy race car driver shifts gears. Do this, remember that, drop off this, check that, call here, go there, make this, and get rid of that. Her brain raced to stay ahead of itself and everyone else. But now her brain was shutting down.

Grace had never thought about ending her life. Not before Buddy died, anyway. Suicide wasn't a word that was in her vocabulary, much less a choice as a solution for life's problems. People died from cancer or heart disease or strokes, but not suicide. At Sunday school she was taught that if you killed yourself (they never used the word suicide), you would go to Hell. After Buddy took his own life, suicide became an option. But when the thought of suicide came into her head, she thought of how it would affect her kids. And her mother. She had experienced firsthand what a suicide does to a family.

Yet today the pull and push in the direction of death overrode the thought of her children. Figuring out who she was and how she fit into the scheme of things was too hard right now. All she wanted was peace. She was sure the world would be a better place without her. She was pushy and bossy and self-centered. And she was so tired of trying to stay one step ahead of the sanity-chasers.

She got out of the car. The wind and snow pelted her face, causing her to scrunch her head down turtle-like into the neck of her coat. She pulled her scarf up over her earmuffs and wrapped it around her neck a couple of times. Guy had bought the scarf for her on one of his frequent business trips to New York.

She walked along the path toward the lighthouse. The wind bombarded her with frozen water coming from the lake. It felt like someone had taken frozen ping pong balls and was throwing them at her face. She thought about walking backward to protect herself from the searing gusts but that would be treacherous as the path was covered with ice and snow. No, she would have to burrow her head into her chest and go. She laughed, thinking how Guy would be appalled at her appearance now, looking like a bag lady or even worse, a fat, middle-aged housewife with her babushka tied around her head.

Her cell phone rang. She hadn't taken it out of her pocket. But she kept walking. It could have been her daughter Kelly, who sometimes used speed dial to call her cell phone to tattle on Austin. It might have been Guy, sounding like a normal loving husband asking her how her day was going. Maybe it was Sheila wondering why she hadn't come over to go over the charity auction. But at that moment, Grace couldn't care less who was calling her. Whoever it was, their call wasn't nearly as strong as the lure of the lake.

Chapter 10

Second Thoughts

Tim felt badly that he'd had to cut his conversation with his mother short. He knew she counted on him to talk to, to help her make sense of the world, and keep his finger on the pulse of the family. After all, in the hierarchy of their family, he was the man nearest the top.

He looked at his watch and decided to call her back after his meeting, right after he called his wife, Helen. He had to call his wife first because if she ever got wind that he had called his mother before he called her, well, she'd put another notch in the "Your own family should come first" pile.

He did put his family first. Helen and the kids were always first on his list. But his mother was important, too. And so were his sisters. They had been through a lot together, things Helen would never understand. And now that his mom was a widow, he had to be there for her when she needed him.

No, it wasn't that he *had* to be there for his mom and for his sisters, he *wanted* to be. He loved them. Even whacky Sugar. The love he had for his mother and sisters was different from the kind of love he had for his wife and kids. It was a deep, caring love, one that had history and understanding. And his mother's love was the only one he had ever known that was unconditional.

Tim looked at his watch again. He had a few minutes before his eleven-thirty meeting. *Maybe I should call Grace,* he thought. But what good would that do if he didn't have time to talk to her? With the short time he had the phone call would be, "Hi, Grace. How are you doing? Sorry, I've gotta run."

So he didn't call. Why stir up something if he didn't have time to help the situation?

He took his pencil and marked on his day planner, "Call Grace." He had nothing scheduled between three and four, so maybe he and his sister could chat a bit and he could find out what was behind what she had said to Mom this morning. He never wrote down when he needed to call Helen or his mom, as he did so by instinct. But not his sisters. Even though he loved them, he didn't contact them very much. Probably not as much as he should. He assumed it was because each of them was busy with their own families. Besides, they didn't call him much, either.

He considered his biggest job as a son was to reassure his mom that everything would be fine. Sometimes he thought she overreacted, especially when it came to family matters. And that's probably what she was doing now with Grace. He knew his sister loved to be a drama queen, straight out of the Lawyer School of Dramatic Court Presentations. "Mom, you take Grace too seriously. You've gotta ease up," he'd say. "You're going to stroke out."

He had noticed how since his dad died, well, actually since Buddy died, his mom held on to every word each of her kids said even more than she did before. She took everything they said so seriously. Even jokes. He sensed that she was so afraid she was going to lose another family member that she held on for dear life. Sometimes her grip was strangulating. He knew he should tell her this but he hadn't found the right time.

Tim kept thinking of what his mother said about Grace during his next meeting. This was not usual. Normally he was very good at hearing information and filing it into the right mental filing cabinet. But something about the conversation with his mother stuck in his craw.

Sales Manager Jacob Crane pointed to a chart showing the last quarter's sales. Tim's eyes followed Crane and nodded in agreement to whatever Crane was saying, but he didn't have a clue as to what the guy was talking about. He was trying to recall his last few conversations with Grace.

He stared at the mural of the tomato fields painted on the wall in the conference room. Lake Erie shimmered in the background of the painting, off behind the tomato fields. The sun shone over the fields. The blue of the sky and lake contrasted beautifully with the red of the tomatoes and the green of the tomato plants. In the corner of the mural was Marblehead Lighthouse standing sentinel over the lake and the fields.

The last time he *really* talked to Grace was, gee, hum, well, he couldn't remember. He knew she had called recently, but he hadn't had time to talk. When was the last time he'd *really* talked to his sister, or more importantly, *listened* to her? The kind of talk where the talkers are connected, the kind of talk that makes you feel that you are tethered together by blood. In his mind, it hadn't been that long ago. Or had it been? It was now the end of January. Had he talked to her much in January? No. They had planned to get together for New Year's but her daughter Kelly and son Austin were sick with the flu so that was cancelled. They'd get the families together soon, they'd agreed.

At Christmas the whole family had gotten together, everyone except Sugar, who always had an excuse why she couldn't come back for the holidays. Bad work schedule. Short on money. He missed Sugar even though it seemed like the big goal in her life was to cause discomfort for those around her. Once, after Sugar had said something outrageous, Tim asked his mom what she'd eaten when she was pregnant with Sugar. Lydia laughed and said, "Obviously, bologna."

The talk in the boardroom turned to cutting expenditures. Department heads were supposed to go employee by employee, job function by job function to see where they could cut any fat. Tim chuckled to himself wondering how you could cut fat from a tomato, a watery vegetable that didn't have an ounce of fat in it.

He would have loved to have said it aloud (he got that from Lydia), but he always remembered he had a mortgage to pay and that was enough to keep his tongue planted firmly in his cheek.

As he sat in the meeting looking at Lake Erie on the mural, he felt himself becoming seasick. Or was it heartsick? He wondered if anyone in the room would notice the color draining from his face as he realized he hadn't *really* talked to Grace or any of his siblings since right after their father died. No wonder his mom was worn out trying to hold her family together.

Tim pushed his chair back from the table, stood, and excused himself from the meeting. "Nature calls," he said, as he walked from the room, not looking back to see if anyone was giving each other the What-the-hell-was-that-about? look.

He strode to his office and closed the door. He called his secretary and told her he was not to be disturbed. Then he picked up the phone and punched in his mother's phone number.

Lydia didn't hear the phone ring. She was in the shower, singing. The hot water melted her body until she felt like warm candle wax. That was one good thing about this house, she thought, the hot water. She had forgotten to mention the great hot water to Bitsy. The water got really hot, and since the house had two hot water heaters she could stand in the shower until Lent and never run out. But as she was leaning down to scrub her ankles, she noticed the grout had fallen out between several tiles and the caulk Walter had put between the edge of the tub and tile seemed to be growing some black form of vegetation or mold.

Even though the water was warming her body down to her bones, Lydia suddenly felt a cold chill. *I should have gotten in the car and followed her.*

After her shower she walked into the bedroom and was about to climb over the mess of clothes on the floor to get into her closet when she noticed the red light flashing on the phone message machine. She hit play. "I hope it's Grace," she said, raising her eyes toward the heavens as if she were making a request to God.

"You have one new message... message one... beep," the machine said, "Mom, it's me, Tim. Was just wondering if you wanted to get together for a late lunch or a cup of coffee or something. Give me a call ASAP."

She was deflated that it wasn't Grace, but when she heard Tim was inviting her to lunch she chippered up. It had been a long time since she and Tim had had lunch together. At least alone. Every once in a while Tim would invite her to lunch, but Helen always joined them and monopolized the conversation with vivid accounts of her latest ailments. Although Lydia never considered herself a prude, she did get offended when Helen mentioned how her doctor had to lance her boil and pus "just flew everywhere," right when Lydia was putting a forkful of chicken salad dressed in mayonnaise into her mouth.

Maybe he'd thought about something Grace said, Lydia thought. Yes, maybe he could shed some light on what was going on in this family.

Lydia kicked a bunch of the clothes out of her way and stepped into the closet. She stepped over a laundry basket that was full of shoes, some she was sure she had had since before Nixon resigned.

"I really should do something with these," she said to Binky. He sat on the edge of the bed, watching Lydia in her quest to find an outfit to wear

Lydia picked up the phone and called Tim. They arranged the time and place for lunch. She finished getting dressed and walked downstairs to leave.

As she was walking out the door to get into the car she heard the phone ring. "I'll bet that's Grace," she said. "Maybe she'd like to join us for lunch."

"Hello, Grace?" Lydia answered, after seeing Grace's home number on caller ID. Thankfully, she had found a pair of her dime-store reading glasses in another purse and put them by the kitchen phone.

"Hello, Lydia, this is Constance, Guy's mother. How are you?"

"Oh, I'm fine. I thought for sure you were Grace. I saw her number on caller ID."

"Sorry. I was wondering if Grace was still at your place. She said she'd be home by ten-thirty or so. She's still not here."

"No. Grace isn't here. Actually, she wasn't here that long." Lydia wished she hadn't said that. She should have just said, no, Grace left about nine. "She left about nine. You mean she hasn't been home yet?"

"No. She surely hasn't been. And her friend from the charity auction called, someone named Cindy, or Sheila or something like that. She asked where Grace was because she was supposed to be at her house for a meeting this morning and she never showed up. Didn't call, either."

"That's not like Grace." Her daughter never just didn't show up.

"I didn't think so. She's always so organized and prompt. She keeps things running like clockwork. Austin, don't stick that pretzel up your nose! Sorry to yell in your ear," she yelled into Lydia's ear. "Listen, I hate to ask you to do this, but I'm going to have to leave soon to take Earl to the doctor; his gout has really been flaring up. Do you think you could come over and watch the kids until Grace shows up?"

Now Lydia was really concerned. Something must be wrong with Grace. This didn't have the appearances of some of what Tim and the other kids referred to as Grace's "drama queen" antics. The kids caught on to Grace's theatrics early on. Lydia had been much slower.

She couldn't be losing another child, could she? God wouldn't do that to her, surely.

"Hello, Lydia. Are you there? I said, I hate to ask you this, but do you think you could come over and relieve me so I can get Earl to the doctor?" Constance repeated.

Lydia didn't say anything. She became aware of her rapidly beating heart. She was thinking. Thinking as quickly as she could. Maybe Grace stopped at the gym. Maybe she went shopping at the mall. Grace told her she needed to buy an outfit to wear to Guy's firm's Mardi Gras bash. Sure, that's what she did. She took that extra time and went to the mall and lost track of what time it was.

"I, um, did you call Guy at work and ask him if he had heard from Grace?"

"No, I didn't want to bother him at work. I'd only call him if I thought this was an emergency. I think this is just an inconvenience, don't you?"

"I'm not sure. This isn't like Grace. If Grace says she's going to be somewhere, she's there. Unless something happened." She could barely say those last three words. "Normally I would come right over but I was on my way out the door when you called. I have to go to—" She stopped herself from saying "lunch with Tim." Constance didn't need to know that. So she said, "I'm on my way to an appointment." Lydia sensed Constance was none too pleased with her answer. "Let me give you a call back in a couple of minutes. Okay?"

"Fine." Lydia heard a distinct "humph" in Constance's voice.

After she hung up, Lydia got into her car and headed for Mikey's Oriental Garden where she and Tim had agreed to meet. She looked at her watch. "Oh no. I'm going to be late. What's Tim's cell phone number? Is it five-three-zero or is it five-zero-three?" She tapped her gloved fingers on the steering wheel. "Dog-on-nit," she said. "I can't remember anything. I wonder if Tim realized how bad it's getting out here."

She made one last attempt at the traffic light to find Tim's cell phone number. Honk! Honk! The car behind her beeped at her when the light turned green. "I'm going. I'm going. Hold your horses."

No sooner did she put both hands on the wheel then she remembered she had told Constance she would call her right back. She reached for the cell phone Tim had given her for Christmas. It was prepaid for a year. Keeping one hand on the steering wheel, she removed the glove from her other hand with her teeth. She punched in Grace's home number. "Geeze, Louise," she yelled as she watched a car slide into a telephone pole. She jammed on her brakes and looked to see if it looked like the driver was injured. It didn't and, anyway, two people from other cars had already gotten out of their car to go help.

Constance answered on the first ring.

"Hello," she said.

"Yes. Constance? Lydia. I'm sorry but I can't get over there for at least an hour, maybe an hour and a half. I'm unable to cancel this appointment."

"Oh no. I don't know what we'll do. I just called Earl. He'll be so upset because his gout is so bad. He can hardly stand. He said he *has* to go to the doctor. *Today.*"

"I'm sorry. Maybe you should call Guy. Tell him he needs to come home."

"I hate to do that. His time is so valuable and he's so busy. And I'm afraid he'll be upset that Grace isn't here."

Lydia wanted to choke her. Nothing personal, but she wanted to say: Perhaps the most valuable use of your son's time today would be to come home and watch his kids and help find out where his wife is and what's wrong with her. "You need to call him and let him decide where his time is most valuable today," Lydia said, not caring if she sounded short. "Sometimes people have to do what they have to do. If you want me to come by later, call my cell phone. Here's my number."

Chapter 11

Sherry's World

"Helter-skelter." That's how Sherry described her life on a survey distributed by Millie Schlee, Office Coordinator at the university. Normally, Sherry dumped office surveys into file thirteen. But this one she filled out. She'd heard from Millie, who sat two desks away from hers, that the college was thinking of offering flex-time. "Flex-time would be a gift from God," she told Millie.

Even she didn't know how she juggled the schedule she did. She worked full-time, drove both boys to football, basketball, and Scouts; Danny to karate and Markey to piano. Every other month she served as Scout troop mother.

Two years ago she'd given up her beloved bath and opted for the three-minute shower when she started her job in the financial aid department at the Port Huron Community College. She worked in data entry. It wasn't what she wanted to do, but she'd quit college before she'd gotten her degree and the jobs she wanted were out of reach. She was quietly trying to remedy that.

She hadn't told anyone, including her husband or mother, that she was taking courses to finish her degree. She took the classes on the QT because if she told her husband, Joe, about the classes he would say, "Why waste your time?" And she didn't tell her mother, because she didn't want or need a cheerleader. This was something she wanted to do herself, on her own terms. So she kept her classes to herself.

She'd gotten pregnant at twenty, fifteen credits shy of earning a diploma. She studied anthropology, much to the chagrin of her dad and Joe, whom she was dating at the time. "Anthropologists barely make a living wage, or they end up working in Timbuktu," her dad had said when she told her parents of her plans. "You should be a teacher like your mother."

Joe was no better. He said anthropology was a waste of time. "Besides, you'll make only a fraction of the money you could make if you would go into business." Of course, he added, "You could be a hotshot lawyer like your sister Grace."

Her mom had taken her dad aside during that discussion. Her mom tried to keep her voice down, but Sherry heard her. "Didn't you see the disappointment in your daughter's face when you belittled what she wanted to do with her life? Not to mention," she said with a harrumph, "teachers barely make a living wage, either."

After her mother chewed her dad out, she took Sherry aside and said, "Darling, you know you can be whatever you want, even President of the United States." Sherry tried not to roll her eyes. She had heard this You-can-be-anything-you-want stuff since she was born. But Sherry had no desire to be president. All she wanted to be was Grace.

Sherry had just gotten out of her eleven o'clock class when she decided to call her mom. She would use the phone in her office. There were few pay phones left on campus since everyone, except her, seemed to have a cell phone. She had wanted one, had asked for it for Christmas and her birthday and Mother's Day, but Joe said they couldn't afford one.

Figuring her mom would just have finished watching "The View," Sherry set her purse and briefcase down and dialed her mother's number.

The phone rang. And rang. Four times and then the recorder came on. Sherry shook her head as she listened to her dad's voice on the message recorder, "You have reached the Calypso residence. If we were here you wouldn't have gotten this message, but since you have and you know we aren't here, please leave your name, number, and a message. Remember, don't ramble and speak clearly."

After leaving a message, Sherry sat at her desk and opened a bottle of mineral water she'd brought from home. She would have rather had soda, but since she had gained seven pounds over Christmas, she had been eating healthier. There were a few minutes before she had to be at her next class so she decided to close her eyes and rest. Her eyes took a break but her mind didn't. She remembered how Grace and her mom had gotten into a tiff, when on Thanksgiving, with the whole family gathered at Lydia's, (except Sugar, of course), Grace mentioned how unnerving it was to have Dad's voice answer the phone when she called.

Lydia was scooping the stuffing out of the turkey when Grace started her interrogation. "When are you going to change the message on the recorder?"

"I've read it's much safer to have a man's voice on your answering machine," Lydia said defensively, plopping another spoonful of the sage and sausage stuffing into the Wedgwood bowl she and Walter had gotten at the Lutheran Church rummage sale.

"Well, for crying out loud, Mom, have Tim or Guy record the message. Doesn't it seem odd to you that it's been over two years and you still haven't changed the message? And you haven't even cleaned out Daddy's closet. Don't you think this is a bit ridiculous? It's time you put Daddy's ghost to rest. Past time, really," Grace said to what had become a silent crowd, except for the grandkids who were in the den.

Sherry thought she would choke on her radish. Normally, she wouldn't have said anything, but this time words popped out of her mouth before her brain knew what was happening. "Grace. Knock it off. This is neither the time nor the place to bring this kind of thing up. It's Mom's recorder and her house. She can do whatever she wants with both. Besides, it's Thanksgiving."

"Here, here," Tim said, lifting his glass of Bud Light as if to give a toast.

"Well, I agree with Grace," Helen said, while looking at her reflection in the microwave, using her finger to get rid of a lipstick smear. "My mother got rid of my dad's things a week after he died."

"Your mom hated your dad," Tim said.

"Not all the time," Helen snapped, giving her husband *the look* that married people give each other when they are ready to kill their spouse.

Guy seemed to want to stir the pot more. He looked at Joe and said, "You double-dipped that carrot. Now nobody else can eat the dip. Real considerate."

Sherry thought Guy and her husband Joe were going to come to blows as Joe pushed his chair back and got up in the direction of Guy.

She could feel the heat of the halo made of anger that had circled Lydia's head. And if all of this wasn't enough, Kelly came racing into the kitchen yelling, "Markey's talking about poopy."

At which point Sherry noticed all eyes were on at her.

"Joe, will you go in there and tell Markey to behave?"

"Why? Kelly's just a little whine bucket," Joe said, looking at Guy. "All kids talk about poop."

Don't, Joe. Just don't.

"They do not," Grace said. "And Kelly is *not* a whine bucket. The problem is Markey is a brat."

"Stop it! All of you. Be quiet," Lydia said, trying to keep the quivers in her voice in check. "If you could hear yourselves. You sound like enemies, not a family."

The room stilled.

"First of all, the voice message stays as it is. Second, Miss Grace, I will clean Daddy's closet out when I am good and ready. Joe, you shouldn't double-dip. And lastly, the grandkids aren't acting any worse than their parents are. Now everyone go into the dining room, sit down, and be grateful we are all together. Tim, you'll say grace. And make it a good one."

Sherry remembered Tim stumbling over the prayer. If she had given the blessing, she was sure she'd have said something like: "Dear Lord, please bless this dysfunctional family. If you can find it in your heart not to have anyone stab the person sitting next to them with a butter knife, we'll consider this a successful Thanksgiving, and we will be extremely grateful. Amen."

Tim was always much better at political correctness, even in prayers.

Sherry complimented him for handling the "grace" situation with aplomb. She was sure it was only through grace that any of them survived that dinner.

Her eyes still closed, she shook her head back and forth. She thought about that meal and its silence. Only the clink, clink, clink sound of water glasses and silverware clanking against the plates made any sound. Intermittently, someone said, "Please pass the stuffing," but chitchat was at a minimum. Virtually non-existent. She was so nervous she could barely eat, so she spent a good portion of the meal watching everyone else. She went from person to person, down the table. Her mom smacked her lips and made a slapping sound like a dog drinking from a water bowl. Guy chewed with his mouth partially open, exposing a mish-mash of turkey and stuffing. *And he thinks he is so cool.* She had to squelch herself from laughing out loud when she saw how Guy and Grace, sometime between the last family outing and this one, had acquired the European style of holding their fork and knife. Her husband, Joe, used his fork like a shovel digging a highway. She watched him scoop spoonful after spoonful of mashed potatoes into his yap like he was afraid someone was going to announce a potato famine was on the way.

Even though it was Thanksgiving, a time to count your blessings, she couldn't help but start to list, in her head, all of the things about her husband that annoyed her. The veins by his temples pulsed. She used to think that was sexy, but now it repulsed her. She couldn't stand the clacking sound he made when he ate. He'd told her it was because when he was thirteen his jaws got knocked out of alignment when he got smacked in the face by his old man. He'd never told her why his dad whomp-sided him, but she imagined it was his snide comments that sent his dad over the edge. She couldn't believe their relationship had gotten to the point where she even hated the slope of his shoulders, how they just sort of fell from his neck and were simply there to hold his arms. She had finally figured out something to be thankful for. That, with any good fortune at all, this would be the last Thanksgiving she would be sitting across the table from him.

Indigestion had set in and Sherry was glad she had brought a roll of Tums with her. The adults sat, each looking at their plate as if they were going to be tested on its contents.

She picked at some turkey and stuffing, complimenting her mom on how moist the bird was. At the same time what was going through her mind was how she would love to give some people at the table the bird, especially Guy, whom she'd never liked and never trusted. But ruffling her mother's feathers was the last thing she knew she wanted to do.

Tim didn't seem to let the earlier proceedings affect his appetite as he piled his plate high with dark meat and stuffing. Lydia asked Helen why she was eating only turkey and Helen boasted that she had begun the Atkins diet the day before and she didn't want to blow her diet within a day after having started it. Sherry had kept her mouth shut about seeing her sister-in-law eating a handful of peanut M&Ms shortly before the group sat down for the meal. Only her mom had taken a serving of everything that was on the table.

Sherry studied Grace, the sister she had always looked up to. The remark Grace had made to their mom bothered her. She knew her sister was strong-willed and sometimes demanding, but she never considered her rude or mean-spirited. Yet that's what she was today.

It was a miracle when Tim broke the silence and mentioned how the biggest tomato *ever* had come into the processing plant last week. "It weighed seven pounds," he said. "Came from Texas. We couldn't bring ourselves to squish it into catsup so we brought it into the dining room and ten of us had BLT's with it for lunch."

Everyone laughed. A bit forced, but it was a start.

Before long, the chatter spread like soft butter. Sherry thought it decent of Guy to try to repent from his earlier comment about double-dipping by asking Joe how his construction business was going, and that he'd seen and liked the new billboard Joe's company had put up near the Home Depot.

Grace asked Sherry how her job was and said, "We really do need to get together for lunch. I could come over to your campus. "That would be great," Sherry said. Looking at her mother, Sherry was glad to see something had made her smile.

Chapter 12

Bowing Out

Lydia pulled into the parking lot behind Mikey's Oriental Garden. "Maybe I should call Sherry," she said, thinking out loud. "Maybe Grace stopped at her house." Then she remembered Sherry was at work. She'd been working long hours since she took that job at the community college and she didn't know how long Sherry could keep on burning both ends of the candle. Especially with the little help she received from her husband, who had done nothing but disappoint her daughter. To this day she regretted the role she played in that fiasco. The fiasco turning out to be her daughter's life.

I'll call her later this afternoon, Lydia thought as she pulled into a space next to Tim's car. Apparently he had already gone inside because he wasn't in his Jeep. Not that there wasn't more than one Jeep in the parking lot. Many people in Port Huron drove Jeeps because of the rough winters. But her son's Jeep was the only one with a logo of a tomato with a happy face on the side.

"Oh Tim, I'm so glad to see you," Lydia said as Tim stood and gave her a kiss on the cheek. She unbuttoned her ski parka and pulled it down over her shoulders and arms and hung it on the back of the seat. The silver parka was adorned with passes from a ski lift in Vail. She had never been skiing but she loved to dress like a skier. Rita had given her the lift tags after she and one of her conquests had gone skiing during a winter break. Lydia's black ski pants and serviceable-looking boots completed the outfit. One time when Grace saw her wear this outfit, she said, "You look like an Ivana Trump impersonator."

Rita had tried to convince Lydia to go on a ski trip with her but Lydia begged out, saying she had as much agility as the Hoover Dam. "Besides, everybody I know who has gone skiing has come back with a broken leg. How about if we go on a cruise?"

"Count me in," Rita said. "Where should we go?" In the next breath, she said, "You mean you would leave the kids and Walter?"

Lydia lifted her eyebrows and shrugged her shoulders. "Why not? It's just Buddy and Sugar at home. They're old enough to get themselves wherever they have to go. Heavens, Buddy will even graduate this spring. Can you believe my little Buddy's graduating?" Lydia didn't wait for Rita to answer as she was mostly saying that fact aloud for her own benefit. Then she added, "And Walter, he knows how to cook and take care of himself. I'll tell you, that's one thing the army was good for. It taught Walter how to survive."

Lydia and Rita went to the one travel agent in Port Huron, Crystal Cruises, owned and run by Crystal Cruze, a former student of Lydia's. Crystal asked Lydia and Rita if they wanted to meet men on this trip. At the same time, Lydia said "No," and Rita blurted out, "Yes!" All three of the women laughed.

So they compromised and went on a cruise that wasn't geared to singles or couples.

"This trip down to Puerta Vallarta is *muy excellante*," Crystal said. "It's a good ship and great ports of call. Sun, surf, a bit of excitement and relaxation, all wrapped up into one nice, affordable package. You'll think you're living in Margaritaville."

Lydia and Rita signed up right then and there. For once in her life she wasn't going to discuss this first with anyone else because if she did, there would be so many imagined obstacles set up that within two minutes, she'd decide not to go.

Her only concern, she told Rita, was "I hope Buddy and Walter get along. They seem to be always at odds."

"Why do you think that is?" Rita asked.

"I'm not sure. Sometimes I think Walter sees too much of himself in Buddy and that bothers him. You know, they really are quite a bit alike. But every time I mention that to Walter, he pooh-poohs what I say. He says from what he sees, he and Buddy are opposites."

"Yeah, right," Rita said. "Even I can see how much alike they are. You know, people see what they want to see. Hell, I know I do!"

Lydia laughed. "Don't we all."

As they drove home from the travel agent, Lydia asked Rita, "What do you know about that phys ed teacher, Ms. Strump?"

"That certainly came out of the blue," Rita said. "What do you mean, what do I know about her?"

"Just that. Do you know anything about her?"

"Why are you asking?"

"Just tell me what you know first and then I'll tell you why I'm asking."

"Well, I know she's a looker. Looks like she's a damn high school cheerleader. She's always got that toothy smile going on and an annoying giggle." Rita went "Gahilt, gahilt, gahilt," imitating the teacher's giggle. You could tell by the look on her face she was disappointed Lydia didn't burst out laughing. "You were supposed to laugh."

"Sorry."

"Okay. 'Fess up. Why'd ya want to know?"

"Because she calls the house asking for Buddy."

"What?"

"I said, she calls the house asking for Buddy."

"Well, is she his coach or something?"

"She coaches girl's track," Lydia said, giving Rita one of her suspicious looks.

"Well, does she say what she wants to talk to Buddy about?"

"She has never identified herself to me. I just happen to know who she is. I recognize her voice from when she was trying to organize that food giveaway."

"So why don't you just come out and ask her what she's doing calling your seventeen-year-old son?"

"I did ask Buddy."

"What'd he say?"

"He said he was just helping her out with some track stuff."

"Yeah?"

"Uh-hum."

"How many times has she called?"

"I don't know. I've answered at least a dozen calls from her."

"That sounds weird."

"Yeah, I know."

"What are you going to do?"

Lydia hesitated before answering. "I guess I'll just see if this is just a passing thing. Probably is. It's just you know how an imagination can be."

"Yeah," Rita laughed. "Some of the best times I've had have been in my head."

"What a day," Lydia said to Tim while she scooted into the booth. "Before I left I got a call from Constance, you know, Guy's mother. She said Grace was supposed to have been home a couple of hours ago and she hasn't arrived. Hasn't called. And she said some lady called, and said Grace was supposed to be at her house and she hadn't shown up. I don't know what to make of it but I'm starting to get worried, what with how she acted this morning. Have you by chance heard from her?"

Tim shook his head. "No, I've been in meetings all morning. Maybe she went to the mall or somewhere and her car got stuck in the parking lot. You know the weather's bad. I almost called to cancel, thinking I was an idiot for expecting you to drive in this weather."

"But she has a cell phone. She would have called," Lydia said, ignoring Tim's protestations about having her come out in this weather.

"Maybe she forgot her cell phone. I do, sometimes. And you know how impossible it is to find a phone booth anymore?" Tim said, still trying to put Grace's possible disappearance into the normal-situations-of-life category. "Or maybe she was shopping and just lost track of time."

"But you didn't hear her voice this morning. It was like, oh, I don't know. I've never heard her like that. Not even after Buddy or Daddy died. Such self-doubt I've never seen in her. It really did frighten me."

"Hi, my name is Xena and I'll be taking care of you," the waitress said. Xena stood with her hip thrust out like a hitching post. Lydia noticed Tim staring at her T-shirt that said Eezee Over and had two fried eggs strategically placed over her prominent nipples. Whenever Xena inhaled or exhaled the yolks rose. Because she was preoccupied, Lydia kept her comments to herself about what an odd T-shirt that was to be wearing while serving in an Oriental restaurant.

"Green tea," Lydia said. "Please."

"Will do."

Tim had already ordered and received a Mountain Dew.

Lydia looked at the Mountain Dew and said, "Does that go with Chinese food?"

"Sure," Tim said. "The Dew goes with everything."

"But doesn't drinking that stuff keep you awake at night?"

"Nah, I sleep through anything. I need it to stay awake."

"I'm the just the opposite."

"So is Helen."

Silence. The normal din of the restaurant was subdued. People appeared to be moving in slow motion. It wasn't nearly as crowded as it normally was at lunchtime. The snowstorm must have kept all but the diehard Kung Pao Chicken fans away. And actually this wasn't Lydia's favorite place.

Lydia looked at her son as he stared out the window at the falling snow.

"That stuff looks like it's in a hurry to get somewhere," he said.

"It is," Lydia replied, "It's in a hurry to wreak havoc, that's what it's in a hurry to do."

"I'm sure that's it," Tim said, razzing his mom. "There's evil written all over that white stuff. God's sending it to make us miserable."

"Wouldn't surprise me one bit," Lydia said. "God has been playing lots of tricks lately."

Tim laughed and shook his head and continued looking out the window. "Sometimes I wonder where you come up with some of this stuff."

"What stuff?"

"Some of your thinking."

"What thinking?"

"Like your comment about the snow, like God is sending it to be a pain in the ass."

"Oh, that. I was just rambling. But sometimes I do think God likes to push people near the edge. See what He can get away with."

"Is that a Methodism?" Tim asked, grinning.

"No. That's a Lydiaism," she said before taking a sip of her green tea.

Sharp light from the reflecting snow streamed through the window. Lydia looked at her son. *You look so much like your father.* Tim's shoulders looked strong in his gray suit. Walter wore gray suits a lot, too. And a conservative tie. Tim's was gray-and-white striped. His lapel held a small tomato pin. She looked at his forehead and noticed worry beginning to settle in. It seemed odd seeing her son with wrinkles. There were a few gray hairs beginning to gather at his temples like people congregating at a bus stop. And his hairline was receding like a beach after a storm. Just like Walter, Lydia imagined Tim would be totally gray or bald (whichever came first), before he was forty. His eyes, although green, appeared slate, probably from the harsh, cold light.

Tim took a sip of Mountain Dew. "What do you really think of Guy?" he asked, taking his straw, stirring his drink, and placing a finger over one end. He pulled the straw, full of soda, from the glass and put the straw in his mouth.

The question caught Lydia off guard. She shrugged her neck back and said, "I don't know. He's all right, I guess. Why do you ask?"

Tim lifted and dropped his shoulders. "Beats me. I guess there's something about him that makes me uneasy. Do you notice the way Grace tenses up when they're together? She doesn't seem as happy-go-lucky around him. And he watches her. Watches her like a hawk."

"Oh, Tim. Now I've got you going off the deep end. You're supposed to keep me grounded, remember? You're not supposed to have awful thoughts like I do."

"These aren't awful thoughts. Just observations I've stuck in the back of my mind."

"So do you think that's what's making her act so strangely? Guy? I thought it was me. I figured I'm annoying her because I'm not doing what she wants me to do."

"Which is?"

"Move. She wants me to sell the house and move. Oh, also, I think she'd like me to become a different person, but that might just be me reading things into things."

"Well, she might have a point about the moving. That house is huge. And expensive to maintain."

"But it's my home," Lydia said defiantly. "It's where we raised our family."

"I know. You say that all the time."

"Not all the time."

"No, just when anybody mentions anything about it," Tim said, his voice changing from easy-going to staccato in rhythm. "I hate to tell you this, Mom, and please don't take it wrong, but everything isn't about you. You know I love you dearly, all of us kids love you to death, but especially since Dad died, you've sort of lost touch with what's going on around you."

Lydia froze. She felt colder than the window with its layer of icy crystals. What was going on? This must be a conspiracy. They're all against me.

"Mom, I can tell by the look on your face what's going through your head. You think it's a conspiracy. That all we kids are against you. But that's so far from the truth. And to be perfectly honest, it isn't just you who has buried your head in the sand. I have, too. I've been so wrapped up in work, with the kids and Helen, I haven't paid attention to Grace or Sherry or Sugar. I've probably let you down.

You hadn't even gotten over Buddy's death and then Dad died. These last few years must seem like hell to you."

Tears dripped from Lydia's eyes. She could feel sobs and that heaving sensation in her chest coming on. "I... I... a... don't... know... what to say," she said between sniffles. "I feel like I've been punched in the stomach."

"Did I ruin your appetite?"

"This whole day's ruined my appetite."

"Then let's get out of here, go for a ride. We need to talk. Whatyasay?"

"In this weather? What are you? Crazy?"

"Possibly. But I've got the Jeep. It can handle this weather."

Lydia wiped her face again with the napkin. She put her coat on while she was still seated. She wrapped her scarf up high around her neck to partially obscure what she was certain was her blotchy face. As she stood, she looked out the window. "But it looks really bad out."

"Mom, I've got four-wheel drive."

Tim placed a five dollar bill under his glass, helped his mom out of the booth, put his arm around her and walked toward the door.

The wind cut through them as they walked to Tim's Jeep.

"Do you think my car will be okay here?" Lydia asked, talking loudly so her voice would be heard.

"What? Somebody's going to steal it in this weather?" Tim laughed.

They got in the car.

"Don't forget your seatbelt."

"Yes, dear," Tim said. It was the same kind of "Yes, dear" Walter would give her when she said something obvious.

There was ice on the windshield. The wipers wouldn't budge. "Damn," Tim said as he reached into the back and grabbed a scraper.

The Jeep took a while to warm up. Lydia blew on her hands, and then blew a breath onto the window.

"Whoa, did you see that ambulance? It skidded through the traffic light and almost hit that telephone pole. The person in the back's probably going to get whiplash along with whatever else is wrong."

The Jeep's wheels spun as Tim pulled out of the parking lot.

"Mom, I just thought of something else that might be bothering Grace. Gosh, I am stupid. I should have thought of this before."

"What," Lydia said, "What is it?"

"She called me right after Christmas. At first we talked about the kids and what all we did over the holidays. And then she—"

Tim's cell phone rang.

"And then what?" Lydia asked, either not hearing or ignoring the phone.

"Just a sec. It's work. Better take the call."

Lydia put her head back on the headrest and closed her eyes.

"Tim Calypso. Hi. What's up? Uh-huh. Sure. Well, that is good news. It's getting worse out by the minute. I think canceling the meeting's for the best. Tell Jared to tell second-shift production that the meeting for this afternoon is cancelled and will take place tomorrow at three-thirty. Anything else?"

Lydia closed her eyes and listened. When he was in his business mode, Tim sounded just like Walter. Deep and controlled, a well-modulated voice. A voice and demeanor that put everyone at ease. She loved to hear that voice. As she sat there with her eyes closed she imagined it was Walter driving the car, that Buddy was alive and happily enrolled in some college that was not too near and not too far, that Grace was home whistling while she played with her children, that Sherry had figured out what she wanted to be when she grew up, and that she and the boys were happy. She envisioned Sugar living in Vermillion, just a hop, skip, and a jump away, running an art gallery instead of being so far away in New York. She saw Walter with his arm on Tim's shoulder, walking to the ninth hole at the Sandusky Country Club. For a moment life was as it should be, not as it was.

"Thanks for calling," Tim said. "I don't think I'm coming back this afternoon and you know, I think you should head home, too. I heard we're supposed to get a few more inches before this is over. See you tomorrow. Where was I?" he asked.

For a second, Lydia couldn't remember, either. In her momentary interlude everything had been fine.

"Oh, yes. Grace." Tim's voice was still in business tone. Then: "Right. Jesus Christ! Did you see that? That truck missed that car by a cat's whisker. It's worse than I thought out here."

Lydia grabbed what her kids called the "Oh hell" handle. "Careful," she said.

She saw the look on Tim's face. Tim's attention was on the road. He jockeyed around parked cars and pedestrians who slipped and slid from point A to point B, many bouncing off point C.

"Mom, has Grace mentioned anything to you recently about her adoption?"

"No. Not a thing. Why? Did she mention it to you?"

"Yeah. I think that might be why she called that day. She asked me if I knew anyone who was adopted."

"She did? Why would she want to know that? What'd you tell her?"

"I told her I knew a couple of people who were adopted. Jason Siegrist and Melanie Pottorf, Skip's wife. You know Skip. He was in my fraternity."

"Yes, I remember him. His mother died when he was young."

"That was his adoptive mother."

"Oh, I didn't know." Normally she would have asked what happened to his mother, how she died, etc. But she was focused on her daughter. "Did Grace ask anything else?"

"She asked if I knew if either of them had tried to find their birth mother," he said with a little less confidence than his business voice.

Lydia didn't say anything for a moment. She thought about what Grace had said this morning. "How could I have been so stupid?" she said.

"Stupid? What are you talking about?"

"Those comments she made today, saying nobody loved her. They must have stemmed from her feelings about her adoption. And I just didn't hear, or listen."

"Mom, don't be so hard on yourself. It wasn't like Grace asked you a question point blank. How were you to know? You know with Grace, she only gives you the information she wants you to have. She's a lawyer, remember."

"But she was my daughter before she was a lawyer and I should have known. A mother should be able to figure these things out. And I didn't. She'd told me a couple of weeks ago, that with the way I was acting, to her it was like when she lost Daddy, she lost her mother, too. And instead of trying to understand, I got angry. Blamed it all on her. Typical Grace. If things didn't go her way, she, well…"

"But that's how she is, Mom. You know that. Grace is different. Very strong-willed. She likes to make people stand trial. It's part of her training. Her personality. And anyway, did she expect you to read her mind? She could have come out and said, 'Mom, I have some questions about my adoption. Could we talk?' You can't blame yourself for everything your kids do or don't do, say or don't say."

Lydia thought about Buddy. What clues did I miss with him? Did he tell me what was bothering him and I ignored it? There had to be clues. People don't just kill themselves without leaving crumbs along the way, hoping to be saved. And maybe I could have saved him. I should have been able to save him. Maybe I shouldn't have gone on that trip to Puerta Vallarta with Rita. How can a mother not save her child? Oh, God. Have I done the same thing to Grace?

Again, Tim read her mind. "You're thinking about Buddy, aren't you? You're thinking you could have saved him. I can see it in your eyes. And I'm going to tell you, don't. Don't do this to yourself. You couldn't help what happened to Buddy. What happened with that accident was enough to push anyone over the edge. He felt responsible for those kids' deaths."

"My head realizes that, but my heart doesn't. The conflict between the two never stops. It might have been his reaction to the accident that made him decide he didn't want to live, but it seemed he was coming to terms with what happened and I can't shake this nagging feeling that maybe it was something else that made him think there was no hope."

"Mom. You've just got to let it go. You're never going to get your life back to any semblance of normal if you keep raising questions like that."

"The day Buddy died, the word 'normal' was eliminated from my vocabulary. There's no such thing as normal anymore. And what if I've missed Grace's cries for help and she—"

"Stop it, Mom. What if, what if. What if a meteorite careens through the air and smacks into Port Huron tonight? Are you going to take responsibility for that? You are good, but you're not God. You've gotta let some things go. You're never going to have all the answers and you're never going to really know what goes on in another person's mind."

"But…"

"But nothing, Mom, Grace is fine. She might be upset. She might have questions she needs answered, but whatever's going on with her isn't your fault. You can't *fix* all of our problems, and you shouldn't even try." Tim took a deep breath. "You and Dad did a great job. You know, there comes a point in everyone's life, even your kids' lives, when they have to accept responsibility for their decisions."

"Sometimes I feel so lost. So alone and scared. Ever since Buddy and Daddy died, I just can't seem to find my balance. Except for brief moments, I feel like I'm not a part of the world. Like I'm constantly hovering over myself, like I'm in a constant state of a near-death experience. Floating over everything. I keep reaching for things that aren't really there. I've replayed the last few years since Buddy died over and over, trying to change what happened. Each morning when I get up I think maybe today, maybe today I'll wake up and hear Buddy whistling the Notre Dame Fight Song in the shower. But I don't. And I think of you kids. I think about how I've failed as a mother. And now I've lost Grace."

Tim pulled the Jeep over to the snow-covered curb, put the gear in park, reached over and took his mother's ungloved, cold hand. "We'll get through this. You didn't fail anyone. The only one who you've short-changed is you. We can't bring Buddy or Dad back, but we'll find Grace and everything will be fine. I promise. We'll get this family crankin' again. And Mom, you're not alone. You've got me and Helen and the kids. And Grace. And Sherry and Sugar. You've got your family. As whacky as we are, you've got us! But what you really need is to figure out what you want to do during this next stage of life. I don't know if you're aware of what an opportunity you have."

An opportunity? Gee. She hadn't ever thought about it like that.

Tim had gotten his mom's ear. "Mom, I know it's not how you planned it, but look, and I want you to take this the right way," he said, leaning toward her, "you've got freedom. Your kids are grown, you don't have to work, and you've got your health. I mean, what are you waiting for? Now is the time for you to do what you want to do and stop worrying about your kids. Let them live their lives. Bottom line, it's time for you to stop worrying." Tim put his gloved fingertips under his mother's chin. "Mom, would you like me to lift your jaw up off the ground? It's dragging."

"What did I do to deserve you?" Lydia asked.

"I could say the same thing, you know."

"What's that?"

"What'd I do to deserve you?"

Lydia smiled. "I think I'll take that as a compliment."

Tim laughed with her. "You should take it as a compliment because it was given as one."

"Do you really think Grace is okay?"

Chapter 13

The News

"*H*ola," the voice on the phone said.

"Hello? May I speak to Grace?" Tim asked.

"Meez Grace eez not here."

"Who am I speaking to?"

"Maria. Meez Grace's housekeeper. Who eez dese? *Por favor*?"

"It's Grace's brother, Tim. Is Grace home?"

"No."

"Is Guy home?"

"You mean Meester Mumford?"

"Yes." Tim's patience was slipping like his tires on the ice.

"Yes. Is Mr. Mumford home?"

"No. Heez not home."

"Do you know where he is?"

"Heez at de how you say eet, hos-pital?"

"What hospital? What for?" Tim said, his voice going back into business mode.

Lydia and Tim looked at each other. Lydia leaned her head toward the phone and tried to hear the conversation.

"Meez Grace. Sheeze had an acceedent. Sheeze in thee hos-pital."

"What hospital?"

"I dunno."

"Who's watching the kids?" Tim asked.

"Iyam," Maria said. "Meester Mumford called and asked me to watch *los ninos*."

"Thanks," Tim said, folding his cell phone, automatically shutting it off. "Grace is in the hospital. She's been in some kind of accident."

"Oh, my God! I knew it. I just knew something was wrong. Is she okay? What kind of accident was it?" Lydia asked, her face stiff with panic.

"I have no clue. That was the housekeeper who Guy asked to watch the kids. She didn't know anything other than Grace was in the hospital."

"What hospital?"

"She didn't know."

"She didn't know what hospital? For Pete's sake. I can't believe this. I knew it. I should have gotten in the car this morning and followed her. I knew it, I knew it, I knew it. I never make the right decisions. Never."

"Mother, don't overreact. It might be next to nothing."

"I'm not overreacting, Tim. A mother can sense these things." Lydia looked at Tim. "How are we going to find her?"

"Well, there are only two hospitals in the county. Good Sam and County. We'll start with the closest one. Good Sam." Normally he'd take the highway and they could get there in ten minutes, but with this snow… he'd do better to go down Rte 2 and cut over to Ben Franklin Highway to Coomer. Sure. He could get there that way and it would probably be faster.

Driving was slow. "Get out of the way. Come on. Come on," he mumbled as he willed their way through traffic. He glanced over at his mom. Her eyes were closed. Her lips were moving.

"Dear Lord," Lydia mouthed. "Please be with Grace. Help her be okay. If something happens to her, I don't know what I'd do. I'm so sorry for not being a good mother, being so absorbed in my own world, my own problems. I have more to talk to you about but I'll talk to you later if that is okay. Amen."

Lydia's cell phone rang.

"Lydia? Guy. I'm at the hospital."

"Which hospital?"

"Good Sam."

"What's happened to Grace? Was she in a wreck? Is she okay?"

"All I can tell you right now is that she's alive. Can you get over here?"

"I'm on my way. I'm with Tim. We just called your house and the housekeeper told us Grace was in the hospital. Guy? How is she? What happened?"

"I'm not sure. No one's sure. We'll try to figure it out when you get here. Just go to emergency. I've got to go."

Click.

Neither of them said a word as Tim dodged cars and tried to see through the snow that blew sideways, making him dizzy.

Lydia's thoughts wreaked havoc on her. She was thinking about the last time she was at Good Sam, with Walter. As she walked past one of the EMTs who was leaving the Emergency Room as she was walking in, she heard him say, "That poor guy didn't stand a chance." She knew he was talking about Walter.

By the time he pulled into the parking lot, Lydia looked whiter than the snow covering the cars.

Chapter 14

Another Day, Another Bill

Sherry threw her keys on the counter, sat on the edge of a chair and took off her boots, then carried them to the mud room and laid them on a towel. She slipped her feet into her fuzzy slippers and walked back into the kitchen to get a cup of coffee, stopping on her way to raise the thermostat to sixty-eight. The community college had for once closed early because of the snow. It didn't do that often. Not often enough, anyway. She'd thought about stopping by Mrs. Grayson's house and picking up the boys, but she'd decided she'd love to have a couple of hours to herself. She needed to chill, even if she did have to pay Mrs. Grayson for the privilege.

After flipping through the mail, she sorted the bills into one pile and junk mail in the other. Junk mail and bills were the only mail they received anymore, since everyone emailed everything, else, including birthday greetings. She even got an email this week from Cassidy Bakewell, who worked two cubes over, inviting her to her wedding. Tacky but thrifty, she'd thought. She opened the Port Huron gas and electric bill and peeked into the envelope: $227.63. She shook her head and put it in the bill pile under the Visa bill and the bill they got from Dr. Batsche, the dentist. She didn't dare open that as she knew the bill was going to be nearly a thousand bucks for the two root canals she'd had.

The microwave beeped and she took the steaming cup of coffee out of it. She dropped two teaspoons of sugar into the cup along with a generous pouring of Carnation Vanilla Cream, which her husband said made her look like a yuppie.

She sipped her coffee and paged through the *Cosmopolitan* magazine that Ginger, the secretary with the frisky, salmon-colored hair, had given her. She rarely read magazines these days, what with life's platter being so full. Besides working full-time and going to school clandestinely, she did all the housework. Joe never lifted a finger to help, not with the housework, cooking, and rarely the boys. The only thing he took part in was the boy's football, which she'd rather they didn't play.

Danny's peewee football team was called the Comanches. Political correctness had not yet ventured into the world of peewee football. Sherry thought it was ridiculous to play such a sport at such a young age. She worried about brain damage and broken legs and arms and knocked-out teeth. She'd expressed her concern to Joe, but she might as well as have been talking to a tree. "What? You want him to play the p-i-a-n-o and be some sissy twit?" Joe had sneered. "Football will make him a man." And Danny wanted to play. So she acquiesced. Of course, she was the one who ended up driving him to and from practice as Joe always claimed he was too busy. But then on game day Joe would show up at the game wearing his own high school varsity football jacket. Standing on the sidelines, he looked like he was ready to go in for the kickoff.

Sherry often watched the games from the car where she sat studying. Sometimes she stared at Joe. From behind and from a distance, Joe looked good. There was no denying he had a good body. He stood with a coach's posture, legs spaced about a foot and a half apart, arms crossed tight, square-jawed, observant, watching their son's every move. She hated it when during the game Joe called Danny over to where he was standing, and got in his face and told him to "toughen up." Sherry had heard him say once when she was standing beside him, "Don't be no sissy boy. You get back in there and rip that kid's head off." That was another reason she sat in the car, to be away from Joe. She couldn't stand to hear him talk to their son like that.

One time Sherry confronted Joe about being such a jerk on the sidelines.

"You know, Joe, how you talk to Danny when he's playing isn't helping him. Haven't you noticed that the more you call him over and yell at him, the more hostile he gets?"

"Well, then I must be doing something right."

"How do you figure?"

"Because he's getting more hostile. Developing that killer instinct. That's what's going to get him into the pros."

"He's nine-years-old, for Christ sake!" She didn't have her mother's angst about swearing. She tried not to swear in front of her kids, at least not if she could help it. But in her mind swearing beat throwing things, which beat hitting people, which beat killing people, all of which she sometimes felt like doing. "And he's not only hostile on the field, but here at home, too. And at school. Did you read the note from Mrs. Simon, his gym teacher? She said Danny was bullying some kid, pushed him up against a locker, and told him something ridiculous like if he didn't stop looking at him funny he'd rip his lungs up through his mouth. She said next time she would have to send Danny to the principal's office. And he told Markey, I mean threatened him, that if he didn't go downstairs and get his math book, he'd 'beat the snot out of him.'"

"He's just being a boy."

"He's just being a bully. The other day he tried to bully me. Got up in my face and said I *had* to take him to his friend Jason's house *now* and that if I didn't, I'd be sorry. And when I said 'No' he'd have to wait 'til I finished what I was doing, he threw his fist into his hand and sneered at me."

"Well, what were you doing that was so important you couldn't take the boy?"

"That's irrelevant!" Sherry screamed.

"Maybe if you'd just support him a bit more in his football he wouldn't treat you like that. He doesn't act like that with me."

"You're a moron," she said, then under breath whispered, "A fucking moron."

She knew from past experience that trying to discuss something with Joe was fruitless. He derailed everything, turned the tables and made her end up feeling like she was the idiot for thinking the way she did. She had argued with him throughout most of their marriage, but driving to work one day there was a sign on the marquee of the First Baptist Church that said, "If you argue with a fool, there are two fools arguing." And even though she didn't have much use for the Baptists, she'd found that saying to be quite true. So she tried to solve things herself. And those things that couldn't be solved, she put behind her because if she kept them in front of her they would keep her from doing what she needed to do. And that was to get herself to the point where she could take the boys and leave.

She picked up the phone to call her mom. Even if she was too tired or had nothing to say, Sherry called her mom as often as she could. As much as her mother could drive her to distraction, Sherry found the sound of her voice reassuring. It seemed to her that her mother was the only person in her life who was truly excited to hear her voice.

Sherry listened patiently as her father's voice told her no one was home and she should leave a message. Unlike Grace, the message didn't bother her. Actually, she enjoyed hearing her dad's voice.

"Hi, Mom, it's me, Sherry. Give me a ring, okay? I've got news. Luv ya. 'Bye."

She hung up the phone and went to the pantry and pulled out a Little Debbie. She wasn't wild about them but the boys loved the little chocolate cakes packed in their lunches. And at this time of the month, it wasn't a matter of choice as to whether she would eat chocolate or not. It was a necessity.

She turned on the TV. "My, my, Oprah's looking good," she said. Oprah was giving out a check for some ungodly amount of money. "Damn, I wish someone would hand me a check like that," she said.

"What I wouldn't give for some money. Money equals freedom. Maybe I should start a charity. A charity for women who have dickhead husbands. Hmm, that probably wouldn't be considered a charity, but a club, maybe the largest club in the world. And if I charge a ten-buck membership fee once a year I will be, well, not up there with Oprah, but I'll be rich. Damn rich." She laughed at her creative thinking. She turned the volume on the TV down, got her cup of coffee, her Little Debbie, and *Cosmopolitan*, and settled into the big, old, crinkled leather recliner that they'd gotten when Joe's mother died. She didn't dare sit on "the throne" when the king was home, but the king was at work or wherever. She really didn't care.

She thumbed through the magazine, removing the cardboard inserts and dog-eared an article about how to get your husband to volunteer to do housework. Uh-huh, right. When hell freezes over. She read it anyway and of course in the end, the solution was blow jobs. "Cosmo," she said. "They think blow jobs fix everything in a relationship. If it were only that easy."

Page seventy-eight. The title was "When You Fall In Love With Your Best Friend's Husband." Under the title was a photo of a sultry, dark-haired girl with legs up to her armpits, draped around a man whose suit coat lay in a pile on the floor. The top two buttons of his shirt were unbuttoned, revealing a few perfectly coiled hairs and his hands cupped the girl's bottom. The article began, "I didn't mean for it to happen. It just did. I fell in love with my best friend's husband. And lost my best friend."

"Well, duh," Sherry said, as she read the article aloud, intonating as though she were reading for the radio. "We started out as friends, or not even that. You know, that third wheel in a two-person relationship. Out of the kindness of a heart, you are invited to enter the circle of friendship. At first the boundaries are clear. Concrete. Then they begin to crumble as does your resistance. The slight, at first, inadvertent touch. The conversation shifts from the general to the specific. You already know many of the intimate details. You know he loves kisses in certain places because that was confided to you after too much wine and too many years of sharing secrets. And then comes the shifting of sides. You try to see the world from his vantage point because it's new and different. You connect on levels that your best friend has become blind to... Slut. That's what you are when you fall for a married man. A slut." She talked back to the article, which had begun to read like a novel. Of course, when she thought about it, if any of her friends wanted Joe, they could have him. They'd have to be a fool. She laughed at the prospect for a second. But then realized it wasn't really funny.

Her marriage had become disposable, which ate at her heart like ulcers ate the lining of her stomach. Her dreams were no longer of Joe, the man who shared her house, her bed, and the last ten years of her life. She dreamed of another man, one whose face was obscure but whose kindness and strength engulfed her. She knew she wasn't like many of her friends who had gotten divorced and didn't care if they would ever marry again. She wanted marriage. A good marriage. Someone to share things with.

With her cup empty, Little Debbie eaten, and Oprah signing off, Sherry sighed, knowing it was time to fix dinner. She got up, carried her cup and saucer to the sink and put her hands on her hips as she looked out the window. She walked to the pantry, got out a box of Hamburger Helper, grabbed a pound of ground beef from the freezer and threw it in the microwave. Then stopped in her tracks.

She grabbed the copy of the magazine and flipped it open until she came to the page of the article she had just read. She looked at the name of the writer. "I don't believe it," she said, "Rita Goin-Guccione." Then she said, "Could that be mother's Rita?"

Chapter 15

Do Not Leave Children Unattended

"Where's Grace?" Lydia asked when she saw Guy standing at the coffee machine in the hall adjoining the Emergency Room.

"She's getting a CAT scan. She cracked her head and they're trying to see what's going on," Guy said as he blew on his coffee. "And frankly I'd like to know what's going on in her head, too."

The comment seemed inappropriate to Lydia. "What do you mean she hit her head? Was she in a wreck? Is she going to be okay?"

"We're not sure what happened, but there wasn't a wreck. She was out at Marblehead Lighthouse for some reason," he said.

"Marblehead? What on earth was she doing at Marblehead in this weather?"

"I have no clue. I told you, we don't know what happened and we won't know until she regains consciousness." He took a sip of his coffee. "Shit," he said as he spit it out, some of it spewing down the front of his shirt. "Still too hot. Christ, I have a meeting to-night and now I won't have time to go home and change," he said, walking away.

Lydia and Tim looked at each other.

Guy came back. He had found a napkin and was wiping off the front of his shirt.

"Consciousness, you mean she's unconscious?"

"Yes, Lydia, she's unconscious. If you want to know any more, you're going to have to track down a doctor."

Lydia turned and strode to the nurse's station. She thumped her purse on the counter. "Hello, I'm Grace Mumford's mother. I hear she was brought in with some sort of injury. Where can I find her?"

The receptionist fumbled around on the computer then said, "What's your daughter's name?"

"Mumford. Grace Mumford."

Although Lydia wasn't very adept at computers, she wanted to push the lady out of her seat and check the computer herself. She was sure she would be faster.

Scrolling down the screen the receptionist got to the "Ms" and began muttering, "Madison, Mitchell, Morgan… "

"It's Mumford," Lydia said abruptly, "Grace Mumford. M-U."

"I know it's M-U, ma'am, but I can only go as fast as the computer lets me."

Lydia didn't say, "I'm sorry."

"Mumford, Grace. Yes. She's here. Apparently she's getting a CAT scan."

"I know that. I wondered where I might be able to find her."

"Well, you can't see her when she's getting a CAT scan. But if you take a seat over there, I'll call you when you can see her."

Lydia looked at the receptionist's eyes and saw nothing but a person putting in her eight hours. Even in the frenzy of the moment she couldn't help but recognize the difference in attitude of this receptionist versus the one the woman at the desk had when she came to this same hospital when Walter had died.

Defeated, she walked over and sat down.

Sirens blared as flashing lights from an ambulance went by the window. She listened to sick people cough. A mother told her son, who was crying, to sit still, that squirming around wasn't going to make his injured shoulder feel any better. Lydia listened to his sniffles and studied his navy-blue snow pants and the matching snow jacket that lay on a chair beside him. His mother noticed Lydia staring. "Sled riding. Ran into a tree." The words broke into Lydia's gaze. Most of the people waiting stared blankly at the two televisions that hung like piñatas from the ceiling. She'd had a piñata at a couple of Grace's birthday parties, a touch of Mexico to celebrate Grace's Hispanic heritage—until Grace vetoed such celebrations.

Lydia looked around the room. It hadn't changed much since she'd been here with Walter. The same uncomfortable chairs with cold, chrome armrests that attached one seat to the next. The same linoleum-tiled floors that showed every slushy footprint and tread mark from wheelchairs. The smell was the same, a mixture of disinfectant and people. And the lighting, the fluorescent lights that allowed no clue as to whether it was day or night. Ghastly. Ghostly. Even the people looked the same; some leafed through the pages of out-of-date magazines, while in the kids' corner fretful children played with the plastic toys in various primary colors, red, blue, yellow, that were scattered across the floor. The sign above said "Do NOT leave children unattended."

Lydia noticed an elderly woman, all in black, wrapped from head to toe, sitting in a chair, weeping. *Isn't she dying from the heat? She must be in her seventies.* A middle-aged woman, possibly her daughter, gaped at the soap opera on the television; no sound came from the television. In order to know what was going on you had to read the subtitles. The younger woman wasn't watching it; it was just a diversion. Lydia saw the same look in the middle-age woman's eyes she had seen in her daughters' when Walter died. Grief, sorrow, panic. She also saw the questions: What will happen to Mom? Without knowing the older woman, Lydia still knew her story and why she was there. It was her husband, her husband of perhaps forty-fifty years. The only man she'd been with. The only man she had ever loved. Well, loved enough to marry. He'd had a heart attack. Possibly shoveling the sidewalk, though his wife had told him not to. Just like Walter had done. Just like most men do. Stubborn fools.

And she felt for that lady because she knew her husband wasn't going to make it and this poor woman's life was going to change just like hers had and she felt lonely for her because she knew what lay ahead in the old lady's life.

"Mom. M-o-m," Tim said.

"What?" Lydia rose from her seat, grabbing her coat.

"Nothing. Just making sure you were still somewhere here on this planet."

Guy approached Lydia. "I just talked to the police. The only thing they know is that some guy from the Coast Guard went to the lighthouse to check something and when he was walking up the path he found Grace. The doctors think she might have slipped on ice and fallen and hit her head. She was covered with snow and the doctors said her fingers and toes showed signs of frostbite."

"Frostbite? That can be dangerous. Did you find out when we can see her?" Lydia asked Guy. He seemed less belligerent now. Maybe he had just been taken aback by the shock of the situation, she thought.

"I guess when she gets back from the CAT scan," he said, looking at Lydia. Then he glanced at his watch.

On the way back from the drinking fountain Tim stopped and looked at a bulletin board covered with articles on health issues, cancer support groups, heart rehab happenings, and a contest for people to vote for the friendliest person at the hospital. Then he walked back to where his mother was sitting.

"Grace should be back out from the scan in a couple of minutes. The nurse said the doctor will talk to us then," Tim said to Lydia.

Tim sat down in the chair next to his mom, and then Guy came over and sat in a chair facing them. All three of them stared at the television. Stock prices scrolled across the bottom of the screen.

"Procter and Gamble's up three bucks a share," Guy said to Tim. "Not bad."

"Who gives a shit?" Tim snarled, glaring at Guy.

"Good Lord, where'd that come from?" Guy asked. Lydia wondered the same thing.

"You're a jerk, that's all," Tim said. "God knows what's happened to your wife and here you are sitting here getting excited about some stupid stock going up three bucks a share."

"Who made you my judge and jury?" Guy asked, his belligerence fully returned. He got up and walked away.

"Why'd you blow up at Guy like that?" Lydia asked

"I've just had it with him. His attitude. He acts like this whole thing is a ploy by Grace to mess up his tidy little lawyer world."

"Maybe he was just—"

"You're much too charitable, Mom," Tim said.

"It's not that I'm being charitable, it's just that I feel there's a time and place for everything and right now we need to come together as a family, not rip each other to shreds."

"You mean sweep feelings and unacceptable behavior beneath the carpet."

Lydia let the remark slide.

Several minutes passed. Quiet minutes. Guy returned and sat down several seats away from Tim.

Tim rolled his hands and rubbed his knuckles while Guy cleaned his fingernails with a folded piece of cardboard. Lydia stared at a water leak on the ceiling tile, seeing through it and the floors above, past the snow-filled clouds and into the heavens. She was looking for strength. She needed to talk to God. Right now. She prayed, *Dear Lord. Please be with Grace. Make her well. Make her whole. Make her at peace.*

"I'm going to go call Sherry," Tim said, interrupting her prayer. He stood up and stretched his arms over his head, then bent forward toward his toes. Lydia smiled slightly when she heard something creak.

"Getting old," Tim said, realizing his mom heard his bones creak.

"Aren't we all?"

"Want any coffee?" Tim asked, looking at Lydia and then saying it a little louder for Guy to hear. "Coffee, you want any coffee, Guy?"

Guy shook his head.

"Mom? Did you say you want some?"

Lydia shook her head.

"Sure you would. You've gotta be freezing, I am. Or maybe you'd like some hot chocolate. That's what I'm going to have."

"Yes. That will be fine." She figured if she sent him to fetch hot chocolate, then she could continue her prayer.

When Tim returned and came around the corner he saw his mom, Guy, and what appeared to be a doctor standing in the middle of the hall, talking.

"This is my son, Tim. Tim, this is Dr. Brewer. He's been taking care of Grace."

Tim nodded and raised the cups he was carrying.

"Why don't we get out of the hallway," Dr. Brewer suggested as he took Lydia's elbow and nodded toward a door that led to a "Quiet Room." They followed the doctor into the small conference room that had the Lord's Prayer and Praying Hands on the wall. Otherwise, the walls were empty. Tim pulled out a chair for his mom as Guy scooted in around the other side of the table so he'd be sitting opposite Tim.

"First let me tell you, Grace's CAT scan appeared to be normal."

Audible sighs of relief came from around the table. "Thank God," Guy said.

"Your wife sustained a hard blow to the head," the doctor said, looking at Guy. At this point we're guessing she slipped on the ice and cracked her head a good one on a boulder or a stone or something. Quite frankly, she's lucky she has a hard head. That's the good news. The bad news is that she *is* unconscious, and we're not sure yet of the extent of the head injury."

"But you said the CAT scan looked fine. Wouldn't that have shown brain damage?" Guy asked.

"Yes and no. Brain traumas are funny things. Sometimes everything looks normal on the tests, but when you're dealing with the human brain, weird stuff can happen."

"What do you mean 'weird' stuff?" Guy asked tersely.

"I mean, tests aren't a hundred percent accurate. There are other factors that can affect a person's recovery."

"What fac—" Guy began.

"The other issue we're very concerned about is the baby."

"Baby?" Lydia asked. She looked at the doctor as he asked, "You didn't know your daughter was pregnant?"

Lydia turned to Guy, the look on her face a martini of confusion and anger.

"Yes, Grace is pregnant, again," Guy said with a hint of disgust in his voice.

"Why, well, why didn't...?" Lydia stumbled, trolling for words.

"We didn't tell you because we weren't ready to tell anyone yet. There were some issues we had to address before we went public."

Lydia began to boil. "'Go public'? We're not talking about a company issuing stock certificates," she said, anger binding her voice. "You're talking about my grandchild."

"We're talking about something between Grace and me. It's not your grandchild until it's born."

"What do you mean by that?" Lydia said.

Guy shook his head and said, "Nothing, Lydia. I meant nothing. When can I see my wife?" he asked the doctor.

"When can I see my daughter?" Lydia asked at the same time.

It was obvious by the doctor's fidgeting demeanor that he would have rather been anywhere but here in the middle of this family squabble. He looked at Lydia and took her hand. "I think it's best if we let her mother go in first. I want to see if by you talking to her she might come around. Then, Mr. Mumford, you can see your wife."

Tim watched the tug of war between Guy and his mother. He could see that Guy's ego was taking a beating. Guy was always the one giving people orders. It was obvious by the twitch in his left nostril, that he didn't like this. Not one bit. Tim decided to go to his car and use his cell phone to call home. Lydia had also asked him to call Sherry.

The only noise he heard when he walked across the parking lot to his car was the sound of ice crunching beneath his feet. Like dry cereal. Snow had silenced the world. That and worry. He tugged at the door of his Jeep. He'd only been in the hospital about an hour and the door had frozen shut in that time. Finally, it opened. He sat in the driver's seat and started the car. His windshield wipers groaned as they brushed off the top layer of snow, skimming over the ice. He was going to have to scrape the window so he could see. He'd call his sisters. Their numbers were in memory on his phone. First, he'd call Helen, and then he'd call Sherry, since she was local and he could pick her up in a few minutes. Then he'd call Sugar.

When he called Sherry's, the call went to Sherry's answering machine again.

"Sherry, this is Tim. Please give me a call ASAP. There's been an accident. Call my cell phone. 'Bye."

Tim turned the heat on and dialed Sugar's number. He was about to hang up when someone answered.

"Hello? Sugar?"

"No, it's Sidney, one of Sugar's roommates."

"Oh, hi. May I please speak to Sugar?"

"Just a minute. I'll get her."

Tim could hear Sidney yelling to Sugar.

"Who is it?" Tim heard Sugar say.

"I have no idea."

"Hello. This is Sugar."

"Shoogs, it's Tim. Your long-lost brother."

"Hey, bro. What's making you call on this beautiful day?"

"Beautiful day? You've got to be kidding. We're having an awful snowstorm. We've had seven inches of the doom and gloom. Not to mention freezing rain."

"Aah. That's too bad. It's gorgeous here in the Big Apple. Sunny and nearly forty. So to what do I owe the pleasure of this call?"

"Actually, Shoog, it's not a social call. Something's happened back here."

"What? Did something happen to Mom? Tell me nothing's happened to Mom."

"No. Mom's fine. It's Grace."

"Oh," Sugar said. "What happened? Is she okay?"

"We don't know much yet. She's unconscious. It appears that she fell on the ice and cracked her head on a boulder."

"A boulder?"

"Yeah, she was out at Marblehead."

"Out at Marblehead. What was she doing out at Marblehead? Especially if there was a bad storm."

"We don't know. All we know is that some man who was checking something at the lighthouse found her. She was partially covered with snow. They said it would be a couple of days before we know the extent of the damage. Mom's with her now."

"Did the doctor say how long she'd be unconscious?"

"They don't know. They did a CAT scan and it appeared fine, but they're concerned that she hasn't gained consciousness. Plus, she's pregnant."

"She's pregnant again? You've got to be kidding."

"No. Not kidding."

"Should I come home?"

"I don't think so. Not now. Let's see how things progress. I'll keep you posted."

"I'll bet Mom's a mess."

"Surprisingly, she's keeping it all together. I don't know if it's because she's been through so much already or what. She's been praying a lot and I think that's helping her."

"That's good. I'll go meditate and send positive energy Grace's way. Keep me posted. If you need me, I'm just a plane ride away. Tell Mom that, too. Okay?"

"Will do. Take care, kiddo."

"You too."

Tim decided to drive over to Sherry's house. It wasn't that far and it was after five so even if she wasn't home, she should be soon.

He grabbed he scraper out of the back seat, pulled his collar up, put on his gloves and got out and scraped the front window. In the minute it took him to scrape the ice, he felt as though his temperature had dropped five degrees. Grace was lucky she hadn't frozen to death.

Chapter 16

Sugar

Sugar had done her best to rewrite her family history. Sometimes she'd tell people she was an only child. Other times, when she thought she'd never see the person again, she might tell them she was the oldest of seven children she'd had to raise nearly all by herself because her mother had abandoned the family and her daddy was a drunk. She didn't see these as lies, but stories that were meant to entertain and deflect questions that she knew would be asked if she told the truth. Even her roommates Sidney, Brianna, and Sam were unaware that Sugar had a brother who had committed suicide.

"What's the matter?" Sidney asked, seeing the look on Sugar's face after she hung up the phone.

"Nothing."

"Didn't sound like nothing."

"Let's just say it was nothing I can do anything about."

Sidney shrugged and said, "Well, if you want to talk."

Sugar's reply was a shrug of the shoulders and a turn to walk away.

"Suit yourself," Sidney said under her breath as Sugar left the room.

It wasn't that Sugar didn't want to talk, it's just that she didn't know what to say. A lot of times that didn't stop her from flapping her lips, but today it did. Talk of family did that. Clammed her up.

She walked toward her bedroom and then turned and walked back into the living room, or the room that Sugar and her three roommates had designated the living room.

Out of the blue, she blurted, "Do you like your family?"

As Sugar asked the question, Brianna, another roommate, an aspiring actress whose last gig was a housewife with lobster hands for a dishwashing detergent, walked into the room dressed in her robe and a towel wrapped around her wet hair.

"Who you asking?" Brianna asked, leaning over and taking the towel and rubbing her long, red, curly hair.

"It's up for grabs," Sugar said.

"That's an odd question. And very complex," Sidney said, as she pulled off the cucumber eye mask she'd placed over her eyes when she lay down on the funky, worn, purple leather couch that was held together by duck tape. Sidney "worked in publishing" or that is what she told people. In reality, she was a sales clerk at a bookstore called Grasshopper, over in Soho. Anyway, Sidney rolled on her side and said, "It might depend which part of my family you're talking about. I have one father, two stepfathers, two stepmothers, another pseudo-mom who's only one year older than I am, not to mention a brother, a half-brother and two stepsisters. And lest I forget, my mother's mother, who my mother didn't talk to for three years because she thought her mother, my grandmother, was making passes at her then husband. "As I said, it's a very complex question." Sidney rolled on her back and placed the cucumber mask back over her eyes.

Sugar laughed as Brianna said, "Doll, you ain't got nothing on me. The word dysfunctional didn't exist until my family invented it and submitted it to Webster's. Look it up in the dictionary and you'll read: dysfunctional; noun: referring to the Hardwick family of Burlington; fucked up to their armpits; best secret-keepers in the state of Vermont; many members wouldn't know the truth if it bit them in the ass. What else you want to know?" Brianna rewrapped her hair, pulled her robe belt tight and sat on her knees on another chaise lounge that looked like it had been chewed on by a rodent.

"Damn, I think my tongue's infected," she said as she removed an earring from her tongue. "Thith thuckin' thing hurths." Sugar studied Brianna as she talked. Even with her hair wrapped in a towel, sans makeup, infected, swollen tongue and in a beat-up gray robe, Brianna was beautiful. Sugar sometimes thought how unfair it was that one person would be blessed with a face so beautifully shaped and such well-proportioned features, a flawless complexion and a body that had men and women at her feet.

The word "secret" stuck in Sugar's mind. She had a few secrets of her own. Her struggle with bulimia was one of them. She'd taught herself how to vomit silently so even if you were sitting in a bathroom stall next to her, you would never hear her. She'd told no one that she hadn't had a period since she was eighteen. The first few months when it didn't come, she feared she was pregnant. But eventually, no period became normal for her.

But those were little secrets, small compared to the one she'd kept for seven years, which was so heavy it threatened to ground her being into gravel. And it was only now, with the help of a therapist, that she realized that unless she came to terms with Buddy's death and told the truth about the secret she had been carrying, she would not be able to live the life she was meant to live.

"Do you like your family?" Sidney asked, looking at Sugar.

Sugar shrugged her shoulders and said, "Not really. Oh, I guess my mom's all right and so is my sister Sherry and brother Tim, now that I think about it. But I don't like my oldest sister, Grace."

"Why don't you like her?" Brianna asked as she lit some bayberry incense.

"Because she... because she, well, I don't really want to get into it. There's too much back story. But basically, I think the girl's an egotistical, self-serving witch."

"Gee, tell us how you really feel," Sidney said, laughing. Brianna laughed, too. Sugar didn't.

"Not that I was eavesdropping, but wasn't that phone call something about Grace?"

"Yeah. She was in an accident or something. They don't really know what happened but she's in the hospital. Tim said she was unconscious."

"Was it a car wreck?" Sidney asked.

"No. She was out at Marblehead in a bad snowstorm. Typical Grace. Couldn't just stay home and play with her kids or bake cookies like a normal mom. No, she has to drive out to some deserted lighthouse in the middle of a snowstorm and cause everyone all sorts of angst."

"Gosh, Sug, you aren't very sympathetic."

"Why should I be? The girl's never had sympathy for anyone else. Everything's always been easy for her. She got good grades, was popular, was gorgeous, and went around acting like she was 'the chosen one,' just because she was adopted. Not to mention, she treated my brother Buddy like he was nothing, just because she didn't understand him. Maybe nobody understood him, except me. And even I couldn't save him." Sugar's voice trailed off. She went and stood by the window crisscrossed with a fire escape. On the outside ledge were three pots covered in gold foil that during the holidays had held poinsettias. All that was left now were plant skeletons, one which was bent over so badly it looked as if it had a bad case of osteoporosis.

Brianna and Sidney looked at each other. It was obvious from the expressions on their faces that they didn't know whether asking Sugar what happened to Buddy would make things better or worse.

"Buddy committed suicide," Sugar said, as she turned around and faced her two roommates. "He was seventeen and my best friend in the whole world. He's who I told all of my secrets to. Then one day I found him hanging in the garage. He'd taken a rope we used to use to pull each other with on sleds, threw it over a beam, stood on one of my dad's car lifts, tied the rope around his neck, and jumped off. And that was it. He was gone from my life."

Brianna's face had turned white. Sidney had tears rolling down her cheeks. Sugar looked as though she had stepped out of her body and gone into a different world. Her face suddenly looked gaunt and gray and within a few seconds had aged ten years.

"I'm sorry," Brianna said. "I'm so, so sorry."

Sidney said nothing. Her tearstained face said it all.

Sugar inhaled and exhaled deeply. "I like that bayberry smell," she said, as if that were the most natural comment to make after such a revelation.

Finally, between sniffles, Sidney asked in a soft voice, "Does anyone know why he did it?"

The question shook Sugar back to reality. "He felt responsible for the deaths of two of his friends," she said. "There'd been an accident." Her voice trailed off. The rest of the story wasn't ready to pass through her lips.

Brianna, also in a soft voice, asked, "Did he leave a note or anything?"

Sugar shook her head. "No, no note. There was no note." Turning her head away from both Sidney and Brianna and returning her gaze out the window, Sugar said again, in a strong, firm voice, "No, there was no note."

But as she stared out the window, her mind whirled as it had done for so long as she tried to figure out why, seven years after Buddy's death, she still lied about the suicide note she'd found in Buddy's top drawer. The note she'd never told anyone about. Not the police, not her siblings, and not even her parents.

Chapter 17

A Gaggle of Geese

L ydia hated the smell of hospitals. Disinfectants collided with alcohol to produce a toxic mix of fear, helplessness, and death. She walked with as firm a foot as she could over the still-wet tile floors that had just been mopped.

She and the doctor strode past the nurses' station. She glanced at the big wipe-off board on the wall and saw the name Grace Mumford, Bay 3, Dr. Brewer. The last time she'd seen her daughter's name on a hospital board was when Grace had Gigi. Lydia took a corner too close and bumped into an empty gurney. She didn't feel it. She looked into bay number two and saw a black man's toes hanging off the end of the bed. He was moaning.

Dr. Brewer pulled the adjacent curtain back.

Lydia's bottom lip trembled when she saw her daughter lying in the hospital bed. An IV was hooked into her arm. Her skin, normally a healthy earth tone, was devoid of color. Not gray, not white, just sort of pale pastry.

She walked over and watched Grace's chest rise and fall. When was the last time she saw her sleep? It was unnatural for her to see her daughter so still. Grace had boundless energy. She and Walter sometimes called her their Mexican Jumping Bean, that is, until she became sensitive about her race.

"Thank you," Lydia said to the doctor as she pulled a chair near Grace's bed so she could sit down.

"You're welcome. I'll be back to check in a bit," he said as he bowed out.

Lydia sat in the chair and bowed her head. "Dear Lord, please be with Grace. Please make her wake up and come back to us. I'm trusting that you'll let her know that whatever has been eating at her heart, I'm here for her. And you are, too. You tell her that, Lord. Please let her know she's a wonderful daughter and mother and she has so much to live for. Amen. Oh, and God, I can't lose… oh, never mind. You know."

She stopped just short of telling God that she couldn't take it if she lost another child. No one should have to have that happen. It was against the law of averages, right? But she had read in the newspapers and seen on television stories where all of a family's children were killed in a house fire or car accident. And at those moments it was all Lydia could do not to rail against God and his injustices.

"Grace, darling. It's me, Mom," Lydia said softly into her daughter's ear. "Can you hear me? I think you can. I think you can hear everyone but you're so tired and confused you don't have the energy to respond. And that's okay. Although I would love it if you could give me a sign that that is what's going on."

She couldn't take her daughter's hands because they were wrapped in mitten-like coverings because of the frostbite. So she stroked her forehead, pushing Grace's dark brown bangs off her face.

"It seems you had a nasty fall and conked your head a good one. The doctors said everything in the CT scan looks good. But I don't think it's your head they needed to check. I think they would have found out more by taking a scan of your heart."

Lydia spoke with a controlled voice. No histrionics. Just kind and caring.

She took her pointer finger and ran it along Grace's eyebrow, along her temple, down the side of her face, to her lips. She traced her daughter's lips, then her nose, then moved her finger to Grace's ear and traced it. She used to do this when her kids were little and they loved it. "Nose, nose, eyebrow, eyebrow," she would say as she traced the features on their face. Then she'd rubbed the temples in a slow, circular motion, almost hypnotizing her little one. Now she did the same thing to Grace as she lay there, still, frozen in time.

"Tim will be here soon, dear. He wants to see you. He's called Sherry and Sugar and I'm sure they send their love. You know, like the soap operas, how they always send their love. Tim and I were out to lunch today, but we didn't eat. We ended up driving around in this wild snowstorm. Well, I guess I don't have to tell you about the wild snowstorm. You were in it. Speaking of which, just out of curiosity, why were you out at Marblehead on a day like today?

"Do you remember how Daddy and I used to take you kids out to Marblehead for picnics and how you and your brothers and sisters loved taking your shoes and socks off, letting the water creep up between your toes? I can still hear your little voices giggling with delight. And Daddy would yell, 'Shark!' and all you kids would squeal and pull your tootsies out of the water and then Daddy would laugh and say, 'There aren't any sharks in Lake Erie.'

"Remember how Daddy quizzed you kids on the names of groups of animals? A gaggle of geese. Then you'd all start honking and daddy would laugh and I'd say, 'Enough already, you're driving me batty," and then daddy would ask, 'Okay, kids, what's a group of bats called?' And he'd think he was so funny and all of you would giggle and forget you were tired and hungry. I'll bet you even remember what a group of bats is called. You always knew the answers. You were so smart. I bet you don't know this but your brothers and sisters all wanted to sit by you because sometimes you'd whisper the answer in their ears so they could yell it out. Okay, Gracie. What's a group of elephants called? Come on, that's an easy one. You know what it is. A herd. And this one, which I couldn't believe you knew: Seals. You knew it was a pod. That's when I knew you must have been a genius. I still do. And you were brave, too.

"Remember when Buddy got up on that rock, yelling 'I'm king of the mountain' and how he slipped off the rock and fell into the water? You, without thinking, jumped in and tried to save him even though you didn't know how to swim. Eventually, Daddy and Tim had to jump in and fish both of you out of the lake.

"I can still see you standing on the edge of the lake, shivering. 'I just wanted to save my Buddy,' you said. And you know what? You might have. Daddy and I were so busy setting up the picnic that we didn't even notice Buddy was gone."

The doctor poked his head in the room. "We better let your daughter's husband in. He's getting rather impatient."

Lydia shook her head and said, "He'll just have to wait a few minutes more."

The doctor moved his mouth to the side and nodded his head. "I'll stall for a few more minutes, but the guy certainly seems in a hurry."

"You're right. He's always in a hurry. In a fast rush to go and do whatever he wants to do no matter how it affects anybody else."

"I'll just tell him—"

"I'm so sorry. I shouldn't have said that. Must be my nerves run amuck."

"Don't worry, hospitals stress out the best of families. You take your time. I'll handle the husband; he's a challenge. I did want to ask you something, though, if you could step outside for a moment."

"Certainly," Lydia said, rising from her chair and following the doctor to another area of the room.

"Is your daughter by chance accident prone?"

"Accident prone?"

"I mean, does she trip over things and bruise herself easily?"

"No. Grace was a ballet dancer. She does yoga and runs. She's as sure on her feet as I am sitting down. Why do you ask?"

"She has what looks like remnants from bruises."

"Wouldn't the bruises have come from the fall?"

"Possibly," Dr. Brewer agreed. "But from what I've heard, the man who found her said she he found her on her back. That would account for the head trauma and maybe bruises on her hips or legs.

I'm talking about an area on her abdomen. Has she ever mentioned any type of abuse?"

If her bones hadn't have held her up, Lydia would have been a puddle of flesh and on the floor. "No. Grace has never mentioned anything about that." Her mind raced. She searched for clues.

Her whole life had turned into a game of searching for clues. *Maybe that's what's had Grace so wired up. Maybe it wasn't the adoption. Maybe she wanted to tell me about the baby or maybe she wanted to tell me her husband was abusing her. Maybe, maybe, maybe...* "Are you going to say anything to Guy?"

"Not right now. I think we have to be careful with him. He seems to be quite upset.."

Lydia grabbed the door frame. Yesterday her major concern was deciding which Lean Cuisine she should eat and today she was in the hospital wracked with worry about her unconscious, pregnant daughter, who was possibly in an abusive marriage.

She walked back to Grace's bed. The room was filled with beeps and chugs and whispers and telephones ringing, and stress, which in itself made its own noise, but all Lydia heard were the shallow sounds of her daughter breathing. She rubbed Grace's arm, and said, "Gracie, I love you. I love you more than life itself. Daddy and I always said you were our special, chosen child. And when I took that first look at you, it was the happiest day of my life. Your creamy, angel-kissed skin, your wonderful brown eyes that held all of our hopes and dreams for having a family, your curly hair... oh, Gracie, you were so gorgeous. You still are. And each day since then my love for you has grown. There's no way I could ever not love you. There's no way anybody could not love you," she said, her voice trailing off.

Lydia watched for any twitch or movement under her daughter's eyelid, any sign that Grace heard what she had said. But Grace lay still as a closed book. She patted her daughter's arm again.

"Grace, darling, you rest." Although she didn't want to, she said, "It's time we let Guy come in to see you. He's been waiting. I'll be back in a little while."

She gave her daughter a kiss on the forehead and ran her finger down to the tip of her nose, then tweaked it. She rose from her chair and ran her hand over the sheet covering Grace's leg. She patted her knee. "You'll be fine, Gracie. I know you will be because God has told me so."

But what she didn't tell her daughter was that right now, she didn't trust God.

She staggered into the hall feeling like someone had spiked her drink. She was dizzy, light-headed. She walked over to the visitor's lounge where Guy was pacing back and forth.

He looked at his watch and at the clock on the wall and said to Lydia. "I didn't think you were ever going to come out of there. What took you so long? I've got a meeting with a new client at six-thirty, and I've got to shower and shave and Jesus, I hope Mrs. Sanchez can stay with the kids. If she can't, can you watch them?"

Guy's insensitive words snapped Lydia out of her stupor. If looks could kill, Guy would have been six feet under. Her nostrils flared and temples throbbed. "I don't give a damn about your meeting and you shouldn't, either. Your wife's in a coma. She might be losing your baby. And if, and if that—" She wanted to threaten him. With what, she wasn't sure. But as she had told Tim earlier, now was not the time or place. She did say, "Guy, this morning your wife was in tears asking me if anybody loved her. And you know what? I think she was referring to you, and—"

"Lydia, you're upset. Grace knows I love her, even though sometimes she's not easy to love, especially when she's pregnant. I'd told her I didn't want any more kids. She can't even seem to handle the ones we have." In spite of the fact he was a lawyer and should have known to keep his mouth shut, he kept digging himself in deeper and deeper.

"Is that why she has bruises across her stomach? Because you love her?"

His eyes narrowed and his jaw edged out like a rock. "I am not going to dignify that accusation with a response. I'm going to go see my wife. Now, if you'll excuse me."

He clipped her shoulder. She believed he did it intentionally, like a pitcher who beans a batter to show who's in charge. She watched him walk down the hall. She'd never noticed how cocky his walk was; how slick he looked. Her eyes followed him until he was out of sight.

Feeling nauseous, she said, "I need some fresh air."

Chapter 18

Maybe It's Better Not To Know

The hospital halls were like the corn maze at Orkin's Farm Lydia took her grandchildren to. She always got lost. And, now, here she was walking down one hall only to have to figure out whether she should go left or right down another hall that always seemed to end up at Oncology. This way to the cafeteria, that way to X-ray. All she wanted to see was a sign that said, "This way out."

Finally, she saw a door to the outside that looked like the one she had come through several hours ago. MERCER STREET EXIT, it said. "Thank God."

The snow was still falling. She pulled her scarf up over her head, walked out the door, and heard snow shovels grate along the sidewalk. Snowplows grunted down the street, throwing salt, throwing snow.

"Evening, ma'am," a man said as she walked by. "Watch your step."

"Evening," Lydia said back.

Despite the harsh weather, the parking lot was crowded. Lydia walked down the sidewalk, then stopped. She looked out over the expanse of cars, many of which looked like moguls, white bumps popping on a mountain.

"Where did I park my car?" she wondered aloud. She couldn't remember. She couldn't even remember walking into the hospital. Somehow she was just there. Now stop and think. Retrace your steps. When did you get to the hospital? Oh, God. Tim brought me. I don't have my car here. In the confusion, she had forgotten that Tim had driven her to the hospital. Her car was still in the parking lot at Mikey's Oriental Garden, if it hadn't been towed.

"Cell phone. Where's my cell phone?" she said as she rummaged through her tapestry purse. She loved the look of this purse, but she'd recently decided to change to a leather one with compartments because everything she put in this purse fell to the bottom. She leaned against a car as she felt her knees beginning to weaken. "Come on, come on, where are you, cell phone?"

She found it. It had become entangled in some red ribbon she'd been carrying in her purse. As she unwrapped the ribbon, she heard a voice.

"Hi, Mom, I'm back," Tim said. He gave her a kiss on the cheek.

"Oh, your nose is cold."

"Hi, Mom," Sherry said, as she gave her mother a hug.

"What are you doing out here?" Tim asked. "You do remember you don't have a car here?"

Lydia didn't say anything. She shrugged her shoulders.

"Whadya do, go out in the parking lot and look for your car?"

"I was upset," Lydia said. "Upset about Grace. I needed some fresh air, that's all."

Tim looked at her.

"All right, so I forgot I came to the hospital with you."
"I told you I was going to go get Sherry and then I'd come back and get you."

Lydia's eyes went heavy with worry, fatigue, and embarrassment.

"Ease up, Tim. She's been through a lot."

"I know," Tim said. "Sorry. You're doing a great. Considering. If I were you I'd be crumpled in a little ball in the corner." He took his mother's hand and squeezed it.

"Can't we go inside?" Sherry asked, resuming her trudge through the parking lot. "It's like a blizzard out here. Anyway, I want to see Grace."

"I think Guy's with her and they're restricting visitors," Lydia said, trying to pull her scarf higher over her head.

"But I'm her sister. I should be able to see her," Sherry said, bracing herself against the wind. "Wish I would have worn my other coat."

Lydia walked arm and arm with Sherry, then stopped abruptly. "Grace is pregnant," she said, believing she was offering new news.

"I know," Sherry said. She resumed walking.

Lydia looked confused. She began walking again, too. "Oh, I guess Tim told you."

"No, Tim didn't tell me."

"Well, how did you know?" Lydia asked, half shouting because the wind drowned out her voice.

"Grace told me!" Sherry shouted.

Finally, they made it to the hospital door. Tim, so far not involved in the conversation, held the door open for his mother and sister. All three stood in the vestibule, shaking and stomping off the snow.

"You mean Grace told you she was pregnant but she didn't tell me?"

Sherry stomped the last of the snow off her boots and began walking without responding.

"How long have you known?" Lydia asked, her voice rising slightly.

"Just a couple of weeks."

"Well, why didn't you tell me?" Lydia had to double-time it to catch up with Sherry.

"Because she asked me not to."

Lydia caught up with her daughter and looked her in the eye. There was something else Sherry wasn't saying.

"What?" Sherry said to her mother. "Why are you looking at me like that?"

"You know something else, don't you? You know why Grace didn't tell me."

Sherry wanted to keep moving but they had reached the elevator. "What floor is Grace on?" she asked, looking at Tim.

"She was in emergency. That's up a floor."

Sherry turned to push the button to call the elevator. Lydia grabbed her arm. "Sherry, you didn't answer my question. Do you know something I need to know?"

"She asked me not to say anything."

"Listen, Gracie's in a coma. If there's something I need to know in order to help, you've got to tell me."

Turning away from her mother, Sherry mouthed something.

"I didn't hear a word you said," Lydia said. "What'd you say?"

Turning toward her mother, Sherry grit her teeth and said, "Grace wasn't sure she wanted to keep the baby. She and Guy, well, they're having trouble. Guy wanted her to have an abortion. She called me because… well, she just did."

"My God," Lydia cried. "Oh, my God." She could barely keep her balance. How could she have missed all of this? Did she know anything about her family? Her mind stumbled. How could God be doing this? "Poor Gracie, poor Gracie."

"Mother, please don't 'poor Gracie' her. That's the last thing she wants or needs. One of the reasons she didn't tell you things were going haywire in her marriage was because she doesn't want your pity."

"Is that what she told you?" Lydia asked, surprised.

"Yes, Mom, it is. I didn't say that to hurt you, it's just that, as you said, we've got to think of Gracie."

She was thinking of Gracie. But she couldn't help feeling a wave of sadness. She had always been her children's confidants, the hub of the wheel, the first to know the "big news." She was the person they called in a crisis. When Tim was having trouble deciding whether to propose to Helen, he came to Lydia to discuss some "issues." When Sherry got pregnant with her two boys, she called Lydia first. Lydia knew she was told first because when she asked Sherry if she had told Joe yet, Sherry had replied, "No, I'm telling you first." With that bit of knowledge Lydia pranced like a peacock for days. And Grace still had the letter from the bar association in her hand when she had called her to give her mother the news that she had passed. She gave Lydia permission to pass the news to everyone. And pass it she did, to everyone she saw for the next week. Whether she knew them or not.

Finally, the elevator opened.

Chapter 19

Divine Providence

Four weeks later, Grace awoke from the coma. The day after she'd arrived at the hospital, and while still in a coma, she'd miscarried. Lydia, Tim, and Sherry thought they would vomit when they found out Guy had acted disconsolate about the loss of the baby. They were even more chagrined that Grace appeared to have bought his act. When Lydia tried to console Grace about the baby's loss, her daughter shrugged her shoulders and said, "What will be, will be," and then asked her mother never to mention the subject again.

As she went about her daily routine, Lydia wished she could think of some way to bring her family all together. She wanted to do something special. Celebrate something. But things to celebrate seemed few and far between.

Tim called to check in every day. Her grandson Brady was elected to Governor's Court, so Lydia was invited over to dinner to celebrate. Helen was Helen. She complained about how preparing the meal had made her back ache. She popped pain pills with such flourish Lydia thought about telling her she really should try out for community theatre. Brady seemed very pleased to have his grandma there. He took Lydia to his room to show her how he had cleaned and organized his closet, going so far as to line up his shoes according to height. She was quite impressed that a nine-year-old was so well ordered. "I certainly wish my closets were as clean as yours," Lydia said, giving Brady a big hug.

Sherry, perhaps feeling badly that she had chastised her mother for pitying Grace, asked Lydia if she could pick the boys up from school on Wednesdays for the next month. She was "overwhelmed" at work and "it would really help me out," she'd said.

So on Wednesdays at four, Lydia made her way over to Berry Elementary and sat in the parking lot reading until she saw Danny and Markey run toward her car.

"Hi, Grandma," they'd say, practically at the same time as they winged their book bags in ahead of them. "I don't know how you boys can even lift those things," she said, listening to the book bags thump down on the seat. "Aren't they awfully heavy?"

"We're tough," Markey said.

Danny sat up front with Lydia because he was oldest.

"Put your seatbelt on," she said as she handed each of them a brown bag she had on the seat.

"Oh, goodie," Markey said, opening the bag. "Puckerballs."

"Thanks, Grandma," Danny said, pulling out a bottle of Gatorade. "I like when you pick us up."

On those days that she picked up Danny and Markey, Lydia made dinner and delivered it when she dropped off the boys. Joe was always a fan of her meatloaf and Danny and Markey yum-yummed about the hash brown recipe. Danny told her that if she was going to bring dinner every Wednesday, could she please bring the hash brown casserole every time?

For the first week after Grace had gone home from the hospital, Lydia prepared dinner for her family, too. Of course Mrs. Sanchez told her that that was not necessary because she could cook for the family. But Lydia said, "*Au contraire*, it is necessary. I'm Grace's mother and this is what mothers do."

Mrs. Sanchez rattled something in Spanish that Lydia was sure wasn't complimentary.

Cooking for Grace's family was more stressful than cooking for Sherry's. Sherry thought Hamburger Helper was heaven sent, whereas Grace would rather have her family starve than serve them such "unhealthy, gastronomically awful" food. Grace had gone so far as to say that she was convinced processed foods were going to be the demise of this country.

So Lydia took pains to steam vegetables, broil fish and meat, and use whole grain everything when preparing a meal for the Mumfords. She laughed when she thought about the reaction she'd get from Danny and Markey if she brought them broiled fish and steamed vegetables.

She hadn't heard from Sugar since she'd called her to let her know Grace was out of the hospital and doing okay. She asked Sugar if she had sent her sister a card "or anything." And she was none too pleased when Sugar's reply was, "Eeeh, I forgot. Been busy." In the middle of Lydia's families-need-to-support-each-other-in-times-of-crisis speech, Sugar abruptly interrupted her with, "Gotta go, Mom. Later."

The next day, Friday, around nine-thirty, Lydia put on a pair of stretch pants and a sweatshirt and drove to Albers Grocery Store. Whether she needed anything or not she walked up and down every aisle. Slowly. Sometimes just for fun, she'd pick up a can of peas and study the label. One time she counted all the kinds of salad dressings. One hundred thirty-three different kinds. If she was having a good day she'd say hello and make chit-chat with other people in the aisle. Sometimes she wanted to blurt out, "Do you want a new friend?"

"Do you know where the balsamic vinegar is?" asked a lady with a baby car seat atop the grocery cart.

"Sure," Lydia said, thinking for a second. "It's in aisle five, right next to the cider vinegar." She knew the store better than many of the employees.

She followed her nose to where a woman, who looked like she would rather be anywhere than here, was cooking sausage links in an electric skillet. Lydia's stomach growled. She grabbed a toothpick and poked it into a piece of sausage. "Very good," she said. "Maple-flavored."

The woman with the tongs looked at her. Lydia was desperate for another piece of sausage. She threw her toothpick into the trash bag on the floor and picked up another toothpick. She was about to spear another sausage bit when the woman with the tongs snapped, "One per customer."

Lydia felt like she had been caught robbing a bank. She dropped the toothpick and moved on. She was too rattled to sample the soup and cheese cubes she soon passed.

In aisle nine, while putting a bottle of Marzetti's French dressing into her cart, she stopped suddenly. She had an idea. Why didn't she invite all of her children over to brunch some Sunday and have a celebration. Yes! This was a brilliant idea. Divine providence. She'd have her kids over, sans spouses and grandchildren. She'd make everyone's favorite dishes, guacamole for Grace, Mimosas for Sherry, and lots of bacon for Tim. She'd call Sugar and get her to come home, too. They would laugh and bond and catch up on each other's lives. It would be like old times at the Calypsos. Yes, that's what she would do.

She was so excited she nearly crashed her cart into a pyramid-shaped stack of toilet paper. At least if it fell, it would be soft. She whizzed her cart past mayonnaise and ketchup, and past the cooking oil that was on her list to buy.

"Oops." She accidentally pushed her cart into some woman's rear end. "Sorry," she said as she scooted by. The bumped woman gave her a dirty look. Lydia smiled.

She raced down the aisle as if she were one of those goofy television shows where they have supermarket races. Finally she was at the checkout. "Drats," she said, "only one lane's open." She stood in line, tapping her toes and thumping her fingers on the handle of the cart. To distract herself from her impatience she grabbed a tabloid. Hum, Joan Rivers has had how many plastic surgeries? Another tabloid had a photo of a half-horse, half-man that even Lydia realized had been computer-generated.

Then it dawned on her. If they were going to have a celebration, she would have to think of something to celebrate. The glitch in her freshly hatched plan almost caused her to panic. But instead, she grabbed four four-for-a-dollar Snickers bars, put them in her cart and said, "Oh, I'll worry about that tomorrow."

Finally, it was her turn to check out.

Chapter 20

Two Birds, One Stone

"Tim, can you come over March first, at about ten? It's a Sunday," Lydia asked. Zippy was the only way to describe her tone.

"What's going on on the first?"

"Well, it's sort of a surprise and sort of not."

"That clears things up."

"Actually," Lydia said, "we're celebrating."

"Celebrating what?"

Lydia couldn't understand why Tim's voice wasn't as excited as hers. There was going to be a celebration, for Pete's sake.

"Celebrating what, I ask?" Tim repeated.

So excited about her idea, Lydia had forgotten to decide what they were celebrating. She kept her stammers within her mind. "Spring cleaning. That's what we're celebrating. Yes, spring cleaning."

"Spring cleaning? That's what the celebration's about?"

"Yes, I think it's a perfectly fine thing to celebrate," she said, fully aware Tim was thinking she'd gone 'round the bend.

"Mom, I think you've gone 'round the bend."

She laughed. Not that he'd said that she was going 'round the bend, but because she knew he was going to say it. "Possibly, but it's

a bend I need to go 'round. And I think our family does, too. It will
be good. You'll see."

"Oh, I'm sure," Tim said with a hint of laughter slash sarcasm.

"Now, Tim, don't be like that. This will be great," she said as she
took a drag on her straw. "There's only one thing."

"What's that?"

"I'm not including spouses or grandkids. This time it's just for
my kids. Okay?" She scrunched her neck up when she said that no
spouses or kids were invited. She knew Helen would be none too
thrilled about not being included.

"Hey, Heather. Don't jump on the couch, you're going to fall into
the coffee table," Lydia heard her son say. "Sorry about that. Hope
I didn't yell in your ear. These kids must have eaten straight sugar
for breakfast. They're bouncing off the walls. And the furniture.
Heather, I *said* stop it!"

"Sounds like a circus over there," Lydia said.

"It is. Unless the kids are asleep, it's always a circus. But that's
okay. I like it that way."

She believed her son did like it that way. He had told her one of
his disappointments was that Helen didn't want to have any more
kids. Growing up, he used to say he wanted to have his own baseball
team. Nine boys.

"So, you've got this all planned, have you?" Tim said. "You know,
Mom, Helen might be hurt she isn't included. Actually, there is no
'might' about it. She's going to be downright ticked."

"Tim, dear, you know it's not my intention to hurt anyone. But
this time Helen will just have to understand. When we clean out
these closets, some of the stuff we find might be emotional. Besides,
most of this stuff will be meaningless to anyone who doesn't know
the stories behind it."

Lydia's voice changed from excited determination to one of
explanation and pleading.

Tim raised no more questions. "Don't worry. I'll be there."

"Yes!" Lydia said after she placed the receiver in the cradle. She
took both of her arms, and like a kid who just scored a goal, pushed

one arm forward and yanked the other arm back to declare victory.

She drummed her fingers on the table, rolled her neck, and then stretched her arms over head. She picked up the phone and punched in Sherry's number. The phone rang four times. Lydia was about to hang up because she knew that on the fifth ring the answering machine would pick up and she didn't want to leave a message. But just as she pulled the phone away from her ear she heard a winded voice.

"Hello."

"Sherry? It's Mom. Are you busy?"

"Well, actually I am. I just got in the house, my hands are full of groceries; for some reason the stove buzzer is going off and the damn dog pooped in the middle of the kitchen. Can I call you back?"

"Oh, okay. Call me back when things settle down." Lydia's bubble wilted. She wrinkled her nose as she hung up the phone. She pondered. "Binky, do I dare call Sugar? Do you think she'll think I'm nuts if I call her and tell her she needs to come home to help me clean closets?"

Binky hopped up onto the counter and headed toward an empty can of tuna.

"Get down from there. You know you're not allowed on the counters."

Binky hopped off the counter and scurried out the door and into the living room.

"A lot of help you are," Lydia said as she got up out of the chair and took her teacup to the sink.

She walked back to the table, took a deep breath and picked up the phone. She had to look up Sugar's number because she didn't call it often. She checked her watch. It was iffy if Sugar would be home, but she was going to give it a try anyway.

She was surprised when someone answered the phone after the first ring.

"Hello."

Lydia didn't recognize the voice. "Hello," she said. "May I please speak to Sugar?"

"Sugar? You must have the wrong number."

"Are you sure?"

"No one named Sugar lives here and I swear you must call once a month asking for Sugar. When are you going to remember the damn girl's number?" Click.

Ouch. "But I looked it up… and I still can't punch in the right numbers. I must be getting doppish. Let's try this number, Bink. Who knows, I might reach the White House. I wouldn't mind talking to Laura Bush."

Two rings. Three rings. Three and a half. "Hello."

"Sugar?"

"Yep, sugar and spice and everything nice."

"I like your greeting. It's Mom."

"I know it's you, Mom, that's why I said the greeting."

"Oh, right. I get it." Lydia could imagine Sugar rolling her eyes and making goofy faces at the phone. She always did. But she was glad Sugar sounded like she was in a good mood. "How are you, dear?" The next question she wanted to ask was, is your hair still magenta? But she didn't.

"Eh, okay. Fighting a cold. Doubled my dose of Echinacea. Hope that helps. Other than that, peachy keen. Say, did Grace ever tell you what happened, how she got knocked out?"

Talking to Sugar was always interesting. She never used the pronoun, "I." She spoke in phrases and always sounded as if she were being chased by a tiger.

"No, she still hasn't mentioned a thing. Just said it was an accident, that's all."

"That's hard to believe. Grace remembers everything. For better or worse."

"I know. But the doctor thinks that when she fell, it might have affected her memory."

"Seems bizarre. And it certainly doesn't seem like Grace. Being out there at the lighthouse and all during a huge snowstorm. The girl must have gone loopy." Not waiting for a response, she added, "And pregnant, to boot. Ridiculous."

"Are you still smoking?" Lydia asked. She could tell Sugar was inhaling.

Sugar ignored her mother's question.

"Don't you think it was ridiculous that Grace was pregnant again? My God, the girl's a rabbit."

"Not to change the subject, dear, but I called to ask you something."

"What's up? What's the question?"

"I need you to come home."

"Say what? All right. Who has cancer?"

"Cancer? Who said anything about cancer?"

"Why else would you call and want me to come home?"

"Perhaps because I miss you and want to see you?"

"Uh-huh."

"Sugar. Why would you respond like that? Everyone wants to see you."

Since Sugar had moved away there was barely a day that went by that Lydia didn't miss her, or at least the thought of her. But now, in the short span of this phone call, she felt the angst that came with having a conversation with this daughter. Sugar had a habit of making something out of nothing, looking for ulterior motives, and making snide remarks. Still, Lydia wanted Sugar home.

"We're having a celebration," she said.

"What kind of celebration? Did Grace win the Nobel Peace Prize or something?"

"No." She wanted to ask, Why don't you ease up on Grace, she's been through enough, but as sure as she'd say that, Sugar would accuse her of always taking Grace's side. "I thought I'd have you kids home and we'd celebrate our family, just the five of us. I also thought we could clean out some of the closets. I think it's time to do it, but it's such an overwhelming task that I need some help."

Lydia heard Sugar guffaw. "Let me get this straight: You want me to take time off work and fly home to help you clean closets?"

"Yes."

"Just get some garbage bags and pitch the shit. Call Goodwill.

Salvation Army. Call the Merry Organizers or somebody. Anybody but me. I don't want to go through that crap."

Lydia said nothing.

"I mean, you know what it would cost for a plane ticket to come back? And I can hear me tell my boss, 'Sorry, I can't work because my mother insisted I come home to clean my closet.'"

"Sugar. Will you help me?"

"Does what I just said lead you to believe I'm going to drop everything and run home?"

Lydia was thinking, *Why did I bother calling?*, but she said, "I'll pay for the ticket. I'll give you my credit card number. "

"But I've got meetings Monday and Tuesday. And I'm not sure when the flights are."

"Sugar, if it's that much of a problem for you, just forget it. I just thought maybe, oh, never mind."

"Can I call you back tomorrow and let you know?"

Lydia took a few seconds to answer. "Really, Sugar, if it's going to cause you that much inconvenience and stress, I really don't see the point. My goal wasn't to make you miserable, you know."

"I know, Mom. It's just that… "

"It's just what?"

"Oh, never mind. It's nothing. You know how goofy I am."

"Sugar dear, you're no goofier than the rest of us."

"You're being kind, Mom."

"No, I'm not. I'm telling the truth. We all have our little eccentricities. That's what makes our family and life so interesting, don't you think?"

Sugar didn't answer. She simply said, "I'll call you tomorrow."

Lydia looked at the receiver in her hand. She slowly pushed the disconnect button.

Lydia waited for Sherry to call. One hour went by. Then two. Three. Instead of sitting by the phone waiting for it to ring, Lydia went on about her day as if all of the arrangements had been made.

She wanted a cookie. But when she opened the pantry door

she couldn't find the cookies. What she did find was a mess. With her hands on her hips, she stared at cereal boxes that hadn't been touched since Walter died, shelves strewn with so many crumbs they looked like calling cards for a cockroach convention, and a can of prunes with a lid that looked like it was going to explode. Walter had bought the prunes the last time his parents had visited… seven years ago.

She grabbed a yellow gingham-checked apron from the hook inside the pantry door, hung it over her neck and tied the strings into a bow behind her back. She went over to the radio, turned it on, pushed the garbage can close to the pantry, took a deep breath, grabbed the can of prunes and pitched them in the garbage.

How many open packages of crackers did she have? There were wheat crackers, garlic chips, butter crackers, sesame rounds and crackers shaped like fish. She found a box of snack cakes hidden behind a stack of about ten cans of hot and spicy chili beans. She wanted to have the cakes in the house in case she had a sweet-tooth emergency, but she had forgotten about them. She wondered if they were still good. Looking at the expiration date, she said, "My gosh, Binky, these things expired a year and a half ago. They're probably fossilized." She pitched them. Clink. Thud. Clunk. She pitched all her spices that had crusted over, hardened, or turned disgusting colors. "*Adios*," she said to the can of hominy she had bought because Walter said they should try something new.

It was nearly six when she realized Sherry had not returned her call.

She removed her apron and put it down the clothes chute and put the kettle on for a cup of tea. She was tired of coffee. She walked into the living room while waiting for the water to boil. She sat down and put her feet up on the edge of the coffee table. She closed her eyes.

Just as she was dozing off, the tea kettle whistled and the phone rang. In her half-conscious state, she thought the tea kettle was the smoke detector. She bolted up. She didn't know which way to head. Then she realized the screeching sound was coming from the tea kettle, so she settled down.

It was Sherry on the phone. She, too, seemed to think coming over to clean closets was an odd sort of celebration. "But hey, I'm game," she said. "As long as you return the favor."

"Be glad to," Lydia said.

Three down, one to go. Tim, Sherry, and Sugar were all in line. Now she had to ask Grace, and she would be the hardest nut to crack.

Lydia drove to Grace's to see how she was doing and to tell her that Sugar was coming into town this weekend and that she had invited Tim and Sherry to brunch Sunday, sans spouses or kids. Lydia wanted to extend Grace's invitation in person.

She'd brought along a cinnamon twist roll covered with caramel and pecans. She knew Grace would have a pot of coffee brewing. Grace drank more coffee than she did.

Mrs. Sanchez, the housekeeper, answered the door.

"Good morning, *señora*," Mrs. Sanchez said.

"Morning," Lydia replied, stepping inside, uncomfortable being greeted by a housekeeper, especially at her daughter's house.

"Miss Grace eez in zee kitchen with zee children."

Lydia shook off the cold and removed her coat. She started to walk through the foyer.

"*Senora*, would you mind removing your snow boots? I just waxed zee wooden floor in zee hallway."

Lydia looked at her boots. They didn't appear to her to have slush or snow on them. Still, she bent over and took them off, holding onto the door handle to keep her balance.

Mrs. Sanchez watched to make sure Lydia didn't sneak down the hallway without removing her galoshes.

"Hello, darling," Lydia said to Grace, taking her daughter's head into her hands and giving her a kiss on the forehead. Grace was seated at the table feeding Gigi her bananas and oatmeal.

"Hi, Grammy," Austin said, mouth full of Cheerios. Kelly got up out of her chair and ran around the table and gave her a big hug.

"Hello, darling," Lydia said, scooping Kelly up into her arms. "My, you're getting to be such a big girl."

"I know," Kelly said with delight. "My birthday's coming soon."

"It is?" Lydia grinned.

"Uh-huh," Kelly said, eyes glowing.

"You mean 'yes,'" Grace said to Kelly. "Uh-huh isn't a word."

Lydia shivered inside when Grace scolded her children for such minor transgressions. She wanted to tell her daughter "uh-huh" was in the dictionary. But she figured that bit of knowledge wouldn't be appreciated.

"I mean, yes, Grammy. My birthday's in March."

"Ooh, that's coming up soon. What would you like Grammy to get you for your birthday?"

"I want a new Barbie Ballerina," Kelly said, without pause.

"Kelly, you already have three other Barbies. You don't need another one," Grace said, not looking at Kelly. She concentrated on the spoonful of bananas she'd put in Gigi's mouth.

"I don't think a little girl can ever have too many Barbies," Lydia said, cheerfully. "If I remember correctly, Grace, I think you had about ten Barbies."

"Nine. I had nine Barbies. But that was a long time ago. I don't think Barbies are good role models for today's young girls."

It was obvious to Lydia that Grace had recovered from her accident. Her memory and tongue were working quite fine.

"But their hair's such fun to play with," Lydia said, winking at Kelly.

"Oh, Mother, you don't understand. Girls don't grow up wanting to be beauticians."

Contrary. The girl's so contrary. "I beg to differ. A lot of bright young women want to be beauticians, manicurists, and massage therapists. Carmelina Zurich's daughter is going to beauty school."

Grace rolled her eyes and continued to stuff bananas into Gigi's mouth.

Kelly sat on Lydia's lap, buttoning and unbuttoning the buttons on her sweater.

"I want to be a beauty people when I grow up," Kelly said, "I like playing with hair." It was true.

Lydia loved it when Kelly stayed all night and they played beauty parlor. Kelly's little hands would hold a big brush and stroke Lydia's hair. Then Lydia would put a spot of rouge on Kelly's cheeks and have her pucker her lips so she could apply lipstick. The ritual was complete when Lydia dabbed a touch of perfume behind Kelly's ears and allowed her to go into her closet and choose a pair of high heels to wear.

"You're not going to be a beautician," Grace said, looking at Kelly. "You're smart enough to be a doctor or a lawyer. You're going to be self-sufficient."

Lydia looked at Kelly. It was obvious that she didn't have a clue what her mother was talking about.

Kelly hopped down from Lydia's lap and went back to her seat to finish her now soggy cereal.

"Help yourself to coffee," Grace told Lydia.

"Will you join me?" Lydia asked as she got up to get herself a cup. "I brought cinnamon twist roll. Want me to slice you a piece?"

"No, thanks. I'm not hungry. And don't you remember? I don't eat that stuff anymore."

Things weren't going as Lydia had planned. But they rarely did when the plans included Grace. There was so much she wanted to say, but she was too afraid to say anything. "I suppose Kelly or Austin couldn't have a piece?"

"No, too much sugar," Grace responded. Lydia rolled her eyes as she turned toward the counter. As she was slicing a piece of cake, she said, "I've called Sugar and asked her to come home."

"What for?" Grace asked. Gigi had spit out the last two mouthfuls of bananas. Grace finally figured out the baby was full, so she quit feeding her.

"I asked her to. She asked how you were doing. She said she was sorry she couldn't come when you were in the hospital."

"That doesn't matter."

"Well, she felt badly."

"I doubt it. She didn't even call or send a card."

"You were in a coma, Grace. You couldn't have talked if she had called. I will admit she should have sent a card."

"Mother, you needn't defend her. She is the way she is. She just doesn't care."

Lydia breathed a heavy sigh, the kind that altered the barometric pressure of a room. "Of course she cares. We all care, Grace. Anyway. I was hoping you could come over Sunday morning for brunch. I thought it might be nice if the five of us got together. And I was hoping we could kill two birds with one stone by going through some of the closets and clearing out some of the clutter. That's one thing Bitsy's visit certainly did do, let me see how jam-packed the closets are."

"You want us to come over and help clean closets? Why don't you just go through them and pitch the stuff? Why would you need us to help?"

"Because the thought of going through everything alone overwhelms me. And I thought since everyone seems to want me to move on, maybe you'd all be willing to give me a little help. Just one Sunday, that's all I'm asking. Besides, I thought it might be fun to relive some of the memories. You know your flute is still in your closet and so is your cheerleading sweater. I thought now might be a good time for everyone to go through and get what they want out of the closets."

"You mean transfer junk from your house to ours." Grace snickered.

"Well, I didn't mean it like that. I just thought, maybe, oh, I don't know, maybe I just don't want to go through some of that stuff by myself." Lydia felt like she was pleading her case before a judge. "Besides, I still say it could be fun."

The look on Grace's face was skeptical. *Perhaps I should explain what the word "fun" means*, Lydia thought.

"What time and how long do you think it will take?"

"I thought I'd serve brunch around ten-ish or so. Have a nice, leisurely meal, then head upstairs to 'treasure city.' With all of us working I can't imagine it will take more than a couple of hours."

"I've got to see what Guy has planned. Maybe I'll see if Mrs. Sanchez could watch the kids. Did you talk to Sherry and Tim yet?"

"Yes. They're coming. They think I'm nuts, but they're coming. Think you can make it?"

"I'll try," Grace said.

"Thank you. I promise you, we'll have fun."

"Austin, don't put those Cheerios up your nose," Grace said. "You could suffocate."

"Mommy's right, Austin. Your nose is to breathe through, not to eat through," Lydia said. She thought she was doing Grace a favor by backing her comment.

"I'll handle it, Mother."

"I wasn't trying to 'handle' anything. I was offering reinforcement."

"I'm sorry. I'm still not feeling all together all right," Grace said, looking at her mother.

"I'm sure it's going to take a while to get back to normal. That was quite a fall you took. And with you losing the baby and all…"

"Stop mentioning that baby! That whole thing was a mistake. Will you ever let me put it behind me?" Grace snapped, her tone sounding like the prelude to a summer storm.

Lydia put her fork down and looked at her daughter. Kelly and Austin looked up at their mom, their eyes wide with surprise.

"Uh-oh, Grammy's getting in twouble," Kelly said to Austin.

Lydia was glad to get into her own car and out of her daughter's world. Being with Grace could be exhausting. *And I thought it took so much energy to be with my kids when they were little.* She shrugged. She remembered her mother telling her that kids had fewer problems as they got older, but the ones they had were bigger. She was right.

She sat in the driveway thinking about her mom. She wished she were here. As Lydia started her car, she said, "She would have known how to handle Grace."

Chapter 21

Buying Time

The call to come home had come as an ugly surprise to Sugar. At first she resented the intrusion into her schedule and her life. But then, as she listened to the sound of her mother's voice, she'd felt so conflicted. And then her therapist's voice kept ringing in her ears: "Until you come to terms with Buddy's death and tell the truth about the secret you've harbored all these years, the life you live will not be your own."

Sugar hated spiders. Not just your normal, "I don't like spiders," but a response so frantic it bordered on phobia. Of course that knowledge hadn't prevented Buddy from occasionally placing big black rubber spiders on Sugar's pillow or in her drawers. "Buddy!" Sugar would scream, knowing he was the only one who would do such a thing. But even though he played pranks on his sister at home, when they were at their cave hideout, if Sugar squealed the word "spider" Buddy would come running and squash the eight-legged intruder.

Sugar hated spiders so much that she almost never ventured into the old wooden garage. The poor-postured structure filled with old tree branches, grass clippings, and overgrown shrubs was a haven for spiders, flying cockroaches, and an occasional snake.

Her mother wasn't too fond of the old garage either and only made trips out there sparingly. She called it "Walter's World," that masculine domain of tools and testosterone.

Walter was the only one who regularly opened the creaky, heavy, double doors and ventured in. He'd go in and putter at his workbench that he'd built along the back wall. Belts, pipe wrenches, hammers, and whatever other tools could be bought at Sears hung from the rafters like garlands. Over the wooden rafters were rounds of rope that were used to pull trees away whenever Walter felt the need to cut them down. And along the side wall under a window were lifts that Walter used when he changed the oil in the cars. He let everyone know that taking the cars in for service was a waste of money.

Walter would go to his hangout and fix conked-out scooters, tinker with broken gears on bikes and occasionally build birdhouses, complete with security guards to keep squirrels at bay.

When Tim was younger Walter would invite him into the garage to work alongside him. But when Buddy attempted to go into the garage, he'd get shooed away. "Run along," his dad would say, "you have a habit of getting in my way."

Once, Buddy, with a dejected look on his face, ran to his mom after his dad had refused his help. "Dad won't let me work in the garage with him," Buddy cried. "He says I'll just mess things up."

Lydia marched out to the garage and said, "Walter, you're hurting Buddy's feelings. Why can't you just give him a little hammer, a piece of wood, and a nail and let him stay with you?"

"Because he talks constantly," Walter said. "And I come out here for peace and quiet. Not to be driven nuts by a chatterbox."

Buddy did have a habit of talking nonstop. He talked about anything, bugs, cars, baseball, bodily functions, rockets, treasures, and girls. "He'd talk a hole through steel," Walter said.

That is, until after the accident, when words had ceased to be his friends.

"Sugar, I need you to go to the garage and get my set of pipe wrenches," Walter said. He knew Sugar hated to go to the garage and usually he didn't ask her to go out there because by the time she got done squawking he could have just as easily gotten whatever he needed. But now he was stuck under the kitchen sink holding a busted pipe together, and he didn't want to let it go.

"But, Dad, there are spiders out there."

"The spiders won't bother you, Sugar. Now go get my wrenches or you're going to be grounded."

Normally, Sugar would have screamed to her mother to try to get her to intervene, but Lydia wasn't home. She'd gone shopping at the mall with Rita.

"But, Dad."

"But Dad nothing. Get my wrenches. I can't hold this thing forever."

"If I get bit by a black widow and die, you're going to be very sorry," Sugar said as she opened the back door in a huff and purposely let the screen door slam.

"Nobody's going to die," Walter shot back, "except you if you don't hurry up!"

"Son of a bitch," Walter said when he heard Sugar scream. "Knock it off, Sugar," he said, trying to turn his head to wipe sweat from his eye on his shirt.

But the screaming continued.

"If it's a spider, I'm going to ground that girl 'til she's thirty-five." Walter waited.

But Sugar didn't come back.

"Dad, Dad!" he heard Sugar yell. "Help! Please help! It's Buddy!"

Walter could barely make out the words. "Shit!" he said as he let go of the pipes and wriggled out from under the sink, banging his head on the cabinet. He stood and looked out the window. He didn't see Sugar, but he heard her screams more clearly. "Dad! Dad! It's Buddy! Help!"

Walter grabbed a towel off the counter and dried his hands on the way out the door. At first he walked with his normal speed but as his daughter's screams became more blood-curdling, he broke into a trot and then a full-out run.

"Jesus Christ!" he said when he opened the door wide enough so he could see into the garage.

"Daddy! Daddy!" Sugar was screaming and crying. "Buddy! Buddy! No, Buddy! Daddy help me!" Tears rolled in torrents down Sugar's cheeks.

Sugar, all five-foot-three of her was standing under Buddy's limp body, holding his legs, trying to give slack to the rope that was tight around his neck. She had her head tight against his legs.

Walter tried to push Sugar out of the way but she wouldn't let go. "Sugar, go call nine-one-one," he yelled as he literally ungripped Sugar's hands from Buddy's legs. He grabbed his son's legs and lifted them. "Go! Sugar, go!" Walter said.

Sugar stood there looking at her brother's face. His eyes were open and his face frozen with panic.

"Go! Sugar, go!"

"Budddddyyyy!" Sugar cried all the way to the house. "Buddy, don't leave me!"

Two months to the day after Buddy died, at night, during a bad lightning storm that had come off the lake, the fire department was once again called to the house on Chippewa Street. The Calypso's garage had burned to the ground. After a discussion with Walter, the fire marshal declared the fire was caused by lightning. But the Calypso kids knew better.

Sugar hung the phone up from talking with her mother and called her therapist. She needed to discuss her mother's phone call. Maybe now was the time to go home and set the family record straight.

When she told the therapist that her mother had asked her to come home and help clean the closets, the therapist smiled and said, "Maybe your mother isn't the only one who has closets that need to be cleaned. Don't you think it's about time you clean out the closets of your mind and heart?"

Sugar sat on the chair, chewing on her fingernail.

"But what can I say? So much time has passed. And I promised Buddy." She rose from the chair and walked over to the aquarium.

"I've spent so much of my life pushing these people away, my mother, sisters, and brother. They think I'm a jerk," Sugar said as she traced the path of one of the goldfish with her finger. "Hell, I am."

Sugar's already pale skin took on the cast of a ghost, gray and translucent.

"Sugar. You've done the best you could. Your brother put you in a really bad position making you promise to carry his secrets. He wasn't well when he did that. You have to understand that. If he knew how what he asked you to do had affected you, he would never have asked you to do it. I have to believe he would want the truth to come out. He would want his child to know his family."

"But what do I say, 'Hi, Mom. Sorry about this, but I've known you have a grandchild for several years and I haven't told you about him?'

"Sugar, the right words will come," the therapist said.

"That's easy for you to say. You are trained to know what to say. I'm programmed to screw it up." Sugar gave a sigh that said more than words could.

"And that's why you need to do this. Build a real relationship with your mother and the rest of your family. It's time for you to be who you are, not who your brother wanted you to be."

Sugar said nothing.

"Sugar, don't you think the purpose of keeping this secret is long past? For whatever reasons your brother made you promise to keep this information from your family are no more. And you harboring this information is adversely affecting your life. It has destroyed your relationship with your mother and your siblings. And I believe it has turned you into a person you don't really want to be. I see you as a flower trying to open up and blossom but instead you're wilting in the hothouse of secrecy."

"You think I'm a nut case, don't you?" Sugar said with a bit of a fearful smirk.

"Anything but. I think you are a lot stronger than you realize. I only wish you'd realize it."

"Thanks."

"I mean it, Sugar. Break free. And as trite as it may sound, the truth will set you free."

After her appointment with the therapist, Sugar called her mom and told her she would indeed try to get home. She also said, "I will need money for the ticket."

Chapter 22

Sandbox

"Hold on, hold on, I'm coming," Lydia yelled. She threw the three bags of groceries she was carrying down onto the table and raced for the phone.

When she picked up she heard a dial tone. "Drats. If it's important, they'll call back."

She removed her coat, laid it over a chair and began putting groceries away. She'd had fun buying food to cook instead of just heat. It appeared she had purchased enough food to feed a family of twelve for a month. She took the apples out of their bag and placed them in a basket on her counter. Not a bad alternative to fresh-cut flowers. She washed a bunch of grapes, pulled two off their stems and put one in her mouth. "Mucho delicioso," she said.

She put the slab of bacon in the refrigerator, along with the two dozen eggs, a pound of sausage, milk, and butter. The menu she had written before she left was on the table. She had forgotten what it was like to shop for so many people with so many different tastes. Sherry was allergic to garlic, and Tim wretched at the thought of goetta, but Grace loved it.

While putting the cheese in the butter bin, she found a yogurt that had taken on a life of its own. "Looks like the Blob," she said. The lid looked like it had blown partially off and goop had dripped all over a container of cottage cheese. On further examination, Lydia discovered the cottage cheese had expired some time after the first frost, which was four months ago. So instead of shoving the old stuff deeper on the shelves, Lydia cleared a counter and emptied her refrigerator. She pulled out an open can of pears. She found an unidentifiable casserole. Hum, a breeding ground for botulism or E coli.

The phone rang. Lydia was right. Whoever called before was calling back now. She was sure of it.

"Yo, Momma, it's me."

"Hi, Sugar."

"A, I've got a problem," Sugar said.

Lydia said to herself, *Yeah, I've got a problem, too. You didn't bother to call me back.* "What problem?"

"I need your credit card number so I can book the ticket. Can you give it to me?"

"Is everything all right? You sound strange."

Sugar said slowly, "I'm just tired, that's all. It's been a long week. Listen, I've put a ticket on hold. If you give me your card number, I can confirm it. Let me get a pencil."

Sugar put the phone receiver on the table. Lydia put her receiver on the table, too, and walked to the desk and got her wallet out of her purse.

"Hello. Hello," she heard Sugar yell through the phone. "Are you there?"

"Just a sec. I'm getting my credit card." Lydia huffed and puffed into the phone after running back. "I've got the card. Ready?"

Sugar repeated the number back to Lydia.

"Good. You're all set then. When should I pick you up?"

"My flight gets in at four-thirty. But if you're busy I can just take a taxi."

"Like heck, you'll take a taxi. I'll be there at four-thirty. With bells on. What's your flight number?"

"Don't know. Never pay attention to flight numbers until I'm at the airport. It's a Delta flight, though. It'll be coming from Pittsburgh."

"Is there anything special you'd like me to make for you?" Lydia asked.

"How about some cabbage and noodles? I love them but I can't cook them here because my roommates hate the smell of cooked cabbage. And cornbread. Make some cornbread. Love your cornbread."

"Will do. A big batch of cabbage and noodles and cornbread coming up."

Late in the afternoon when the temperature and shadows fell, Lydia decided she'd better get to cleaning. She spray-polished the wood furniture, mixed a vinegar and water solution for the picture window in the living and dining rooms, wiped down the woodwork around the door frames with a solution of oil soap and dragged out her canister vacuum. When the living and dining rooms were in order, she rewarded herself with a chocolate bar with almonds—the pieces melted in her mouth, square by square. She had only one more day to eat chocolate. Lent was starting and as she did each year, she gave up chocolate.

At least for a week.

"Hi-ho, hi-ho, it's off to work we go," she whistled as she walked over to the mahogany hutch. She opened the doors of the buffet and peered inside. She pulled out an oblong silver tureen with little legs and a glass bowl. Perfect for the egg casserole. She found a similar container but round in shape. She pulled that out, too. This would be terrific for the sausages. She got down on her knees and looked way back inside. In the back corner, she reached for a silver pitcher and pulled it out. It was tarnished, but with a little polish it would shine beautifully. This would be perfect for ice water. She pulled out a small silver tray from the other side of the hutch. She decided it would be just right for the croissants.

As she pulled out her fine serving dishes she remembered how much fun entertaining could be. But those same serving pieces also reminded her why she and Walter quit having dinner parties. Since Vietnam Walter had pretty much resisted alcohol because, as he had told Lydia, "I don't want my kids to grow up with a pickled herring for a father, like my mother was." But after Buddy died, so did his will to not drink. First it was one beer. Then two. Then a six-pack. Then he began to buy liquor. And then one cocktail became two, two became three. Not to mention after dinner drinks.

It was one thing for Lydia to put up with Walter's drinking when no one else was around. But to watch Walter drift into a morose toad when guests were at their house was more than she could handle. When he drank, he endeared himself to no one. First he went quiet, then belligerent, and finally, he turned into a bully.

It wasn't that none of their friends drank, but with everyone else, at least on most occasions, once food was served, sensibility kicked in. Lydia saw the martini shaker in the corner of the lower shelf. She pulled it out, took the glass stirrer between her fingers and rolled it around inside the glass. It was as if she were stirring the argument that had concluded the social chapter of their lives.

All the guests had left except the Hendricksons. Lydia had mentioned to Ralph Hendrickson, privately, that she might need help getting Walter to bed.

She was right.

Ralph helped Walter to the bathroom. He stood outside the door while Walter vomited. He helped clean the vomit off Walter's shoes, then walked him upstairs to the bedroom. "I can take it from here," Lydia said.

She remembered how she slept in Grace's old room for several nights.

She was humiliated by how Walter had acted toward one of their guests, Meredith Beacon.

"Your class's standardized test scores were pretty pathetic this year," Walter said.

If ever Lydia had ever wanted to punch him, this was it. She couldn't believe he had breached not only personal etiquette, but professional standards as well.

When Walter sluggishly rolled out of bed the next morning, Lydia had already had her coffee, and eaten her toast and strawberry yogurt. She'd cleaned up the dishes from the night before. She seethed as she tried to clean the red wine stain out of the tablecloth her mother had needle-pointed for her. Walter had knocked not just one glass of wine onto the table, but two, causing red stains the size and color of a liver to form on the linen.

She stood at the kitchen sink watching the linen soak in a pot full of club soda, a remedy she'd gotten from *Good Housekeeping*. Walter walked up behind her. He walked quietly, but Lydia heard him. When he got to her, he wrapped his arms around her waist, nuzzled his face into the crook of her neck and whispered, "I love you." His breath smelled like old damp rags.

Instead of melting when she heard those words, Lydia threw her arms back to break his embrace, spun around and got nose to nose. She looked him in the eye and said, "Well, I'm not so sure I love you."

Walter took a step back. His hangdog look disappeared. He squared his shoulders and his head and stood rigid; alert. It was as if someone had taken a bucket of ice cold water and dumped it on his head. "You don't mean that."

"Maybe I don't and maybe I do. All I can tell you is how I feel now."

"You're just angry."

"Angry? You think I'm just angry? Try mad as hell. Furious!"

"For what? I had a bit too much to drink. Ease up. You're making too much of this."

"Do you remember what you did last night? Do you? How you got so drunk your words slurred one into the other, you spilled two glasses of wine, one on Connie and the other on yourself? Do you remember tripping into the buffet and saying 'fuck' in front of our guests? Or humiliating Meredith, telling the whole table her class's results from the standardized tests? Do you remember any of that? Do you remember having to be walked to the bathroom and undressed so you wouldn't vomit all over yourself? Do you recall any of it? If not, I do."

"Don't you think you're exaggerating a bit? As I remember, Connie had just as much culpability in knocking that glass of wine over. You know, she's no slouch in the drinking department."

"Walter. The end. I'm tired of you acting like a non-stick skillet. Everything slides off you. It's always everybody else's fault. I don't understand it. You go to your office every day and tell administrators, teachers, and students to be responsible for their actions, but anymore, in your own life, you don't follow that at all."

"What is this, bash Walter morning? I simply had a bit too much to drink. It won't happen again."

"That's what you said last time. And the time before."

Lydia grabbed the stained area of the tablecloth from the pot and began scrubbing. She scrubbed and dipped, scrubbed and dipped. She began to say "Walter, you need—" When she turned around he was gone.

That afternoon Walter attended his first AA meeting.

Chapter 23

Husbands Who Cheat on Their Wives

Sugar's flight from Pittsburgh was delayed due to bad weather. Estimated arrival time was now six forty-three. Lydia could choose to go back home and then turn around and come back or walk around the airport, pick up a magazine at the bookstore and sit and drink a cup of coffee. She opted for the second choice.

The airport was quiet. It was a Saturday night so there weren't many business travelers. Lydia walked along the concourse past a shoe-shine stand. The shoe-shine man sat alone in one of two chairs. She couldn't imagine how he stayed in business. He nodded as she walked past. She nodded back. She felt guilty for not getting her shoes shined, supporting the man, but she had on hiking boots.

The food court scents surrounded her. Hot grease and salt. They were an invitation, but she wasn't hungry because she'd had a sampling of cabbage and noodles and cornbread before she came. A foreign currency sign grabbed her attention. A man stood at the counter. She was close enough to hear the word Euro mentioned. The word Euro excited her. She thought about Europe, Ireland, actually, how she and Walter had planned to go there but it didn't work out. Something about the house. Something broke and took the money they had saved for the trip, but she couldn't recall what it was, other than a hurtful disappointment. She stood still for a moment and looked at the countries listed on the exchange rate board; England, Italy, Germany, Ireland, France, Hong Kong, Thailand, Australia, Russia. Look at all of the places people travel. She squeezed her hands, got a strange sensation in her stomach and began to walk again.

She came to a bookstore and walked in. She looked for the magazine rack. There was no reason to look at books since she had only a couple of hours to wait. Of course, there was Oprah staring her in the face. Along with Cindy Crawford and at least five Jennifer Annistons. She saw a magazine with Katie Couric on the cover and grabbed it. Lydia hoped the story would be about Katie's life without her husband. It wasn't. The article was on colon cancer screening. She decided to buy the magazine anyway. There was an article on the cover titled, "Husbands Who Cheat on Their Wives." She suspected Guy might be cheating on Grace. Although it upset her to think such a thing, maybe this article would have information that would help.

She was light in step as she paid for her magazine and a container of breath mints. Across the concourse was a place called the Eagle Deli. Perfect for a cup of coffee.

A waitress came to Lydia's table to get her order. "What can I getcha?"

"A cup of coffee, please."

"Regular or decaf?

"Regular, eh, no, decaf," she said after remembering what time it was.

"Anything else?"

"Just cream."

"No, I meant like a sandwich or salad or anything to eat."

"No. No, thank you. I'm just waiting for a plane."

"Most people here are," Miss Snippet said as she turned on her heals and went to another table.

Lydia laughed. Normally if she just had a cup of coffee and sat at a table longer than called for, she left a generous tip not based on the bill, but on time. But this little chickadee, well, Lydia would fix her. She'd leave her a nickel if her attitude didn't improve. She got comfy, well, as comfy as she could in the orange plastic chair. She was certain all of the orange plastic chairs on earth were left behind by Martians. She hung her coat over the back of the chair, got the magazine out of the bag, and flipped through it. First she removed all of the loose inserts that irritated her no end. Next she sniffed for scented samples; they caused rashes on her face. She found one. A man's fragrance, called UncomMANly Yours. She ripped it out and pitched it the garbage receptacle next to her table. Lastly, she thumbed through the magazine and ripped out cardstock pages that disrupted a smooth thumb-through. Now she could read her magazine.

She paged to the Table of Contents. It was a toss up. Should she read the Katie Couric article first, or should she go to the cheating-husband story? She moved down the page, using her finger. She figured both stories would be in the feature section. Uh-huh. KATIE COURIC BATTLES COLON CANCER, by Nancy Fields, page one twenty-three. Lydia was disgusted the title of the article might make people think Katie Couric had colon cancer. She moved her finger down more until she saw HUSBANDS WHO CHEAT ON THEIR WIVES by Rita Goin-Guccioni, page ninety-seven.

"Rita Goin—!" Lydia said out loud, just as the waitress set her coffee in front of her.

"Nope, I'm not Rita Anyone," the waitress said.

"I know. I was just thinking out loud."

"Anything else?"

Lydia shook her head. She took off her glasses and wiped them with a napkin. She didn't believe what she'd seen. Her fingers tingled as she opened the magazine and looked for page ninety-seven. "Husbands Who Cheat on Their Wives," by Rita Goin-Guccioni. She flipped back to the front of the book where contributor's photos and credits were listed. Her eyes went back and forth down the page until, there she was: Rita. Hair a bit shorter. The black and white photo didn't give away Rita's hair color but Lydia assumed it was brown. Maybe she could detect frosting or highlights, but she wasn't sure. But her face did indeed look the same, few detectable lines, eyes bright and mischievous and that classic smirk.

The notes said: "Rita Goin-Guccioni is a freelance writer whose articles have appeared in various local, regional, and national magazines. She has a Master's Degree in Journalism from American University in Washington. She recently returned from Italy where she lived for the last year. Her new novel, *Why This Marriage Can't Be Saved* will be published this summer. This Illinois native now resides in New York with her husband and one year-old twins."

If someone had poked her, Lydia would've fallen down from the ceiling.

A man walked by and tripped over Lydia's purse. He lost his balance and grabbed her chair.

"Oh, I'm so sorry," she said as she tried to help him unhook the purse strap from around his ankle.

At first he grumbled something unintelligible. But after he straightened himself he looked at Lydia and saw she was more embarrassed than he was.

"That's okay," he said, "No worse for wear."

He appeared to her to be sixty-ish, but Lydia had gotten so bad at guessing ages, he might have been only forty. Their eyes caught, then ricocheted away. He held a briefcase in one hand and struggled as he tried to maneuver his coat over the same arm.

"Let me help you," Lydia said as she rose, took his coat, folded it nicely and laid it over his outstretched arm.

"Thank you. You needn't have done that."

"It's the least I could do after nearly breaking your neck."

"Nah, it wasn't that bad. Not that bad at all." He looked at his watch. "Got a plane to catch." He gave her the impression that if he didn't have to catch a plane, he might talk to her. "There's never enough time when you need it," he said.

"I know what you mean."

"Later," he said as he pushed the chair next to Lydia in toward the table, "and watch that strap. You never know what you might catch."

He walked down the concourse going the opposite way of the others. A flight must have landed. The concourse filled. People in a hurry to get home to their loved ones. At least that is how Lydia envisioned it in the movie that played in her mind.

Then she wondered, Was it my imagination or did he wink at me?

"Yo, Momma," Sugar said when she saw Lydia.

They hugged.

"It's good to see you, dear," Lydia said.

"You too."

"Do you have any checked bags?"

"No. Just this carryon. I always say 'travel light.' Makes escapes easier."

Lydia chuckled nervously. Why was she feeling so nervous? This was her daughter, for Pete's sake. "I guess you're right about that."

They walked down the concourse.

"What a nightmare of a flight. We sat on the runway at Newark for forty-five minutes and then at Pittsburg for another forty-five. And, Jesus, the screaming kids. A whole damn family of brats, two rows in front of me. Wanted to strangle the lot."

Lydia laughed. Sugar's tolerance level still wasn't perking to the top of the coffee pot. It was hard for her to notice as they walked, but Lydia thought she'd observed some changes in Sugar's appearance. She looked out the corner of her eye. The magenta hair, gone. Now it was a deep shade of brown. It was cut short, well, shorter. And it didn't stick out every which way. Of course the shorter hair made the multiple piercings in her ear more noticeable. And of course the ring in her left nostril was still there. And, was that a shiny silver thing on her tongue?

Lydia couldn't understand why anyone would want that many holes in her head, not to mention the belly button and other pierced parts Sugar had told her she had. Lydia wanted to crane her head around to look at the other side of Sugar's nose to see if there was a nose ring in that nostril too, but she knew that would be too obvious. Despite her curiosity, she was determined to play it cool.

"So what's happening with you?" Sugar asked. "Other than dealing with Grace's dramas."

"It wasn't a drama. Grace was really hurt."

"Oh, I know, but her life is always so dramatic. She's such a drama queen."

"Life gets dramatic when you have kids." Lydia laughed.

"Yep, that's why I don't have any."

"All in due time. All in due time."

"Yeah, like never," Sugar said in her best Valley Girl voice.

"We'll see."

"How are Tim and the kids and the shrew?"

"You mean Helen?"

"Yeah, the shrew. Don't tell me you don't think she's a shrew."

"Helen's not a shrew. She's just different. Had a very difficult upbringing." She'd only been with Sugar a few minutes and already she was talking like her, speaking in phrases.

"So, Cinderella had a wretched upbringing and she was still nice."

"That was a story, Sugar. A Walt Disney movie."

"I know. I was just making a comparison. Anyway, remember when she got pissed off at you that Christmas?"

"The car's this way," Lydia said.

Sugar followed. "Remember? She cornered you and said she was really disappointed you didn't give her a piece of jewelry like you did your daughters? Thought I'd barf. What a cow. I was tempted to say 'Listen, Hon, when you stop acting like such a shit-head, maybe you might get a piece of jewelry.' She really made me mad. You pissed me off, too."

"How's that?"

"You acted like a victim. Being a victim is beneath you. You should have stood up for yourself. Anyway, that girl's an ungrateful cow."

"But I didn't want to make it bad for Tim. He has to live with her."

"Trust me, Mom, Tim can take care of himself."

"Ah, cabbage and noodles. I can smell them. Good job, Mom. You're the best," Sugar said, dumping her duffel on the chair in the living room and making a beeline for the kitchen. "Uh-uh-um, they smell great. I'm starving. Can we eat?"

"They might need to be heated."

"That's okay. Can you say 'microwave'?"

Lydia was excited that Sugar was excited. Uh-uh-um was music to her ears. "What would you like to drink?"

"Have any wine?"

"Wine with cabbage and noodles?"

"Wine with anything. It's good. Red, white, I'm not fussy."

"I think I've got some Chianti."

"That'll be great."

The phone rang. It was Sherry.

"Hi, Mom. What's up? Sugar home yet?"

"As a matter of fact, she is. We just got in from the airport a couple of minutes ago. She's sitting right here. Want to talk to her?"

"Sure, in a sec. But I wanted to tell you I've got a problem about tomorrow, or at least a potential problem."

Lydia's stomach sank. Two seconds ago she was on top of the world and now the rug was being pulled out from under her. She could sense it. "What's the matter?"

"It's Markey. He's got a fever of a hundred and two. He goes from sweaty to cold and feels awful. Looks awful, too. I just don't know how well he'll be doing tomorrow morning and if he's not any better, well, I won't be able to leave him."

"Poor baby. Have you tried Tylenol? A cool bath?"

"Tylenol, yes. Bath... not yet. I was giving the medicine a chance to work. He hates when I try to make him take a cool bath. I just wanted to give you a heads up in case I have to cancel for tomorrow."

"But can't Joe watch him for a couple of hours?" Lydia felt a twinge of guilt after she asked. She knew she sounded insensitive. And selfish.

"I'm trying to get him to, but he's acting like a jerk. As usual. I've got tonight to work on him and if Markey's fever is a hundred or less, Joe should be able to handle it. The only thing he'd have to do is give him fluids and his medicine. I'll give you a call in the morning, okay?"

"That's fine, dear. Take care of your family. And yourself. Okay?"

"Will do."

Sugar slurped her noodles like a ten-year-old and drank her wine like a scholar. "I thought Sherry was going to say hello," Sugar said, slurping a noodle between her lips.

"Egad, I totally forgot. Sorry. She was talking about Markey. He's sick. High fever and feels awful. Hopefully, you'll see her tomorrow."

"Hope so. I like Sherry. Always have."

The phone rang again.

"Hi, it's me. I forgot to say hi to Sugar. Can you put her on the phone?"

"Sure, here she is."

Lydia handed Sugar the phone. "It's Sherry. She called back to say hi."

It was after nine when Lydia got the kitchen back in order. Sugar had gone upstairs to get settled and then she was going to go out clubbing with some friends from high school.

Although she was glad to see Sugar, Lydia needed a break from her already. Sugar was exhausting. Besides, she had preparations to take care of for tomorrow.

Tonight felt like the Wednesday before Thanksgiving or Christmas. Though tomorrow would be March first, Lydia put on some Christmas music. And she sang. "O Come all ye faithful. Joyful and triumphant."

There was no one to tell her she was nuts or to shut up. "You could wake the dead," Walter used to say when she sang. He'd laugh when he said it but it wasn't funny to her. She loved to sing. But the kids didn't help, either. "Oh, Mother, please. You're hurting my ears," they'd say. But tonight she would sing. She'd sing Christmas carols if she chose and then perhaps move onto Broadway tunes. Lydia had told Rita one time that she swore that when she was in the bathtub singing "Memory" from *Cats*, she sounded just like Betty Buckley. Rita said, "Don't get too cocky. It's probably the tile."

Chapter 24

Timing is Everything

Sugar sat on the edge of her bed, playing with the earring in her nose. "Phew," she said to Binky, who had followed her into her room. "Acting as if everything is okay is exhausting."

She looked at the clock. It was getting late and her friends were waiting for her. But she didn't really feel like going clubbing. She was tired and emotionally exhausted. Besides, clubbing in Port Huron wasn't exactly like going clubbing in Manhattan. In New York they could go to a new place every night for years. In Port Huron you had your choice of the Bada Bing Bar or the Sailor's Delight.

Besides, she had to figure out when, where, and how she should tell her mother what she knew.

Chapter 25

Charades

Lydia fell into bed about midnight. Exhausted. She ran down a mental checklist. Mexican egg casserole with chilies? Mixed and in the fridge. Ham and sausage? Cooked and ready to go. Ingredients for homemade biscuits? Check. Coffee-maker ready? Check. Brown-sugar ham? Cooked. The smell from the ham ran through the house all evening. It was better than incense. The dining room table was set.

Closing her eyes, she hoped for easy slumber. But then Rita flashed into her mind. Seeing her name in the magazine had brought her right back into Lydia's life, at least mentally. If only she could talk to Rita. She would love to be able to discuss how her life was and how her kids were acting.

She would have told Rita about the comment Sugar made when she came into the house. Sugar looked at the dining room table and said, "Geeze, looks like somebody died. All the good stuff's out." Typical Sugar.

As a child, Sugar knew exactly the right thing to say to try to push someone over the edge. She was born strong-willed. All three of her other kids came out in a normal fashion, head first. But not Sugar. She came out feet first, nearly taking Lydia's uterus with her. She and

Walter and the older kids laughed because instead of sucking her thumb, Sugar loved to suck her toes.

Walter told Lydia, "That girl was born with her foot in her mouth and she hasn't taken it out since." They both thought it was funny, at least at first, but as the years went on the foot-in-the-mouth theory became more prophetic as Sugar's penchant for saying all the wrong things became a family undercurrent.

She saw the "message waiting" light flashing while climbing into bed. She pushed the playback button.

"Hi. It's me, Jan. Just called to get your recipe for crab cakes. I lost the one you gave me and I've tried three other recipes and none are as good as yours. Call me. I need the recipe tomorrow."

She hung up, turned off the light and wished her sister still lived in town. Then she wondered why every time she thought about Jan, she thought about Rita, too. Actually, she wondered why she had a tendency to think about people she had lost more than the people she still had, which made her feel ungrateful.

That's the kind of feeling Rita had been so good at helping her get over. When they were on that cruise and had days to be together without being interrupted by phones and kids and life's demands, they talked about everything, from God to love, to marriage, to being single, to parents, to siblings. Of course not everything they talked about was serious. They roared with laughter when trying to determine a proper word for the shape of the captain's body, howled themselves into near convulsions while mimicking two Brazilian men, who, Rita informed Lydia, were gigolos, who sat on loungers near the pool in their thongs, drinking martinis and making chit-chat with any female who passed by.

Nothing was off-limits in their discussion, which was such a treat to Lydia. It wasn't until then that she realized how her thinking, questioning, and outlook on life had become censored. In her efforts to be a good wife and mother she had closed some of the closets in her mind that contained her natural curiosity for life.

By then Walter had ceased even feigning interest in how she saw the world. He'd gone on his merry way with his life, which he tried to keep as ordered as military ship. He skimmed the surface, trying to make as few waves as possible. And she, in order not to rock the ship, had thrown part of herself overboard to remove anything from the marriage that might cause conflict.

Lydia was exhausted but wired, the way she used to be the night before holidays. Norman Rockwell's paintings of families had nothing on the picture Lydia had in her mind of how she wanted her family to be. Before Walter died, Lydia would spend days, sometimes weeks, making plans, menus, place cards, and clever napkin rings with turkeys and Santa Clauses made of felt. When Helen, Guy, and Joe came into the family, Lydia had visions of everyone gathering in the living room after dinner and playing games like Trivial Pursuit, Scattegories, Balderdash, Pictionary, and Jeopardy and, her favorite, Charades. She had great visions of hilarity and camaraderie. When the grandchildren came along, she bought little favors for them, bottles of bubbles, sets of magic markers, and Etch-a-Sketches. She walked from person to person with a video cam, asking everyone to share their favorite holiday memories.

Walter tried to tell her the kids hated having that video camera in their faces, but she said it was important to record family events for future generations. Invariably, Lydia wound up in tears when the kids winced, ducked, and dodged the camera. One time she found Grace, Sherry, and Sugar hiding in the bathroom, giggling. Angry, she exploded. "I've worked so hard to make this day special and, and…" she said, tears welling, "and no one participates!" She finally retired her camcorder after Sugar thrust her middle finger in front of it and said, "Bugger off."

Participation in the game department was rather dismal, too, because Walter, Tim, and the sons-in laws nearly trampled each other racing to get the best seats for the football games. The two leather recliners were prize. None of the men ate dessert because if they did, that might put them at a disadvantage toward getting one of the leather recliners. One of the recliners was reserved for Walter, but the other was up for grabs.

The scene was the same every holiday. The men bolted, the grandkids fled to the basement to play, and Lydia and the girls were left to sit at the dining room table alone.

But each year, by the first of November, Lydia had forgotten last year's disappointments. As she plowed forward preparing for that year's festivities, Walter would say, "You're either a saint or a glutton for punishment."

Lydia remembered she had not said her evening prayer. It was tempting to let it go, to promise she would say an especially good one in the morning, but she felt that was like short-sheeting God.

"Dear Lord, I'm so exhausted, I don't even think I can remember the Lord's Prayer, so if you don't mind, I'm just going to wing it tonight. First of all, I want to say how glad I am that I turned my life over to you. Thank you for getting Sugar here safely. I didn't really mind waiting for her. It gave me a chance to slow down. So thank you for thinking of that.

"I'm not sure if I should thank you, though, for pointing me toward that magazine that has Rita's article in it. I mean, now that I know how to get in touch with her, I think I should. But what if she doesn't want me to? Was that a sign or something? Did you do that intentionally? If it was, you're going to have to give me more clues about how to deal with this, because I'm torn. And with the family coming over tomorrow and all that's going on right now, I hate to do this, but I have to question your timing. Couldn't you have waited to bring Rita into the mix until after this weekend? Forgive me for second-guessing you, but you know how I am by now.

"Thank you for getting Sugar to tone down the color of her hair. It must have been you who got her to change it because heaven knows she never listened to me. But those piercings… goodness gracious. You need to work on those.

"Please be with each of the kids and let them be as excited about getting together tomorrow as I am. Please give them all hints to be on good behavior and to show their love for one another. Have them feel the sense of family and history.

"It makes me really sad that Walter and Buddy won't be here. I still can't get used to that. I wanted so much to ask Walter to run some errands for me when I was cooking and I wanted to ask him to help me extend the table. And when I sat in the living room resting for a few minutes, I looked at the fireplace and in my mind I saw Walter bending in front of it stacking kindling, methodically making little logs of newspaper and striking the match. Thinking of him doing that was lovely, but it didn't take the chill out of the air.

"I would love for him to be here to talk to Grace. She and Walter always had a special relationship. They talked the same language. Sometimes when I'm talking to Grace, I feel like I'm talking Greek and she's talking Russian. And it kills me.

"Walter would love to see how well Tim is doing. And he would love seeing the grandkids grow.

"And Buddy, my Buddy. It's been seven years since he's been gone. You know, just last week at bridge the women were talking about a Missy Delord. Her five-year-old was killed when she was hit by a school bus. One of the women, I think it was Delores, said something like, 'It's an awful thing, but time will help her find closure.' I don't know what got into me, but before I knew it I found my mouth moving faster than a kite on a windy day. I said, 'Closure. What closure? The one who died is the only one who experiences closure. All you can do is pray that the holes in the heart of the living heal. Because trust me, they never close.'

"I suppose I don't need to tell you about the looks I received and the gasps I heard.

"Oh, I'm rambling. No wonder you had someone come up with the Lord's Prayer, so you could hear from everyone in a concise fashion. It must drive you to distraction when you get a rambler like me. I hope you don't take this as an insult, but the Lord's Prayer does seem a tad too pat.

"I pray you will tell Buddy I still miss him and think about him every day. I don't want to think about him too much right now because I'm so tired all I would do is cry and then my nose would get stuffed up and I'd never get to sleep. Just tell him 'hi' for me. Amen.

"P.S. Please make sure my Mexican Egg Casserole turns out tomorrow."

Chapter 26

The Comprehensive Guide to Grief and Getting on with Your Life

The alarm sounded at six forty-five, but Lydia didn't hear it. She was in the shower. Excitement had awakened her before her alarm did. "We gather together to ask the Lord's blessings," she sang in a confused voice. Some notes came out alto, some inched toward soprano, and others were unrecognizable. No matter how sour the sound, she sang with gusto. "He hastens and chastens His will to make known."

Lydia knew her song selections were always a bit suspect. At Easter she found herself singing Christmas songs, at Christmas, she'd be singing "Take me Out to the Ballpark," and it was anyone's guess when she'd burst out with a little Temptations.

She turned the water off, stepped out of the shower and grabbed a towel. She'd always hated these towels. They were avocado green, Walter's favorite color. She could have thrown the towels away or given them to the Salvation Army after Walter died, but she thought that would be frivolous and both Walter and her mother had instilled in her that frivolity would lead straight to hell.

She looked into the steam-covered mirror. First she drew a smiley face with her pointer finger, then wiped the steam from inside the circle. She peered closer. She still couldn't see much because she didn't have her glasses on.

She opened the door and felt the cold rush of air. She heard the alarm screeching. She dropped her towel and grabbed the robe that hung on a hook behind the door. Walter's robe. Grace had bought her parents matching robes for Christmas one year. Lydia's had a big "L" embroidered on the upper left breast. She'd told Grace, "This makes me feel like Laverne in Laverne and Shirley." Walter's robe had a "W" over the pocket. Walter's robe was several sizes too big for her, but after he died, his was the robe she always wore.

She switched the alarm button to off, put on her slippers and headed downstairs. "Today's the day, Bink," she said as they both pranced down the stairs. She had assembled an assortment of cardboard boxes in the den, along with five gigantic Rubbermaid tubs, complete with lids. Grace, Tim, Sherry, Sugar, and Buddy's names were written in permanent marker on the lid and sides of the containers. She envisioned her kids lovingly and happily packing away their childhood treasures.

Lydia noted a message on the recorder. "Hi, Mom, it's me, Sherry. Markey's fever is below a hundred so I can come over. I'm not sure how long I'll be able to stay, but I'll be there. I know you're looking forward to this."

"She must have called when I was in the shower," she said. She looked at the time the call came in, six-twenty-two. "Wow, she was up early for a Saturday," Lydia said to Binky. "Poor thing."

Lydia couldn't help but think about Walter as she was getting ready for her company. She didn't know how or why it happened, but each day since Walter died, her love for him had grown. Sometimes she saw her marriage through a gauzy film. Perhaps her imagination had edged out reality.

Within two months after Walter's death, she'd been besieged with books on mourning and grief. Madeline, a friend who worked for a foot surgeon, gave her a book titled, *From Mourning to Morning... How to Wake Up Each Morning and Be Glad You Are Alive.* Her hairdresser, Carol, lent her two books on grief. Carol told her they had been a huge help when she had to put her beloved poodle Maximilian to sleep after he developed a bowel obstruction after ingesting half a tennis ball.

Lydia, at a loss for words, had simply said "Thank you very much."

Even her kids had gotten into the act. Especially Grace. For Lydia's birthday Grace had come armed with not one, not two, not three self-help books, but *five*, with titles such as *Sail On... The Comprehensive Guide to Overcoming Grief and Getting On With Your Life*, published by Inspiration Cruise Line. Another title was *Death Among the Living... How to Live a Full Life After a Loved One Dies.* And the *coup de grâce* was the one titled *Getting Your Groove Back after Grief,* with the subtitle, *Don't Dress Like a Widow.*

Tim's gift was the same railroad, different line, titled, *The Single Women's Guide to Handling Minor Household Emergencies.*

The only gift that brought a smile to her face and didn't involve changing her life was from Sugar. She'd sent an As Seen on TV talking fish on a walnut plaque.

Chapter 27

The Roundup

Sherry's house

Sherry set a tray with a plastic glass full of crushed ice and ginger ale by Markey's bedside. She sat on his bed and felt his forehead.

"How's my boy?" she asked, rubbing his head. "Your fever seems to have gone down a bit."

Markey looked at her and took his hand and waved it back and forth like a plane tipping its wings.

"Not so good, huh?"

"I'll be okay. How long are you going to be gone?"

"Oh, not real long. I'll just be at Grandma's."

"How come you have to go to Grandma's anyway? Can't you just tell her I'm sick?"

"Grandma asked me to come over. Sugar's in town. So she wanted to spend some time with all of her children."

"Children. You guys aren't children. You're grownups."

"But to Grandma, we're still her children."

"Even when you're old like you and Uncle Tim?"

"That's right, even when you're old like Uncle Tim and me are. And guess what."

"What?"

"No matter how old you get, you'll always be my baby boy."

"I'm not a baby," Markey said, skewing his face.

"Oh, yes, you are. You're my baby." She kissed her son on the cheek and said, "Here, if you need anything, ring this bell. Daddy has instructions that if he hears the bell ring, that means you need something. Kapish?"

"Kapish. You think daddy will really come if I ring it?"

"Of course he will. Just make sure you ring it loud enough that he can hear it over the TV. 'Bye, luv."

" 'Bye, Mom. Tell Grandma I love her."

"I will," Sherry said. She swallowed and it caught in her throat. If everyone in the world could be as sweet as her Markey, it would be a grand place.

Tim's House

"I still think it's stupid and extremely rude that I wasn't invited," Helen said to Tim, her nose turned up like a light switch. "You know, I've been a part of this family for over ten years. Frankly, I think your mom never liked me."

"Oh, come on, Helen. Mom loves you. My mother loves everyone. But this doesn't have anything to do with you."

"I beg your pardon?"

"This has to do with her. Not you. I think she just wants us to work on some family business. Don't you understand? This is progress."

"I still don't see why I'm not invited. It hurts my feelings."

"Jesus. Everything hurts your feelings."

"Excuse me?"

"Honey, you need some thicker skin. You take it personally if our mail goes to the wrong house. You think the whole world's against you if you break a fingernail. Lighten up, hon. Be grateful Mom's not asking if she can move in with us or have me move back home."

"But she's serving brunch. That sounds quite social to me."

"She's feeding the help."

"I could have helped, you know. I'd like to see what's in those closets. I have a vested interest in what goes on in that house. Besides, I might like some of the stuff."

"Now the real deal comes out. You think there are gold doubloons hidden in the closets that're going to be showered upon those who are present," Tim said, with a chuckle.

"You're making fun of me."

"Yep, I am. It's between that and getting pissed off at you. Take your choice."

Helen ignored that remark. "Well, if she starts giving away the good stuff you better put your dibs on the set of Waterford Crystal goblets and the silver tea service."

"For Chrissake, she's cleaning the closets, not dying. Sometimes… sometimes…"

"Sometimes what?"

"Sometimes, it's just that, oh, never mind. I'm not going down this road," Tim said as he stood up and shook his legs one at a time to get his pants to hang right. He rolled his neck. "I'm leaving. I've got to pick Grace up. She still isn't supposed to drive. I'll be home when I get here."

He left without kissing her.

"Fine. Just be that way," Helen said.

Grace's house

"How long are you going to be at Lydia's?" Guy asked in an early-morning grumpy voice as he sat on the edge of the canopy bed, pulling on one of his socks.

"I'm not sure. Why? You're taking the day off, aren't you? That's what you said last night." She turned and looked at him as she pulled on a pair of jeans.

Guy stared at her as she tugged at the zipper. "It's a simple question. Just tell me what time."

She looked at him, twitched her head and gave a sigh of disgust. Before she answered, Guy added, "You're not wearing those jeans are you?"

"I'm not sure what time I'll be home. And, yes, I am wearing these jeans. It's freezing out," she said with authority. Then with a more doubtful voice, she said, "There's nothing wrong with these jeans, is there?" She turned her body first to the right and then to the left, looking for any rips or stains.

"No. They make you look fat. You look better in the gray tweed slacks."

"Guy, I'm old enough to decide what clothes I want to wear. You promised you'd stop doing this."

"Stop doing what? Being interested in how my wife looks?"

"No. Undermining my confidence." She pulled her maroon sweater over her head.

"You know I say these things because I love you."

"Bullshit. You say those things because you want to control me," she said, now standing with her hands planted firmly on her hips.

"You're just hormonal."

"Would you knock it off with the hormone comments? They're so lame."

"I thought that was pretty good of me to suggest it was hormones and not just a bitchy personality."

"I've had it. I'll be downstairs waiting for Tim."

Lydia's house

Sugar tromped downstairs in her short nightshirt that had on it a picture of two people in a Kama Sutra pose.

As she walked by her, Lydia got a complete, unobstructed view of the tattoo of the crucifixion that rose up the outside calf of Sugar's right leg.

"Morning," she said to her mom as she poured herself a cup of coffee. "What time's this shindig?"

"Soon. I thought we'd eat at eleven. I told everyone to come between ten and ten-thirty. So you'd better get dressed."

"I will. Have to have my cup of coffee first. Then I'll take a shower and put my party clothes on. You know, crinolines and patent leather shoes and all."

"Oh, yes. Don't forget to wear your tiara, too."

"Wouldn't you just be surprised?"

"Not at all."

The kitchen smelled wonderful, except for the residual cigarette odor Sugar had dragged in with her. The Mexican egg casserole was cooking nicely, scenting the air with sausage, onions, and red peppers. Lydia took the croissants out of the bag and put them in a silver basket, and placed lemon slices on the rims of the water glasses. She still had to fill the glasses with ice. Or maybe she would have one of the girls do it when they arrived.

The iron skillet on the stove was hot, waiting for the hash browns. Lydia poured the potatoes in the pan. The hot oil jitterbugged out of the skillet. It crackled and spit and carried on. Lydia stepped back from the stove. "Whoa," she said as she turned the heat down.

She took a spatula and scattered the potatoes so they'd brown evenly. She began to multi-task as she added the cilantro to the salsa, pinched a peach slice from the fruit salad, and wiped the counter. "Hum, Bink, should I add maraschino cherries to the fruit salad or not? I think it needs some color. What do you think?"

She didn't wait for Binky to answer. This was a management decision. Although Tim didn't like maraschino cherries, she knew he wouldn't say anything. He would just pick around them. Sherry would try to spoon as many pieces of pineapple out of the salad as she could. Grace would go for the peaches and pears and Sugar would opt for eating a banana, saying processed fruit caused diabetes.

She was quite pleased with herself for how much she knew about her kids.

The dining table looked like a page out of House Beautiful. If her arms were longer she would have given herself a pat on the back. She lit the candles in the silver candelabra in the center of the table and turned on the stereo. She put in a Johnny Mathis CD in and he commenced singing "Chestnuts roasting by an open fire."

"Uh-oh, wrong CD. Better change that, Bink. The kids already think I'm in a time warp."

She went through her short stack of CDs and found one she loved, "Johnny Mathis—Johnny's Greatest Hits."

"I love this," she said as she put the disc in the stereo and fast-forwarded it to track number seven. She closed her eyes when she heard, "You ask how much I love you, need I explain." She listened a moment with her eyes closed. "Until the twelfth of never."

"Walter," she said softly as she walked over to the fireplace. Newspaper, matches, kindling. Everything was set. She was going to ask Tim to light a fire, the first one in the fireplace since Walter had died.

She went into the bathroom to make sure there were fresh hand towels. She fluffed the lavender potpourri in the small Chinese porcelain bowl she and Walter had bought at an estate sale at an old farmhouse by the lake. They'd been told it was an antique, but Lydia had later seen one just like it in the Old Time Pottery store. She flushed the toilet, releasing a cascade of blue commode cleaner into the bowl. She stood and watched it swirl and commented to herself on the miracles of science.

"I should get a new rug for this bathroom, Binky. This one is looks a bit ragtag."

Lydia was certain she heard Binky say, "Yes, you certainly should."

She walked back through the living room and plumped a couple of tapestry pillows on the couch. She noticed the fringe on one of the pillows was ripped. She tucked it under and gingerly placed it behind another pillow. She slid the screen shut. "Waste not, want not."

"What the hell do you have playing?" Sugar said. Her voice sounded like she was trying out for the *Exorcist*.

Lydia jumped and turned around. "You scared me."

"Well, this funeral-parlor music scares me. Can't we listen to something a little more upbeat? Like Coldplay?"

"Cold what?"

"Coldplay. A band. Never mind. I'll find a station." By then, Sugar had turned Johnny off.

"Why did you do that?" Lydia asked. "I love Johnny Mathis."

"Oh, I'm sure you do. But if you play that, I'm outta here. It offends my sensibilities. I'm turning the radio on."

Lydia did a slow burn. Obviously, Grace wasn't the only controlling daughter she had. It was just that since Sugar lived out of town she wasn't exposed to her obnoxiousness on a regular basis. It was obvious Sugar's quiet demeanor on the phone the other night was a temporary lapse.

"Fine, change it," Lydia said, "but don't put any rap or bip-bop on, and don't play it too loud."

"Mother, it's hip-hop not bip-bop." Sugar rolled her eyes.

Lydia turned around and rolled hers right back at her daughter. "What in the world is that?" Lydia asked. "That's not music."

"Sure it is. Gotta get with it, Mom," Sugar said as she bogeyed over to where her mother stood. "Get down, Momma. Get down."

Lydia watched wide-eyed as Sugar bumped and ground her way around her. She felt her bump her rear end, which nearly made her lose her balance.

"Yo, Momma, you gotta loosen up. Shake that booty of yours." Sugar shimmied, and as she did, her considerable breasts bounced right in front of Lydia. She grabbed her mother's arms, pulled them out to her sides, and said, "Come on, Momma. Shake it baby, shake it."

Lydia pulled her arms back down to her side. "If I shake anything it will fall off," she shouted at Sugar.

Sugar continued shimmying around the dining room table, stopping only long enough to pluck a few ripe olives out of a bowl. She wiggled her hips as she placed the ripe olives on her thumbs and pointer fingers and played them like they were castanets. She danced back into the living room. Lydia shook her head and laughed.

She hasn't changed a bit, she thought, as she looked at Sugar. Well, of course she had. Look at the hair, the body, the piercings, and the tattoos. But she was still fun. Still obnoxious and rude but full of zest for life. Sugar's personality was larger than this house, larger than this family. Sugar needed her own state; her own country. Although Lydia laughed at Sugar's dancing and loud behavior today, that wasn't the way it had always been. But she didn't want to think about that today.

Sugar danced her way into the hall bathroom and shut the door. She stood in front of the vanity, put her hands on the edge of it and leaned forward toward the mirror. She looked at her reflection and then closed her eyes. "God, this is hard," she said, referring to her act that made her mother think everything was fine. Sugar knew if she acted any different than her "old" self, her mother would suspect something was wrong and she would start asking questions. And Sugar wasn't ready for that. She had to be certain of her timing, and now was not the time.

She opened her eyes, and looked into the mirror. She moved her head closer so she could see her eyes. Even though she was focused on seeing into her own soul, all she saw was Buddy. And it had been that way for seven years.

"Oh, God." She lifted the toilet seat and leaned her head over it. "I can't do this," she said. And then she vomited.

Chapter 28

Arrivals

"Am I at my mother's house or at dance club?" Sherry asked, mock-shouting as she walked in, unwrapped her scarf, and removed her coat. She held it in her arms while she came over to give her mother a kiss on the cheek. "Sounds like the party's started."

"Oh, it has, dear. Let me take your coat."

"Sure. This is for you from Markey. He made a bow tie out of tissue and he wanted me to give it to you. And he said to tell you he loves you."

"Ah. He's such a cutie, my Markey."

"Sugar. It's been a long time," Sherry said, seeing Sugar come into the living room. Sherry walked over and gave her sister a hug.

"Can we maybe turn the music down a bit?" Sherry asked. "I can't hear anything."

"Ah, you're turning into an old fart, too," Sugar said, laughing, going back to the role she had assigned herself for the visit.

"I'll turn it down," Lydia said. "It's giving me a headache." She turned the music off. Not down. Off. She knew if she didn't, Sugar would hear a song she liked and would go over and turn the volume up full blast.

"You're looking good, Sis," Sugar said to Sherry.

"So are you, my dear. New hairdo?"

"Nah, I've had it several months. But I guess it's new to you since I haven't seen you for... how long has it been?" Sugar's hair was cut asymmetrically, the left side about two inches shorter than the right side.

"A bit over two years," Sherry said, "since daddy's funeral." Sherry looked at her mom. Lydia had on one of her nervous smiles. Her mouth was pretty much straight across, but the corners turned up ever so slightly.

"Show Sherry your peacock tattoo," Lydia said, trying to make conversation. Lydia hated tattoos but she was trying to appear accepting and hip.

"Sure." Sugar tugged down the back of her hip-hugger jeans and leaned her hip toward her sister. "It's the NBC peacock. I got it when I was working with Brokaw."

"Are you still working with him?"

"No. I got fired."

"I'm sorry. What happened?"

"Don't be sorry. I was glad. I tried to get fired. That way I could get unemployment while I chilled for a couple of months. Corporate America isn't for me. I'm working at a gallery in Soho now. I've also started painting."

"I didn't know that," Lydia said, looking at Sugar.

"Well, Mom, there's probably lots you don't know," Sugar said.

"I'm just interested in my kids. Nothing wrong with that, is there?"

Sherry decided it was time to change the conversation when she was saved by the bell, or at least Grace and Tim coming through the door.

"It's a miracle. The door's not locked," were the first words out of Grace's mouth.

Lydia knew the remark was intended for her. "Wonders never cease."

Tim leaned over and gave his mother a kiss and a hug. His cheeks were painted with the wind. But Grace, Grace looked a bit pale to Lydia. Her kiss seemed tentative. And she wouldn't look her in the eye.

"Look who's here," Tim said, seeing Sugar. "My long-lost sister from New Yawk."

"You mean your Broadway Baby?" Sugar laughed, and gave Tim a big hug. Grace stood back a bit, nodding hello.

"I mean where the hell have you been? Shame on you for never coming back to see me," he said.

"Like, you don't think the roads and jets go to New York, you creep?" Sugar asked, still laughing.

"Only a little four-letter word is stopping me, you know," Tim said. "And no, it's not the word you're thinking. It's 'kids.'"

"And what word did you think I was going to say?" Sugar asked.

"Never mind," Tim said. "I know exactly what evil thoughts lurk in the mind of the deranged."

Sugar laughed.

"Grace, dear, let me take your coat," Lydia said. "Tim, give me yours, too, and I'll put them both in the den."

Grace unbuttoned her coat. Tim already had his jacket off. "I'll take them," Tim said, but Lydia replied, "No, that's fine. I'll get them. You stay here and visit with everyone."

She took the coats and scarves and walked to the den. Binky followed closely. It was as if he wanted to hear any comments Lydia might make. But she said nothing. She was too busy chewing on her lip, and feeling the knot form in her stomach. Her excitement had turned to nervousness. When she went back to the living room, she said, "Who would like something to drink? I've got soda, lemonade, tomato juice, coffee, tea, and the ingredients for Mimosas."

"Gosh, Mom, you've outdone yourself," Sherry said.

"Do you have any vodka?" Sugar asked.

"No," Lydia said. She had gone over this scenario in her head earlier. Oh, not the request for vodka, but Sugar asking for something that wasn't offered. She always did that. No matter what was served, Sugar would ask for something else. Just to get a rise.

"Damn, I wanted a screwdriver."

"I'll get ya a screwdriver," Tim said. "I brought my toolbox."

"Ha-ha. Always the wiseass," Sugar said.

"Look who's talking," Tim replied.

Lydia couldn't believe it. It had been over two years since the family was together and within five minutes, everyone was regressing to behavior from when they were ten. It's like they had checked their adult selves at the door. But in a way, wasn't that what she had wanted? Wasn't part of the reason she was doing this was because she wanted to believe she could relive and perhaps alter the past?

"Sure could use a cigarette," Sugar said, tapping her fingers on the piano.

"I thought Mom told me you quit smoking," Tim said.

"I did. For three days. But when the Nazi mayor put that smoking ban in place, well, that's all I needed to light up again. Next thing you know he's going to outlaw Big Macs. It'll be called the 'Lard-Ass Law.'"

"Smoking kills," Tim said.

"Everything kills," Sugar said. "And hell, we all gotta go sometime."

"Gee, this is a cheery conversation," Sherry interjected.

"Mom, why in the hell do you have Katie Couric's photo up here with the family photos? Did you adopt her, too?" Sugar asked.

Grace glared at Sugar.

"Drinks, anyone?" Lydia asked. She'd learned that sometimes the best response to Sugar was no response. "What if I make Mimosas for everyone? I watched Emeril make them the other day."

"Emeril?" Sherry asked. "Who's Emeril?"

"Emeril Lagasse. Food Network. He's great. Like a little Buddha," Lydia said.

"Television gives you cancer of the brain," Sugar said, adjusting her nose ring.

"That's a lovely thought," Lydia said. "Can't you do your ring business somewhere else?"

"What doesn't give you cancer?" Sherry asked.

"Yep, you can't drink the water and you can't breathe the air," Sugar said. "And you can blame that on big business and this administration. We're not going to have a livable, breathable environment left by two thousand twenty-five."

Sherry rolled her eyes and laughed. "Oh, no, Sugar's getting on her political soap box."

Tim chimed in, "I can see it now, 'Sugar Calypso, President'! I'll be your campaign manager if you let me stay in the Lincoln Bedroom."

"The only reason I'd want to be president," Sherry said, "would be so I could fly on Air Force One. Oh, and to have all of my meals cooked and house cleaned." She chuckled. "I could only imagine my family in the White House. Danny and Markey would draw mustaches on the portraits of past presidents. No doubt Joe would want Pamela Anderson invited to every State dinner and I'd get PMS and want to nuke everyone. Hey, forget you, Sugar, maybe I'll run."

They were all laughing. Except Grace, who barely squeezed out a patronizing grin.

"Grace, you're awful quiet. Are you feeling all right?" Lydia asked.

"I'm fine." She sat on the couch with an expression on her face that looked as if it were the first time she had met any of these people.

Lydia had thought Grace might behave one of two ways today: Either she'd be back to her old self, telling everyone what to do, rearranging the table ever so slightly, maybe just taking the napkins off the tops of the plates, folding them and putting them under the forks. Or she might try to gather the forces of the other kids to lead the so-called grief intervention. Even though both Tim and Sherry denied hearing of such a plan, she wouldn't put it beside Grace to organize one on the spot. It was disconcerting to Lydia that Grace just sat there silent. Resolved. Alone.

"Grace, would you mind helping me with the Mimosas?" Lydia asked, while walking toward the kitchen. "Tim, if you could start a fire, I'd appreciate it. There's such a chill in the air."

Grace didn't answer but rose up off the couch and followed Lydia.

"Sure, I'll start the fire," Tim said.

That Tim didn't bat an eye when his mother asked him to start a fire was a testament to the healing powers of time because for years the mere mention of the word "fire" to any of the Calypsos brought looks of suspicion.

"How are my two little delinquent nephews?" Sugar asked Sherry.

"You mean my two little angels? Well, Danny's fine. Markey's sick. Has a cold. Fever. I wasn't sure if I was going to be able to come today, well, you know, I talked to you last night, but luckily Markey's fever came down a bit. He's been sick a lot this year. He's had Strep twice, and, well, you don't need to know all his ailments."

"I don't know how you do it. Working, two kids, and a husband who, well, how the hell is the slug? I mean Joe."

Sherry rolled with it. Like her mother, she too had long since learned to gloss over Sugar's comments.

"Joe is Joe. Work comes and goes. Right now he's working a job at some mall they're building on Wainwright. Keeps him out of my hair and out of the house," Sherry said laughing, grabbing a handful of nuts. "Atkins diet. They're allowed."

Tim toyed with the fire, methodically rolling newspapers and setting the paper logs just so among the wood logs that he had stacked just like has dad and Scouts had taught him. He made sure there was good airflow. When everything was set he lit a match and ignited little fires throughout the assemblage. The wood was so dry it caught immediately.

Lydia and Grace were in the kitchen getting the Mimosa ingredients together. The orange juice, Brut champagne, and Lenox flutes set on a silver tray. Grace waited for Lydia's instructions. This unnerved Lydia. Grace never waited for instructions. She was always one to plow in and read instructions only as a last resort.

"You want to pour the orange juice or champagne?" Lydia asked.

"Doesn't matter."

"Well, then. I guess I'll pour the orange juice and you can pour the fun stuff." She handed Grace the bottle of Brut.

"Can you open this? My fingers have a hard time gripping," Grace said.

"Oh, I'm sorry. I forgot. How stupid of me," Lydia said apologetically, face turning pink. She had forgotten all about the frostbite and how the doctor had told Grace it might be months before all of the feeling returned and that even then she might have weakness in her fingers. The doctor had told Grace that she had been "One lucky lady" because her frostbitten fingers would eventually return to normal. "A few more minutes in that snow and I hate to think what the results would have been," he'd said.

Lydia took the bottle of champagne. "You know, I've never opened a bottle of champagne. Daddy always popped the bottles."

Grace said nothing.

Lydia unwrapped the foil. "Oh great," she said. "Why do they have wire around this plastic corky thing? I need some pliers... hum. Where are my—? Oh, forget the pliers. I've got a better idea. Tim? Tim, can you come here?"

"At your service," Tim said, sneaking up behind her. "Fire's going gangbusters. How old is that wood, anyway? From when Dad was alive?"

"Yes, actually, I guess so. Well aged, huh?"

"Most soitenly is," he said in the Bugs Bunny voice he sometimes used to entertain his kids. Lydia laughed.

Grace rolled her eyes. "Does anybody in this family ever grow up?" she asked, as she turned and walked out of the kitchen.

"Well, she's in a mood," Tim said. "Must be hormones."

"Why do men think everything's hormones?" Lydia asked, obviously perturbed with his remark. "Can you please open the champagne?"

"Sure."

"I better go see what's bothering Grace. If she doesn't get out of this funk, brunch will be ruined."

"I think you should let her go," Tim said. "Just give her space and a few minutes. She'll be fine. Well, as fine as she gets these days. You want me to make the Mimosas?"

"Sure. That'll be great. But, I'm going to just check on her."

"Not a wise move, Mom. Not a wise move. You'll be lucky to come back with your head still attached."

"Oh, I'll be fine. I can handle Grace."

"That's what you think," Tim said under his breath as Lydia walked out of the kitchen and Sherry came in.

"I caught that," Sherry said. "That's what you think, what?"

"Oh, nothing."

" 'Fess up, Tim. What's cooking in this kitchen?"

"Oh, Grace is in one of her moods and skulked out of the room. Mom said she was going to go see what the matter was. I told her to let it go. But as usual, she didn't listen. You know Grace. You catch her in a snit and you can get chewed up and spit out like a bad radish."

"What's with Grace anyway? Did you ever talk to her after she got out of the hospital? Has she ever told anyone why she was out at Marblehead or what happened?"

"No, not to my knowledge. I mean, she might have talked to Mom about it, but she hasn't mentioned anything to me. I'm sure she's still sad about the miscarriage, though."

"I don't know about that. I think the miscarriage was a relief."

"What? Why do you say that?"

"I really can't say. I just think Grace is in a very hard place right now. I don't think her marriage is as it appears to those of us on the outside."

"Hey, what's going on in here?" Sugar asked. "Are these sissy drinks ready?"

"Why do you have to belittle everything?" Sherry asked, obviously perturbed by Sugar's rude interruption. "They're not sissy drinks. They're nice drinks."

"Whoa, what put you in such a state? It was a joke. Ah, but I forgot I'm in the 'Oh so serious' house. Speaking of oh so serious, where are Mom and Grace?"

"In the other room."

"Are you two going to tell me what you were talking about when I came in? I thought I heard someone say something about Grace and her marriage?"

"You certainly have big ears," Tim said.

"I prefer to call it 'in touch' listening," Sugar said. "Anyway, what's wrong with Grace's marriage?"

"Why do you ask that?" Sherry asked.

"I have my reasons," Sugar said.

"I was telling Tim that I think Grace might be having some problems at home."

"Pff. I could have told you that," Sugar said.

Tim and Sherry ignored the remark.

It was apparent Sugar wasn't taking their concern about Grace seriously when she said, "And here we have Dr. Sherry on her radio phone-in talk show, 'Can This Marriage Be Saved?'" Sugar grabbed a flute and the bottle of champagne and poured champagne to the tippy top of the rim. "Why are you two talking about Grace's marriage anyway?"

"It's called concern, Sugar. A concept you apparently haven't heard of."

"No, it's called butting in and nosing around someone else's business."

"Sugar. Why don't you take your drink into the other room so Sherry and I can finish our conversation? In other words, scram."

"Fine. Who wants to listen to this family stuff anyway? Would it kill this group to try to discuss something other than themselves? How about discussing a little art or music or politics? No. We've got to discuss f-a-m-i-l-y. Boring. I'll be in the living room looking at the book on the charming doors of Boston that's been there since Lincoln was president. *Adios*."

"My God," Tim said. "Is she a loose cannon or what?"

"I can only attribute it to a hospital mix-up," Sherry said.

"Back to Grace. What do you think is up with her and Guy? You think they get along?"

"In my opinion, Guy's a shit. A total shit. Oh, he can play cool when he wants, but I think there's stuff that goes on in that marriage we don't know about."

"Well, that could be said about any marriage, couldn't it? That no one knows what really goes on behind those closed doors?"

"Well, sure. But sometimes it's much more ominous."

"Why? What do you mean? Are you referring to Grace's marriage or marriages in general?"

"Grace's. When Grace was at the hospital, Guy was a complete jerk."

"You mentioned that."

"I know. But there's being a jerk and being a JERK. He was being a JERK. He showed no sympathy for Grace. Thought the whole thing was her fault. And he was obnoxious with the doctor and the hospital staff. Mr. Criminal Defense Lawyer."

"Yeah, he can be that way. But Grace never says anything. She doesn't moan and groan about it. But... "

"But what?"

"I heard something from Teresa, Joe's mother, that made me wonder."

"Wonder about what?"

"Whether Guy cats around."

"Cats around? What's that?"

"Has affairs."

"Why do you think that?"

"Teresa works at Identity, the beauty salon down on Mitchell. And you know how beauty salons are. Cesspools of information. Well, Teresa has a client, a young blonde lawyer, a prosecutor, who confided to her that she has been having an affair with a married criminal defense attorney she argued a case against. Besides hearing more than she wanted to about his sexual prowess, she also found out he is about six-two, has dark hair, blue eyes, and loves racquetball. Don't those characteristics sound just a bit too familiar to you?"

"I don't know. It could be someone else."

"Another six-foot-two, dark-haired, blue-eyed criminal defense attorney in Port Huron? Who loves racquetball? I think not."

"Do you have proof? Or is it just hearsay?"

"God, now you sound like a lawyer."

"That's accidental. But still. It's just rumor, speculation. You can't approach someone with that."

"That's why I haven't said anything. Besides, even if I had proof, I'm not sure I'd tell Grace about it. It's the messenger who always gets shot."

Sugar walked into the living room with a flute of champagne in hand. She took a long drink and then put her glass on the coffee table. She held out both of her hands. They were shaking. "Jesus," she said. "I don't know if I'm going to make it."

The fire was going strong as it crackled and popped and hissed. For a moment she was mesmerized by two flames that were synchronistic in their leaping. It was as though they were dancing the tango, each one knowing the move of the other. Then one of the flames disappeared. She walked toward the fire, picked up the poker and pushed the logs around as if to find the flame that had disappeared. She looked up. She looked at each of the family photos that lined the mantel. Her eyes stopped on Buddy. She picked up the photo.

"I don't think I can do this, Buddy. You know, for so long I thought I owed it to you to keep the secret because you said I betrayed you before. But that was never my intention. You had to know that. But then on top of that, you asked a broken-hearted sixteen-year-old to betray herself and her family. My God, Buddy. Did you think my head and heart were made of stone?

"Just out of curiosity, did you think about me or about Mom at all before you killed yourself? Did you think for one second what your death would do to your family? I mean, I know you were mad at Dad. I was, too, but poor Mom. She's never gotten over your death and I doubt she ever will.

"You were my hero. I thought you knew that. Not many brothers let their little sisters tag along. You did. No other brother I know let their little sisters into their lives like you did. And then you went and hung yourself. Damn you. What you did was so selfish. You know, I've never said that. I've always just felt sorry that you felt so bad. But I'm angry, Buddy, downright pissed. And maybe it's time you knew that.

"You said I betrayed you. Well, listen, Buddy, you betrayed me.

"But you must understand what I'm going to do isn't going to be done in anger or because I'm mad at you. It's not a betrayal, and please, don't try to make me feel guilty. I've felt guilty for seven years. That's got to be enough.

"I love you Buddy, but I've got to tell the truth so that I can finally let my memory of you rest in peace."

Sugar put the photo back on the mantle. She took in as deep a breath as she could, which wasn't as great as she thought it would be. She started coughing. "I've got to quit smoking," she said, as she picked up her glass of champagne, tipped it toward Buddy, and said, "To you. And to me."

When Lydia walked into the guest room Grace was standing with her hands in the front pockets of her jeans, staring out the window. "I wonder if winter will ever end." Grace offered no response. "Grace, dear," Lydia said softly, "are you feeling all right? You look a bit peaked."

"I'm fine."

Lydia had known that was the answer she'd hear. "You're awful quiet. Are you sure everything's all right?"

"I'm fine, Mom."

Silence.

Lydia waited for Grace to say something more.

Finally Grace said, "Since you're having us over to help clean your closets, does that mean you've decided to sell the house?"

Lydia moved her head from side to side. But Grace didn't see it because she was still looking out the window. "No, dear, not necessarily. I don't know what I'm doing with the house. It's my home. I can't decide that just yet. But what I did realize when your Realtor friend Bitsy came over was that I do need to clean out some of these closets. Get rid of some of this stuff. And I thought that instead of me just going through it all, pitching stuff you kids might want, I thought it would maybe be a good idea and fun to have everyone over to go through things. Give you all a chance to take some of the things from your past to your own homes."

"That might not be a bad idea, but why do we have to all be here to do it together? And why now? Personally, I think it's only going to dredge up a bunch of bad memories."

"Bad memories? But Grace. I thought you all had good childhoods. I thought you kids had good memories of this house."

"Some were. Some weren't. And you know Sugar's going to be a shit about everything. Why'd she have to come back?"

"Because she's my daughter. Your sister. A part of this family. And she deserves to be here."

"She's a jerk. Always has been. Always will be."

"Grace Mumford. What is up with you? What has made you so hateful and intolerant?" Lydia bit her lips closed as if she were afraid if there was any space between them strong words would fly out. And she didn't want that to happen. All she wanted was a nice day with her family and here she was trying to defend herself.

Grace stood silent. She turned from the window and looked at her mother. "I guess I just can't figure out why you put so much effort into this charade of us being this wonderful, close-knit, happy family. It's only in your mind that we all get along. And trying to force us to act like we're one big happy family is almost more than I can take. Just for one flipping second, I'd love it if you could deal with reality."

Lydia took an involuntary step back. She leaned onto the edge of the open door. She reached behind her and grabbed the door handle and shut the door.

"Hey, are you two finished playing Dr. Laura?" Sugar yelled from the living room. "The fire's cozy. And I'm finished clipping my toenails."

"You're disgusting!" Sherry shouted.

"I was kidding!" Sugar shouted.

Tim laughed. "We'll be there in a sec. We've moved on to solving the war in the Middle East. Maybe we'll send you over there to deal with Admadinejad. If anybody can handle him, I'm sure you can."

Sherry shook her head. "How do you do that?"

"Do what?" Tim asked.

"Avoid wanting to kill her?"

"She's my sister. You don't kill family."

"Are you kidding? Most murders are by family members," Sherry said as she and Tim took their Mimosas into the living room.

"Was'sup, Sugs?" Tim asked giving Sugar a noogie.

She smacked his rear end when he walked by and sat on the couch next to her. Sherry sat in the wingback chair. Of course no sooner had

Tim sat down than he told Sugar to hold his drink so he could tend the fire. No one seemed to notice Sugar's red-rimmed eyes.

"What's it like living in New York?" Sherry asked.

"Cool, cool, cool," Sugar said. "Lots to do. People everywhere, you know, people and rats, rats and people, and some of the people are rats, and I suppose some of the rats are probably people. You never know."

"It's really expensive, isn't it?" Sherry asked.

"Mucho. *Muy grande expensivo*," Sugar said in her brand of Spanish. "Bet you're wondering how I can afford it, aren't you?"

"Actually I was wondering how anyone could afford it, unless you're Barbara Walters or Katie Couric. Have you ever seen Barbara Walters?"

"Yeah, I've seen her. She doesn't look half bad. Great legs. Good bod."

Tim and Sherry looked at each other.

Sherry said, "Perhaps that's more information than I need to know."

"I don't know," Tim said, "I find it fascinating."

"Where *are* Mom and Grace?" Sugar asked. "I'm starving."

As soon as she got to the "g" on starving the buzzer in the kitchen sounded.

"Mom, the buzzer's going off," Sugar shouted.

"She's with Grace, trying to figure out what's wrong with her," Tim said as he poked and prodded the logs.

"Well, if that's what's she's doing, we won't be eating 'til hell freezes over," Sugar said. "Or later."

"Grace, sit down," Lydia said.

"I prefer to stand."

"Do as you like. You always do. But I want to get something straight. I'm not sure what's going on in your life, in your house, or in your mind, but whatever it is, I'm sick of having you take it out on me. You talk about me and how I don't deal with my life. Well, dear, I think that's the pot calling the kettle black. And even though I'm your mother and I love you dearly, I will not listen to you put down my family, which may I remind you, you are a part of."

"That's the thing. I'm not a part of this family. I don't look like anyone else, think like anyone else, or feel like anyone else. And you make me feel like an outsider, too."

"An outsider? I make you feel like an outsider? Oh, come on. You make yourself feel like an outsider. For some reason, and I have no clue what it is, you've alienated yourself from our family, your family. And you've made it a guessing game for me to try to figure out what's wrong and frankly I don't have the energy to play those type of games."

"So you think I'm playing games?"

"I'm not sure what you're doing. At first I thought this was all about me, something I had done, hadn't done, something I could fix if I just did what you wanted. But I don't think that's it anymore. Grace, I don't think this is about me at all. It's about you. It's not about my unhappiness. It's about yours."

"I am perfectly happy," Grace said with a scowl.

"Oh, yes, dear, you are the epitome of happiness. The halo of your happiness is damn near blinding me." Lydia put her arm up over her eyes as if to protect them from a bright light.

"You're not my mother."

"Excuse me?"

"You heard me. You are not my mother. My mother would never laugh at me if she thought something was wrong."

Lydia froze. It was the first time Grace had ever said such a thing. Even after bitter arguments during her teens, Grace had never, ever brought up the subject that Lydia was not her mother.

"I-I don't know what to say to that. I'm not laughing at you, Grace. After all these years you'd think you'd know I wouldn't do that. I don't think this is funny at all. As a matter of fact, I find it terribly distressing. But Lord help me, I haven't known what to do. And whether you believe it at this moment or not, I am your mother." It was only by the grace of God that Lydia remained standing.

"But don't you see? The reason you don't understand me is that you're not my mother. Not my real mother, my biological mother," Grace said, her voice trailing off near the end.

"Do you really think this has to do with biology?"

"Maybe. I think a real mother knows instinctively what's wrong with their child."

Lydia's mind was doing somersaults. There was part of her that wanted to take the blame, say something like, *Oh, Grace dear, I'm so sorry you feel that way. It's all my fault. I am your mother. I should understand. I'll try harder in the future.* Or perhaps she should console her and say, *Grace, I'm so sorry you are miserable. I'll fix it and make it better*, like she'd done so often when Grace skinned her knees or broke her arm after falling off a swing. Yet there was also a part of her, the angry part of her, that wanted to slap her and say, *How dare you say something like that to me? Do you not realize how much love and time I have invested in you?*

Instead, she said calmly, "Obviously, this has something to do with your adoption." She chose this road to separate herself from the emotion of the situation.

"Yes, I guess it does. It's just that right now I don't feel like I'm a part of this family. And I don't know where I belong."

"Grace. You're a part of me as much as anyone out there in that living room. You have to know that."

"Do I?"

"Yes, you do. I've done everything in my power to make you feel special, wanted."

"Maybe that was the problem. Maybe while you were trying to make me feel special, all I ever wanted to feel was just the same as my brothers and sisters."

"I hate to burst your bubble, Grace, but your father and I tried to make each of you kids feel special. It had nothing to do with whether you were adopted or part of a litter."

"A litter?"

"Well, I was just using that as an expression. I meant one of the other kids."

"But why am I feeling like this? Why do I feel like I'm not part of this family or a part of my own family?" Grace burst into tears.

Lydia put her arms out and walked toward her. Grace leaned

into her arms and sobbed into her shoulder. "I don't know, dear. I don't know."

Sherry knocked on the door. "Mom. The timer went off so I took the casserole out. Is there anything else you want me to do?"

"Thanks, dear. I'll be right there. It would be great if you could put the ice in the glasses."

Lydia wiped a tear from Grace's cheek. She was crying, too, only her tears fell inside, deep in her heart, where Grace couldn't see them. It was Lydia's policy to have only one person be in crisis at a time.

"I'm going to go and get the brunch on. If I don't, I'm afraid Sugar will come in here and try to eat us both alive. You go to the bathroom and fix your face."

For the first time in Lydia didn't know how long, she looked into Grace's eyes and saw her daughter standing there. Not a bossy stranger, but a daughter who was lost in a world of problems she couldn't identify and didn't understand.

As she walked out the door, she stopped and said, "Gracie, you'll get through this. We'll get through this. You're just caught in one of life's little mazes right now. But trust me, there is light at the end of the tunnel."

"I hope so, Mom. I really hope so."

Lydia was spent. All she wanted to do was go to bed and wake up just in time to see her life flash before her eyes, then die. But she couldn't. She had a house full of kids. She'd gotten what she wanted. And it was killing her. How much of a heart did she have left, what with it being broken in bits and pieces and chunks? She could feel her heart racing. Unnaturally. "I'm having a heart attack," she said softly.

Then she remembered to breathe. *Why do I always forget to do that?*

She didn't feel herself walk into the kitchen. But suddenly there she was standing in front of the big old oven looking at an over-cooked Mexican egg casserole. She heaved a heavy sigh as she moved the casserole from the stovetop and placed it on the counter. What else did she need to do? She had made a list but she couldn't remember where it was. Her brain cells were as flaky as the croissants she was serving.

"Shit," she said under her breath.

"What's the matter, Mom?" Sherry asked.

"Nothing. Everything's fine."

"You don't seem fine."

"I just can't talk about it. So everything is fine. Okay?"

"Okay, then. What's wrong with Grace?"

"I really don't want to talk about it now. Did you put the ice and water into the glasses?"

"Cross that one off your list. I took care of it."

"Thanks, dear."

"Grace is complicated," Sherry said softly so no one else could hear. "And I think she's got a lot of stuff going on in her life. Just remember. You are not responsible."

Lydia knew Sherry was trying hard to help. "But I'm her mother. Although she doesn't seem to think so right now."

"I'm sure no matter what she said, her problems aren't with you."

"What do you mean?"

"I mean, maybe she's taking whatever's wrong in her life out on you."

"Are you trying to tell me something?"

"What I'm saying is perhaps Grace needs to take out whatever's eating her on Guy, since he's the source of the problem."

Lydia stopped in mid-scoop. "Sherry. What are you talking about? Are you suggesting what I think you are?"

Sherry started coughing like she was choking. Lydia turned around. Grace had just walked in the room.

"Ah, there, you look much better," Lydia said. "I think we're ready to eat."

"I'm starving!" came a cry from the living room.

"Well, then come and help carry the food to the table," Lydia yelled back. *If it doesn't kill me it will make me stronger*, she said to herself. She thought about saying a prayer as she spooned orange marmalade into a cut-glass bowl. Obviously it would have to be a silent prayer and a quick one at that. *Dear Lord, please help me get through this brunch, this day, this life. Please put me in a better humor, quickly. I pray you help me enjoy my family. Or at least not feel like killing them. Amen.*

Sugar came into the kitchen. "Any ketchup?"

"Ugh. You still eat ketchup on eggs?" Tim asked while sticking his finger down his throat in mock disgust.

"It's for the hash browns, you 'tard," Sugar said.

"I've moved on to steak sauce. It's for the much more refined palate," Tim said, opening the refrigerator door to see if he could spy some. "Any steak sauce, Mom?"

"No. I didn't know you liked that stuff."

"Never mind. I just remembered I brought my own. It's in my jacket pocket. Where'd you put the coats?"

"In the guest room. On the bed."

"He brought his own steak sauce?" Grace asked, surprised out of her own mood.

"Have condom-ment will travel," Sugar said, laughing hysterically at her quip.

"I'm not really related to her, am I, Mom?" Sherry asked, nodding toward Sugar.

"No, I'm the one you're not really related to," Grace said.

"Grace, I didn't mean to imply or infer anything other than that Sugar's an idiot," Sherry said.

"I know you were joking," Grace said, "But your joke is my reality."

Lydia felt like she was Tommy in the Who's pinball game. Boing. Boing. Boing. Words bounced off her brain, out of her head, against the ceiling and floor. Was this what it was like before? she wondered. What had happened to everyone? Is this what her family had become? An argumentative group of strangers who, if left to their own devices, would never speak to or see each other again? Except maybe at her funeral?

"All right. Let's eat." Maybe if they all had food in their mouths there wouldn't be an argument.

Tim marched into the dining room carrying his bottle of steak sauce. "What's going on in here? Looks like someone died," he said, hoping that would break the glazed trances everyone seemed to be in.

"Nobody died, Tim. Everything's fine. Let's eat," Sherry said.

Lydia was still in the kitchen as everyone else assembled at the table. She really didn't want to face any of them. She turned the faucet on. Steam came from the hot water. It burnt her hands. But the pain she felt wasn't in her hands.

Lydia sat at one end of the table facing Tim. Grace and Sherry sat on one side and Sugar sat on the other.

The clink, clank of spoons sounded in the air as everyone filled their plates.

"Please pass the croissants."

"Could you please give me a spoonful of casserole?"

"If you could please hand me the butter."

"Orange marmalade?"

"The bacon smells great."

"Where did you get these sausages? They look wonderful."

Everyone's plates were filled. There was a pause. Hands were placed on laps and heads bowed. All but Lydia's. She just picked up her fork and took a bite of egg casserole. Then a bite of bacon. The kids looked at her.

"Aren't we saying grace?" Grace asked.

"You're welcome to," Lydia said, matter of fact.

"I mean, we always say grace," Grace said. "Don't we?"

Grace looked at Sherry and Tim looked at Grace and Sugar shrugged her shoulders. "Fine by me. Let's eat."

"No. We're going to say grace," Tim said. "Mom, I'll say it."

"Suit yourself," Lydia said, placing her fork on her plate. She closed her eyes and bowed her head.

Sherry and Grace looked at their mother and then bowed their heads.

"Dear Lord," Tim said. "Please bless this food that we are about to receive. May it nourish our bodies and souls. We thank you for bringing our family together. Although we sometimes act like nitwits, the truth is, we really do love each other. We may not like each other sometimes—a little humor there—we do love each other. And we thank you for giving us our mother, who although she doesn't realize it, is the best mother any one of us could ever have. Amen."

"Amen."

Lydia kept her eyes closed to keep the tears from falling after the "Amen." After a moment, she opened her eyes.

"Suck up," Sugar said out the side of her mouth, looking toward her brother.

"Shut up, Sugar. The prayer was very nice, Tim. And I agree," Sherry said.

"My God, it was a *joke*. Just like the one he said to God in his prayer. I mean, even God has a sense of humor. It's just too bad no one at this table does," Sugar said, dropping her fork down on the table.

"Not everything's a joke," Grace said, regaining her best lawyerly voice. "And why you think everything is, is beyond me."

"I don't think everything's a joke," Sugar said. "Why is everyone on my back? I don't need this, you know. I came all the way from New York, hoping against hope that maybe, just maybe, things would be different than they were, but I see they're obviously not."

So much for the fifteen seconds of joy, Lydia thought.

By the time brunch was finished everyone at the table had pretty much retreated into her own world, except Tim, who gamely tried to get a conversation going. He and Lydia talked about the weather, with Grace and Sherry agreeing by nodding their heads.

"It's been a long winter, hasn't it?" Tim commented.

"Very long," Lydia agreed.

"Wonder when spring will get here," Tim said.

"I wonder that, too. The groundhog saw his shadow so it could be a while, not that I believe in the groundhog prediction," Lydia said.

"He's usually pretty accurate," Tim said between bites of chewy egg casserole.

"Food's good, Mom," Sugar said.

Lydia said "Thank you," waiting nervously for the other shoe to drop.

Grace picked at her food. Sherry bypassed the croissants and the marmalade and the hash browns but piled on the bacon and sausage. "Atkins," she said when she could see Tim was about to say something.

Lydia took a few bites of casserole but even after she swallowed, it wouldn't go past her gullet. How could the vision of the family she had in her head be so different from the one that sat before her at the table?

The phone rang.

"I'll get it," Lydia said, removing her pink damask napkin from her lap and setting it on the table. "Hello?"

"Lydia? Helen. Are you finished with brunch?"

"Just finishing."

"How was it?"

"Delightful."

"I'm starving. Can I talk to Tim? I thought maybe he could bring me some leftovers."

"Tim, it's for you," Lydia said, rolling her eyes before turning around. "It's Helen."

Sherry had begun to clear the dirty dishes from the table. Grace followed. Sugar said she had to go to the bathroom. "Some things never change," Sherry said. "She'll come out when the dishes are done."

"Helen? Is something wrong?" Tim said into the phone. "Then why'd you call?... Well, if you're hungry make yourself something to eat.... No, I'm not bringing leftovers home.... Uh-hum. No. We haven't started cleaning the closets. We're going to go do that next; at least I think that's the plan... Helen, I am not asking my mother for that. I told you before, I'm not going to ask her for the silver service," he said in an attempted whisper. "Go make yourself a peanut butter sandwich. I've gotta go." Click.

Lydia caught the essence of the phone call as she walked back and forth between the dining room and the kitchen. *If that's not typical Helen*, she thought.

"So are we really going to clean the closets?" Sherry asked when Lydia came into the kitchen. "Or was that just a ruse to get us over here?" Sherry and Grace had gotten a nice rhythm and conversation going while doing the dishes. Lydia even thought she heard Grace laugh.

"Yep, we're going to clean a few of these closets. It's time to move this stuff from my house to yours. Time to clean house. And you guys are cheaper than hiring a cleaning crew."

"Oh, so the truth comes out. We're just cheap labor," Tim said. "Well, you know, you get what you pay for."

"That's what I'm afraid of," Lydia said. She had regained her composure. "I've got a plastic container for each of you in the den. I thought you could put your treasures in those and then haul them to your homes."

"Where are they?" Grace asked.

"In the den."

Grace, Tim, and Sherry each had their plastic tubs and were awaiting instructions. Sugar had charged ahead, declaring she would do the hall closet. Lydia had thought about whether each person should be assigned a closet or if it wouldn't be better for them all to work on each closet together or if perhaps two by two would be a good idea and she could go back and forth. She had decided that it might be best if two people did each closet. She pulled out a list she had stuck in her pocket. "Sugar, I'm going to have you and Tim work on the hall closet and Grace, you and Sherry, you two work on the closet in your old room. You both still have a lot of things stored in there. Then I thought we'd all go through Buddy's closets together. If we can get just those done this go 'round, that would be super. Then maybe we can tackle the rest of the linen and bathroom closets next week. Oh, I forgot the 'official' junk closet, too."

Sherry looked at Grace, Tim at Sugar.

"Next week?" Tim whispered to Grace. "I thought this was a one-time shot."

"What? Is something wrong with that plan?" Lydia asked.

At first, no one said anything but Lydia saw a wave of shrugged shoulders and skewed facial expressions.

"Buddy's closet? I mean, I don't want to seem disinterested or unwilling to help, but Mom, Buddy's closet? I just don't know if I want to go there," Sherry said, softly, lowering her head and closing her eyes.

"I'm not up to it, Mom," Grace said.

"Mom, how about you and I go through Buddy's things? I'd sort of like to do that," Tim said.

Just as Lydia was about to accept Tim's offer, Sugar said, "No. I'll do Buddy's closet. I want to do it. He was closest to me."

All eyes turned to Sugar.

"That's fine with me," Tim said.

Lydia nodded. "I think that's a good idea. Sugar and I will go through Buddy's closet."

"No, Mom. If you don't mind, I need to go through it myself. I won't throw anything away until you see it, but if you don't mind…"

"Don't you think Mom has the right to go through Buddy's closet first?" Grace asked.

Sugar shook her head. "You just don't get it, do you?"

"Don't get what?" Grace asked. "You don't know what I get or don't get because you—"

"All right, girls. Stop it. At some point in your lives you're both going to have to let the past go. Just sort out your feelings and give each other a break. Life's too short for this kind of squabbling. And after all the things that have happened in this family, I was hoping you'd all realize that by now."

Lydia had on her school teacher face and voice. She scanned her children's faces, then said, "Sugar, that's fine. You go through Buddy's closet first. I don't have a problem with that."

Lydia avoided Grace's glare. She'd already had enough of it for one day.

Chapter 29

Cleaning Closets

Sherry and Grace dragged their empty plastic tubs to their old bedroom. Grace dropped her container by the closet and sat on the edge of the bed. While Sherry went straight to work, Grace looked around the room.

The walls were still painted a pale pink. "Fair Maiden," Grace said out loud.

"What?"

"Fair Maiden. That's the name of the color of paint. Do you remember that?"

"Not at all. I can't remember what I ate an hour ago, much less the name of a paint chip from the dark ages. I do remember Dad wouldn't let us put up any posters or anything on the wall."

"Yeah, he was anal about a lot of things."

They both laughed.

"I always remember stuff like that. Things that don't really matter," Grace said.

"You do. You have a photographic memory. I've always envied that."

"Oh, phooey. You know what a photographic memory does? It never lets you forget. Memories, facts, dates, linger in the gray matter and fight for space. My shrink said it creates conflict."

"Shrink, I didn't know you were seeing a psychiatrist." Sherry stretched to reach some boxes that were high on the shelves. "Rats, I'm going to need a chair," she said, walking over and grabbing the vanity chair that went with the dressing table. "Hope this holds me."

The vanity chair was the same one that had been in the room when Grace and Sherry were at home. They both hated it but Lydia had loved it. "It's so feminine," Lydia told them, "Just like little girls should be."

"Ah, don't worry. It will hold you. Besides, even if it doesn't, you won't fall far," Grace said, her eyes lighting up. She rolled over on her side and looked around the room. Not much had changed since she'd left. The beds had the same pink-and-green-checked spreads; each bed had two pillows, two shams, and a couple of throw pillows. One bed had a green coverlet and the other bed had a pink one. The dressing table had a green-and-cream-plaid skirt that draped all around. A great place for hide-n-seek. The top of the figure-eight-shaped table was a mirror. There was also an oval mirror above the dresser that leaned against the wall. Walter wouldn't even allow the wall mirror to be attached to the wall. A couple of orange and chartreuse leis hung from one side of the mirror. Next to the dresser, on the wall, was a large frame filled with Grace's school pictures, all in order, kindergarten through high school. And on the other side of the room, above another dresser, was the same-sized frame filled with Sherry's pictures. Interspersed among the photos were notes written by a young hand. Grace got up and walked over to the frame that contained her photos.

"Did you see these?" she asked.

"See what?" Sherry asked as a couple of boxes plopped to the floor. "I'm afraid I'm having an avalanche here. Can you give me a hand?"

"Sure." Grace helped Sherry unload at least ten shoeboxes of varying weights.

"What in the world could be in these?" Sherry asked as she climbed down off the chair and placed an armful of boxes on the bench at the end of one of the beds.

"Take a look at these," Grace said, walking back to the framed photos. "These weren't here when we were, were they?"

"No. I've never seen them. Mom must have put them up after we moved out," Sherry said as she walked to where her photos were. "What a hoot. And these notes that are in here. I didn't know she even saved them."

"Oh, my God. Did I have some ugly years? I can't believe I really went around like that. I look like a drunken chipmunk. And that's when I was in high school and I thought I looked so hot," Grace said, looking as though someone had taken their two fingers and pulled the corners of her mouth as far to the side as they could.

"At least you had a time when you thought you were hot. I always thought I looked like a dog. A complete bow-wow. Of course, what should I expect? I had boobs the size of Tunisia, hair that was wired for sound and a constellation of zits. Oh, and braces. I had almost forgotten about the twenty-four months of pain and torture I suffered through, wearing those braces."

"You're crazy. You were always cute. Little and cute. Except for your boobs, which I always envied. You had big boobs and light skin. What more could a girl have asked for? I tried to believe I was hot but I hated being so dark and flat. I can't tell you how many times I'd leave the house with my bra stuffed with soccer socks. And I was always darker than anyone else. I hated that. I'll never forget Ricky Snead called me 'nigger girl.' And he wasn't the only one," Grace said, studying the photos. "But I wasn't that dark."

"I never knew anybody called you that. That's awful. Did you tell Mom and Dad?"

"No."

"Why not?"

"They would have had the kid in a noose. Made a big scene and that would have made it worse. Besides, I didn't want them to think they'd made a mistake by adopting me. I thought maybe they hadn't noticed I was that dark. I didn't want to embarrass them."

"My God, Grace. You didn't tell anyone? You carried that all by yourself?"

Grace shook her head. "It's no big deal. But it wasn't just outsiders who called me that, either."

"What do you mean?"

Lydia walked in. "How's it going in here?"

"When did you put these photos up?" Grace asked.

"Shortly after daddy died. I'd wanted to earlier but you know your daddy and holes in the walls." They all laughed. "I've pounded a lot of holes in the wall since your daddy died. It's quite good therapy," Lydia said. "I can't really stay here because I've got to go see how Sugar's doing. I'll be back in a few minutes to see if you need any help. Toodles." Lydia whistled her way out the door.

"I haven't seen Mom this happy in quite a while," Grace said.

"I know. It's nice. But getting back to what we were talking about before she came in. What did you mean when you said it wasn't just outsiders who called you the N word?"

"Just forget I mentioned it. It doesn't do any good to bring up stuff like this."

"I think you're wrong. I think sometimes you need to face this kind of thing, resolve it, and then move on; not just bury it. No wonder your head is full." Sherry's voice softened. "Now who else called you a nig— I can't even say it."

"Darling Buddy."

"Buddy? You mean our Buddy?"

"Yes. Our Buddy." Grace nodded. "We got into an argument. I'd just gotten my driver's license. He wanted me to take him somewhere, maybe to the go-cart place, and I said no. He kept bugging me. 'Please take me, please take me.' I kept saying no. No. No. I said I didn't want to be seen with anyone who acted like a snot-nose baby. And that's when he said, 'Go ahead. Be that way, I don't want to go with a nigger anyway.'"

"Buddy said that?"

"Yeah. And I told him to drop dead." Grace walked over to the bed and ran her fingers along the lace-edged canopy. "Quite a prophetic response, don't you think? Few days have gone by since Buddy died that I haven't thought of that. I've always wondered if that had any part in him trying to kill himself."

Sherry gave a short laugh.

"What's so funny? I feel responsible for our brother's death and you're laughing?" Grace asked, angry.

Sherry cut her laughter. "For Pete's sake, Grace, I hope you don't think what you said had anything to do with Buddy's suicide. That was how many years before he died, five? Besides, we were always telling each other to drop dead. We said it as many times as we brushed our teeth. That's what kids say. None of us meant it. Don't you remember, we called people queer before we had any idea what queer meant? We called each other fat, ugly, stupid, retards. One time Tim called me 'turd face' after I'd licked a chocolate brownie bowl. Of course, he waited 'til Mom left the kitchen, and when I tried to rat him out she said she didn't want to hear it. We were all pretty brutal. And I'm sure I told Buddy to drop dead at least a dozen times because he was so annoying. Don't you remember, Mom thought Buddy was so perfect? But we all knew better. He always reminded me of Eddie Haskell. 'Yes, Mrs. Cleaver. Of course, Mr. Cleaver.' He'd suck up to Mom and Dad and then he'd come outside and threaten to put firecrackers up our butt. We were all just goofy kids."

"But why do I keep thinking it was my 'drop dead' that made him kill himself?"

"No offense, Grace, but I think it might be because you think God put you on earth to feel guilty for everything that goes wrong. You and Mom."

"What?"

"You've always try to fix everything and everybody. I hate to be the one to break the news to you, but you're not God. And guilt doesn't need to be your middle name. I know you're going to hate me for this, but when people ask me if I have any sisters, and what their names are, I tell them I have a sister named Grace whose middle name is Guilt. And I'm guilt by association."

"No, you don't."

"Oh, yes I do. That's part of the reason I had to quit calling you or trying to be close with you. You've always made me feel so guilty.

You were always trying to tell me what to do and how to do it. And that took away my confidence. I decided when I could choose who I wanted to be around, I would choose people who made me feel good about myself, and," Sherry's voice was soft and apologetic, "and you weren't one of them."

Grace was silent for a moment. Then: "I had no idea. I've never seen myself like that. I always thought I was being helpful. I only wanted what was best."

"I'm sure you did, but who knows what's best for another person? Hell's bells," she said, borrowing her mother's phrase, "we don't even know what's best for ourselves. And to assume we know what's best for others is, well, arrogant."

Grace sat back down on the bed. "I am arrogant, aren't I?" she said, looking only to herself for the answer. "And bossy."

"Now don't go beating yourself up. You've got lots of good qualities, too. And all of us Calypso kids are arrogant to a certain degree."

"Why do you say that?"

"I mean, we were brought up being told we could be anything, do anything, and that we were the Calypsos and we were special. Mom wanted us to all have good self-esteem and that's how she thought a person developed it, by being told how wonderful they were. Didn't you ever look at the shelf of books in the den that were all about self-esteem? Geeze. I can still see them, *The Self-Esteem Workbook, Self-Esteem Comes in All Sizes, Building Self-Esteem in Boys.* Self-esteem this, self-esteem that. It was the parenting mantra of the times. Still is. And we, as kids, well, it was a free ride to the Big Head. And that confused me for so long. I never understood why I could be told I was so good and so special and so talented and still feel like a worthless cow. But finally, taking my psychology courses the last couple of years helped me figure it out."

"I didn't know you were going to school."

"Nobody knows. Except the school. Working at the college makes it easy. It's free and I make my hours around my classes."

"You haven't told Joe, or Mom?"

"No."

"Why not? Wouldn't it be easier if you got some support? I mean, I know Mom would help with the kids and all."

"I didn't tell Joe because he'd pooh-pooh the whole idea. And I don't want to deal with that."

"But why not Mom? She'd be your biggest booster."

"That's precisely why. I don't want a booster. I don't want a cheerleader. I just want to do this myself. On my own. I've realized that's what helps me build... oh, I hate this phrase, but yeah, it's helping my self-esteem. Making my own decisions, having my own successes, and even failures. And in a way, I've altered my definition of success. Damn, sometimes just getting out of bed and brushing my teeth is a success."

"Am I really that obnoxious?" Grace asked, pulling the conversation back to herself.

"I told you, you have lots of good qualities, too."

"Such as?"

"Such as you are very generous and you put all your energy into whatever you do. Your kids are always clean and beautifully dressed. I've never seen snot hanging from any of your kids' noses! I'm serious. My kids always ran around with gunk falling from their faces and even when your kids have been sick, they were snot-free. And you are smart, too. If I needed a lawyer, I'd come right to you."

"That's because you'd think you'd get a sister discount."

"No. It's because I think you're a good lawyer. And if you weren't on the Mommy-track, you'd be the best. You're competitive and fearless. Even when I think you're dead wrong, you do it with gusto. I find it inspiring that when you believe in something, you put your heart and soul into it," Sherry said, exhaling in a puff. "Is that enough?"

"It's a start," Grace said, laughing.

"I've always wished I had your self-assuredness. I'd give anything to go through one day without going back and forth fifty times saying, 'I'm okay. No, I'm not. I'm smart. No, I'm not. I'm an idiot. No, the rest of the world's an idiot.' I have these conversations in my head. I've realized the best I can do is put one foot in front of the other and keep moving forward more times than I move backward. That's just going to be my journey through life. It's taken me almost thirty years, but I've finally learned to drown out that committee in my brain that always says, 'Better not do that, or you might get hurt, or what would your Daddy say, or, Lord, I could go on and on. It's a wonder any of us ever figures out who we are."

"Believe it or not, I think that's a big part of my problem," Grace said. "Although it has appeared I have a lot of confidence, I think a lot of it is false bravura. I've never had a clue as to who I am. I've just faked it." She rose from the bed and walked over to the pictures on the wall. "I look at all these photos and I see someone who's always tried to be something and someone she's not. One of the Calypsos."

"Oh, Gracie. Come here." Sherry took a step toward her sister and put her arms around her. "I never knew you felt like that. You've always seemed so confident. So sure of yourself. If there's one person I ever thought knew who they were, it was you." She took a step back and looked into Grace's eyes. "And here I was thinking I was the only Calypso kid who didn't have a clue."

"At least you know your heritage. You *are* a Calypso. I can't even say that."

"But you *are* too a Calypso. Maybe not by birth, but you're just as much of a Calypso as I am or Sugar or Tim or Buddy," Sherry said. Then with an impish grin, she added, "And if you really think about it, when you look at this bunch, aren't you just a tiny bit glad that you aren't in the gene pool? This bunch does have its share of nitwits. I mean, do you really think it makes me feel better knowing Sugar is a blood relative? Not. Do you think it makes me sleep any better at night knowing that I have some of the same blood as Uncle Cash, the lech, or Aunt Dottie, the kleptomaniac, who never wore her own underpants one day of her life? And I could go down the whole list. You should thank your lucky stars you have some degree of separation from the lunatic farm."

"You've got a point," Grace said between sniffles that had turned into a cocktail of laughing and crying. "But at least you know. You know what you're dealing with. What if my mother regrets that she gave me up and wonders where I am? Did she have any regrets? What were the circumstances behind her giving me up? Or did she just not want me? I just need…"

"To what?"

"To find out. I just need to find out who my birth mother is. Find out why she gave me away. Why she took the easy way out."

"Where in the world did you get the idea that giving a baby away is taking the easy way out? Women, mothers, don't give babies away because they want to. She carried you for nine months. If she didn't want to give you life, she could have aborted you. Just because she didn't raise you doesn't mean she didn't love you. You know what? I think what you're feeling is perfectly normal. I'd venture to say that I'd feel the same way if I were you. I'd want to know where and who I came from."

"You would?"

"Of course. I think it's natural. We all want to know how we fit into this world. Even if we were born to a serial killer, most of us would want to know. Some things we just *need* to know. Have you mentioned this to Mom?"

Grace shook her head. "In a way. Before we ate I did. Perfect timing, huh? She has us all over for a good time and I tell her that she really isn't my mother."

"You didn't."

"I did."

"What'd she say?"

"She was upset. Probably more upset than I realized."

"I'm sure it stung and hurt her, at least temporarily. And I must say, your timing was a bit off, but I'm also sure that after the sting wears off, Mom will understand. She's always wanted what's best for us kids even though what she's wanted for us and what we've wanted for ourselves hasn't always coincided."

"I know. I know. It's hard, isn't it? Being an adult. Being a parent. I swore I wouldn't make the same mistakes Mom and Dad made, and I think I haven't… I just make different mistakes."

"Okay. We've both established the fact that we're both screwed up, at least partially, so how about if I solve your problems and you solve mine? I'll handle Guy and your kids if you tell Joe I want a divorce? Okay?"

"You want a divorce? My God, Sherry. I didn't know."

"No one knows. The time's not right. I need to get my degree first. I should have that by spring, and then *adios*, Joe Blow."

"But you and Joe seem happy, or at least content," Grace said, her face registering confusion.

"That's because you rarely see us. The truth is, I'm not happy."

"How are you not happy?"

"Let me rephrase that. I'm not happy with the marriage. But I am relatively happy with life. I've learned to separate the two, at least for the time being. And doing that allows me to choose to be happy in the parts of my life that I can control."

"You seem to have so much of this 'stuff' figured out. How'd you do it? I mean is this how you've always thought?"

"Lord, no. I was half nuts for a long time. I suppose you could say I had a mini-breakdown after Markey was born, you know, post-partum depression that really wasn't just post-partum. I even went to a shrink once."

"Is that what helped you?"

"Heavens, no. That guy was more nuts than I was. I mean, I was depressed, but not nuts. I got out of there fast when he thought the answer to my problems would come if we 'role-played' some sexual fantasies. Actually, I think I knew a lot of what was bothering me. A bad marriage and not finishing getting my degree left me feeling trapped. And you know I had an abortion before we were married. I felt really guilty about that."

"You did what you had to do," Grace said.

"No. I didn't have to have an abortion. I chose to. I wasn't, I mean, we weren't ready to have a baby. We didn't even know if we were going to make it at the time. And would you believe, I was stupid enough to think that Joe would love me more if I made this decision? The things I've thought. And done. Anyway, even while I was getting the abortion, I knew this was a decision I would have to live with."

"And have you?"

"Have I what?"

"Learned to live with your decision?"

"It took a long time, but I'd have to say, 'Yes.' Why do you ask?"

"I don't know," Grace muttered.

"But I think you do know," Sherry replied.

"Maybe I ask because, well, because, I feel guilty about my miscarriage."

"Why? A miscarriage is not something you *do*, it's something that *happens*. Not to sound too holy-rollerish, but a miscarriage is God's plan, not yours."

"But what you don't know is I prayed for the miscarriage. I prayed it would happen because I knew Guy didn't want the baby. I wasn't even sure *I* wanted the baby. So I prayed, and punched myself in the abdomen to try to cause a miscarriage. And even when I was in the coma, subconsciously I prayed that this baby would go away. Not exist. And now I feel like that will haunt me forever."

"It will haunt you until you resolve it. Sometimes it is time that heals, but in your situation, like in mine, I think there's more to resolve than just that one issue. Some people talk to therapists, some feel better after they talk to friends, and others converse with God. And not to sound like Mother, but that's where I finally found the answers I needed. Not to mention I can afford God's fee."

"Why'd you go away on that cruise with Rita?" Sugar asked, catching Lydia totally off guard.

"What?" Lydia asked, her face looking like a bitter pill had begun dissolving on her tongue.

"I said, how could you go on that cruise with Rita when you knew Buddy's life was falling apart?"

"Sugar, what are you talking about? And what brings this up?" She walked over to the far end of Buddy's bed, to establish a distance between herself and Sugar.

Sugar leaned on the door of Buddy's closet, her arms folded, her posture slouched.

"You mean when Rita and I went—"

"Yes, that one. The one you took shortly before Buddy died."

"I went because I needed to get away. Rita understood that. I hadn't slept in months. That whole episode with the accident and taking care of Buddy and lawyers and being worried sick about everything, I just had to get away."

A soccer ball had rolled out to the edge of Buddy's closet. Sugar lifted her foot and placed it on the top of the ball and rolled it around. Finally, she said "Harrumph."

"What was that for?" Lydia asked as she leaned over and picked up a navy-and-rust-colored pillow that had fallen off the bed and onto the floor. She held the pillow in front of her as if it could somehow protect her from the onslaught of Sugar's pointed questions.

"Don't you feel just a little guilty that you went away and then a month later Buddy killed himself?"

Mother and daughter locked eyes. Sugar's eyes were wide like a full moon. Lydia's long and narrow like a mail slot.

"I don't think I like what you're implying."

"Most people in this family don't like what I have to say," Sugar said.

"Well, when you make accusations like that, how do you expect people to react?"

The room filled with an eerie silence, the kind heard on a battlefield where there is no peace, just the reloading of weapons.

"Are you saying I was responsible for Buddy's death?"

"Partially."

The expression on Lydia's face had changed from puzzlement to anger. Instead of sitting on the bed and having a nice chat as she'd planned, she was up and pacing, trying to dodge the blows of a street fighter. "How dare you bring this up now and make such an accusation? Do you think I haven't rethought and replayed everything I ever said to Buddy? Do you think there's a day that goes by when I don't question what I did as a mother and try to figure out how I could have saved him?" Her voice rose with every syllable. She took the pillow she was holding and slammed it on the bed so her finger was free to point it directly at her daughter. "You have no idea what Buddy's death did to me, and unless it happens to you, God forbid, you'll never know what it's like to wake up every morning hoping each day before was a bad dream and today when you go downstairs to the breakfast table, all your children will be there. But they never are. So you learn to deal with your losses the best you can."

Throughout the years, whenever her kids had lashed out at her, Lydia had always tempered her answers so as not to sound personally retributive. She took the brunt of the attack and tried to diffuse the situation. But with what Sugar had said, she could feel herself removing her kid gloves because Sugar was opening wounds and burrowing with her weapon of choice, her tongue.

"You had to have seen Buddy was a mess. You had to have heard him cry, see the sadness in his eyes. Notice that he had withdrawn. And yet you left and went on your merry way to save yourself instead of saving your child."

"I didn't leave Buddy parentless. Walter was here. And as far as I could tell, Buddy was handling the situation as well as could be expected."

Lydia heard Sugar "harrumph" again.

"Knock it off with your grunting, Sugar. How dare you stand there judging and accusing me. The fact is I asked Buddy a million times, 'Are you okay? Is there anything I can do? Is the therapist helping? Are you taking your medicine?' and he'd say 'Yes, Mom, I'm doing fine. I'll get through this. No, Mom, there's nothing you can do. It's up to me. Yes, the therapist is helping a lot,' and 'Sure, I'm taking the meds.' How was I supposed to know any different? I took what he said at face value. That's all I could do. Why are you dredging all of this up now, after all this time? It's like you're trying to get back at me for something."

"No, Mother. I'm just trying to get to the truth. Trying to talk about something that's been swept under the rug for too long." She nudged the soccer ball back into the closet. "After Buddy died, you and Dad acted as though he'd just got hit by a car or died from a heart attack, but he didn't. He took his own life and the way I see it is everyone in this family is to blame for his death. Grace treated him like shit. It was as though Tim could do no wrong and Buddy could do no right and anyway Tim was too busy being everything Dad wanted him to be to get his hands dirty with his little brother. Sherry saw what was going on, how Grace treated Buddy and she did nothing about it. And you, you saw how Dad treated Buddy and you did nothing about that," Sugar said, pointing her finger at her mother.

Lydia walked over and grabbed Sugar's hand. "Don't you ever point your finger at me."

Sugar jerked her wrist out of her mother's grip.

Knowing she had better get some space between herself and her daughter, Lydia walked back to Buddy's bed, then turned and said, "And you, Sugar, where do you put yourself in this blame game? Have you absolved yourself from any responsibility? My God, Sugar, it's like you've spent the last seven years dealing out guilt cards to each of us—"

The door to the room had closed which it had done for years because the walls were out of plumb. Tim, Grace, and Sherry peeked in and then Tim opened the door wide and all three entered Buddy's room.

"What's going on here?" Tim asked. He scanned the room, his brows furrowed when he looked at Sugar. Then he looked at Lydia.

Lydia's face had the expression of a drowning person, sheer panic. "Sugar just accused me of being responsible for Buddy's death," Lydia said, her voice quivering.

"What?" Tim yelled; throwing his arms, palms up, open.

Grace and Sherry muttered the same thing. Grace shook her head and breathed a noticeably heavy sigh. Then she said, "Don't be a jerk, Sugar."

"It's not just Mom who's responsible. We all are," Sugar said, casting her eyes over everyone in the room.

"What brought this on?" Tim asked, walking over to the corner where his mother stood with her arms crossed.

Sherry pulled out a chair from Buddy's desk and sat down. She picked up a pencil and pushed the lead tip on the desk, then ran her fingers down to the other end of the pencil and then flipped it over and pushed the eraser end over end on the desk, a nervous habit she'd picked up when she was small.

Tim continued. "Of course we all feel bad that Buddy killed himself, and yes, we probably all wish we would have said or not said something to him, but seven years later, to be shooting arrows at people, that's not fair."

"That's what I was talking about, Mom, how cavalier everyone is. Sure, everybody's sorry about Buddy, well, almost everybody," Sugar said, looking at Grace. "And—"

"What are you looking at me for when you say that?" Grace took a couple of steps closer to Sugar.

Sugar quit leaning on the door frame and stood erect, feet about a foot apart and clenched her arms. "Because you could care less that Buddy died," Sugar said smugly, moving her head back and forth, inching it closer to Grace. Her eyes dared Grace to come any closer. "Buddy was an inconvenience to you. You never liked him and you've never liked me."

"How dare you say I don't care that Buddy's dead? You have no idea how I feel about Buddy. I loved him as much as you did."

"Yeah, right," Sugar said, breaking her focus on Grace and picking up Buddy's baseball mitt off the closet floor.

"But I must say you are right on the other account. I don't like you. You've always been a spoiled brat, Sugar. And if anybody's responsible for Buddy's death, it's you!" Grace said, taking her finger and pointing it at Sugar.

"You bitch! You self-serving bitch," Sugar said as she made a fist, held the glove a couple of inches from Grace's face and punched it. "That's how you've always operated. Throw it back at me. You've blamed me for everything. You hated it if Buddy and I had secret. You couldn't stand it that Buddy and I actually liked to be together and that he liked me better than you and since you couldn't get him or me to act the way you wanted us to, you did whatever you could to try to get us in trouble. Rat here, rat there."

"You got yourselves in trouble," Grace said, as she pushed the glove out of her face. "You need to be on medication. I think you've lost it."

"*I've* lost it? I'm not the one who drove out to Marblehead in a blizzard, pregnant, and ended up in the hospital. Of course that was probably your plan. Anything for attention."

Lydia grabbed the headboard of Buddy's bed. It was as though she were at a movie watching some family dissolve on screen. For a couple of seconds she dissociated herself from what was happening around her. She looked at the back of her hands and noticed the age spots. She felt cold, as if someone had poured a bucket of ice water on her. And for that instant, she felt numb. She heard people talking but she wasn't listening to what they said. *Is this what I've lived my life for?* she wondered.

Tim watched his mother and placed his hand over hers. But Lydia pulled away.

"I'm not sure what's going to be solved by everybody making accusations," Sherry said.

"Oh, Sherry, quit trying to be the little peacemaker. At some point, somebody in this family has to say 'enough is enough' with pushing things under the rug and you have your share of blame in this whole equation," Sugar said.

"Me? What did I do?" Sherry asked in a voice that was so shrill with hurt it brought Lydia back to witness what she was sure was the dissolution of her family.

"It's not what you did, Sherry. It's what you didn't do," Sugar said as she played with the leather lace strings on Buddy's mitt.

"What didn't I do?" Sherry asked as she put the pencil she had been playing with down.

"You never stood up for Buddy. You saw how Grace treated him, how she belittled him and you said nothing. All you wanted was Grace's approval," Sugar said she removed the mitt from her hand and placed it under her armpit.

"Isn't this clever, Sugar, how you have everything figured out," Grace said as she walked over to where Sherry was sitting. She placed her hand on Sherry's shoulder but Sherry stood, breaking Grace's grasp. Grace put her hands in the front pockets of her jeans and continued. "I'm not sure when or where you got your degree in psychology, but I hope you didn't pay much for it because it stinks."

Lydia moved away from the bed. Beads of sweat sparkled like sequins on her forehead. She wrung her hands. "I've heard enough," she said.

But Tim began talking as if he hadn't heard her.

"Grace is right, Sugar. What gives you the right to attack all of us? Buddy wasn't just your brother. You weren't the only one who loved him. And all I can think is by the way you're dealing out guilt and blame, you must feel awfully responsible for something. You're trying to master the art of deflection and you're failing miserably. But the problem is that your take-no-prisoner approach is vicious and totally unfair."

"Yeah, Sugar. What are you hiding? A mountain of guilt? Hum? What little secret is eating away at you that you're willing to destroy a family to protect yourself? You and Buddy always had secrets. Is that what's playing out here?" Grace asked. Then she looked at her mother. "You know, this could have been avoided if you and Dad had smacked this girl years ago."

"Be quiet Grace," Lydia said. "I'll not stand here and listen to my children destroy one another. Tear down everything I've worked so hard to build."

Lydia put her hands in front of her and clasped them together. She stared into Buddy's closet. His clothes still hung from the rod. The floor was piled high with old gym shoes and cleats. She couldn't bear to look anymore. She turned away and looked out the window. "Why, Buddy, why?" she asked of no one.

The room went silent. Nobody moved. The balloon of hope Lydia had worked so hard to fill had deflated and all that was left was a spent family. She tried to move but her feet felt so leaden she was certain she would fall

Finally, Tim broke the silence, and said, "The bottom line is, this isn't going to get us anywhere. We'll never really know why Buddy killed himself."

"There you go again, trying to take the easy way out. Why don't any of you fight to try to find out the truth? Wasn't Buddy worth trying to understand what drove him over the edge, damn it?" Sugar yelled, pounding her fist on the closet door with her "damn it."

"We did, Sugar. We all searched our souls and hearts for answers. And we all came to the same conclusion. It had to have been the accident. He felt responsible for the death of his friends," Sherry said.

"That's the easy way out. Just assuming that was the reason," Sugar said.

Lydia sensed Sugar had a point she was trying to make. She honed in on Sugar. "So why are you taunting us? None of us will ever know what was going on in Buddy's mind because he didn't tell us or leave a note. All we could do is make our best guesses and try to understand. But that doesn't seem to be good enough for you. And I'm not sure why, other than that you must know something that we don't know and you're just waiting for me to get down on my knees and beg you to tell me, which I did over and over right after Buddy's death. Either that or else you're just playing a cruel, cruel game. Now which is it? Do you know why Buddy killed himself or are you just screwing with our minds?"

"Yeah, Sugar, what is it?" Tim asked as he got up off the bed and folded his arms, posing an intimidating gaze at Sugar.

"Quiet, Tim. I'll handle this," Lydia said. "Sugar, what do you know about Buddy's death? If you know something, tell me now so we can finally put his memory to rest. And if you're hiding something from me and don't tell me, I'm telling you, I'll never forgive you. This is your last chance. I will not discuss this again."

Lydia couldn't believe the words she heard coming from her mouth. She'd just told one of her children she would never forgive her. And she knew, as soon as the words came out of her mouth, it was the wrong thing for her to do. She'd backed Sugar into a corner, literally and figuratively, and now all she could do was fear the results.

All eyes were on Sugar. Lydia could see her hands were shaking. Nobody breathed. Then Sugar kicked at the door frame, looked at Lydia and said, "Buddy did leave a note. He left *me* a note."

The room was silent.

"I knew it. I knew it," Grace muttered.

Everyone watched as Lydia walked toward Sugar.

"I'm sorry," Sugar said. "I should have—"

But before Sugar could get the rest of her words out, Lydia slapped her.

"Mom, Mom!" Sugar held her cheek. She looked around at her brothers and sisters, then said, "Mom, Mom."

But she was too late. Lydia had gone to her room and slammed the door.

"Mom, *Mom*," Sugar said, banging on the door. "Let me explain. I need to explain."

She tried opening the door. It was locked.

"Mom," Sugar said, her voice softer yet increasingly more pleading.

"Go away," Lydia said. "All of you please just go away."

Chapter 30

Aftermath

L ydia was certain that if she saw anyone or if someone touched her, she would explode and splatter all over her bedroom. And she didn't care.

She'd left four strangers in the other room. Her own children. People she'd born and raised. But strangers nonetheless.

She took off her apron, threw it in the corner, kicked off her shoes, low heels she'd worn to try to show Grace that she wasn't a total old frump. As she kicked them into the closet she said, "Wearing those was a waste."

Then she threw herself down on the bed and slammed her fist into the pillow. If she punched the pillow one time, she punched it ten.

"All this time Sugar had a letter," she said. "And she never told me. She's let me go on playing back scene after scene in my mind, guessing what happened. And now, after all this time, she steps forward. What kind of demon is my daughter? Oh, God, How could you do this to me?"

Sugar ceased pleading and walked back down the hall past Buddy's room. She looked in and saw Tim standing like he was a soldier at parade rest, Grace leaning over, looking into the mirror, removing lipstick from her teeth and Sherry, seated at the desk, fiddling with the pencil again. She heard them whisper but she couldn't make out what they said, although she was certain they were waiting for her to come back in the room so they could finish her off like lions picking at a hyena's carcass. She knew the interrogation about the contents of Buddy's letter would be swift and brutal. But she had no intention of telling them anything that was in the letter. She knew she'd screwed up everything with her mother and all she wanted to do was run away, just like she'd done when anything in her life had gone bad.

Maybe suffocating myself isn't a bad idea, Lydia thought, as she realized that with the pillow pulled so tightly over her head it was difficult to breathe. She removed the pillow and pounded it. Then she pounded it again. And again.

"Damn you, Sugar! Damn you kids! Damn you, Walter! Damn you, Buddy! Damn you, Rita!" she screamed, her voice throbbing with pain. "And damn you, God!"

She grabbed the pillow she had just punched flat and pulled it to her chest. She stared at the ceiling and looked at it as though she could see straight through to heaven. "Damn all of you. All any of you have done is let me down," she cried in a trembling whisper. "Damn you, Walter, for not being here when I need you. You promised you'd never leave me. And you did. You left me all alone.

"And you, Buddy. I've never said this, but what you did was so unfair. I've tried so hard to rationalize that you were sick, that you were in pain, and that it was some sort of demon that made you kill yourself. But it was so selfish. Look what your death has done to our family. And I asked you over and over to go get help, see a counselor after the accident. You lied to me and said you were fine."

Her tears fell uncontrollably. She had never been this angry. The bedspread where her head lay was soaked from tears that had been dammed up for years. Her mind was in overdrive. She removed the pillow from her chest, then folded her hands as if she was going to pray.

"You know what God? I'm sick of you. I don't know why I bother to pray to you. Habit, I guess. Each morning when I get up, I pray. During the day, I pray. At night you won't let me sleep unless I pray. And for what? For a life spent getting up each day, drinking coffee, talking to a cat, and a person on the television who doesn't even know I exist?

"Is it written somewhere in the Bible that the ratio of sadness to happiness is a hundred to one? Because that's what it seems like. Maybe that's why I'm afraid of happiness, because I don't trust it, and I don't trust you. I know if I am happy about something, you'll come and take something else away.

"Tell me, God, why do you give us families and not allow us to find happiness in them? I was brought up to believe you were a loving and merciful God, that you want *us* to love and be good to each other. But where is *your* love? I don't see it. I don't feel it. I really don't. Where is your love and compassion for the people I deliver meals to and those in the nursing home who you've crippled with illness and disease? Do you get a kick out of seeing people suffer? It must be a game you call, 'Let's see how sick I can make people before I let them die.' Can you tell me, God, where this love of yours is when you have one of my children find their brother hanging from a rafter in our garage? What kind of God would make a child experience that? What kind of God makes a child, who believes in you, feel so helpless that he takes his own life? And even with that, God, I tried to understand. I listened to people say, 'It's God's will,' and 'Now he's at peace,' and all that other bullshit.

"The only thing I think I've ever really wanted in my life was to have a loving family. Watch my children grow and become adults. Have them come to my home, enjoy each other's company and laugh and solve our problems together. Be friends now and after I'm gone. But no, you couldn't let that happen. Then you make me witness my family throwing shards of glass at each other.

"The bottom line is I'm not sure you really exist. And what's more, I don't even care. The way I see it is I would have been better off all these years making a pact with the devil. At least I'd have known who and what I was dealing with."

Lydia was so into her rage that she didn't hear what was going on in the other rooms. She didn't see Sugar walk out of her room, down the stairs, and out the door. She didn't hear the other kids decide it was best if they left her alone. She was unaware that Tim and Sherry both had to leave to get back home; Tim to his complaining wife and Sherry to her sick son.

She didn't hear Grace clear the table off, put the food away or do the dishes and she didn't get up to cover herself even though her body had turned cold.

Chapter 31

Holy Smokes, Cat

"What time is it?" Lydia asked aloud when she opened her eyes. It took a moment to focus because her eyes were matted and swollen. She looked at the clock. A quarter to six. She yawned and stretched and rolled over to her side and noticed light coming from behind the shade. Her tongue felt thick, like she had dragged it on the carpet.

The house was quiet and its temperament calm.

She'd fallen asleep denouncing God, her family, and her life, but instead of waking up in a continued state of angst and regret, she was surprisingly composed and clear-headed. Which surprised her greatly.

Normally, an episode like she had just experienced would have sent her into a tailspin. She would have second-guessed everything she had done and said. *Why did I even have this brunch? Should I have had Sugar come home from New York?* She would have beaten herself up for slapping Sugar. And she wouldn't have simply focused on what happened today. She would have gone back and questioned her judgment all through the years.

But this time the urge to do that was gone. *It was as it was,* she said to herself.

She was stunned she didn't feel guilty about talking to God the way she did. As she railed against Him, she had this underlying suspicion that she would be very sorry she talked to Him as she did it, but that hadn't occurred, either.

She thought about Sugar's revelation. She'd been so angry when she found out that indeed, Sugar had a note from Buddy that might have answered the questions she'd asked herself all of these years, but now, after the shock had worn off, she thought about the burden Sugar had been under. Yes, she was still angry with Sugar, but until she found out why Sugar withheld this information for so long, she'd try to reserve judgment.

Although Lydia had cleared the air with God, and put her judgment about Sugar and Buddy's letter on hold, she knew the Calypso family was more unsettled than ever. But even so, what was finally clear to her was that she had spent most of her life living for or through other people's lives. But why? And for what?

Growing up, she had lived to please her parents, especially her father, who'd denied that he was demanding, but was. Then, without missing a year, she'd gone straight into Walter's life, and supported him through his military years and school and his career. After the children came, she lived for and through them. Her goal was to build a family that Norman Rockwell would have given his eyeteeth to paint.

Eventually, she had lived through Rita, too. Vicariously, maybe, but still, her view of the world was through Rita's eyes and not her own.

Then after Buddy died, she'd believed it was her destiny to give herself over to God, let him have responsibility for her life. If things went well, it was divine providence. If things didn't go well, that, too, was God's will. After what she'd been through, it seemed like the right thing to do. She was exhausted from trying to make sense of Buddy's death. But deep inside, she knew she was also looking for an easy way out. Life was hard. And if the God was responsible for her life, wouldn't that take some of the burden, the responsibility, off her?

But that was before today. That was before she saw what she'd seen, what she'd heard, and what she'd felt. If God was angry at her, so be it. She told herself that if He was any God at all, He'd understand. Perhaps God had even given her that raging voice, a voice that finally spoke what she was feeling and thinking. And maybe the reason she was able to wake up without feeling awful about what she'd said to God was that she had the sense that He was relieved that she was finally going to accept responsibility for her own life and not place all that burden on Him.

She got off the bed. It pleased her that she wasn't weeping and crying for Walter or Buddy or Sugar or Grace or pleading with Rita to come back into her life. Instead, she thought about herself. What did she feel like doing now? Tonight? Tomorrow? With the rest of her life?

"Well, first," she said, "I need to get something to eat."

Downstairs, Lydia saw that the dishes had been done; the china and crystal had been laid in rows next to the silverware on the dining room table. The kitchen counters were clear of leftovers. Even the floor was swept. On the table was a note. Actually, she noticed it was a piece of her stationary that was addressed to her. A flash of trepidation seared her stomach, but then she decided she wouldn't succumb to that.

But she didn't open the letter right away. Instead, she made herself two pieces of toast, got out the butter and jam, poured a glass of juice, sat down, and ate.

She wiped her hands on a napkin to remove any grease and then she opened the letter.

Dear Mom,

I'm sorry. I'm so very sorry. I know I've been putting you through a lot. I've been unfair and selfish. To say I didn't realize I was acting like I have been wouldn't be true. I know I've been a thorn. And what you said earlier today was right, my problem isn't with you, it's with my life. Right now I'm not sure which end is up. I don't know who I am, where I really come from (and please don't take offense at that and note that I didn't say I didn't know who my real mother is). I mean I don't really know where and who I come from, both genetically and culturally speaking.

And although I don't want to go into it right now, I think my marriage isn't what I thought it was and I don't know what to do. I feel betrayed and trapped.

Please don't let what was said today by Sugar, me, Tim, or Sherry make you feel like you have failed. You haven't. We have. And hopefully time and understanding will help us work at building the family you want us to be.

I've done my best to try to clean up the mess, at least the physical one. I double-wrapped most of the leftovers. I did throw the egg casserole out because it, to be honest, was quite dry. But don't blame yourself on that either. You were trying to sort me out.

I just want you to know that I do love you and you are the best mother a child (adopted or not) could have. And if you would like me to help you go through the closets, just let me know.

Love always,
Your daughter, Grace

Lydia was surprised at her reaction to Grace's letter. Instead of being absorbed in Grace's praise for her as a mother, she thought, *Isn't that funny, she didn't mention a thing about Buddy's letter.*

She walked into the living room and checked to see if there were any coals still burning. She took the poker and pushed some charred logs. A slight orange cast appeared. She took a piece of newspaper that had been on the floor, rolled it up like she had seen Walter and Tim do, and placed it under the grate and blew. A puff of smoke billowed. She blew again and inserted another rolled paper and blew yet again. Poof. An orange flame appeared. She adjusted the logs and added a couple of smaller pieces of wood and then sat down in the wing chair and put her feet on the coffee table.

She worked on thinking about nothing. She closed her eyes and tried to envision a single flame and concentrate on it. No past, no future, no present. Just peace. That was all she was looking for.

She breathed long and slow, inhaling deeply through her nose and exhaling through her open mouth.

Eventually, the flame in her mind's eye faded, as did the fire. She got up and closed the glass fireplace doors and decided to go upstairs. She had work to do. She needed to get her own life. And the first step on her new journey would be to stop living on the surface, going through the motions. In order to move on to the future and learn to live in the here and now, she had to deal with the past. And where would she find much of her past? She knew. But this time, when she opened those closet doors, it wasn't going to be to placate a daughter or a real estate agent. She was going to do it for herself.

It dawned on her as she was going upstairs that she hadn't seen or heard Sugar since she got up. Lydia couldn't imagine Sugar was still here. She probably went to stay with one of her friends, which was just as well, Lydia thought, because she was not ready to see her.

As she walked by Sugar's closed bedroom door, Lydia noticed an envelope was taped to it. "Mom," it said on it. "Please read." The irony of receiving two letters in a matter of minutes when the most important letter had not been mentioned for seven years did not go unnoticed by Lydia.

She removed the envelope and then opened the door to Sugar's room. It was empty. Sugar's suitcases were gone and the bed was made. "Boy, she did feel guilty," Lydia said. "That girl's never made her bed a day in her life."

She tucked the envelope in her pocket and walked into her room. There hadn't been a day that had gone by since Buddy's death that she didn't ask "Why?," but now that there was a possibility she could learn the answer to that question, she wasn't sure if she wanted to know. She moved a stack of magazines and books from the floral chaise and sat down. She rubbed her finger across the word, "Mom."

"That's a strange word," she said. "I probably should have looked it up in the dictionary years ago, before I had kids."

She sat listening to silence, watching her stomach rise and fall with every breath she took. The she put the letter back in her pocket.

Chapter 32

Spice Up Your Life

If there was anything positive that had come out of the family fiasco, it was that Lydia had learned she couldn't count on others to sort out her life, heal her past, or make plans for her the future. She'd have to do it.

"If there was an award for the Slow Learners of Life, I'd win it," Lydia said as she sat in the chaise deciding what she wanted to do with her future, which she decided was now.

She closed her eyes and pictured herself standing over the Cliffs of Moher, gazing out into the ocean. Then she thought of herself sitting in a pub listening to traditional Irish music and then wowing the locals with her magnificent rendition of "Danny Boy." She laughed. It had been so long since she'd had dreams that weren't threaded with worry. Then out of the blue she said, "Ah-ha."

A marathon, that's what she'd have, an overnight cleaning marathon. Instead of a morbid reenactment of her life, she'd celebrate what she found. In order to do this, she knew she'd have to set some ground rules for herself. She'd read an article in a magazine that said that if you didn't use a particular item in a year, you should get rid of it. She could do that. But what if she *loved* an item? And what if that item had memories? Could she get rid of it? Should she get rid of it?

She questioned whether she should give what she didn't want to the Goodwill or the Vietnam Vets or the Salvation Army. Should she put the stuff in garbage bags or plastic tubs? Should she sort the stuff by size or just place it in heaps?

"One step at a time," she said.

There were three closets that she knew would be the most emotionally draining; hers, Walter's, then Buddy's. She decided to tackle her own closet first.

"Let's go Binky, you've got to help, too," she said, as she opened her closet door. It was eight in the evening and she wasn't going to stop until she was finished. "I'll pull an all-nighter like I did in college."

She opened the top of the small boombox she had in her room and placed a CD of Celtic music in it. She loved the flutes. "This will be great," she said to Binky just before she opened the door to her closet.

"Holy smokes, cat," she said, taking a gander inside. Stuff was everywhere. She rumpled her face like an old shirt. For a split second she thought it might be easier to close the closet door and not clean out her life, but then she pulled her shoulders back, sucked her chin into her chest, and walked in. "I've got to do it."

She'd also read that it was best to start cleaning from the top, which was fine, but the floor had so much junk on it she decided to begin there.

She kicked some clothes out of the way and cleared herself a place to stand. She bent over and picked up some scattered clothes: a turquoise jogging suit, gray sweatpants, a sweater with elves on it, (whose is this?), a couple pair of satin-like underpants, a handful of yellow silk lilies, and a tambourine. She banged the tambourine against her hip. "This must be from my Mamas and Papas era.

"Laundry, laundry, Goodwill, laundry, no, I'm going to throw these out, Bink," she said, referring to the boxy underpants. "What do you think? Should I make a flower arrangement? No, I want real flowers," she said, tossing the fake flowers out of the closet. "And I've got to save this tambourine."

She looked in the corner of her closet and saw a tall stack. "Records," she said, "the dinosaurs of the music industry."

She kicked a box out of the way and moved toward the records. She sat on the floor beneath clothes that hung like wave-mitter curtains at a car wash. She and Walter had bought most of the albums at garage sales. Of course there were Johnny Mathis, Nat King Cole, Dean Martin, Frank Sinatra, Ella, (Walter had bought Ella during his jazz phase, a period Lydia couldn't whatsoever understand his attraction to), several Beatles records and the Monkees. "Hey, hey," she said picking up the Monkees record. "I can't believe I used to be in love with Mickey Dolenz." Then she spied a Herman's Hermits record. "And Herman, too. Bink, I was a real groupie."

She pulled the Nat King Cole album out of the stack and took the record out of the album cover. It was well worn. She ran her finger very lightly along the grooves of the record, remembering how she and Walter used to try to dance to "Unforgettable." And that's what dancing with Walter was, unforgettable. Not that he was good, but because he had no rhythm and two left feet. Six weeks worth of lessons at Arthur Murray hadn't helped one bit.

"I can't throw these away," she said, but she knew she didn't have a record player. But to throw away memories like that, hum. Then she remembered Tim collected old records. "Guess what, Timmy Boy," she said, "it's your lucky day."

She got up off the floor, tried not to tangle her head in the clothes that hung from the rods, picked up the heavy stack of records and moved them out of the closet and into a pile she now designated as Tim's.

She grabbed other stuff, whether it was on the floor, hanging from a rod, or on the shelf above. Standing on a stool she had long ago painted with a picture of a toad (the reason why, she couldn't remember), she reached onto the shelf and pulled down a handful of stuff.

"Oh, my, gosh," she said, sifting through the soft pile of garments and finding a girdle. A girdle! Then another girdle. This one even had those doohickeys that attached nylons. She ran her hand along the front panel. It was like a steel wall. "I can't believe I used to wear these. How'd I breathe?" Although it was in reasonably good shape, she couldn't take this to Goodwill. "Heck, Bink, this belongs in the Smithsonian, in the torture section."

She moved along at a much better clip than she thought she would. Pink dress, size fourteen? Gone. Pumpkin-colored corduroy jumper, size sixteen? Out of here. Bright green sweater with the shamrock on it she had bought because it was only $2.59? What was I thinking? A pair of leopard-print pants, size ten? Was I delusional?

Shoe after shoe she threw out of the closet; blue, pointed-toe shoes that had been custom-dyed to match the dress she wore to Tim's wedding. She tossed a pair of hiking boots she'd bought because her New Year's resolution that year was to walk across Ohio during her summer vacation (the best laid plans—she'd changed her mind about the hike because the boots gave her a blister), and three single shoes whose mates had been lost years ago. But she had saved the mate-less shoes just in case the shoe fairy decided to bring their companions back during the middle of the night.

She sorted yarn of various colors; crimson red, tangerine orange, daffodil yellow, royal blue. "Maybe I'll knit some potholders." Then partway through rolling the old yard into balls, she decided that yes, she might make some potholders, but no, she wasn't going to use this old yarn. So she threw an armful of the dusty yarn on the pile of things she would take to the nursing home. The arts-and-crafts lady was always begging for things like yarn and empty milk cartons. A half-finished needlepoint piece? Never again, hurts the eyes.

"So *here's* that scarf," she said, referring to a cream-color knitted scarf and hat set she swore she'd bought Sherry for Christmas the year before last. She put that in a "Sherry" pile she started.

"Kid's School Papers," the box said. It was a huge box. She tugged and moved it to the center of the floor and sat on the toad stool. "That's why I decorated it with a toad, so it would be a toad stool. I should go through all this and sort it into piles and give it to the kids."

She couldn't remember why she hadn't had Walter get rid of this box along with the other boxes of school stuff.

"Dear Mommy," she read. "We had to write our first leter today so I decided to right to you. Luv Buddy."

Her heart responded by beating more quickly. "Buddy," she said softly. She held the paper for a moment and then carefully laid it in a pile next to her. "Buddy's pile," she said. Then she moved on. She knew if she stopped now and let her mind do what it wanted to do, she would never move forward, never get these closets clean and her life in order.

She picked up a faded piece of red construction paper that had a Santa, whose beard was made of cotton balls and had a bubble coming from his open mouth, drawn in black pencil that said, Ho, Ho, Ho. "I love Santa," someone had printed. Whose was this? Tim's? Grace's? "I remember it was Grace's," Lydia said. The clue that told her whose picture this was was the small drawing of a sled in the lower right-hand corner. That's all Grace had said she wanted for Christmas that year. Lydia felt a pang of regret when she remembered that she had forgotten, forgotten that Grace had asked for a sled.

There was a stack of Sherry's report cards. She opened one, then another. Most of the grades were average, which she remembered Sherry always being embarrassed about. Sherry knew Grace got A's and Tim got B's. Never mind that Buddy and Sugar got D's and occasionally F's. The comments from the teacher were good, though, and Lydia remembered she had pointed them out to Sherry. "Sherry's a delightful girl to have in class," Mrs. Woliver said each quarter. Miss Henderson said, "If I ever have a daughter, I would like her to be just like Sherry." But Lydia knew those compliments didn't make Sherry forget that Grace's and Tim's grades were better than hers.

"You know, Bink, Memory Lane is a long and winding road," she said as she stood and carried the just-emptied box out of the closet.

Along the back wall stood a pile of fabric. Bundles of fleece, denim, corduroy, wool, and linen. All from the sewing years. On top of the pile of fabric was a bag full of patterns. She quickly rummaged through the bag. "Nursing home," she said. She put her arms around the large stack of fabric, hoisted it up, and tried to open and put it in a garbage bag. "I need three hands," she said.

She walked back to the rear of the closet. Under where the fabric had been was a box. It looked like a plain shoe box.

She grabbed the box, put it on her lap and opened it. "Oh, my word," she said, her face turning redder than the Santa Claus felt she just threw out. Inside the box was a vibrator. A big, pink vibrator called the Twist and Shout. She'd forgotten all about it. She picked up the vibrator as if her thumb and pointer-finger were tweezers. She laughed as she remembered where she got it.

It was at Georgia Huddleston's Spice Up Your Life party. She'd told Walter she was invited to a Pampered Chef get together because she didn't want to have to explain what a Spice Up Your Life Party was.

"I can't come to a party like that," she said to Georgia, the party hostess. "What would it look like if the party was busted by the cops and a teacher was found in attendance?"

"Oh, for crying out loud, Lydia, we're not doing heroin. We're just having a little fun. And you are over twenty-one, aren't you?"

"Very funny."

"Besides, other teachers are coming."

"You're kidding. Who?"

"Just come and find out."

Lydia was dying to go. It had been a long time since anyone said sex and fun in the same sentence. It wasn't that she thought a sex toy could or would spice up her and Walter's sex life. "It is what it is," she used to say to herself.

But those days when she thought about sex, she wasn't thinking about Walter. She thought about Carl Goodstock, a divorced biology teacher ten years her junior, who actually looked at her when they talked, laughed when she told a joke, and opened doors for her.

Although she felt guilty, it was, to this point, only an affair of the mind. Lydia spent a lot of time dreaming about Carl. They ate lunch together. When she needed help moving desks in her classroom, he volunteered. When she mentioned she had a problem student she wasn't sure how to handle, he told her he'd think about a good way to handle the situation. And he did.

One day when Lydia stayed late to grade papers, Carl stayed late, too. It was dark by the time they left.

Carl said, "May I walk you to your car?" She had said yes.

Normally, she would have walked briskly to her car, step, step, step, there. But this time she walked as though they were on a stroll in a park.

When she was with Carl, all of her senses became acute. She heard each step he took. She smelled the scent of the wintergreen breath mints she'd noticed he repeatedly put in his mouth when he was talking to her. If their hands touched due to coincidence, a shiver of excitement ran up her spine like she had touched an electric switch while standing in water. And when she looked at him she saw life.

When they reached her car she fumbled with her keys until he calmly took them from her hand, which caused her to look at him instead of the car. Instead of opening the door immediately, Carl lifted her chin and bent down and kissed her as passionately as she'd ever been kissed.

It was the first kiss she'd received from another man in almost thirty years.

The next day was Georgia's party.

"I can't believe the size of that thing," Rita said. "It reminds me of Raoul."

Everyone laughed.

Lydia couldn't believe how many teachers bought more than one item. Carolyn Joseph, the high school music teacher, bought two kinds of vibrators and three pair of crotchless undies.

Throughout the evening, Lydia kept thinking about Carl's kiss. Suddenly she blurted out, "Do these things come in unmarked wrappers?"

"Of course," Georgia said.

Paula B., (she never gave out her last name), the representative from Spice Up Your Life, brought up the subject of the "Big O," which was not once that night called an orgasm. "Has anyone here not had a "Big O?"

The women got their best poker faces on, none going to say aloud whether they had or had not ever had the "Big O."

"It's no sin not to have had one," Paula said. "Everyone does know what the "Big O" is, don't you?"

"No," Rita, said, calling the woman's bluff, "can you explain to us what it is?"

Paula cleared her throat then rummaged through her clipboard. "The "Big O," according to the dictionary, is 'intense or paroxysmal excitement; especially: an explosive discharge of neuromuscular tensions at the height of sexual arousal that is usually accompanied by the ejaculation of semen in the male and by vaginal contractions in the female.'"

"To hear it put like that, I'm not sure I want one," someone in the group said. Everyone laughed.

Paula told the group about some products that were available to help women achieve "a more intense 'Big O.'"

The discussion moved along to the topic of "What is an affair, and is it an affair if you're not having sex?"

Lydia said nothing but was a rapt listener.

"Of course you can have an affair without having sex," Carmine, another teacher said. "There are emotional affairs. And I think those are an even worse betrayal."

"That's a bunch of hogwash," Rita chimed in, "If there's no sex, there's no affair. The end. It's called a friendship."

"But what if the people tell each other things they don't tell their spouses? Is that an affair?" Carmine asked.

"Nope," Rita said.

"Yep, it is," Elizabeth said, one of Georgia's neighbors.

"Well, which would you rather have your husband had: an emotional or a physical affair?" Carmine asked.

"Neither. I'd kill him if he had either," Marnie said.

"I wish my husband would have an affair," Georgia said, causing heads to turn. "Maybe he'd learn something."

"Just send him to a prostitute then," Rita said.

"How about a sex therapist?" someone else suggested.

"Or just get a video," Paula said, obviously glad someone had given her the perfect segue into talking about another product she sold. "There's a bunch of videos in the catalog. Here's one. *Didi Does Denver*, and another called *Getting Rid of Frigidity Forever*."

"What do you think, Lydia?" Rita asked. "Which do you think would be the worst betrayal, if Walter had an emotional or physical affair?"

At first Lydia acted like she didn't hear what Rita had asked. The question made her feel like she was pinned between two cars that had smashed together. Of all the things she had told Rita during their friendship, she hadn't been able to tell her about Walter's betrayal, which had happened nearly ten years earlier.

Lydia had been doing the laundry as she always had, going through Walter's pockets, removing coins, receipts, sticks of gum, Rolaids. She hadn't noticed anything out of the ordinary on his pants, but she did notice something different about his shirts. For weeks she wondered what that difference was, and then she figured it out.

Well, she didn't, Grace did. Lydia had asked Grace to run upstairs and get a load of clothes and take them down to the basement so she could run them through the wash. She thought about asking Sugar to do it because she was already upstairs and could have easily brought the clothes down, but Lydia didn't want a confrontation, which is what happened every time she asked Sugar to do something.

"Why can't Sugar bring them when she comes down?" Grace asked as she sat at the kitchen table eating a Pop Tart.

"It's just easier if you do it," Lydia said.

"Easier for you, maybe."

"Grace, watch your mouth."

"Why don't you ever tell Sugar to watch hers?" Grace asked, not in a nasty way but as an honest-to-goodness question.

"It's too hard to explain," Lydia said, but then she quickly added, "I do tell her to watch hers."

Grace finished her Pop Tart and went upstairs, taking two and three at a time. On her way back down, while going through the kitchen with her arms full of Walter's dirty shirts, she walked by her mother, who was standing at the kitchen sink, and said, "When did Dad start wearing Tabu?"

Lydia dropped the paring knife she was using to cut apple slices. "Let me have those," she said to Grace. "I'll take them downstairs."

"Gladly," Grace replied, "I've got to get to school."

At first Walter denied the affair, but then in a bout of guilt he broke down and confessed, saying, "It didn't mean anything. It was just physical."

"But it means something to me," Lydia had said, rage and sadness filling her face.

The flowers Walter sent every week for the next two months were lovely, but instead of making her feel better, they were a constant reminder of his betrayal.

"Lydia, you didn't answer the question," Rita said, now many eyes cast in her direction. "Which would bother you—?"

Then seeing the look on her best friend's face, Rita backed off.

By now the proceedings had fallen into cackles and calls for the pineapple upside-down cake to be served. But the conversation had gotten Lydia thinking. Was her infatuation with Carl one of real interest or some sort of Freudian revenge? Maybe he filled a need that wasn't being met.

On the way home from the party, Lydia, with John Lennon's "Imagine" playing on the radio, decided her flirtation with Carl was wrong and against her moral code. And so she ended the affair before it began.

By two in the morning she had her closet pretty well organized *and* she still had her wits about her. Both were pleasant surprises.

Feeling herself fade, she said, "I need some caffeine." She walked downstairs to get some cola, but when she opened the fridge she saw champagne. Grabbing a flute from the dining table, she popped out the cork and poured away. She held her glass up in the air and made a toast.

"To life," she said as she tapped her glass on the refrigerator door. Then she took the bottle and went back upstairs.

She placed her champagne flute and the bottle on her end table and lay on her stomach across her now cluttered bed. Walter's side was completely covered with stacks of books, clothes, and a bag of orange-can-sized hair curlers. She took one of the yearbooks she'd put on the bed and opened it. The book's spine cracked like a fresh-cooked lobster, the pages stuck together like a long married couple reluctant to separate. Lydia gingerly fanned the pages apart. The book opened to the Men's Varsity Basketball team page. Lydia laughed. "Look at how short their uniforms were," she said to Binky, who was asleep on top of a pile of her old jeans.

There's Bobby Hoolihan, Chester Cheese, whose nickname was Cheddar Cheese, and Duncan Nuxall. "Duncan Nuxall," she said, rubbing her finger up to his face. "I wonder where he is now."

Duncan Nuxall was her first steady boyfriend. He'd given her his class ring (she'd wrapped it with dental floss that she'd painted with nail polish), his varsity letter jacket, and her first passion mark. He was also the only other boy beside Walter to say, "I love you."

Whether it was the champagne or thinking about Duncan and some of the funny stuff they had done, Lydia was laughing. She rolled her eyes, shook her head, then closed the book. She thought for a second about beginning to attack Walter's closet, but when she stood up, the effects of the champagne made themselves clear. So instead of continuing on, she lay down on the bed and fell instantly asleep.

Anybody Home?

"Mom? Mom?" Grace yelled from the bottom of the stairs. "Mom?"

There was no answer. The cuckoo struck eight times as Tim and Grace came into the house.

"Should we go upstairs and see if she's in her room?" Grace asked. They had come in separate cars because if they found everything was okay, he would go right to work.

"Mom," Tim yelled. "Are you there?" he said, as he slowly opened the door to her bedroom. He and Grace were tentative in their approach.

Tim turned the overhead fan off. Grace opened the shades. Lydia moaned.

"Are you alive?" Tim asked.

Lydia opened her eyes and rolled over. Opening her mouth slowly as if it might be full of terrycloth, she said, "What time is it? Heck, what day is it?"

"She *is* alive," Tim said facetiously to Grace.

"I suppose you could call it alive," Grace said, nodding her head toward the empty champagne bottle lying next to her mother on the bed.

Lydia got up on her elbows. "Ugh, my head hurts."

"I imagine it does," Tim said, giving her a hand so she could sit up.

"Did someone say what time it was? What day is it?"

"It's eight, Monday morning," Grace said as she surveyed the room. "Did a hurricane come through here last night or what?"

"What? You don't know a little closet cleaning when you see it?" Lydia joked.

"I'm just hoping there aren't any bodies under all that," Tim said, looking at a huge pile of clothes heaped in a pile in the corner. "Do you want some coffee? I'll go make some and then I'd better get going."

"What are you two doing here anyway? You should be at work," Lydia said, looking at Tim. "And where are the kids?" she asked, eyes trying to focus on Grace.

Ignoring her question, Grace said, "I tried calling all night, up until midnight and you didn't answer. Tim and Sherry tried calling, too, and you didn't answer or call back." Grace sounded like a perturbed mother.

"Oh, I turned the phone ringer to zero rings and sent everyone to the recorder. It was between that and sending everyone to... oh, never mind. As you can see, I'm perfectly fine."

"You scared us to death. I thought maybe you'd gone to bed early but then you didn't answer this morning, either, so I called Tim. My next call was going to be to the police."

Lydia stood up and made a strange horse-like sound.

"What was that?" Tim asked.

"I was clearing my throat," Lydia said. "I feel honored that the rescue committee has showed up but since it's obvious I am fine, Tim, you should get off to work and Grace, you should go back home to your kids. A cup of coffee and a few aspirin and I'll be good as new."

Tim looked at Grace and then his mother. "You sure it's okay if I leave? I've got a meeting and I'm going to be late as it is."

"Please, go. I don't want you missing your work," his mother said. "And you can go, too, Grace. No need to worry about me. As you can see, I'm moving on."

"But I want to talk to you," Grace said. "There are some things I think we need to clear up."

"Please, Grace, you don't need to stay on my account."

"But I want to stay. I need to stay," Grace said in rebuttal.

"Well, if you two don't mind, while you figure out who's staying and who's going, I'm going to bid you both *adieu*," Tim said. He gave Lydia a kiss on the cheek and then put his arms around her and gave her an unexpected hug. "You look like hell," he said as he walked out the door, laughing.

"I'm absolutely disgusting," Lydia said. "At least let me wash my face and brush my teeth."

Grace said, "Go ahead and take a shower. I'm in no hurry. I'll go brew a pot of coffee. I'll bring our cups upstairs when they're ready."

"Don't you want to sit downstairs at the table? This place is, well, you see what it looks like."

"Nah. I'd rather come up here. Some of this stuff looks intriguing. Besides, I brought the paper in so I'll take a look at that."

"Suit yourself," Lydia said. "I'm going to get cleaned up."

Lydia was confused by Grace's newfound charm and longing to please. *Is this the same Grace who was so morose and contrary two days ago, or am I having a bad reaction to the champagne?* she thought as she went into the bathroom and shut the door.

Grace made herself at home. She brewed a pot of coffee, unwrapped the poppy seed roll from yesterday, got two mugs down from the cupboard and placed everything on the creamy lemon-colored wood tray she found leaning between the pantry and the refrigerator. She remembered the tray. It was the same one her mother used to bring hot tea and honey on when she was sick. She needed to get a tray like that for when her children were sick. Right now she just used a small floral enamel tray she kept on top of the card table.

She carried the goodies and a newspaper upstairs and into her mother's room. It took some doing but she eventually found a place to set the tray. She took a sip of her coffee and a bite of poppy seed roll. My, did the slice of roll taste good. She hadn't had a slice of anything like that in so long. "So what if it's not good for me?" she asked the air.

"What did you say?" Lydia yelled from the bathroom. She had just turned the shower water off.

"Nothing really. I just said this poppy seed roll tastes good. That's all."

"Oh. Glad you like it," Lydia yelled back.

With her hair up in a towel, Lydia walked out of the bathroom. She sensed the mood was peaceful and perhaps now would be a good time to ask her something that had been on her mind. "Grace, why did you have a Realtor come to my house even though you knew I didn't want you to?"

"Because I thought it was time for you to move on and you weren't listening to me. And I knew Bitsy would help you. She's good at what she does."

"In other words, you were trying to run my life for me because you thought, or you still think, I'm not doing a good job of running my life myself?"

"There you go again," Grace said, adding, "You're so hostile to me anymore."

"Why do you think I'm being hostile just because I ask a question?"

"It's the way you ask it. It's so, so accusatory."

"Grace, lately, if I ask you what time it is, or what the weather is outside, you think *that* is accusatory."

"You're exaggerating."

"No, I'm not. It's like nothing I say is right with you. I say the sun is out, you'll argue that it's overcast. Remember a couple of weeks ago when we were eating lunch and I said 'I'm not hungry,' and you said, 'Yes, you are,' like I didn't even know how to read my own stomach."

Neither said anything. Eventually Lydia turned and switched on the hair dryer.

Grace put the paper down, took another sip of coffee and got up and walked across the room to one of the piles of things that had been tossed out of the closet.

"When did you do this?" Grace asked, raising her voice over the high-pitched sound of the hair dryer.

"Last night," Lydia said, her voice straining over the hairdryer.

Grace saw a pile of stuff that had a piece of paper with her name on it. Leaning against her pile were a few scattered boxes.

"Is this stuff for me?" she asked.

"If it has your name on it, it is," Lydia yelled,.

Grace noticed a pile of papers of various sizes and shapes. She picked up part of the stack.

Lydia switched the hairdryer to low speed.

"I can't believe you saved all this," Grace called out. "These are my school papers from the beginning of time. Oh, my gosh, did I write this?" Grace squealed, looking at a four-line poem written in big letters on a piece of wide-lined paper. She read it aloud. "Roses are Red, Grass is Green, Did someone Eat, My Jellybean? Wasn't I just the poet of all time? Elizabeth Barrett Browning, in the making." She laughed.

"Actually, I thought it was pretty good."

"Oh, Mom, you thought everything I did was good."

"Well, was that wrong of me?"

This could be the opening Grace had been waiting for or at least an opportunity for her to segue into what she really wanted to talk about.

"Well, was it?" Lydia repeated. She stopped brushing her hair. She put the brush on the table and shut off the hair dryer and looked at Grace. She was about to say never mind when it dawned on her she was going down a road she didn't want to take. If there was anything she had learned after Saturday, it was that she should choose the roads she traveled with her kids more carefully.

"I don't think it was wrong, but it was perhaps naïve," Grace said. "And maybe that approach wasn't healthy."

Now Lydia wished she hadn't asked at all. She was sick of analyzing and rehashing her parenting skills. "Well," she said, her voice becoming more terse, "should I have said 'What you wrote was crap,' or 'My gosh, how could you make such a lousy drawing?' or 'Boy, you sure are awful at baseball or dance or whatever?'"

"Here we go again. You're taking what I said the wrong way. You always do."

"Yes, here we go again, everything's my fault."

"Mom, I didn't say that."

"Yes, you did. If not with words then by inference."

"The 'inference' is coming from you, not me. All I was saying is that maybe it would have been better if you would have given us a more honest assessment of our abilities than building us up to believe we were better than we actually were. That's all I'm saying."

"As far as I was concerned those *were* honest assessments. They were what I saw."

"Or what you wanted to see? The problem for me is I think I carried that blind optimism far into my life and marriage." Her expression melted like the cheese on a grilled sandwich. "I don't want to blow this by making it sound like I'm blaming you, but Mom, I'm so confused. That's what I wanted to talk to you about. Not you, or what you did wrong or right as a parent but what's gone wrong in my marriage and... in my life." Tears welled in the outside corner of her eyes.

Lydia, for a split second, turned whiter than the bleached muslin curtains in her room, but then regained her color as she went into mother mode. She wasn't used to seeing Grace cry.

"What's going on in your marriage?" Lydia asked, walking over to Grace, putting her hand on her shoulder, and then sitting on the edge of the bed. Grace had cleared herself a spot and was sitting on the floor.

Lydia had a vague idea of what could be wrong. When Grace was in the hospital she saw some of what she believed had to be Guy's true colors come out. But she didn't want to lead this conversation. That was up to Grace, because if she accidentally misspoke, seemed intrusive or judgmental, she knew her daughter would shut down and they'd never get to the bottom of what was going on. So she waited for Grace to speak.

Grace picked up a long scarf that was on the floor. She twisted it through her fingers, undid it, and wrapped it around her wrist, and then looked up at her mother. "Here goes," she said under her breath. "It's Guy," she said, her voice thin and unsure. "I'm not sure if he's the same man I married and didn't know who he was or if he's changed. Everything's a blur."

Lydia nodded slightly but remained silent.

"I think I've been blind to a lot of things." Grace scrunched her face and pulled her eyebrows together like a gathered skirt. "I think he's been having an affair. No, I think he's been having affairs. Plural. And he's so erratic nowadays. One minute he says he loves me and can't live without me and the next minute he calls me names and tells me he hates me. I feel like I'm on a roller coaster. And when I asked him if he was having an affair he said no and I believed him because I wanted to and I couldn't face the rejection of being discarded again. But he makes me feel so worthless and ugly."

The tears fell readily, but she wasn't sobbing. It seemed to Lydia she had still not gotten to the bottom of what was hurting her. And she was right.

"When I found out I was pregnant he wanted me to have an abortion. An abortion. He said I was incapable of handling any more kids and that if I had the baby, as far as he was concerned, he would consider the child a bastard. I didn't know what to do. Mom, I couldn't bring myself to have an abortion but I was so afraid to have the baby that I punched myself in the stomach and threw myself down the basement stairs trying to get rid of it and I feel so horrible and guilty and I know I caused my miscarriage. And why? Why did I do it?"

"You did it for survival, Grace. You survived the only way you knew how." Lydia wanted to say, "I wish you would have come to me," but she didn't want to add a layer of guilt to how Grace already felt.

"But I killed my baby," she sobbed.

Lydia got up from the bed and sat on the floor next to her daughter and embraced her. Grace's tears soaked Lydia's robe. Grace cried openly and loudly. Lydia stifled her own sniffles. "No, you didn't. If you had had a healthy pregnancy, neither of those events would have caused a miscarriage." She'd read articles about women who were pregnant who'd suffered violent, traumatic experiences yet still maintained a pregnancy, but now seemed hardly the time to mention that.

"You don't know that for sure."

"And you don't know for sure that you caused the miscarriage."

Lydia's mind was working as fast as it would be if she were trying to escape a burning building. "You probably don't know this because you were young and besides, Daddy and I never discussed this kind of thing with you kids, but I had two miscarriages. One at six weeks, about the same time you had your miscarriage, and another at ten weeks. The doctor explained to me then that miscarriages are God's way of taking care of fetuses that don't develop properly."

"I had no idea you had miscarriages," Grace said, her sobs becoming quieter.

"As I said, we didn't tell you kids about it. We just didn't think it was something you'd understand or needed to worry about."

Lydia handed Grace a couple of tissues she'd grabbed from Walter's bed stand.

"But I know *I* had the miscarriage because I prayed for it. I got what I prayed for and now I'm being punished by God."

"That's not how God works."

"How do you know?"

"Because I've dealt with that fellow a lot longer than you have. And I know that just because you ask Him for something doesn't mean He's going to give you what you want. He has His own plans."

"Obviously the pregnancy wasn't in Guy's plans. He blamed me."

"Of course he blamed you, because he didn't want to take responsibility himself. But Grace, dear, just because Guy or anybody else wants to make you feel a certain way, it doesn't mean you have to accept that."

"But when that's all you hear, 'You're looking fat, you're lazy, you're a bitch, when did you turn stupid on me?' it's hard not to believe it."

"I know. I know. For a good part of my life, up until I moved away from home, I dealt with a lot of that. I was told I was too tall, my hair was 'mousy,' I wasn't cute like Jan or smart like Regina or outgoing like Jackie. If I got a B on a school paper my mother would chastise me for not getting an A, and when I sold more Girl Scout cookies than anyone except Betty Hurt, instead of mother saying 'Good job,' she said, 'Humph, if you'da tried harder you coulda finished first.' And it was then that I vowed that when I had kids I would never do that to them, make them feel less than who they were. So I suppose I went overboard the other way and when I should have given you kids a swift kick, I didn't. I rationalized when I should have just acted."

"I think I'm acting more like your mother with my kids," Grace said.

"I've noticed that, but I didn't want to say anything. I wasn't sure if it was my business. Besides, I was afraid to say anything because I knew you'd bite my head off. Funny how a mother can be scared of her own daughter. But let's get back to Guy. What he's doing is abusing you."

"That's what my therapist says."

"Well, what does she say to do about it?"

"Leave."

"Then why don't you?"

"You say that so cavalierly, like it's easy to do."

"You didn't answer my question. Why haven't you left him?"

"Because I have three babies, no place to go, and no way to support them."

"That's not true, Grace."

"It is too. Where would I go? How would I support my family? And, there's another reason."

"What's that?"

"I, uh…"

"I, uh, what? You still love him?"

"Part of me does. And part of me hates him. That's why I'm so confused."

"Have you tried counseling?"

"He won't go."

"That doesn't surprise me. Let me ask you this: If you stay with Guy, what do you think your life will be like in five years?"

Grace hesitated. "Mom, I barely get by thinking an hour ahead, much less five years."

"You might want to think about that. Think about it real hard. Ask yourself if you're building the life you want, the life you want for your children. It might help you see a bigger picture. Did you tell the therapist you suspected Guy was cheating on you?"

Lydia remembered what Sherry had started to tell her in the kitchen, that she had heard a rumor about Guy and, well, someone.

"No. I think I've been in denial. I suspected he might be having an affair, but then I thought it was my imagination. But I guess I did have a gut feeling. And then there were a few times when I was getting his shirts together to take to the cleaners that I smelled a strange scent. Not a strong one, but a hint of fragrance that wasn't familiar. And that made me think of when I was carrying Daddy's shirts downstairs and I mentioned they smelled like Tabu and you went ghastly pale and I learned later that was when Daddy had one of his affairs. And it hit me like a rocket that I might be going through the same thing you did. But when I asked Guy about it, he denied it, said I was 'delusional,' and that if I would ease up in the bedroom and be more 'experimental,' then maybe I wouldn't have to worry about such things."

Wait a minute, Lydia thought after listening to Grace. She heard everything. She was sure that Guy wanted Grace to be experimental in the bedroom, that he thought she was delusional... but what else did she say? "After one of Daddy's affairs." Affairs, plural? But maybe it was just an accident. Maybe Grace just misspoke and meant affair, singular. But how could she ask that question without taking the focus off Grace's problems? "What did you mean when you said Daddy's 'affairs'? Did you mean to say affair? Singular?" she blurted out.

Grace froze. She and her siblings had agreed not to mention the rumors they'd heard about their Dad's other affair. "How'd we get to talking about Daddy?" she asked, obviously trying to divert the conversation away from the watershed she accidentally steered it to.

"We weren't talking about him, but something you said startled me. Did you mean to say Daddy's affair, singular or affairs, plural?"

"I shouldn't have said affairs," Grace said, still sounding evasive.

"Don't make this a matter of semantics, Grace. Is there something you know that I don't?"

"I don't know. I'm not sure," Grace said as though she was verbally doing a Michael Jackson moonwalk.

Lydia's eyes burrowed into Grace's. "All I'm asking is for you to honestly tell me what you meant, what you know."

"Mom, it's not about anything I actually know for certain. It's just that, uh, there were rumors."

"Rumors about what? Who?"

Grace looked at her mother. "Rumors that Daddy and Rita were having an affair. But like I said, they were rumors and you know most rumors aren't true and that was years ago and Daddy's dead and—"

"You can stop, Grace. You don't have to give excuses. Do you remember who you heard these rumors from, or who told you?"

"I'm not sure I even remember. It was a long time ago. But I guess I might have heard it from Sherry, but like I said, I'm not sure. Mom, I didn't mean to say anything about this. Really."

"Sherry told you?" Lydia noted, pursing her lips. Then it hit her like a January electric bill: Oh, my God, that's why Rita moved away without telling me.

It was nearly noon by the time Lydia and Grace finished talking and going through the papers and treasures in the pile Lydia had put aside. They resumed their discussion of Grace's problems in her marriage, but with this new information about Rita rumbling through her head, Lydia felt as though any information she proffered about building a healthy marriage and relationship was a farce. But she put on a game face even when Grace brought up the subject of her adoption and how she didn't think she could ever "totally" move on with her life until she found out who and where she came from. Grace told her mother that her desire, no, her *need* to know this information was in no way a reflection of something Lydia had done or didn't do, that it only had to do with her and her place in the world.

"It sounds like this is really important to you. And I think it's a good idea. If I were you, I'd want to know, too." She paused for a couple of seconds, then added, "I've known this day was going to come for a long time. Frankly, I'm surprised it didn't come sooner. You know there was a part of me that wanted to mention that it might be a good idea for you to look up your birth mother, but as much as I hate to admit it, my insecurities got the better of me."

"And I'm sure I didn't help matters either," Grace said. "In my mind it's always been about me, not you. I think I've often thought about you only through my eyes, not yours. Maybe it's not you who needs to change. It's me." A tear formed in the corner of one of Grace's eyes. " Mom, you are my emotional beacon. You've always been here for me, even when I've tried my darndest to push you away. Nobody could ever take your place. But my birth mother, birthparents, are my genetic history and they're a piece of my life's puzzle. I-I just feel they might provide some missing links to who I am, that's all. And I think it's important for my kids, too, you know. They have a right to know their heritage. It might help me answer some of the questions they ask when they grow up," Grace said, her hand resting on Lydia's.

"You know, your kids are always going to ask you things you can't answer," Lydia said, with a glint of laughter in her voice. "And they'll answer things you won't want to hear, too. Like you did when you asked me, in front of Nadine Simpson, 'Mommy, why does that lady have a beard?'"

"I didn't," Grace said.

"You did. And there were many more times. You were quite inquisitive, you know. Actually, most of what you asked, I wanted to know, too, but I never had the nerve to ask questions. That's one of the things I've always admired about you, that if you want to know something, you're not afraid to ask, no matter what the answer is. Maybe I didn't ask the questions because I was afraid of the answers. Well, aren't I rattling on?"

For a second, Lydia thought about the unopened note she had from Sugar.

Grace and Lydia agreed that while Grace went home to check on the kids, Lydia would go through the strong box in Walter's closet and pull out any information she had pertaining to Grace's adoption.

"We can decide how to proceed after we see what information we have," Grace said, sounding like her best lawyer self. Lydia was pleased that her daughter said, " 'We' can decide…" Just to make sure she was understanding her daughter correctly and not just reading what she wanted to hear into Grace's statement, Lydia said, "Did you mean *we* as in you and me? Do you want me to help you?"

"Of course I meant *we* as in you and me, Mom. I wouldn't do this without you."

Grace left and went home to eat lunch with her children. She told Lydia she'd come back about three when the babies took their nap. "Mrs. Sanchez can stay at the house until six or so."

Not five minutes after Grace left, Lydia opened the door to Walter's closet and walked in. She didn't go into her weepy, wimpy routine. Sure, she had had a few false starts going into Walter's closet, but this was different. She had a purpose.

After nearly two and a half years and repeated promptings by kids, relatives, and a pushy Realtor, what finally gave Lydia the impetus to go into her husband's closet was she needed to get something out of it. It was as simple as that. She needed to find something, something important.

She knew Walter had put their daughter's adoption papers in a large safety box in his closet. "That way if there's a fire, they'll still be safe," he'd told Lydia. Although she had thought it best to put them in the safe deposit box at Port Huron First National Bank, Walter had said he thought it best to keep them close at hand. "One of these days she's going to want to find out about her birth parents," Walter had said. "Maybe she won't ask," Lydia had said, "Hopefully we'll be good enough parents that she won't have that need."

Walter was right, Lydia thought, as she opened the door to his closet and walked in. Racks of suits and shirts and pants and belts hung on the right side of the closet. On the left side were shelves full of shoe boxes, and stacks of *National Geographic* magazines. Lydia looked at the magazines and laughed as she remembered how she had caught Buddy sitting on the floor of his dad's closet scouring the *National Geographic* for photos of topless tribeswomen.

The floor was scattered with remnants from a time that, to Lydia, now seemed long ago. Before when she had walked in the closet, even when she had stepped into the closet six weeks before, in hope of cleaning it, it had seemed too soon, such a short time since Walter had died. But now when she entered, it felt right

She stubbed her toe on a set of golf clubs. She walked around a black-and-white bowling ball bag. Then she stopped and turned back around and unzipped the dust-covered bag. She rolled the ball around until the three holes appeared on top. Above the holes were the initials, WAC, Walter Arthur Calypso. She saw his bowling shoes. And remembered how he always had to wear bandages on his heals because he got blisters from the shoes. "They make bowling shoes smaller than regular shoes," he'd said. Lydia smirked, wondering how she could remember such a comment made so long ago when she couldn't remember what she'd eaten for breakfast. She did remember how she never went bowling with Walter even though he'd asked her to. "The bowling alleys are too smoky," she'd said. Now she wished she would have gone.

She kicked a pair of gray sweatpants out of her path. She had forgotten how much she hated seeing Walter in those pants. "They make you look like an old fart," she'd told him, "especially when you have the waist hiked up so high." She cringed at what now seemed less like a joke than a cutting comment. She got an icky tingle in her stomach as she recalled how, although she had tried hard not to hurt the kids' feelings, Walter sometimes wasn't so lucky. She recalled seeing the look on his face after some caustic comments that she had tried to disguise as "jokes."

She couldn't dwell on this now, though. If she did she'd turn into a blithering, guilt-wracked idiot. And that kind of behavior had no place in her future.

Against the back wall, covered with a stack of phone books Walter had insisted on saving for God-knew-what reason, there was the security box. "The combination," Lydia said, "Bink, where did Walter say he kept the combination? Ah, carumba, it's got to be, let me think, where did he say he put it? I know it was in the closet, a place where a burglar wouldn't find it. Yes, yes, it's in Walter's hat, the gray tweed hat I'd bought for him to wear to Ireland. He said he'd make the combination look like a European hat size. Yes."

Sure enough, she found the combination on the shelf in a gray tweed hat. She was glad it wasn't a combination lock like she'd had in school, the kind where you go left and right and left, which always confused her. All she had to do was set four numbers on this one. Walter had chosen the numbers, "One-nine-six-eight," she said as she rolled the tumbler to the number.

"Nineteen sixty-eight," she said, her voice catching. "The year we were married. Keep going forward. Oh, my word," she said, when she opened the door and the contents of the safe began spilling out. Papers, envelopes, stubs, receipts. She couldn't believe how much stuff had been packed in there. "Thank God I didn't have to go through this when Walter died," she said, being grateful all the papers she'd needed were in the desk or in the safe deposit box at the bank. "Would you look at this, Bink? What a mess. I had no idea Walter's pack-rat-itis extended to the security box, too. How am I going to find the adoption papers in this mess?" She wiggled her hand and then her arm into the jumble of papers like she was drawing a winning postcard from a spinning bin on a game show.

"And the winner is," she said as she blindly pulled out a large manila envelope she thought possibly might have the adoption papers in it. There was nothing written on the back so she turned it over. "Rita's Letters" was scribbled in Walter's hand on the front.

Lydia's palms instantly turned sweaty, yet cold. She closed her eyes, because if she didn't, she would pass out. She might pass out anyway. Her morning coffee inched up her throat.

The envelope was sealed shut; for half a second she thought about not opening the envelope. She was, after all, looking for Grace's adoption papers, not trying to drag up the past. But even as she was thinking that, her fingers worked to undo the glued-down flap.

She thought about dumping the contents of the envelope out on the floor, but the closet felt as if it were closing in on her, so she took the envelope, walked out into the bedroom, and dumped the contents on the bed. She picked up one envelope and then another and then another. The word "Walter," in Rita's handwriting was scrawled across the front of each one. "They don't have an address, Binky. She must have given these to him in person." But when? How and when could this have taken place?

She watched as her hands opened an envelope and pulled out pink stationery. It was embossed in the top center with roses. Lydia brought the stationery to her nose, noticing a faint fragrance. Her stomach churned at the smell.

The two pages were folded in half. Lydia opened them and began reading.

Dear Walter,

I know it shouldn't seem like I need to "talk" to you after spending those two sweet hours with you last night. It was wonderful to have a man to talk to. You know, Lydia never mentions how funny you are. I'm still laughing about that comment you made about family vacations. It feels so good to laugh and I seem to be able to laugh around you so easily.

By the way, you left your necktie here. I have it hanging in my closet. You can get it next time you come over. I don't want to leave it out because Lydia might drop by.

I must confess though I do feel guilty. I know that what we have is just a special friendship, but you are the husband of my best friend and I am starting to get feelings for you that are more than just friendship. Maybe we can talk about this soon.
Fondly,
Rita

Setting the letter down, Lydia put her head in her hands and wretched. "Oh, my God, Binky, I've been so stupid. They were having an affair and I didn't even know it."

Binky knew something was wrong. She tilted her head and looked at Lydia, then hopped on her lap and sounded an agonizing meow.

Lydia had thought she had experienced all of life's emotions: happiness, joy, contentment, grief, hopelessness, heartache, and loneliness. She had felt utter devastation when Buddy died and she was crushed when Walter died. She had felt hurt and anger when she found out Walter had had an affair, but this was different. This was a betrayal beyond her comprehension. An emotional betrayal. "Damn you, Walter. Damn you, Rita," she said, picking up her pillows and slamming them on the bed, the loud plump and whoosh of air causing Binky to scatter.

She picked up another letter and opened it. It was dated May 18, 1998.

Dear Walter,

I just want to thank you for the wonderful dinner and evening. It's been a long time since I've felt so comfortable with anyone. If only you weren't Liddy's husband, it would have been a perfect evening. You were a much better listener than I thought you would be. Liddy is one lucky lady.

Hugs,

Rita

P.S. I forgot to give you your tie. Guess you'll have to get it next time.

Lydia's hands trembled. She put the letter down. She wondered if this were a dream she could wake up from. But then she looked down at a stack of what had to be at least twenty letters. "This is real," she said. Then she flipped through to the last one and opened it. Like finishing a novel, she wanted to see how this ended.

Dear Walter,

I've been doing a lot of thinking about our relationship. Well, not just our relationship, but the relationship I have with Lydia, and the one I've developed with you over the course of the last few months. You know I love Lydia like a sister. And I've always cared for you like a brother.

But when you gave me a ride home after that curriculum meeting in February and we stopped for a cup of coffee and you seemed so sad and lonely, I thought it was my duty as Lydia's and your friend to try to help you.

But I was wrong.

I've been around the block enough to know what lending an ear or a shoulder can lead to, and yet I continued meeting with you. As you know, one thing led to another, at least with the sharing of personal information and some secrets. I'd be lying if I said I didn't feel your attraction for me growing and that I wasn't flattered by it.

I pretended to myself for a long time that we were doing nothing wrong. Hey, we were just friends, right? But what I had done, as I've done so many times before, is make my own rules to justify behavior that I knew was wrong.

Now I feel we are at a crossroads. If I stay, I'm afraid of what will happen between us. Your need and my desire are a dangerous combination, destined to blow up in flames and scorch the lives of people we love.

So I have come to the conclusion, I must leave. With the secrets you've shared with me and given the fact I promised not to tell anyone, I feel the only thing I can do is leave. You've put, or I should say, we've put each other in very precarious positions.

I will write a letter of resignation to the Board citing family issues back in Illinois. It will be up to you to tell Lydia why I've left. I will understand if she never wants to talk to me again. You can tell her that. All I ask of you is two things: First, turn to Lydia to help you find your way through life. She has loved you and still loves you with all of her heart and she deserves to be the one you

share your soul with. And secondly, you owe it to Grace to tell her
you are her father.
Fondly,
Rita

"Oh, my God!" Lydia screamed. She read the last line of Rita's letter again. And again. "You owe it to Grace to tell her you are her father. What's this about?" Lydia's mind ricocheted inside her head. It jumped from now to the past to back again. "What was Rita talking about? Grace's birth certificate. Where is it? I saw it myself. Walter's name wasn't on it. This can't be right. I swear I must have been walking through my life blind, with my eyes and ears closed." Lydia got up off the bed and strode to the closet. "The birth certificate," she said to Binky, who had followed her into the closet. "I've got to find Grace's birth certificate."

Getting down on her knees, Lydia rummaged through the strong box. She pulled out Walter's army release papers and bills and receipts which she didn't bother to look at. She threw them helter-skelter on the floor. "Where are you?" she said as she ransacked the box. "I know you're in here."

She had just about reached the bottom of the box when she saw an envelope with the words, Grace's Birth Certificates.

"Here it is," she said.

She pulled the envelope out and stood up. The envelope was sealed. She stuck her finger where there was a slight opening and then ripped. She pulled out a stack of folded papers. She pressed them open. On the top it said BIRTH CERTIFICATE. Lydia speed-read down the lines. Mother's name. Hospital name. County of birth. Date. Time. Until she got to the line she wanted to see, Father's name: Manuel Garcia.

"Thank God," Lydia said. "Maybe Rita was meaning that Walter should talk to Grace and explain how even though he wasn't her birth father, he still was her father."

That's what she wanted to believe, anyway.

There were many copies of the birth certificate behind this one.

Walter had made several copies of each of their kids' birth certificates so that didn't seem unusual. But for once, instead of taking what she saw at face value, Lydia thumbed through each birth certificate. Manuel, Manuel, Manuel, they all said. That is, until the last one, which Lydia assumed was the original because it was a couple of shades darker than the others.

"Oh, no," Lydia sobbed. She read the line that said father: Walter Arthur Calypso.

Lydia dropped all the other certificates and fell to the floor, clutching the one that bore Walter's name.

"This was a house full of secrets," Lydia said between howls. "And everyone knew them but me."

Chapter 34

Missing Links

Lydia stood up slowly, like a ninety-year-old. She bent over and picked up the birth certificates that lay scattered on the closet floor. She placed all of the ones that said Manuel Garcia back in the envelope. The other, the one with Walter's name on it, she placed on her dresser.

She looked at the clock. It was going on two. "I've got to get a hold of Grace and tell her not to come over," she said. "I can't face her right now."

But it was too late. Grace didn't answer her phone.

"Dear God, what should I do?" she prayed.

Even without praying, she knew what she had to do. She had to tell Grace. "Maybe this will help Grace," she said. "For her it has to be good news. But how will I tell her? How do I tell her that her father lied to her and to me?"

The front door opened at two-thirty. "We're here!" Grace yelled.

"Oh, Lord, who's 'we'?" Lydia said as she splashed cool water on her face and patted it with a towel. She even went so far as to dab Chanel Number 5 behind her ear.

"Look what the cat dragged in," Grace said, nodding toward Sherry.

"Oh, hi, dear. Don't you have to work this afternoon?"

"I went in early and didn't take a lunch. We now have flex-hours. They figured that was a good way of getting out of giving us a raise. But actually, it works out well. Of course, it just started today." Sherry laughed as she removed her coat. "I'm here to work." She rolled up her sleeves to show she was eager to get busy. "Let's rock and roll," she said.

"No coffee first?" Lydia asked, trying not to look either daughter in the eye. She knew her face and eyes were puffy.

Sherry and Grace both said, "Nah."

"Diet Coke? Mountain Dew?"

"Nope. I picked up a drink at a drive-thru. Actually, what I need to do is use the bathroom," Sherry said. "You two go on up. I'll be up in a minute."

Grace was already heading up the stairs. "We need to put a fire to it because Mrs. Sanchez said she needs to be out of there by six or shortly after, so I have to leave by five-fifteen. But I think we can get a lot done."

"You know, we don't have to do this today," Lydia yelled upstairs. "Actually, I'd rather not. I'm very tired. Exhausted." She wondered if her girls would hear the quiver in her voice.

"That's okay, Mom. We'll just plunge in and get this done. Getting this taken care of is almost like a miracle to me. I didn't think we'd ever get you to do it," Grace said, her voice trailing off as she went around the corner upstairs.

"Miracle," Lydia said as she trudged up the stairs, feeling as though with each step she took she gained a hundred pounds.

"You know, Mom, until today I hadn't been in here in ages," Sherry said. "It feels and looks almost the same as it did when Buddy was here."

"But it's changed a lot, really it has," Lydia said. "I put on new bedspreads and changed the furniture around. And the dresser, it's new. Well, it isn't new, new, but it's not the same one we had when Buddy was here. And the curtains are different, too."

"I guess I just have a photo etched in my mind," Sherry said. "You know how the mind sees things the eyes don't. And it even looks different than it did a couple of days ago, when, well, you know, when we were all in here."

Grace agreed with both her sister and her mom. "Is it possible that it's changed and yet stayed the same?"

"I suppose," Lydia said. "Whenever I come in here I see Buddy sprawled across his bed, looking at hunting magazines. He'd insist I come over and ooh and ah at a picture of some huge buck with antlers so large they'd make a good coat rack at an orphanage." Lydia chuckled. "He was a character."

All the while she talked Lydia was having two conversations going on inside her head, the one she was participating in and the one she knew would come.

"Damn, I mostly remember coming in and yelling at him because he'd leave his stinky, dirty clothes in the bathroom. Made the whole room stink. So I'd pick them up with a big fat yardstick and stand here at the door and throw them on him and tell him he lived in a house and not a barnyard," Sherry said. "Of course he'd turn around and oink at me." Sherry laughed as she made an oink sound.

Both Lydia and Sherry looked to Grace to see if she was going to join in this miniature remembrance ceremony. But all she said was, "Time's a-wasting." She opened the closet door.

Lydia closed her eyes a brief second. "God help me," she said under her breath.

"I didn't know Buddy was into ballet," Sherry said as she pulled a pink tutu out of the closet, causing everyone to laugh.

"That's mine," Grace said. "I was wondering where that thing was. I was going to see if Kelly could wear it." She held the tutu up to her. "I don't believe I was ever this small."

"You were a tiny little thing," Lydia said. "And cute as a button. All you kids were cute as buttons."

"Oh, there she goes," Sherry said, amused.

Sherry set herself on the floor, right inside the door of the closet. She began pulling things out.

"Nice roller skates," Grace said. "He would have been in hog heaven if he'd've stuck around for the inline skates."

"He would have been one of those kids who do those tubes and chutes and that stuff," Sherry said. "He was one wild and crazy dude."

Lydia listened. It was fascinating for her to hear how her other kids saw Buddy. She'd never really known how any of them saw each other. She'd always wanted so much to be a part of their conversations she never just observed her kid's interactions.

"I can't believe he saved all these stupid things," Sherry said, hoisting out a stack of Deer Life and racing magazines. She flipped through a couple of them. "How gross," she said, holding up a photo of a dead deer hanging from a tree, his guts splayed open.

"Would you please close that thing?" Grace pleaded. "I just ate lunch."

Grace and Sherry bantered on, apparently not realizing how quiet their mother had become.

"I'm not touching that thing," Sherry said, pointing to a rifle that was leaning against the back corner of the closet.

"It's not even put together," Grace said.

"I don't care. I hate guns. You get it out."

"For Pete's sake. Get out of the way, you wimp."

"Well, if it were a spider, you'd be the wimp," Sherry countered.

Grace pulled the gun parts out of the closet. "What do you want me to do with these?" She held the pieces of the gun like they had cooties. "Mom, what should I do with these?" she asked again, causing Sherry to look toward her mom, too.

Seeing their mother's face, both Grace and Sherry looked as though they knew where their mother's mind had gone. And now they might now be forced to go there, too.

"It's been over seven years since Buddy's been gone," Lydia said. "Yet when I'm in here it feels like yesterday."

"I'm sure it does, Mom. I don't know how you handled Buddy's death as well as you did," Sherry said quietly. "I don't think I would ever function again if something happened to Danny or Markey."

"What makes you think I handled it well?" Lydia asked, not combatively, but with a touch of curiosity in her voice.

"You carried on. You got out of bed each morning and continued to raise your family. I don't know if I could have done that."

Grace nodded.

"I had no choice. Only God knows how many times I didn't want to get out of bed. But I had four other children in my family. I had responsibilities," Lydia said, her voice calm and reflective. She had been standing, watching the girls empty the floor of Buddy's closet, but as she was answering Sherry's question she moved toward one of the twin beds in the room and sat down.

"We don't have to talk about this," Grace said.

"No, we don't. And I shouldn't have made that comment," Sherry said.

"Sure, you should have," Lydia said. "You were saying how you felt. You're allowed to do that."

Nervous quiet filled the room.

"Do you want to talk about Buddy?" Sherry asked. "If you do, we, or at least I know I would be glad to listen. Maybe it would be good for you, good for Grace and me, too, to talk about what happened. We've never done that, you know."

"I know," Lydia said with a hint of apology in her voice. "But I don't know where to start or what to say." Lydia sounded like a young child confessing a misdeed to a principal.

"Maybe Sherry and I could start," Grace said. "We could say something we remember about Buddy." For the second time in a day, Grace's eyes welled with tears. "Buddy was so goofy and silly and he could be such a nitwit, too." Grace began talking about the time she took Buddy to Cedar Point Amusement Park to ride rides. "Oh, not that I wanted to," she said.

"I only took him because you paid me," Grace said, looking and laughing at her mother. "I got ten dollars and a month's worth of free gas. That was the payment. Of course I made sure none of my friends were going to the Point that day. The last thing I wanted was to be seen with my dweeb brother who thought he was the official Deer Hunter."

Both Sherry and Lydia paid rapt attention to Grace's story. "And you know what? I thought having to take him there would be the worst day of my life, but it wasn't. In fact, we had a great time. We rode almost every ride. He rocked the ferris wheel so much I thought we would flip over. And you should have seen his face after his third corn dog. And you know, with Buddy I didn't have to act cool or try to look like a movie star. As a matter of fact, if I tried to act cool, he ragged on me. 'Who do you think you are, Cindy Crawford?' he'd say. Of course I almost died when on the way home, he mooned the people who were sitting at that outdoor café right down the road from the Point. But that was Buddy."

"Yep, that was Buddy," Sherry said. "Once we were both locked out of the house. Of course we were both supposed to be *in* the house, asleep."

"What?" Lydia squealed. "I'm not sure if I want to know where this is going."

"Ah, it's so long ago, Mom. And it really was amusing."

"I'm listening," Lydia said.

"I'd snuck out the front door to go meet Meredith and Joy. I was grounded for some dumb reason like not cleaning my room or the bathroom, I don't remember which. But my friends and I had decided it was urgent that we get down to the Monkey Shack. We'd heard there was going to be a fight, Port Huron's version of the Jets and the Sharks. And as I was standing on the porch trying to sneak back into the house, who should I see walking toward the house in his camouflage? Buddy. The crazy kid had his bow and arrow and was holding a squirrel by the tail. Of course, I thought he was some deranged mass murderer and I started to scream when he said, 'Shut up, you idiot, it's me, Buddy.'"

Both Lydia and Grace cracked up.

"So I asked him, 'What the hell are you doing out at this time of night, in that type of getup? You know if the cops see you they'll haul your happy ass to jail, that is, if they don't shoot you on the spot. Where have you been anyway?' He held that dead squirrel in my face and said, 'Huntin,' and I said 'You're an idiot,' and he said back, 'Well, it takes one to know one 'cause we're both stuck outside and if Mom and Dad catch us we'll be grounded 'til we're thirty-five.' And we were so afraid we were going to get busted, but all we could do was laugh."

"So how'd you get in the house?" Lydia asked.

Sherry nodded toward Grace.

Grace smiled, cupped her hand and blew on her fingertips, then rubbed them on her chest.

"You?" Lydia asked.

"Yep. I kept hearing these little pebbles hitting our bedroom window and these pathetic voices whispering, 'Grace, Grace!' so I went down and let the two stooges in."

"Yes, she did. But do you know what it cost Buddy and me? A week's worth of emptying the dishwasher."

"I'm not stupid," Grace said.

All three laughed. Grace had sat on the other twin bed and Sherry sat in an orange beanbag chair in the corner.

Lydia said, "You know Buddy loved working at Froto's. He said when he was there he felt like he was at the Indy 500. He asked me if I was sure Mario Andretti wasn't his father. And he loved it when I told him that was a definite possibility." Then, without any transition, she said, "He died long before Sugar found him hanging in the garage."

Neither Grace nor Sherry said a word. It felt as if they were both holding their breath.

"He never got over the accident," Lydia said. "I doubt I would have, either. Not when you feel you were responsible for your two best friends' deaths. Even the most rational, mature adult would have a hard time handling that. You know, Buddy felt great relief when the jury found him not guilty of negligence, at least for a week or so, anyway. But then after the relief that he wasn't going to go to prison subsided, he returned to his own personal prison cell. His own hell. And nothing we could say or do was able to get him past it."

Grace's eyes were glossy while Sherry sat stone-faced. Lydia's voice was matter of fact, as if she were testifying before a grand jury.

"You know he acted like he was fine. He got up every morning, got dressed and went to school. When I asked him how he was doing, which I did at least five times a day, he'd reply, 'I'm fine, Mom. Don't worry.' And I believed him because I wanted to believe him. We'd all gone through so much with the lawsuit and the trial and all of the nosy do-gooders asking us how we were doing and then finding out they were all talking behind our backs. And Dad kept reassuring me, too. 'He'll be all right, Lydia,' he'd say and I wanted to believe he would.

"I didn't find out until after he died that every day after school he'd go visit Carmine and Vince's graves. He'd told Eddie Broomstock that everything was fine and he'd soon be joining 'his brothers.'

"You know Eddie was at Froto's the night of the accident. He testified that Buddy told Carmine and Vince they shouldn't drive the cars. He said Buddy knew they had been drinking because he had smelled alcohol on their breath. But they bullied him. And lied. They told Buddy they'd each just had one beer. One lousy beer and that they were perfectly capable of handling those stupid little cars. And Eddie said he remembered hearing Buddy say, "No, don't do it." But he didn't stop them. He physically didn't stop them. And that's why everyone said it was his fault. He was five-foot eight and a hundred and thirty-five pounds and Carmine and Vince were both over six foot and two-hundred pounds. What was he supposed to do, for God's sake? They said he was supposed to call the cops. That's what their parents said, but he was seventeen-years-old and they said they hadn't been drinking. They said they hadn't been drinking…" Her voice trailed off.

She told the story so clearly that it was obvious she'd repeated it over and over in her head. It was also obvious this was more detail than Sherry had ever been told. Tears fell from Grace's eyes as she recalled sitting in the courtroom, listening to testimony, watching her brother.. Sherry broke into tears. Lydia had pulled a large loop of thread on the green bedspread. She unraveled two rows of it before she stopped.

"I'm sorry, girls. I shouldn't burden you with all of this. It isn't fair."

"Nothing about death is fair," Grace said. "Especially suicide. Suicide makes everybody feel guilty. You know I hate to admit it, but some of what Sugar said on Saturday was true. At least about me."

"What do you mean?" Lydia said.

"I wasn't a very good sister to Buddy. Or Sugar. I think I was so into myself and jealous that they were real Calypsos and I wasn't. I felt that way with them more than Tim and Sherry. I don't know why, I just did. Maybe it's because I was jealous of their relationship and that they knew how to have fun. I didn't know that 'fun' was a good thing. I've mistakenly thought that life is all about work and achievement, what you become, instead of who you are."

Sherry was about to speak when Lydia, sensing her opening, cut her off.

"I'm sorry, Sherry, but there's something I've found out that I need to talk to Grace about. Do you mind?"

Both Grace and Sherry looked puzzled. Sherry was about to say "Sure," when Grace said, "It's all right. You can say whatever it is in front of Sherry. She's my sister. And I'm so tired of secrets."

"Are you sure?" Lydia asked.

"Sure," Grace said.

"What I have to say might be what you mentioned before."

"What's that?" Grace said.

"A miracle." Then she said, "I'll be back in a second."

Grace and Sherry looked at each other.

It was no longer than a few seconds when Lydia walked back into the room carrying a piece of paper. "You know, Grace, I said I'd look for your birth certificate this morning?"

Grace nodded.

"Well, I did. I found it in Daddy's strong box. But before I found the certificate, I found some letters Rita had written to Walter."

The expression on Grace and Sherry's face plummeted. Neither said a word.

"In one of the letters, Rita mentioned something Walter had told her." Lydia paused. "Let me back up a bit. Remember, Grace, how you have always said you've never felt like you were part of this family because you weren't really a Calypso?"

Grace nodded. "But I—"

"Just wait a minute, dear. What I have to say is you *are* a Calypso. A flesh-and-blood Calypso."

"Mom, I know. You've told me I'm just as much a Calypso as everyone else. And I'm not going to argue that point. I believe you."

"No, Gracie. I don't think you understand what I'm trying to say."

Grace arched her eyebrows. "I don't get it. What are you talking about then?"

"Walter *was* your father, your biological father."

"What?" Grace said. "Do you know this for a fact or are you just speculating from something Rita said?"

Lydia handed Grace the birth certificate with Walter's name on it.

"Where did you get this?" Grace asked.

After explaining how she came across the birth certificate, Lydia, Sherry, and Grace talked for a while. When Grace asked Lydia how this could have happened, Lydia told her that at this time she could only speculate, but it was possible the conception might have occurred when Walter visited Las Cruces with his army buddies.

Sherry and Grace finally told Lydia about the rumors they'd heard about their father and Rita.

"It might not have been what it appeared," Lydia said. Why she was defending Walter or Rita, she didn't know.

"There's still a question of your birth mother," Lydia said. "Maybe if we talk to Rita, she might know more information that would lead us to her."

"I can't. Not yet. I mean, I've just found out I had a father who really never acknowledged I was his real daughter," Grace said. "I never knew I was living with my half-sisters and brothers. What he kept from me changed me, changed my life. All this time I've spent looking for who I am and the secret has been right here in this house … in a closet."

All three women looked as though someone shot them with a stun gun. No one said a word. The answers discovered in the last several days had only raised more questions. Each was so into what this new information meant to them, they couldn't deal with anything else. Lydia wondered who this Walter was who she had been married to. Grace couldn't understand how Walter could pretend not to be her real father all through the years. Sherry was in conflict over the fact that she found out Grace was indeed her half-sister, yet, her father had lived a life of secrets.

The pain Lydia was feeling from the events of the last few days was only tempered by the fact that indeed, she was a survivor. She'd survived the deaths of her son and husband. She could certainly survive whatever the past threw at her.

She decided to give herself one night to take the blow of what she had learned. Have herself a pity party. Cry her eyes out if she felt like it. "Maybe I'll throw something," she said to Binky. "I haven't done that before." She picked up a pillow and threw it across the room. "That wasn't very emphatic; maybe I should throw something that breaks." She picked up a plate and got ready to throw it at the wall. Then she put it back on the table. "You know, Binky, if I throw this and it breaks, I'll have to clean it up."

Tonight she would not try to justify how anything had turned out. She wouldn't analyze anyone's behavior because she was sick of analyzing. Her whole life she'd tried to read minds, put the pieces of the puzzles of other people's lives together and she was tired of it. And what good did it do? Where did it get her? And she wasn't going to pray. If God had anything to say to her, then He would have to make the first move.

She opened the refrigerator door and stared inside. The smell of the leftovers from the brunch turned her stomach. "All this stuff can go," she said as she began removing the food Grace had carefully wrapped. She dumped what seemed to be half the contents of the fridge into a garbage bag and took it outside to the trash can. Then she took a can of air freshener and sprayed the kitchen. "That's better," she said as she turned off the light to the kitchen. She hadn't eaten more than a piece of toast all day.

"I have a new diet," she said to Binky. "It's called the betrayal diet. It's guaranteed to take your appetite away."

Chapter 35

Goodnight Buddy

The full moon shined through Lydia's bedroom window and reflected off the mirror above the dresser. It was as if a light were on in the room.

Lydia lay on her bed on her back, her hands folded under her breasts. She had put on a clean white linen nightgown, one edged with lace, one that Walter had bought her shortly before he died. It wasn't that she had chosen it to wear. It was more like it had chosen her.

If what she had learned the last three days was what she thought the summation of her marriage and life had been, she wouldn't care if the sun came up again. But as she lay there she tried to put the last three days into perspective of a lifetime of experiences and memories.

She thought about Grace and how this new information might help her find her way through life, at least let her find her bearings. And although the revelation had been like a knife in her own gut, she knew her wound would heal.

She had been angry with Rita when she'd first found the letters she'd written to Walter, but as she thought more about it, Lydia saw Rita for what she was, a great friend but a fallible human being, just as Walter was. Just as she was. Her heart sank when she thought about Walter telling Rita about Grace and not her, but she knew Walter had found in Rita one of her best characteristics, her ability to listen. And it didn't go past Lydia without notice that Rita had stood up for her and told Walter to work on their relationship. "And he did," Lydia said aloud. "Those were the best two years of our marriage."

She found herself actually chuckling when she remembered Rita had asked Walter to do two things, but he only did one. "He never was good at taking orders," Lydia said.

She thought about Rita. The magazine article said she now lived in New York. Maybe she'd give her a call one of these days.

On the mirror, stuck between the glass and the wood, was the letter Sugar had given her. The light from the moon shone on it like a spotlight. Lydia looked at it.

She hadn't talked to Sugar since the revelation about Buddy's letter. She was sure Sugar would call when she was ready. But there was also a part of Lydia that wanted to pick up the phone and call her, to see how she was doing. She couldn't imagine what it must have been like for Sugar to have kept the letter and its contents a secret all these years. "No wonder she's been so unsettled," Lydia said.

She stared at the letter. She was amazed at herself for not having opened it. The old Lydia would have ripped it open immediately. She would have sniffed the letter for evidence, answers, and drama. But the Lydia of today believed that nothing in that letter could change what had happened.

For a second, Lydia laughed when she thought about Tim's wife, Helen, who had been so upset she wasn't invited to the fine family event. "Boy, Bink, she wouldn't have known what the heck to do," she said as she stroked the purring Binky. "Probably, when we were upstairs having our brouhaha, she would have been downstairs stuffing the silver into a felt bag."

She thought about how much Tim had looked and acted like Walter during the family feud. "Did you notice how he pulls on his ear just like Walter did?" she asked Binky.

Of all of the things that had happened, the one thing that made her feel good was how Grace and Sherry seemed to have come together. "Wasn't that nice to see, Binky?" she said as she thought about how Grace had asked Sherry to stay in the room when she told Grace that Walter was her father.

Before Lydia fell asleep she rolled over, tightened the blanket up under her chin and looked at the moon. She stared at the clouds as they passed by the large yellow ball that looked close enough to touch. She took her hand out from under the blanket, stretched her arm skyward, and reached for the moon. "Goodnight, Buddy," she said. "It's time I let you go." She kissed the tips of her fingers and blew the kiss toward the moon.

Chapter 36

The Baseball Mitt

After her morning coffee and a strawberry yogurt, Lydia climbed the stairs to finish cleaning Buddy's closet after two failed attempts. "The third time has to be the charm," she said as Binky pulled her tail from under Lydia's falling foot.

She stopped in her room and turned on the CD player. At first she thought about playing the Righteous Brothers, but good sense prevailed. "No, we need something a bit more upbeat," she said. "How about the Beach Boys? Buddy loved the Beach Boys." She put the CD in and turned the volume up.

As she walked into Buddy's room and opened the closet door she said, "No sorrows," and then she took a deep breath.

Within an hour she had gone through at least three-quarters of Buddy's closet. She was amazed at how well she had done sorting clothes, organizing piles, and throwing out old school papers. Of course there were a few things she couldn't part with: a trophy Buddy had received for accurate shooting at Webster's Shooting Range, two model cars that he had painstakingly put together, and his confirmation Bible. She lovingly placed the rest of his belongings in boxes; one box was to go to Sherry's, where she would see if her boys would want any of their Uncle Buddy's things. Another box would go to Tim's house. That box included articles Lydia had saved from the accident and trial. She wasn't sure if things like that were something that should be kept as part of the family record or destroyed so history could eventually be rewritten. Another box would go to Grace, one box to Sugar, and the rest she'd take to the Goodwill.

"Where's Buddy's baseball mitt?" Lydia asked as she looked under one pile after another. "It was here the other day when Sugar was here. Humph, I was going to give that to Sugar. But maybe she took it already. I'll have to ask her."

As Lydia began hauling boxes downstairs, she said, "You know, Binky, if I would have known what the last few days were going to be like, I would've hung a No Vacancy sign on my front door and taken to bed until summer."

"I'm coming!" Lydia yelled as she came down the stairs carrying the second box. It was a good thing she was coming downstairs or else she would have never heard the knock at the door, what with the Beach Boys blasting throughout the house.

"It's the little old lady from Pasadena," she sang as she walked to the door. "Hope it's not another Realtor," she said to Binky, who was perched on the newel post.

Lydia opened the door.

"Hi," came a voice from outside.

"Hi, Sugar."

Lydia looked at Sugar and the little boy standing next to her. Then she looked at Sugar again. And then at the boy. And then at the baseball mitt. And then at Sugar.

"Hi," the little boy said.

Lydia guessed his age to be about seven. "Hi," Lydia said, her mouth and mind working in slow motion. She studied the boy's eyes and cheekbones and mouth. But it was the hair and skin color that made her stop breathing.

"Mom, I'd like you to meet someone," Sugar said. "Can we come in?"

Lydia couldn't take her eyes off the little boy.

"I have my daddy's baseball mitt," he said, looking at Lydia and holding a mitt that had "Buddy" written on each of the fingers. "Aunt Sugar gave it to me."

Lydia looked at Sugar. Her eyes were confused and misty.

"Brandon, I'd like you to meet your grandma. Mom, this is Brandon, Buddy's son," Sugar said.

"Nice to meet you," Brandon said, removing the ball mitt from his left hand. "Aunt Sugar's told me all about you. Do you know much about me?"

Lydia clutched her heart as she bent over. Then she hugged the little boy. "But, Sugar," Lydia said. "What…"

Sugar put her finger over her mouth. "I'll tell you the whole story later. But now, why don't you enjoy the time with your grandson? He's named after his father. He hasn't acquired the nickname Buddy yet."

Lydia thought for sure she would need someone else to move her legs.

Finally, the three of them walked into the living room. "May I please have something to drink?" Brandon asked.

Lydia couldn't help but be impressed with his manners.

"Why don't we go into the kitchen?" Lydia suggested. She continued to mouth words to Sugar but Sugar again put her index finger to her lips and whispered, "Later."

"Good idea," Sugar said as she led Brandon through the living and dining rooms.

"This sure is a neat house," Brandon said. "Is this where my daddy grew up?"

Sugar said, "Yep, sure is," as she walked with him.

Lydia walked behind.

"Would you like some chocolate milk?" Lydia asked Brandon as he hopped up on a chair

"Sure," he said.

Lydia couldn't help but continue to look at Sugar with questions in her eyes.

And each time she did so Sugar put her finger over her lip and said, "Later."

Brandon had barely drunk half his glass of milk when he said, "Can I see my daddy's room?"

"Sure. It's this way, Bucko," Sugar said, making a grin appear on Brandon's face.

Lydia followed Sugar and Brandon up the stairs and into Buddy's room.

"It's a disaster," Lydia said as they walked in. "I was just cleaning out the closet."

"You should see mine," Brandon said. "It's a mess." He giggled.

With Sugar's help, Lydia arranged for Brandon to stay at her house one day a week. She even talked to Brandon's mom on the phone, knowing that only time would allow her to find out the truth. Lydia couldn't believe how much Brandon reminded her of Buddy, the way he tilted his head to the right when he listened, how he had a slight lisp when he said words that began with ess, and how he did not like to wash behind his ears.

Lydia cleared out her sewing room and turned it into a toy room. She and Brandon played games and colored for hours. She even got him to sing Karaoke.

Sugar went back to New York a couple of days after she brought Brandon to Lydia's. Lydia and Sugar spent most of the next two days of her visit talking about everything they had not discussed since they had known each other. Of course Buddy was a large part of their conversations.

Sugar bombarded Lydia with lots of questions. And some-times the exchanges were heated. "Why didn't we move from this house?" Sugar asked. "Didn't you know what it did to me to have to live there?"

Lydia answered as honestly as she could. "We thought about it seriously, but in the end we decided that this was our home. We knew that wherever we went, it wouldn't erase what happened. And if you think about it, I mean really think hard, our family had many good memories there."

Sugar rebuked the answer somewhat, saying she didn't think her mother or father really knew what finding Buddy had done to her. Lydia listened carefully and surprised Sugar by saying she agreed with her, that maybe she was so blinded by her own grief and fear that she didn't see the toll it had taken on her. But then she added, "You said you were doing fine and the counselor said you were doing as well as could be expected."

Again, Sugar argued and said, "I think you heard that because that's what you wanted to hear. But inside I was dying."

"I see that now, Sugar. And I'm sorry. You have to know I would never want my child to suffer like that. All I can say is that I'm sorry I failed you."

"Maybe part of this is that I always thought of you as the 'perfect' mother. And when all of this happened, I was angry that you weren't."

"Did I ever say I was a perfect mom?" Lydia asked, somewhat defensively.

"No. But I thought you were."

"But I wasn't. And I'm still not. I'm just older than you. I try to get through my day and life the same as you try to get through yours. You know moms are people, too," Lydia said, looking to see if Sugar would find the humor in that statement.

"And so are kids," Sugar said back.

"Touché," Lydia said. "We're both people. How about that?"

Lydia ended that phase of the conversation by saying, "Sugar, was it you who burned down the garage?"

Sugar laughed. "Duh, Mom. It was all of us. All four of us kids did it. Well, Grace wasn't here, but she told us to 'Go for it.'"

Lydia's mouth dropped open like she was just named chief flycatcher.

Sugar told Lydia how she knew about Brandon—Buddy had told her—and that she had told Walter about the teacher Buddy got pregnant. Walter's reaction to the news was to tell Buddy he could never acknowledge the child, and that if he did, the baby's mother would end up in prison and be labeled a sex offender. Lydia turned fifteen shades of fuchsia on hearing that.

"Buddy told me Dad said he had literally fucked everything up and that if any word of this got out, it would cause a scandal since he, Daddy, was superintendent of schools. He made Buddy promise to never say a word about this. And Buddy accused me of betraying him."

"Did this all happen when I was on the cruise with Rita?"

Sugar nodded.

"So that's why you asked me why I went on that cruise. That's why you've been angry with me all these years."

Sugar had a piece of tissue in her hand and she wrapped it round and round her finger. "But Mom, I couldn't live like this anymore. I felt I was betraying you and Brandon and I got so screwed up. I ended up seeing a therapist and she's the one who told me I had to tell the truth."

Lydia's anger with Walter temporarily surpassed her ability to forgive. "So that's really why Buddy killed himself," Lydia said softly. "It wasn't just because of his friend's death or the trial. If Walter wouldn't have threatened Buddy about exposing the teacher, if he would have said, 'we're here for you no matter what,' maybe Buddy would still be alive."

Sugar said, "I hated Dad for a long time after that. But no more than I hated myself. And when Dad died, I transferred my anger to you. For all these years I thought the reason he killed himself was because I betrayed him. But the therapist explained that it wasn't one event that made Buddy kill himself, it was a group of circumstances that made him feel he had no control over his life. And I have to believe that. And you do, too."

Sugar told Lydia she'd been sending money to Brandon's mother even though his mother insisted that wasn't necessary. "I did it for Buddy," Sugar said. She mentioned that the reason she didn't have the money to come home sometimes was because occasionally she'd fly out to see Brandon. "It was Brandon's mom who dropped me off at your house the day I brought Brandon here," Sugar said. "I can see why Buddy fell in love with her. She's kind and a great mother to Brandon. And I've learned about another side of Buddy from her. You really should get to know her. I think you'd like her."

Lydia listened to Sugar not just as a daughter, but an adult. Perhaps Sugar had taken a huge step closer to healing. And maybe what all her kids had been implying to her was right. She hadn't really let Buddy or Walter go.

"Let's make a pact, Mom. Both of us will let the past go and we'll live the lives we were meant to live."

Lydia took Sugar to the airport to go back to New York. As they walked down the concourse, Sugar stopped and looked at her mom. "Do you forgive me for not telling you, Mom?" Sugar said.

Taking Sugar's face in her hands, Lydia said, "Remember this. Life is about forgiveness. We're all imperfect souls making our way through a complicated world the best we can."

Mother and daughter hugged. "You have to come to New York and visit me, you know?" Sugar whispered into her mother's ear. "I want to show you my town."

"Will do," Lydia said. "This summer."

"I love you, Mom," Sugar said as she handed her ticket to the security agent.

Lydia smiled, nodded, and said, "Right back at ya, kiddo."

Chapter 37

Hints of Spring

It was late March when the daffodils finally peeked through the ground in Port Huron. Of course another snowfall came and covered up all but the tips. But seeing even just the tips of the daffodils gave promise that spring would indeed come again.

Lydia spent the last part of the month going through the remainder of her closets. She whistled most of the time. She found a snow globe with a scene of Niagara Falls, where she and Walter had gone on their honeymoon. She wrapped it in paper and put it in a box marked, "The early years." She found a music box that played "Lara's Theme" from *Dr. Zhivago*. Buddy had given it to her for her fortieth birthday. Up until he'd died, it had set on her dressing table, but after his death, she put it in her closet because she couldn't bear hearing that song. When she found the music box she twisted the key and "Lara's Theme" began to play. She held the box for a moment and then set it on her dresser. Then she thought that in a few years she might give it to Brandon.

A pair of pink leather high heels she had bought to wear with a pink leather skirt made her cringe. Both items were sent to Goodwill. "Who knows," she said to Binky, "Goodwill might reject these, too."

She found a box with an eighteen-hour bra inside. "Who in their right mind wears a bra eighteen hours in a day?"

She found more contraptions Walter had bought on television, including a Jack LaLanne Power Juicer, that was used once when Walter made carrot juice and spent the next four hours in the bathroom; an Ab Slide that she nearly killed herself on when she tripped over it in the middle of the night; and Bowdabra, a contraption that makes bows. He'd given that to her "just because."

It was a couple of days after Lydia had emptied the closets and delivered boxes to her kids' houses when Grace called, laughing hysterically.

"What in the world was that vibrator doing in the pile of stuff you gave me?" she asked as soon as her mother answered the phone.

"Oh, my God," Lydia said. "That was a mistake. I put that in the wrong pile."

"You mean you were going to put this thing in Sherry or Sugar's pile?"

Lydia hadn't heard Grace laugh like this in years. "No, I mean, it wasn't supposed to be in anybody's pile."

Lydia explained how the vibrator came to be in her existence.

Grace razzed her, saying, "Uh-huh, right, Mom."

"It's the God's honest truth," Lydia said.

One day when she was doing her nightly walk through the rooms, checking to make certain doors and windows were locked, she stopped in front of the fireplace mantel. She stared at the photos. Something didn't seem right. Her eyes honed in on the autographed picture of Katie Couric. "I hate to do this, Katie, but you've got to go." She removed Katie's picture. "You're a doll, but the mantel is for family," she said as she proudly placed a school photo of Brandon next to the photo of his father. She rearranged the rest of the photos. Instead of having each of them going in different directions, she lined them up, all facing toward the center. "Just a little symbolism, Binky," she said.

Grace continued to feel crevices open in her marriage and life. But with the strength she had received from learning she was, indeed, a Calypso, and from watching how her mom had handled all of the stones life had thrown at her recently, Grace stood tall and did what she realized she needed to do.

Guy continued denying he was having affairs, so Grace did what any smart attorney would do. She hired a private detective. She never realized that the first file she would put together after her decision to return to practicing law part-time would be one on her husband. The file grew at a quick pace, especially after Carly Harding, the lady who confessed her *ménage a trois* at Bunko, finally convinced her that it would be to her benefit to meet.

They met at the nonfiction section of the Port Huron library. Both of them showed up wearing large sunglasses and fashionable clothing. Each had a small tape recorder; Carly's to play a message and Grace's to record it. As they huddled together they looked like two characters in a James Bond movie, especially with Carly's short skirt showing more leg than the library workers had probably seen in a long time.

"I'm really embarrassed to meet you like this," Carly said.

Grace wasn't certain how to respond because she wasn't sure what Carly meant, although she did think it strange Carly had suggested she bring a tape recorder. "I'd wanted to get together with you sooner but I heard you had that accident and then I went out of town and before I knew it, here it was March. And to be honest"—Grace hated it when someone prefaced their statement by saying "to be honest"—"I had second and third thoughts about meeting you and telling you what I know about your husband."

Finally, the subject of this meeting was clear. They were here to talk about Guy.

"What about him?" Grace said, very lawyerlike.

"Um, a, do you remember when I made a fool of myself at the Bunko at Clare's?"

Grace nodded and said, "Yes."

"At the time I didn't know who you were and it wasn't until the next day that I found out from Clare."

"Why would who I am matter?"

"Give me a second and I'll explain. I'm trying to keep my thinking straight here."

The library was noisy as a children's reading group sat in the corner, laughing. A woman dressed as "The Old Lady Who Lived in a Shoe" was reading a book.

For some reason, Grace felt like she knew where this discussion was going to go. It took all she had to make herself sit there and wait for Carly's story to unfold. It was as if she had heard the story before.

And she had.

"Remember when I told you that my husband and I went to the hotel? And that a naked man greeted us at the door?" Carly waited for acknowledgement of Grace's recall of the situation but didn't get any. So she proceeded anyway. "I didn't know it at the time, but that man was your husband."

"How do you know he was my husband?"

"Because, oh, God, this is humiliating, but, I know because that wasn't the only time it happened. And eventually, after the third or so tryst, he told me his real name. He'd never said his real name before. Then he told me he was a lawyer and where he was from and that I didn't need to worry about entanglements because he was married and had three kids and he only did this because, well, you know."

"No, I don't know. Do you want to tell me?"

"No, not really."

"Why are you telling me this? What's in it for you?"

"Nothing's in it for me. Don't you understand? I never wanted to get involved with anything like that. My husband sprung it on me. And the guy said he wasn't married and I thought if I did what my husband wanted, maybe it would save my marriage. But it didn't." Carly removed her sunglasses. "Remember when I first called you I asked if you handled divorces?"

"Yes, I remember."

"I did want a divorce, but that was only part of the reason for the call."

"And this was the other part? You wanted me to know about my husband?"

"Yes. I thought you should know. I know I'd want to know if my husband was doing what yours was. And like I said, I got into the situation by accident."

"But you said you got together several times," Grace said, beginning to sound as if she were cross-examining a witness.

"Yes. And it was wrong. But, like I also said, I was trying to save my marriage. Listen, I know I sound like a horrible person for getting involved with this sort of thing, and I feel awful myself. But at the time, I-I—you have to believe me when I say I'm so sorry."

There was a part of Grace that felt sorry for Carly. She had been duped, duped by a man, her husband, someone she had trusted. Of course the same could have been said for her. But right now she was not feeling sympathy for herself. She had evidence to gather.

Carly played a tape she had made during the last time she, her husband, and Guy were together. Grace listened to the scratchy tape carefully. She made a copy for herself. Before leaving, Grace asked Carly if she had filed for divorce.

"Yes," Carly said, sheepishly. "I did."

"Were these episodes what caused you to get a divorce?"

"That, and the fact I found out my husband is gay."

"Gay?" Grace said loudly, causing a few heads to turn her way.

"Be careful," Carly said. "Your husband isn't who he pretends to be."

On March 31, after the private investigator had supplied her with more evidence than she'd need, Grace filed for divorce. She told Guy he had three days to pack his things and move out of the house. She asked Mrs. Sanchez to move into the room over the garage that Guy had previously claimed as a home office.

Grace found herself a good lawyer. As a matter of fact, he was her old boss. He said that Grace was welcome to resume her career where she had left off. He said he understood her situation and that her hours would be limited because of the children, but he said, "We're going for quality, Grace, not quantity."

At the beginning of April, Walter's mother passed away, so Lydia didn't have to continue to go to the nursing home.

When the weather warmed, she spent time outside picking up twigs and branches that had fallen in the winter. She laughed at herself when one day she walked outside with a notebook, similar to the one Bitsy, the Realtor, had used to write in, and walked around her house and yard, and wrote notes about things that needed to be done. She saw clearly how the gutters needed to be unclogged and painted, some concrete by the steps needed to be repaired, and the handrail that went along the steps to the side stoop need to be tightened.

She went to the garden store and bought three bags of tulip bulbs and came home and planted them in front of the shrubs that she had proudly pruned.

In May, Lydia thought she had received a piece of mail by mistake. It was a graduation announcement. She opened it and read, "The Graduating Class of 2002 requests the honor of your presence on Sunday, May 22, at Perry Convocation Center to witness the graduation of Sherry Calypso Reed."

"What in the world?" Lydia squeaked, tripping over herself to get to the phone.

She dialed Sherry's home number but there was no answer. Then she flipped through her address book to look for Sherry's work number, which she only called if there was an emergency.

"Administration, Sherry Reed speaking."

"Sherry. It's Mom. I think someone is pulling a joke on me. I just received—"

"An invitation to a commencement?"

"Why, yes," Lydia answered, perplexed.

"Well, will you be coming?"

"You mean this wasn't a joke? A mistake?"

"It's no mistake, Mom. I'm graduating with a degree in social work, on May, well, May something."

"But, I had no idea," Lydia said.

"Nobody did. I wanted to surprise you. And it sounds like I did. Aren't you going to say congratulations?"

"Oh, my gosh. Congratulations. But how, when did you do this?"

Sherry told her mom how she had been taking classes for the last couple of years, sometimes one at a time and sometimes more than one. Yes, it had been hard, and yes she was glad it was over, but she was very proud of her accomplishment.

"You should be," Lydia said, her throat closing tight. "I hope you know how proud of you I am."

"I do, Mom. And you know what? I'm proud of you, too."

Chapter 38

Unfinished Business

Even though she didn't have to visit Walter's mother anymore Lydia kept up her trips to the nursing home. When she returned she made a pickle loaf sandwich with mayonnaise and lettuce. Lydia opened a small bag of potato chips and put a chip in her mouth while she cleared a space for her plate on the table. She picked up a stack of magazines and set them on another part of the table. But when she picked up the stack, she accidentally left one behind. She picked it up. It was the magazine that had the article by Rita in it. She'd forgotten that she'd saved it to read later

She poured her diet cola into a glass full of ice, took a sip and sat down. She ran her finger over the cover of the magazine, deciding whether to open it or not. She knew if she opened it, she'd end up trying to contact Rita. But if she didn't open it, well, maybe that would be for the best.

She'd just taken a bite when the phone rang. She answered it. It was Helen. She had called "just to chat." Lydia was suspicious as to whether that was the real motivation behind the call but she decided to take what Helen said at face value. At first Helen asked the regular questions. "How are you doing?" "What have you been up to?" And so on. Then came the real purpose for the call.

"Did Tim tell you we might be transferred to California?"

Lydia stopped chewing. "No, he hasn't mentioned it," Lydia said, afraid her bite of sandwich would get caught in her throat.

Helen sounded gleeful when she said, "Oh, I thought for sure he'd have told you."

"I'm sure he will tell me when he's ready."

She tried to maintain focus listening to Helen babble on about the hardship she would be under if they had to move "all the way to the ends of the earth. Do you think California will fall off into the ocean some day?"

Lydia kept her comment to herself. But as she talked, well, mostly listened, she grabbed the copy of the magazine with Rita's article in it and opened it. She didn't turn to the article but instead thumbed to the page with the contributor's notes. There was Rita.

"Uh-huh, aha, yeah, uh-huh," Lydia said into the phone, not paying particular attention to what she was responding to. Then suddenly she interrupted Helen in the middle of her complaint that she was certain she had a gallstone. "I'm sorry Helen, someone's at the door," she said, crossing her fingers.

"Oh, so you have to go?"

"I'd better. Uh-oh, they're knocking again. I'll talk to you later. 'Bye."

Before Helen could make any more pathetic noises, Lydia hung up the phone.

Lydia had lied. There was no one at the door. But something urgent had come up. She was going to call Rita. During the last month she'd straightened out as many of the relationships in her life as she could. But unless she talked to Rita, she didn't think her life could move on in the way she wanted it to. She felt strong and healthy and she was certain that no matter what Rita said, she could handle it. And besides, no matter what the circumstances of Rita's leaving were, there hadn't been a day that had gone by that Lydia hadn't wanted to talk to her.

If Rita's phone number was unlisted, she'd call the magazine to get it, but she didn't have to; it was listed under her husband's name.

"I can't believe Rita got married," Lydia said to Binky as she punched in Rita's phone number.

The phone rang three, four times when Lydia heard an answering machine come on. She didn't want to leave a message. She was about to hang up when she heard an out-of-breath voice say, "Hello?"

Lydia took a deep breath. "Rita? Is this Rita Goin?" Lydia asked softly.

There was a pause. Then: "Liddy."

"Hi. I can't believe you recognized my voice."

"My God, Liddy, how could I ever forget your voice?"

"How are you?" Lydia asked, not knowing what else to say.

"I'm fine. I can't believe it's you, Liddy." Lydia thought she heard a catch in Rita's voice. "I'm so glad it's you. But, I-I, I didn't think I'd ever hear your voice again, not after leaving like I did. I thought for certain you'd hate me. And what's worse is I knew you deserved to hate me."

"I didn't call to tell you I hate you, Rita. I called because I've missed you every day."

"And oh, how I've missed you, too. But Liddy, I—"

"Don't say anything," Lydia said. "Not now. Now's not the time to dredge up the past. We can try to figure out what happened later, or maybe we'll decide not to figure it out at all and let the past take care of itself."

Lydia was now certain she heard Rita crying.

"You're being too gracious," Rita said.

Lydia didn't miss a beat and said, "No I'm not. I've not become a saint. I'm sure I'll make you pay somehow." They both laughed. "As a matter of fact, I might make a list. Dinner at Tavern on the Green, a couple of Broadway shows, and a trip to Macy's basement. For a start."

"They're yours," Rita said, her voice going back to normal. "Does that mean you're coming to New York?"

"Someday. Maybe this summer after my trip."

"Your trip to where?"

"Ireland," Lydia said. "I'm going to take the trip to Ireland that Walter and I had planned."

"That's wonderful, Liddy," Rita said. "It's about time you went across the pond." She laughed.

Lydia thought she heard a toddler's voice in the background.

"You're traveling and I'm home with two children."

"That's what the magazine said.".

"It's true. I have three-year-old twins. A boy named Carson and a girl named Lydia. Of course we call her Liddy. Liddy, are you there?"

"I'm here. That's wonderful, Rita. I'm so happy for you. I guess I'm overwhelmed. It's just you being married and having children is almost more than I can imagine. I wish I would have taped your mantra of 'I'm never getting married. There's no man who can tie me down.'"

"Don't remind me."

For the next half hour Lydia and Rita talked about their lives now. Neither mentioned the past, at least their common past. Lydia did tell Rita that she had a grandson named Brandon, Buddy's son.

"Oh, my God, Lydia," Rita said. "How'd that—?"

"Shh," Lydia reminded her. "We'll catch up some other time."

Lydia told Rita that Sugar now lived in New York and she thought she might take a trip to see her. She said she had also promised her sister Jan that she would visit her in South Carolina and that she would probably take Brandon.

They laughed about how they had somehow traded each other's lives. Rita now the married woman with kids, and Lydia, now foot-loose and fancy-free. "You've got to go to Italy next summer," Rita said. "Oh, but before you go, I'll have to give you some tips on how to handle the men."

The conversation was eventually interrupted by a crying toddler and a whiny toddler. Rita promised she'd call next week. "You haven't changed numbers have you?"

"No, I haven't changed the number, but I did finally change the message on the recorder."

Lydia knew that last comment had probably gone right over Rita's head. But that was okay. She hadn't said it for Rita; she'd said it for herself.

After she hung up the phone, she played the phone greeting she had recorded the day before. "You have reached the Calypsos. We are busy at the moment, but if you'd leave your name and number, we'll return your call. Have a good day."

She smiled when she heard her own voice.

Chapter 39

Moving On

L ydia resumed talking to God, but she didn't expect the same
things from Him that she had before. She thanked Him for
the life she was given and the one she was about to embark on.
But instead of asking Him to take over her life she just asked for
guidance. She said she would take care of the rest.

The night before she left for Ireland, after she tucked herself
under the blankets, she prayed, "Dear Lord, tomorrow is the first
day of the rest of my life. And I'm so excited. But before I get on
that plane and fly halfway across the world, I want to thank you for
the glorious graduation we celebrated yesterday. That was one of
your best weather days in years. And if you could extend that good
weather the whole length of this trip that would be great, too. It was
wonderful to see Sherry look so happy yesterday. And thanks for not
letting Joe's jealousy spoil it. I'm still not sure how that relationship
will work out.

"I pray you give Grace the courage to do what she needs to do,
and please give me guidance to know how to help her.

"It surprised me when Tim told me the reasons he'd turned
down the transfer to California. He said he'd thought long and hard
about the transfer but in the end, the decisions to move didn't come

down to money. It came down to family. "Family is what life's about," he said.

"I'm looking forward to visiting Sugar in New York in July. Brandon's mother said I can take him with me. I can't wait to meet Sugar's friends and be as much a part of her life as she wants me to be. I know, I know, within reason.

"Brandon has been like an angel to me. He reminds me so much of Buddy. His laugh and the way he talks with that little lisp. He has been a miracle to our family. And I have seen a side of Sugar I didn't believe existed. I think someday she will make a wonderful mother.

"And you know how thankful I am to have Rita back in my life as I've told you that every day. We'll get together when I go to see Sugar in New York; I can't wait.

"As I'm sure you're aware I've recently done a lot of thinking about family. For a while I didn't think we were going to make it. All of these years I've had this vision of what the perfect family should be. Now, I'm embarrassed to say this, but, in my mind, my family never lived up to my expectations. And I blamed myself. I blamed them. I was angry with you.

"It's only been after revisiting the past that I see that what I was looking for doesn't exist. There is no "perfect" family.

"I know we've had our ups and downs, God. I appreciate your patience in teaching me how you work. I now understand that it was never your goal to walk ahead of me through life, blindly leading me on journeys that I didn't understand. I know that all you ask from me is that I allow you to walk beside me. And God, I welcome you walking beside me. If you have as much faith in me as I have in you, we'll be in good shape.

"Please be with me on this trip. I've heard magical things happen in Ireland.

"Of course, please be with the pilots flying our plane and if they have any trouble, feel free to lend a guiding hand.

"Oh, and one more thing, God. I still haven't decided if I'm going to sell my house and move. When I do make that decision, you and

Grace will be the first to know. But until that time, the one thing I can tell you for certain is, I am moving on.

"Amen.

"P.S. Please see if you can arrange for a good sale on Waterford Crystal."